After giving the doctor time to hide herself away in her room, Tetsuro returned to his. He sat on his bed, his back against the headboard, and stared into space, thinking about his doctor. He could sense the vibrations of her desire for him as well as her need to keep her distance. He, too, felt an attraction, one that seemed centered in his chest, not below his waist. From the first moment he saw her beautiful crystal-clear, light brown eyes, he had been heading in such a direction. Tonight's tea ceremony had made it clear. His body and heart ached for McKenna Stafford.

A DRUMMER'S BEAT TO MEND

KEI SWANSON

Genesis Press Inc.

Indigo Love Stories

An imprint of Genesis Press Inc.
Publishing Company

Genesis Press, Inc.
P.O. Box 101
Columbus, MS 39703

ISBN: 1-58571-171-3
Manufactured in the United States of America

First Edition

Visit us at www.genesis-press.com
or call at 1-888-Indigo-1

DEDICATION

"To the memory of my mother, who always believed in me.
To my father, who has always supported my dreams.
To my sister, who has been there and always will be.
To my son and daughter-in-law, who aren't too embarrassed by me.
To my granddaughter, who proves life goes on.
And as always, to my husband, Tom, my everlasting hero."

ACKNOWLEDGMENTS

I'd like to acknowledge the talent and assistance of William J. Higginson, who composed the haiku used in this work. Mr. Higginson is the author of *The Haiku Handbook*, *The Haiku Season*, and *Haiku World*.

Thank you very much, Mr. Higginson.

CHAPTER ONE

With a visible rhythm in his step, Tetsuro Takamitsu walked through the shadowy hallway behind the stage, his fingers tapping out the gentle cadence of his soul against his jean-encased thighs. A beat had always been there. It had been awakened by the pulse of rock and roll in cosmopolitan Tokyo, then refined by the tradition of feudal Japan and its ancient drummers.

Curtains at the wings swung, brushed by Tetsuro's fellow performers who arranged the drums on the stage for practice the next morning. The backstage area teemed with stagehands going about their work without regard to the Japanese performers helping them.

Whenever the group arrived early in the performance city, Tetsuro enjoyed taking in the city's sights instead of crashing at the hotel and seeing only the auditoriums. Taiko Nihon, the drummers' troupe, would give two night performances in Cleveland. He had the afternoons free to attend baseball games of the Cleveland Indians. Tetsuro was not alone in his passion for America's favorite pastime. No matter how far away from the shores of Japan her drummer-sons strayed, the lure and love of baseball was always present. The Japanese love for the game was renowned, at times surpassing that of Americans. Tetsuro looked forward to seeing Kentaro Ikuta pitch for the first time since the phenomenal pitcher from Nagasaki had defected, as the Japanese press called it, to the U.S.

Pulling sunglasses from his jeans' hip pocket, Tetsuro unfolded them around his eyes and exited the theater. The fresh air was energizing after the four-hour plane flight. A gentle breeze stirred the loose strands of straight raven hair draping his neck and shoulders. He ran a hand through his hair as he paused to breathe in the scent of grass and flowers. The heavy hair settled back around his shoulders seconds later.

From behind him, a sultry feminine voice spoke, "*Ohayo, Te-chan.*"

"*Ohayo.*" Tetsuro turned to the petite woman in her late twenties who leaned against the wall beside the door. "Are you not supposed to be unpacking wardrobe?"

"I am taking a break." She pushed from the wall and dropped her cigarette.

Tetsuro wondered whom she thought she was fooling since she merely took the smoke in her mouth before almost immediately blowing it out. He was glad he'd given up the habit before he was twenty. *Man! Had it been twelve years?*

"I absolutely hate caring for those old-fashioned kimono! Have you been stuck with unpacking the drums?"

"It is my turn." Tetsuro kept walking and she fell into step with him.

"Are the truck drivers and stagehands not hired to unload the drums? I do not understand why we have to unload and unpack."

"It is so you respect every element of performing, from the work of the lowest to the highest."

"Yeah, yeah, yeah."

Tetsuro stopped and looked at the woman.

"Kifume-*san*, if you do not like it, why do you study? *Taiko* is an art…every part of it. If you can not respect one element, how can you honor another?"

Kifume snorted softly, then said, "You make it sound like a religion."

"It is…almost." With his rhythmic walk Tetsuro continued down the sidewalk toward the eighteen-wheeler backed to the curb.

"I like the performing!" Kifume trotted to catch up with him. "And, I like one of the drummers!"

"Well, *that* has been over for a while." It was Tetsuro's turn to scoff.

"Not soon enough." Kifume stopped moving.

Tetsuro took three more steps ahead of her, then halted. He'd heard such a tone before when he was twenty. He turned back to look over his shoulder, pulling his sunglasses down his nose to see her clearly.

"What do you mean?"

"I am pregnant."

The tone *was* the same He jerked the sunglasses off in anger. Rage flooded through him.

"You said you were on the pill." Hadn't Emiko taught him not to be too trusting?

"So…I lied." Kifume stared straight at him as she spoke. At home, her eye contact would be considered bold. Japanese women, even in the twenty-first century, weren't brazen enough to confront a man thusly. Kifume's youth, exposure to America and its customs, and the familiarity grown from studying *taiko*, gave her the confidence to be so direct with him.

"We also used protection," he continued.

"Maybe it slipped." Kifume gave a slight shrug of her narrow shoulders.

Furious, Tetsuro turned on the heels of his black leather boots and stomped to the truck. The back door was open and half of the equipment was already in the theater. He hung his sunglasses by the earpiece in his back pocket and stepped into the dark cavern. At the midpoint sat a large crate with the *O-Daiko,* the largest drum, and the centerpiece of the show. He should have had help to move it, but anger and ego clouded his judgment. Once he moved it to the end of the van, the others would be there to help.

Kifume followed. "Are you not going to say anything?"

"I think you have said enough for the moment. Besides, how do I know you are not lying now?" Tetsuro put his hands on the edge of the huge, heavy crate. "What makes you think it is mine? You *like* a lot of drummers."

He wiggled the crate forward. The rollers of the pallet below the large crate allowed it to move easily, almost on its own.

Kifume moved behind the crate and unhooked a strap.

"This will make it easier."

"No! I have had enough of your help." Too late Tetsuro's words ricocheted off the walls of the truck.

The great crate lunged, surging without warning toward the left. Tetsuro gripped the edges, spreading his feet apart to brace himself. Extending his arms wide, he clutched the rough planks with his long fingers, but his attempt to hold the heavy object in place was futile. The crate shifted in the unleveled truck and the edge of the heavy box slammed his left hand into the truck wall. Monstrous pain ripped through his arm and his deep-throated scream echoed in the cavernous truck.

"Tetsu!" Kifume threw her slight weight against the crate. Unable to move it, she clutched the rope strung across the back and pulled. Still unable to relieve any of the pressure on Tetsuro's hand, she shouted in English, "Help! Somebody! Help!"

"What the…?" The returning driver jumped into the truck and grasped one side of the large crate and heaved.

More performers arrived, returning to continue unloading the truck. Seeing the situation, some of them rushed to shove the drum crate away while others bent over Tetsuro. His hand was pinned between the crate and the wall four feet above the truck floor. His body turned into the side of van. Pain ran from his fingers to his shoulder and echoed in his chest with the bounding beat of his blood. His scream gargled back into his throat as intense agony took all the breath from him.

Once the pressure was removed, Tetsuro slid down the wall. Folding his legs beneath him on the floor, he cradled his left hand in his right. Blood throbbed to the injury in a painful rush and a nauseous knot balled up in his stomach, threatening to force the airline meal up. He fought the wave of sickness and struggled not to lose consciousness.

"*Te-chan, sumimasen*," Kifume wept as she reached toward his hand.

"Get away from me!" he growled, refusing her apology.

"We need to get you to a hospital," said a male performer who kneeled to help Tetsuro when Kifume moved away.

"I think you are right, Susu-*san*." Tetsuro battled the pain striving to overtake his consciousness.

Susumu, his best friend, put a supporting arm around his back and helped him stand as Tetsuro held the injured hand higher than his fast pounding heart. He'd already discovered that blood flowing downward increased the pain.

"What about the performance?" Tetsuro groaned, his voice barely audible.

"Do not worry. We will get along without our beloved artistic manager," Susumu ribbed him. "While we are drumming before a nameless audience, you will be making new friends."

"Are you trying to make me feel better?" Tetsuro attempted a smile, but the cutting pain made it difficult.

"Trying to, my friend."

Leave it to Susumu to see the bright side of things. Tetsuro leaned heavily on his friend, happy to have the support. Who knew what the next few hours would bring, much less the following day?

CHAPTER TWO

From her place at the entrance of the living room, McKenna Stafford observed Claire Ikuta, the honoree of the party. She would vehemently deny envying Claire the infant laden abdomen, but the truth was she was fascinated by the rounded figure of her childhood friend.

Why couldn't she be the one receiving best wishes? There was any number of women doctors who balanced career and children. They even managed to stay married! Where was the decent man who would marry her and fill her with new life? While pregnancy today didn't dictate a husband, only sperm which she could find easily, her heart longed for a man to love and to love her, a man who would stand by her in good times and in bad. She would not give up hope, no matter how many years had passed since her personal tragedy.

A well-dressed, tall gentleman approached her. "Nice to see you here, McKenna."

"Hello, Robert." McKenna took the hand Robert Ferris extended. "I couldn't miss Claire's party, although it is a little different."

"Have you known my daughter to do anything conventionally? Especially since she married?" Robert glanced back at Claire with a proud fatherly smile on his lips.

"No." McKenna sipped her drink. Conformity had been thrown out the window with Claire at an early age. Claire, who was Caucasian, had made a point of forging a friendship with African American McKenna that had remained strong through college and postgraduate work and continued into the present. "She enjoys holding court." Claire, quiet, shy, bookworm Claire, had found a wonderful man. Was there another one out there for her-the quiet, shy, medically proficient surgeon McKenna?

"All the attention of being Kentaro's interpreter, and now his wife, brought her out of her shell." Robert turned back to McKenna. "When do we get to hear your wedding bells?"

"You know us surgeons." She smiled. "Too full of ourselves to be married." This was the stereotype, but did she fit it? Her profession hadn't been the problem. She'd done everything to make that work. Everything, no matter how much it hurt.

"You and James have been dating a while. I'd suppose he'd be used to the life of a doctor."

"Years. But he hasn't mentioned marriage." McKenna sipped again. Good ole reliable James. He tolerated calls and long hours in surgery. She tolerated his devotion to his mother. An escort for anything she needed one for and a pleasant companion when she needed that. But husband? She wouldn't go that far. "You'd think one marriage would be enough for me." Hoping to change the subject she said, "It must be nice to have Claire back home, even though it'll be short."

"Sure is." Claire's father sipped his drink. "It was a bit unnerving there for awhile until her bleeding stopped but to have her back in the States where we can take care of her is a pleasure."

"I understand she and Kentaro are hoping to build here in Shaker Heights." Married to a professional baseball player, Claire split her time between Japan and Cleveland. McKenna missed having her readily at hand.

"They've started remodeling a house in Cleveland Heights. Over on Monmouth. It should be ready sometime after the baby's born."

"Ah. Hope it's close." McKenna smiled softly thinking about the chance to visit her friend and new baby. She lifted her glass to her lips and wet them with the cold drink.

"On call tonight?" Robert asked.

"How'd you guess?"

"You're the only one drinking a Sprite."

McKenna chuckled. Dr. Ferris was a noted pediatric oncologist at Rainbow Babies and Children's Hospital and a friend of her deceased father. That was where the similarities between the two men ended.

"*And* the only one wearing a beeper," Robert noted.

At that, McKenna's beeper sent a metallic 'beep' from the vicinity of her waist and, instinctively, she silenced it while pulling it from its plastic holder. She held the view screen at eye level and squinted to make out the number in the dim light of the room.

"Ah, University Hospital's emergency room," she murmured. "May I use your phone? I left my cell in the car."

"Sure. I'll show you." Robert led McKenna down the hallway. "Should be something interesting, since a resident can't handle it."

"Always is." They came into Dr. Ferris's office and McKenna took the phone he offered her. She punched in the number as he left the room. "This is Dr. Stafford," she said into the instrument when a voice answered. "I was paged." Nodding as she listened, McKenna realized she'd have to go at once.

"Claire." McKenna stepped to her friend's side.

"McKenna!" Claire responded, her hands going out to clutch one of McKenna's arms. "I'm sorry I can't bounce up and down as I used to. Sit." She patted the empty chair at her left.

"No. I've come to say I must leave." She rubbed her friend's hands that held her arm. As she always did, she took note of the darkness of her skin next to her friend's. The difference in skin tone was the only significant difference between them. Both were daughters of affluent doctors from wealthy families. Educated in private boarding schools and reared by nannies, they shared the same social calendar and attended the same cultural events. Stripped of their outer covering, McKenna and Claire could be sisters. "Your father told me about the preterm bleeding," she spoke with concern. "You keep your seat and don't stir anything up."

"Spoken like a true doctor. Are you sure you don't want to change specialties to OB?" Claire's light brown hair danced as her head bobbed.

"Nope. Don't wanna go there!" Now McKenna's hair swung across her shoulders. "Ortho is fine with me."

"Daddy said you might be chief. Is that true? McKenna Stafford, the first woman chair of orthopedics and the first African American as well. I like that."

"I do too. But I have to go."

"If I didn't know better I'd think you paid someone to page you." Claire folded her hands across her swollen belly.

"Why'd you say something like that?" The smile on McKenna's face belied her attempt to look indignant.

"You hate things like this. Socializing is not your strong suit, my friend. Surgery is."

McKenna envied the way her friend's green eyes sparkled.

"You're right but this is your party, and I can deal with that. But I really have to go." Claire was so right. She *had* been known to pay someone to page her out of a party or reception. In the OR she was queen of her world, mistress of her domain, in charge and confident. But with a crowd of people not involved in medicine, she was out of her element. Though finishing school had made sure she had the tools to use in society it didn't make the social scene appealing to her.

"Medical business?"

"Of course. Nothing less would pull me away." McKenna leaned and kissed Claire's cheek. "Congratulations."

"Come back if you can."

"I'll try." Both knew it was an empty promise. Once at the hospital, McKenna would remain until she was weary enough to fall asleep with ease.

As McKenna departed the Ferris's stately house on Fairmount, her mindset changed to face the patient she'd been summoned to attend.

"All right, people." McKenna entered the nurses' station of University Hospital's emergency department with a marine drill sergeant set to her shoulders and a bark in her voice. This was her spotlight. She was in charge and comfortable. And she didn't need a husband to do it. "Where's the patient?"

"Exam room three." A nurse carrying a clipboard approached her. "Thirty-two-year-old male with a crushing injury to the left hand. Got it caught between a truck wall and crate. Vital signs are stable. He refuses to take anything for pain."

"Hm." McKenna flipped through the papers. "I presume you have x-rays?"

She looked around to the fresh-faced resident at her left. He gulped before he spoke, obviously working up his courage.

"Right here." The resident doctor pointed to a light box set at the end of the nurses' station counter. "I immobilized and iced it. I felt sure you'd want to be the first to manipulate."

McKenna didn't honor him with a response. Someone, it appeared, had briefed the new intern on the peculiarity of University Hospital's distinguished orthopedist.

A black film with the gray shadow skeletal frame of a hand was displayed for McKenna to study. The fractures of the four bones running from narrow wrist to long fingers were clear to see. Numerous flecks of bone indicated the extent of the crushing injury and a darker gray area over the palm revealed a large pocket of blood.

"Not good," she commented and turned to the nurse. They walked toward room three. "What's his name? *Tet-sue-ro Ta-ka-mit-zue?*" McKenna focused on the top of the chart in her hand.

"He's from Japan. With a music troupe performing at Severance Hall," the nurse explained.

They entered the room. McKenna's attention remained on the clipboard a minute longer. Then she handed it to the nurse and looked at the patient.

Takamitsu lay on the gurney looking calm, but his breathing was shallow, as if the movement of his chest caused pain. His soft eyes, dark circles painted beneath them and cloudy with the torture of his injury, studied her. Long, straight, raven hair fanned out over the white pillowcase in appealing contrast. An IV had been placed in his right arm, inside the bend of the elbow, and a plastic tube to provide extra oxygen made a translucent mustache on his upper lip. A cotton hospital gown, white with a faded blue design, was haphazardly spread over his wide chest, displaced by the lines of the ECG leads.

"Good evening, Mr. Takamitzue," she said, approaching him. "I'm McKenna Stafford, the orthopedic surgeon they called to see about fixing your hand. I hear you had an accident while unloading a truck."

"*Hai*." Tetsuro grimaced as he answered in Japanese. He then changed to English. "Yes."

McKenna looked at, but did not touch, the mangled hand elevated on two pillows resting on his midsection. She'd wait until he was medicated before she manipulated the bones. She could see all she needed to between the ice packs layered under and alongside the extremity to help slow the swelling. The fingers were swollen, looking more like wieners than digits of a hand. The nail beds were black.

"Will you turn your hand over a bit so I can see the underside? I don't want to manipulate it and cause you more pain than necessary."

Takamitsu complied. A painful grimace crossed the exotic features of his face. McKenna leaned over so he didn't have to move much and saw the area of impact. A line along the middle of his palm was deep red and purple with bruising.

The closeness gave her a whiff of a clean, unfamiliar fragrance on his skin. Her usual ER patients were often more hygienically challenged, making close proximity difficult. This case was completely different. The spicy, gentle aroma caused her medical assessment to cloud for an instant and made her want to linger.

McKenna swallowed, straightened and looked into her patient's agony-filled eyes. The movement had caused a thin line of perspiration to break out along his upper lip.

"They tell me you refuse to take anything for pain." Bone injuries were notorious for their pain and patients were equally renowned for frustrating the nurses with requests for more, more, and still more narcotics. For the Japanese man not to be in that group was curious. Did it have something to do with their being typecast as stoic in nature?

"I could definitely use something to stop the throbbing." Takamitsu made a face as an obvious stab of pain moved through his hand after he settled it on the ice pack. "I wanted to know what you plan to do before my senses are clouded with narcotics."

McKenna's attention remained rapt in the study of his face. Dark brown eyes framed by oblong eyelids and thick lashes stared at her from a lean face with full lips. She was caught in his gaze for several seconds before she could speak again. "My plan is to take you to surgery as soon as we get a room open and put your hand back together. Are you one of the stagehands?"

"I am a drummer," he explained through gritted teeth. "I perform with the Taiko Nihon drum troupe."

"A musician who will need the use of his hand," she muttered to herself. McKenna mulled his answer over. This was increased pressure on her skill.

"Can you fix it so that I can drum again?" The dark eyes beseeched her.

"I'm going to do my best, Mr. Takamitzue." McKenna put her hand on his bare shoulder, and the warmth of his velvet skin sent a spark from her fingers through her arm.

"It is '*mit-su*'," he explained the pronunciation of his name. "I place my hand in your hands."

McKenna noticed the smile he tried to give her. She addressed the nurse. "Get consents signed for the open reduction of multiple fractures of the left hand and then push ten milligrams of morphine."

"Yes, ma'am." The young woman turned and left the area.

"Dr. Stafford," Tetsuro spoke.

"Yes, Mr. Takamitsu?" She noticed a faint acknowledgement in his eyes as she spoke his name correctly. A tinge of warmth filled her.

"Will I be able to play the piano after the surgery?"

"I hope so." *Drummer and pianist.*

"Good. I never could before."

McKenna was taken aback by the stale, old joke. She giggled.

"I'll see you in surgery." She left to prepare for the operating room, still smiling at his comment. This man was an interesting patient.

CHAPTER THREE

"Doctor?" A man came to the desk from the waiting room.

McKenna looked up from writing on the chart to find him standing at her elbow. "Yes?" She took a step back, sliding the clipboard toward her.

"I'm John Restor, U.S. agent for the Taiko Nihon. I'm responsible for Mr. Takamitsu."

"Mr. Takamitsu seems responsible for himself," McKenna commented. "As for the bill, you'll have to see the business office."

"I've already made the arrangements. Can you tell me how long he'll be in the hospital? The performers are scheduled to travel to Pittsburgh Sunday morning."

"He'll be in no shape to go anywhere for the next week or longer. I can't say when he'll be able to use his hand again because rehab's going to be a long road and won't start fully until it's healed." A long period of time in which she would be in close proximity to her mysterious patient, a man who was curiously interesting to her.

"Then I'll make the necessary arrangements for him to remain behind."

"The hospital has many programs for foreigners who come for medical care. If you'll talk with Ms. Cage here," McKenna indicated the unit secretary who stood behind the desk, "she'll get social services down here to make the plans."

"Thank you, Dr. Stafford."

"You're welcome." McKenna turned back to her work on Tetsuro's chart.

"Excuse me, Doctor?"

"Yes?" McKenna's tone made it clear she was not pleased to be interrupted by the Japanese woman behind her. She watched as a Japanese man spoke to the woman in sharp words. The woman responded to him in equal fashion, then spoke to McKenna

"I am Kifume Ito. On the American television shows and movies I have seen, doctors sometimes have music playing in the operating room. Is that true?"

"I usually do," McKenna admitted. "It helps keep me relaxed."

"Would you be able to play this?" Kifume handed the surgeon a compact disc in a plastic case. "It is the music Takamitsu-*san* composed and the troupe performs. If you could play it, he will be comforted."

"Very well." McKenna took the plastic case and slipped it into her lab coat.

"*Domo arigato.*" Kifume bowed and returned to the group in the waiting area.

As McKenna looked at the chart on the desk and continued to write her plan of care for the young man, her mind strayed from the progress notes to his personal life. Was this young lady his girlfriend? Why should she care one way or the other? She was just his doctor and her only concern should be strictly his hand, not his heart, soul, or any other part.

"You're looking good, Mac," Rick Ramirez said from the opposite side of the desk.

"Hello, Rick," McKenna answered the fellow doctor and friend. He was dressed in green scrubs and had a stethoscope slung around his neck.

"Haven't seen your hair down in a long time." Rick picked up a chart and began the same kind of scribbling as McKenna.

"I was at Robert Ferris' reception for his daughter and didn't take the time to change into scrubs or put my hair up." She'd grabbed her lab coat from the back seat of her Jeep and pulled it on over her sweater and skirt outfit.

"Was that tonight? My wife was invited. Did you happen to see her?"

"I didn't get to stay long enough to see any one but Robert and Claire." Even if she'd remained for the full evening, she would have been happy to have it that way. Unless people were anesthetized or recovering in a hospital bed, they did not particularly interest her. Yet, her curiosity was piqued about the man she was about to operate on.

"That sweater is definitely preferable to a scrub top. Got that Halle Berry look goin' on."

"Dr. Ramirez, you're walking a fine line here." McKenna grinned at him. Rick took pleasure in pointing out her resemblance to the actress, especially with her hair down. He only did it to rile her. And she rose to the bait each time. "I have to go to the OR. Do you know who's on for anesthesia?"

"Feinburg."

"Thanks." McKenna moved from the desk toward the elevator, her destination the women physicians' lounge.

Once the consent form was signed, Tetsuro was alone to reflect on his situation. After the ambulance attendants placed him on the gurney in the emergency room, he had lain stone still and tried not to think about the throbbing pain and how out of sync he felt. His internal rhythm was loud and erratic, discordant. When Dr. Stafford appeared at his bedside, however, the discord within him had been replaced with a calm beat. The serenity of her sepia eyes had told him he was safe, that he could trust her with not only his hand, but also with his entire body. In her face he had seen determination, knowledge and skill. Yet he'd also seen a tenderness, almost a vulnerability.

"Mr. Takamitsu." The nurse returned to his side, intruding on his thoughts. "I'm going to give you some morphine IV to help the pain. You might feel dizzy, lightheaded, or sleepy."

"I thought you already had," Tetsuro murmured. With the injection into the plastic line feeding fluid into his vein, warmth covered him and his eyelids drooped. The pain in his hand was assuaged to an ache and his internal rhythm became a soothing, tranquil pulse.

McKenna entered the doctor's lounge to find several other physicians in various states of undress. She made her way through, speaking and nodding greetings, until she came to her own locker. Whirling the combination, she opened the metal door.

"Evening, Mac," she heard from behind her.

"Oh, hi, Leslie. You're just the person I wanted to see." McKenna placed her purse and pager inside the locker, then hung her lab coat on the door. She walked to the shelf where scrubs were kept and picked off a pair of size medium pants and a small top. "Do you speak Japanese?"

"I learned when I was a child, but haven't used it in years. Why?" Leslie Furumiya sat on the couch with her feet propped on the table in front of it.

"Are you busy tonight?" McKenna pulled her sweater over her head and replaced it with the scrub top.

"Finished with an appendectomy. Why?" Leslie asked again.

"I have to fix the hand of a Japanese drummer and think he'll respond better to his native language once he's asleep, although he does speak English." McKenna stepped out of her wool skirt and peeled her panty hose over her hips. She pulled on the scrub pants, drew the string tight at the waist and evened out the bunched material. A small size would fit better, but they were always too short. "Could you do the anesthesia instead of Dr. Feinburg?"

"Be glad to. Is your patient one of the Taiko Nihon group? I have tickets for tomorrow night."

"I think so." McKenna bunched her hair at the nape and pulled it through a ponytail holder. "His name's Tetsuro Takamitsu."

"That sounds familiar. They don't have 'stars,' but I think he's one of the prominent players." Leslie put her feet on the floor and rose. "I have an information sheet Fred received when he bought the tickets." She went to her own locker and gave McKenna the fact sheet.

"Oh? Thanks. You just added more pressure to make sure he gets a working hand back." She took the paper and studied it. It didn't have pictures of all of the performers, only a single figure and the large drum at center stage.

"Sorry. I'll go chat with Takamitsu-*san*."

"Thanks. I'll be here. Call me when you're ready."

McKenna lay back against the couch and closed her eyes. She pictured the x-rays of Takamitsu's hand and what she would need to do to repair it.

It would be an intense operation of pins, wires and tiny stitches. Her plan was not only to put the bones back together, but also to give Takamitsu a hand that would function as before. He needed it to close around a drumstick, to pick up and carry a drum, and to write the notes of music he composed.

Did drummers actually have notes?

She wanted him to be able to take his lover's hand in his, to cup her cheek and to hold his infant.

McKenna's eyes popped open. What was she thinking about? She didn't even know if he had a lover or a child! He needed a hand for his vocation.

"Dr. Stafford?" a voice called over the intercom.

"Yes?" McKenna leaned forward. Her hands rubbed her face to disperse the vision of Takamitsu with a baby in his arms. Babies were the last thing she needed to think about.

Dr. Furumiya spoke now. "Your patient's in the OR. Do you want to speak to him before I sleep him?"

"I'll be right there."

McKenna stood and entered the bathroom. It would be a long surgery so she'd best go to the bathroom now to avoid big trouble. On her way out of the lounge, she retrieved the CD from her lab coat.

McKenna pushed the door to the operating suite open and saw her patient, the view starting feet first. The circulating nurse had encased his long legs in a sheet and blanket to prevent his limbs from falling off the narrow table as well as to keep the heat of his body from escaping in the frigid room. As she advanced into the room, McKenna's stare was drawn to the nurse's hand pulling his gown up. There was not an ounce of fat on the waist and lower torso.

"Sir, this may be cold," the nurse said to warn him. Takamitsu flinched as she placed the grounding pad at the side of his waist. The nurse then pulled his gown and affixed a strap over his thighs.

"Hello, everybody." McKenna greeted her surgical team.

Takamitsu's arms were extended out from his sides. The left, with its injury, was nearest her, still encased in ice. His right had its IV fluids.

McKenna came to the head of the table where Dr. Furumiya fiddled with her anesthesia cart after placing the monitoring equipment on her patient. Takamitsu's eyes were closed and his face peaceful and contented. The surgeon noticed the thumb and index finger of his right hand coming together in a consistent fashion.

McKenna nodded toward the digits. "Some sort of spasm, Leslie?"

"Have no idea. Must be an unconscious habit," Leslie Furumiya answered.

"Mr. Takamitsu," McKenna addressed her patient. "How are you feeling?"

Tetsuro's thick black lashes fluttered and his eyes opened to fix on her.

"It's me, Dr. Stafford, hidden behind this." She pointed to the paper mask over her mouth and nose. A surgeon's cap covered her hair.

"I recognize your lovely eyes." The morphine he'd been given slurred his speech slightly. The dosage she'd ordered was just enough to take the edge off his pain and would wear off quickly.

McKenna was taken aback for an instant. Patients didn't talk about their doctor's eyes. She mentally shook the unexpected comment away.

"Dr. Furumiya will make sure you sleep through all of this." McKenna patted his shoulder and noticed his hand still made its movements, through the tempo slowed. "Are you ready?"

"As I ever will be."

McKenna could not break away from his gaze. "Your girlfriend…," she started.

In a quick beat, Tetsuro replied, "I do not have a girlfriend."

"Well, a female friend of yours gave me this." She held up the CD. "It's your work for you to go to sleep to."

"Very thoughtful."

"Dr. Furumiya has a player on her cart." The nurses and Leslie were watching her. Why was she rambling this way? She should be scrubbing and getting on with this operation. "I'll see you afterwards."

"Dr. Stafford," he spoke as she started to leave.

"Yes?" Was he going to make one of those jokes again?

"Are you sure you can put my hand together?" He had a sober look to his face, his eyes abruptly sad.

"I'm going to use all my skill to make sure you have a working hand," she assured him.

"Promise?"

"I promise, Mr. Takamitsu." McKenna quenched the gasp in her throat at her words. Never was a doctor supposed to guarantee anything!

"Tetsu. My friends call me Tetsu."

"Very well. Tetsu." His gaze caught her once again and she was lost in the deep brown pools once more bright with spirit and life. "I'll see you in recovery."

She made no move to depart, trapped in his exotic spell. "Mac?" Dr. Furumiya broke into her thoughts. "You want to get on with this? I'd like to go home sometime tonight."

"Oh? Yes. Right. I'll go scrub."

"You do that." Leslie's eyes smiled at McKenna over the paper mask. "I'll make sure our Japanese friend is kept entertained."

"Don't tell him any of your sick jokes. I don't want him puking during the surgery."

CHAPTER FOUR

After she placed the headlamp on its band around her head, McKenna turned the water on to run into the deep scrub sink and opened the package of the soap-impregnated plastic brush. She studied her hands as she scrubbed the plastic bristles over her forearms and fingers. Her small hands and thin fingers enabled her to do intricate hand and foot repairs. She hoped her skill would be enough for Tetsuro Takamitsu.

She backed into the OR with her hands held up before her dripping water onto the floor. Accepting a sterile towel from the scrub nurse, she dried them while taking in the changes that had occurred while she was out. The soft steady beat of Japanese drum music filled the room and Takamitsu was anesthetized.

With movements so familiar she could do them in her sleep, McKenna slipped her arms into the surgeon's gown held by her scrub nurse, then allowed the nurse to pull latex gloves onto her hands. Garbed for the surgery, she stepped to her patient's extended arm and the scrub nurse took her position across from her.

McKenna looked at the hand. The nurse had unpacked it from the ice and cleansed the skin with an iodine prep solution. Beneath the arm board was a kick bucket lined with drapes to catch the blood. She sat on the stool the circulating nurse held stable, then rolled into position to work. The nurse connected the fiber optic cords and the lamp on her forehead emitted light. Across the sterile field a nurse draped Takamitsu's arm.

McKenna took note of the firm cords of muscle running the length of the arm before it disappeared from sight.

Who would think a drummer would have such muscle?

Leslie Furumiya spoke. "Any time you're ready."

McKenna hadn't realized she had hesitated. She smoothed the drape over Takamitsu's shoulder and Leslie secured it around a pole. The only view of her patient was his swollen hand.

"Do you want me to change the music?" the anesthesiologist asked.

"No." McKenna accepted a tiny bladed scalpel and bent her head over the hand, the instrument poised to cut. The headlamp spotlighted the area. "It's nice."

As if in prayer McKenna held her position over the hand. The beat of the drum mingled with the other sounds of the room…the beep of his heart on the cardiac monitor, the whoosh of the rebreather bag on the anesthesia cart filling and emptying Takamitsu's own breath mixed with oxygen. The girl who had given her the CD had said it was his composition. Now she was about to merge with the hand that had created the delicate sounds.

McKenna placed the tip of the scalpel blade at the start of what palm readers called the love line. She made the first cut to begin to repair the drummer's hand.

Three hours later, McKenna put the last tiny suture into Tetsuro Takamitsu's hand. A precise clip of the scissors and she was finished.

"Nice job, Dr. Stafford," the scrub nurse commented. "You want your usual dressing?"

"Yes, please." McKenna helped pack cotton wadding in Takamitsu's palm and between his fingers. A plastic splint from forearm to fingers followed this. Then it was wrapped with a secure elastic bandage. She applied tape to the end of the bandage as the nurse held it in place.

McKenna stepped back and reached behind herself to break the paper ties of the gown. Free of the cumbersome surgeon's garb, she came to stand near Tetsuro's head; she dropped her gaze to his face. His mysterious eyes, beautiful in their masculine way, remained closed, the lashes shaping sooty circles beneath the lids. His face was peaceful except for the distortion of his mouth by the endotracheal tube taped into place.

"You sure you want to watch?" Dr. Furumiya had finished undoing the securing tape from the tube.

"Huh? What?" McKenna awoke from her daze. Dr. Furumiya had changed the CD from an upbeat jazz back to Takamitsu's songs and the drum music once more filled the room to mesmerize her.

"Pretty boy here won't be so attractive while I pull this out." She indicated the tube. Tetsuro was already coming out of the anesthesia, beginning to buck the tube. "Go write your orders and let me wake the Shining Prince."

"What are you talking about?"

"Prince Hikaru Genji from the book *The Tale of Genji*. First novel in the world and written by a Japanese woman."

"You're just a fount of obscure knowledge."

"I never had an opportunity to share my Japanese heritage before. Now, go away so I can work." Leslie tried to keep Tetsuro from pulling the tube out.

"Are you going to put in a brachial block?" McKenna asked.

"If you would like."

"I don't like my patients to hurt. Thanks." She left the operating room.

"Dr. Stafford, what are you doing in the recovery room?"

"Think I'm out of my territory, huh, Jennifer?" McKenna sat behind the desk and flipped open Takamitsu's chart.

"No, not that. You don't usually come in here after surgery." The nurse, clad in fuchsia-colored scrubs, lounged against the desk, her arms crossed over her chest. Her long blonde ponytail dangled down her back. Several other nurses sat at the desk while two others worked with patients in different stages of recovery.

"I made a promise to a patient," McKenna muttered. She opened her Monte Blanc fountain pen and began to outline her course of care for Takamitsu.

"Did some little kid get hurt?" Jennifer pressed. "That's the only time we usually see you."

"No." Dr. Stafford looked up as she heard the automatic whoosh of the double doors as they opened. "Here he comes now."

Dr. Furumiya accompanied the gurney, pushing at the head of the bed while the circulating nurse guided the foot. They placed the gurney into a bay with its oxygen supply, ECG and blood pressure apparatus ready. The medical team went to work to put the necessary equipment on and around the patient who lay on the bed.

"Wake up, Mr. Takamitsu," the nurse coached as she wrapped the blood pressure cuff around his floppy, uninjured arm.

"*Takamitsu-san, mezameru.*" Leslie Furumiya used her childhood Japanese to reach Takamitsu's subconscious. She focused on her chart, waiting for the circulator to tell her his arrival vital signs.

"Mr. Takamitsu, your surgery's over." Jennifer joined the group working over him. "Wake up."

McKenna walked to the stretcher.

"Tetsu." McKenna was at his head and spoke softly in his direction. Beneath a maneuver to put the oxygen tubing in place, McKenna stroked the raven hair. Why she did it baffled her. Tetsuro moaned and turned toward her. "Tetsu, open your eyes."

Tetsuro Takamitsu fought to raise the lids and focus his dark eyes on McKenna.

"You're in the recovery room," she explained. "Your surgery is over."

"Did it…go well?" His gaze was hard on hers and his voice was dry and throaty. Both sent thrills up her spine.

"I think so. We'll know more when it heals and you begin rehab." Her hand was once more on the soft black hair fanned out over the pillow when Jennifer removed the paper surgery hat. "Rest now."

She should be leaving. Post-op orders already written, she was finished. Time was all that Takamitsu needed now. Why was she having problems departing?

A skilled surgeon, highly thought of in her specialty, McKenna'd done everything necessary for the patient. This Japanese man—*MAN*! Could that have any bearing on her reluctance? *No*. She had one man in her life, James, all she needed. And she wasn't one of those flighty women who went to bed with any testosterone-loaded body.

Yet she hesitated.

"Did you keep your promise?" His lips and tongue were dry and speech was difficult, but his words were clear. "I'll be able to use it?"

"I...hope so," McKenna stuttered. Oh, how she hoped she hadn't lied. Why had she done something so stupid as to promise success when there were so many variables in the equation? Med school 101 had drilled the rule not to do that into would-be physicians' brains. "Rest, Tetsu."

"I look forward to seeing your lovely eyes again." Tetsuro closed his own eyes and his regular breathing indicated he slept.

It was odd that he spoke of *her* eyes since *his* were the unique ones. They both shared a similar color, his a deep brown to her light, but the shape of his was distinctive. Then, again, to *him*, she was uncommon. And why in the world would a patient be so bold as to address his doctor in such a familiar manner?

"I can see why you waited for him," Jennifer commented over her shoulder as she walked back to the nurses' station.

McKenna could only stare after her, her mouth agape. When Dr. Furumiya and the OR nurse left, McKenna was alone at Tetsuro's bedside. She couldn't move and stood watching him fade into the lingering effect of the anesthesia. Now that no one moved his body without his knowledge or co-operation, she saw the tempo had returned to his hand. The fingers lying alongside his blanket-covered hip moved ever so slightly to his own rhythm.

It was safe to leave him.

McKenna returned to the doctor's lounge long enough to grab her purse, lab coat and clothes. She didn't change, wanting only to go home, take a long, hot bath, and go to bed. The white starched garment was heavy on her arm as she made her way to the parking garage and her black Jeep Grand Cherokee at the far end of the lot. Her Reeboks squeaked on the asphalt in a haunting echo making it a relief when she finally arrived at the SUV's door and slid safely inside.

She rushed the Jeep out of the parking building onto Carnegie Street and settled into the night's light traffic. It was almost eleven. Although she was hungry, bed sounded better than food. She'd pass on a take-out meal for something at home to nibble on.

Unexpectedly, a car pulled out and McKenna slammed the Jeep's brakes to avoid an accident. Her lab coat and purse slid from the passenger seat to the floorboard with a clatter. She pulled to the next red light and took a deep breath to settle her nerves as the other driver sped through. The stoplight reflected on a plastic case lying on the seat. *Takamitsu's CD.* Dr. Furumiya must have slipped it into her lab coat pocket after the surgery.

McKenna watched as her hand automatically opened the case and inserted the disc into the player. Within seconds, the gentle beat of the drum song filled the Jeep's interior. A calm settled over her and she relaxed as she continued the short drive home.

On a hill, recessed amid towering trees, the large mansion on Shelbourne Road loomed before McKenna as she drove up the long steep driveway. A few lights shone through the downstairs windows. She always used 'looming' when she described the house she'd grown up in. When she entered the house, McKenna walked through the kitchen. Her Amish housekeeper had left a note on the table with her phone messages. Rebecca had also left a plate with crackers and fruit next to the note and a similar one of cheese in the refrigerator. McKenna picked up a peach and went upstairs to her room.

The ever-efficient Rebecca had laid out her bedclothes and fresh towels hung in the bathroom. McKenna turned on the shower, felt the torrent of water for its temperature, then pulled off the scrubs, bunched her hair up under a cap and stepped into the spray. Quickly, she soaped, rinsed and left the shower.

She smeared a pricey body lotion over her caramel colored skin, then bypassing the nightgown, dressed in sweat pants and an over-large T-shirt. She settled comfortably on the bed to comb her hair. A mish-mash of genetics had joined to give her a head of thick, wavy tresses, without need for relaxers to be manageable. She had a fleeting thought to thank her white great-great-grandfather for the absence of curls. Reclined against the headboard of the bed, her feet beneath the bed-covers, she ate her peach while she flipped the television remote.

Her mind was not on CNN. The delicate elongated eyes of Tetsu Takamitsu floated in her thoughts. The gentle cloudiness of his dark eyes sparkled in her memories. Her fingertips recalled the silkiness of the rich ebony hair. Her lips tingled as she pictured the full curves of her patient's mouth.

What the hell! McKenna's teeth crunched angrily into the not-so-ripe peach. Why was she thinking of him? He was her patient. No more, no less. Why was he haunting her? Why was she entertaining such intimate thoughts? She didn't even know him! He could be a seri-al killer or some sort of pervert! She flung away thoughts of Tetsuro Takamitsu with the blanket as she stood to wash away the peach juice. Her beeper sat on the counter and she carried it back to bed with her. Settling down again, farther into the bed, she was not going to con-template any more thoughts of Takamitsu.

In the quiet darkness after she turned the television and lights off, McKenna swore she could hear the Japanese drumbeat. She tried to convince herself it was only her heartbeat. Her eyes closed and she began to doze.

What seemed moments later, the phone rang.

McKenna answered it. "Dr. Stafford." Seconds later, she said, "I'll be right there," and hung up. The clock showed one-thirty a. m.

Grabbing only her shoes and a sweatshirt with the logo of the 'Rock and Roll Hall of Fame and Museum' emblazoned on the chest, McKenna departed for the hospital.

A million thoughts rushed through her head as she sped the Jeep toward the University Hospital.

What happened?

What did I do wrong?
What did I miss in the H and P?

She had to calm down. Nothing could be fixed as she drove. She'd have facts to work with once she was at the hospital and some good could be done. McKenna parked in the still vacant parking garage and ran to the entrance. Terror made composed thought impossible. In less than three minutes, she was in the Recovery Room.

The large, open room was empty of patients except for one bed. McKenna approached the group of doctors and nurses around Takamitsu's gurney. Papers and discarded equipment littered the floor. The energy level decreased as the emergency abated. She swept her gaze over the gurney, also littered, and studied the cardiac monitor. A green LED line ran across the screen, moving in the jagged pattern reflecting a normal sinus rhythm. Tetsuro's eyes were closed and his breathing even.

"What happened, Leslie?" she asked the anesthesiologist she'd worked with earlier in the evening. Dr. Furumiya was in charge of Takamitsu's post-operative care until he was discharged from the recovery room.

"Can't say, Mac." Leslie Furumiya finished her charting. The Code Team put the crash cart back together and tidied the room.

"How long was he down?"

Leslie and McKenna walked away from the gurney. "He showed signs of an arrhythmia and the nurses alerted me before he actually went down. He responded quickly to meds."

McKenna's thoughts came into words. "His history was negative. He never mentioned a heart problem."

"Sometimes it happens without cause. You know that," Leslie reassured her. "You're a great doctor. Don't go doubting yourself."

"I'll have a cardiologist consult." But she did have doubts. They came easily after a childhood under her father's brutal tutelage. He'd made her question herself too often. According to him, it made her a better doctor. McKenna wasn't so sure. She was a good surgeon on her own merits.

"Be a good idea. I'll see you." Leslie replaced the chart and left the unit.

"Thanks for being here," McKenna said. "Kathy," she addressed the new shift's nurse. "let's keep him here a while longer."

"Sure." The redhead went about her tasks.

McKenna picked up Takamitsu's chart, then returned to his gurney. She pulled the stool nearer and sat. With her cocked-up leg as a prop, she opened the metal chartback and read Dr. Furumiya's notes. She couldn't find a reason for the dysrhythmia. An odd urge caused her to raise her attention from the chart. Tetsuro's drug-glazed eyes were trying to focus on her.

Most seriously, he asked, "Are we sleeping together?"

"What makes you say that?" A hot rush flowed over her throat and face. Her cheeks burned in its wake.

"Every time I wake up, you're here."

"Is that a bad thing?" McKenna was surprised at her frivolousness. What was it about him that caused her to be so giddy and embarrassed? Acting as though she were sixteen all over again.

"No. I did not want to miss the part between awake and asleep."

"You've had a cardiac event and I can't say why." She changed the subject to quell her flighty feelings. "Do you have heart problems?" The tactic wasn't working.

Tetsuro turned his face away from McKenna to stare at the ceiling. "Does having had it broken a few times count?"

"If it does, then I have the same condition." McKenna stood and approached him, her attention on the monitor mounted over his right shoulder. She also took note of the arm dangling from an IV pole by stockinet and the swollen fingers protruding from the cotton batting dressing. "I'll have a cardiologist look at you later today."

Tetsuro gazed at her. "Are you leaving again?"

"Since you do strange things when I'm not here, I think I'll stay around." McKenna touched his uninjured arm.

"I would appreciate that."

Once his eyelids dropped and his chest began to rise with slow regularity, McKenna left his side.

When she approached the desk, Kathy asked, "He's interesting, isn't he, Dr. Stafford?"

"I don't know what you mean," the doctor responded with reserve. Why were people repeatedly telling her this?

"He's kinda cute and mysterious."

"He's from Japan, but…"

"You can't deny it, Dr. Stafford," Kathy chastised.

McKenna slammed the chart on the counter. "I'll be in the lounge."

"Yes, ma'am." Kathy was suddenly professional.

CHAPTER FIVE

On the narrow bed provided for on-call doctors McKenna slept fitfully, worrying about Tetsuro, both his hand and his heart. She welcomed the interruption when just before dawn, she was paged to set the arm of an elderly man who had slipped in the bathroom. Yet as she worked over the fiberglass cast, Tetsuro continued to intrude on her thoughts.

"Morning, Mac."

McKenna raised her eyes from the newspaper. "Hello, Rick."

"Can I join you?"

"Sure." McKenna moved the morning *Plain Dealer* she'd spread out over the table in front of her plate. She had only picked at the food on the dish.

"You're here early." Rick placed his breakfast-laden tray at McKenna's side and sat. "Did I call you in?"

"Yes, I believe one of your first year interns did start all this." Smiling at the resident's open face, she hoped she managed to hide her exhaustion the way the young Hispanic did. He'd been on-call for twenty-four hours to her twelve.

"That hand patient still giving you problems?" Rick spoke around the food in his mouth.

"Since you were there, you know about his arrhythmia, but he's okay. They moved him out of recovery about two hours ago." The sudden rush she'd experienced at Takamitsu's side came now with only slight less intensity. She enjoyed the feeling, even if she didn't understand it.

"Hmmm." Rick continued to eat.

"'Hmmm' what?"

"Just 'hmmm'."

"Think I'll go make rounds. After that I'm going to enjoy my Friday off." McKenna stood.

"I wish! I have two more days on."

"You'll survive," McKenna assured him and took a step away. "We all did."

"Doesn't mean I'll like it!" Rick called behind her.

McKenna still wore the sweat pants and sweatshirt she'd been wearing when she rushed to the hospital early in the morning. Her hair was freshly brushed and back into a lengthy ponytail. As she emerged from the elevator on the orthopedic floor, nurses greeted her warmly and the charge nurse came to her side.

She resisted the urge to make rounds on Takamitsu first. Something unfamiliar nagged at her about him. She liked the weak-kneed feeling she experience in his presence. The shiver it sent along her spine was new and, in her opinion, not too professional. She deliberately went in the opposite direction of the Japanese man, taking charge of her vague feelings.

"Morning, Diane," McKenna greeted the nurse who approached her.

"Hello, Dr. Stafford. You have eight patients today." Diane Mitchell gave her a computer printout listing each patient's name, room number, and diagnosis. The nurse pulled a cart laden with charts along behind her as he followed the doctor along her rounds. "Do you want to start with room 1043?"

"Which patient is that?" McKenna read the printout.

"The hand from last night."

Without thought McKenna whispered, "Tetsu."

"Excuse me?"

"Mr. Takamitsu." McKenna roused herself. "No. I saw him earlier this morning in recovery. Let's start with Mr. Hill. He should be able to go home today."

McKenna followed Diane through the hallway toward the eighty-year-old man's room. Five days before, she'd performed a hip replacement, a rare operation for her. Her skill was with hands and feet. However, she had once before done work on the man's foot, so when he'd fractured his hip, his family had requested she be his surgeon. Although hip replacements were not her favorite procedures, she complied. Making rounds here first was not what she wanted either. Though a force drew her toward Tetsuro, she resisted.

One after another, the nurse led the doctor to her patients. McKenna examined each patient, charted progress notes and wrote orders, all the while conscious that with each completed chart, she was that much nearer the Japanese drummer. They returned to the nurses' station an hour later.

"Your patient from last night is the only one left," Diane commented.

"Has Dr. Whitman been notified of the consult?" She could use the cardiologist as her excuse to postpone seeing Tetsuro. *But do you really want that?* She ignored the tiny voice that squeaked the question.

"Yes. He'll be in this morning."

McKenna hesitated. She needed to make a professional visit to check Takamitsu's hand, but apart from that she wanted to *see* Tetsuro. Her good sense shouted for her to run the other way, *fast*, not seek him out. Tetsuro Takamitsu caused her to forget her medical persona. She didn't want to be affected by him.

Or did she?

"Diane, I'll see him later. I'm going home."

And with that, McKenna left the University Hospital.

By Saturday morning, Tetsuro Takamitsu struggled to forget where he was. Over the last twenty-four hours, the hospital personnel had awakened him for any number of things—his blood pressure and temperature; to remove the IV line; to change his bed; to prop pillows behind him; to change the position of his arm. It seemed to be one thing after another. Then an old, stern doctor had visited and asked every question in the world, then ordered an ECG. After the procedure, all the places where the sticky discs had been applied itched. He was thankful he had no *Ainu* genes as the aborigines of Japan were much more hirsute than the average Japanese native. Removing the adhesive dots would have been more painful than a bikini waxing.

And meals. A tray appeared, laden with different foods, if not unknown, unappealing. Yet he couldn't admit he was dissatisfied. Complaining was not his nature. From childhood he'd been taught to take what was handed out and make do. The Japanese thought to criticize was impolite. So he subsisted on fruit juices.

"Mr. Takamitsu."

A soft voice awakened him by calling his name in the American manner.

"Hai?"

The teenage blonde smiled sweetly at him. "Hi yourself."

"Iie. No. What I said was 'yes,' as in, 'What do you want?'" Tetsuro explained.

"I've brought your lunch." She turned her back and placed the tray on the over-the-bed table at his side.

Once Tetsuro'd turned more onto his back, she adjusted the tray so it was over him. His hand, the one suspended from cloth on the pole, swung slightly and began to ache. The pain awoke visions of Dr. Stafford. Her perfume filled his senses even without her presence and the clear brown eyes were ever fixed on his. The halo of thick dark brown hair tempted his fingers even in his imagination. He'd heard that a black person's hair was wiry to the touch but Dr. Stafford's looked silky soft. He was eager to make his own assessment.

"My name is Belinda."

The teenager's voice dispatched all thoughts of passion.

"I'm a volunteer. The nurse asked me to help you," she chattered on as she worked. "Since you haven't been eating, she thought maybe you couldn't feed yourself."

"I can do it." As Belinda raised the head of his bed, he wiggled into a more erect position while trying to keep his hand from swinging on the pole. He wished she'd leave so he could think about his doctor. She intrigued him in many ways.

"Well, I can at least set it up for you."

"Very well." Tetsuro eased back against the pillow and watched the eager young woman fuss over the tray. His hand throbbed in cadence with his internal beat.

Belinda opened the milk carton and stuck a straw into it. She pulled back the foil on the juice container. Tetsuro took the plastic cup and drank while she busied herself with seasoning and buttering everything she felt needed such attention. Tetsuro let her. He wasn't going to eat anyway.

This was his sixth visit to America, on tours lasting months. Since he and the troupe often ate at American restaurants, he was familiar with the cuisine. The hospital food left much to be desired. In restaurants, he could order fresh vegetables, salad, fruit and meat without the thick sauces and gravies. He hated to fall into the trap of being so stereotypically Japanese, but he'd kill for a bowl of *gohan* and *shoyu*!

"There," Belinda finished proudly. "Can I help with anything else?"

Not unless you have a bowl of rice and a bottle of soy sauce in that pinafore.

"Iie," he voiced aloud. "No. Thank you." Tetsuro moved his head forward in a slight nod of a bow.

"Okay. Just call." Bubbly Belinda bounded out.

Tetsuro pushed the over-the-bed table away but kept the apple juice within reach. Through the large glass window at his right he took in the view of Cleveland's skyline. However, being awake and moving around made his left hand hurt more, so when the juice was finished, he lowered the head of his bed and tried to go back to sleep. Dreams of Dr. Stafford began anew.

"Takamitsu-*san*!"

"Tetsu!"

"Te-*chan*!"

A clamor of Japanese voices roused him. Tetsuro opened his eyes to find several of the drum troupe entering his room.

"What some will not do for a day off!" Susumu greeted. He placed a small box and large Styrofoam cup on the table. Tetsuro supposed Belinda had been quieter in her return since the lunch tray was gone. "How are you, my friend?"

"All right." Tetsuro changed his position as they approached him, pleased to see his friends. The heavily muscled Susumu performed the strenuous ritual with the large *O-Daiko* in the show, the same drum that had slammed into his hand and led him to meet Dr. McKenna Stafford, who was now consuming his thoughts.

"This looks terrible!" Kifume, the one who'd indirectly caused the accident, peered into the bandage on his hand.

"You should be on this side." As he spoke an ache started in the left side of his chest. It passed and he forgot about it.

"Where is your smile, my friend?" Susumu asked.

"I left it in the back of that truck. How was the concert last night?"

"Not too bad," Susumu answered. "Arima-*san* managed to keep up. It will be nice to have you back though."

"I do not know when that will be," Tetsuro sighed. He inhaled deeply to compensate being short of breath. "My doctor says it will be some time before I can use my hand again." Once the hand was healed, he would have no reason to see Dr. Stafford. The idea was bittersweet.

"We thought you might be hungry so we brought you some *sushi*." Kifume opened the containers on the table. "Can you use *hashi*?"

"That was thoughtful of you." Tetsuro watched Kifume go through the same motions Belinda had earlier, but he was more excited about the results. She soon had small pieces of rice, fish and seaweed arranged perfectly with a small mound of *wasabi* alongside a cup of *shoyu*. Then she took the eating sticks from their paper casing and, after breaking them apart, rubbed the sticks together to dispel the splinters so common to disposable, restaurant *hashi*. Then Kifume moved the table across him so he could reach it easier. When Tetsuro sat further erect to accept the traditional eating implements, the movement hurt his hand and chest.

"It is a great little restaurant," Susumu told him. "We had lunch there."

Tetsuro carefully stirred *wasabi* into the *shoyu*. He then took a small glob of rice topped with a piece with shrimp between the sticks and dipped it into the mix before putting it into his mouth.

"It is good," Tetsuro agreed after he swallowed.

"Here is some tea, but it is lukewarm."

"Anything would be a nice change from the juice I am about to float away with." Tetsuro took a sip after another piece of *sushi*.

"Ki-*chan* wanted to get you a mix of *sushi* and *sashimi*," Susumu continued. "I reminded her you did not like *sashimi* all that much."

"I am glad you did. What is all of that?" He pointed to the suitcase, duffel and other things another of the drum troupe had carried and set inside the doorway.

"Your things," Susumu answered. "We will check out of the hotel in the morning since the plane to Pittsburgh is at nine."

"Because we don't know how long you'll be in the hospital," John Restor, the troupe's agent, inserted, changing the language of the conversation to English, "or how long it'll be before your doctor releases you to return to Japan, we must leave your things with you. The hospital assures me you'll be cared for after dismissal. They have apartments where you can stay. Right now, there's no vacancy, but they'll work with your doctor. Your visa's good until the end of the year." Ever the efficient manager, Restor had covered every aspect of the event. "Hopefully, by then you'll be well and can go home."

"I would hope my hand's usable in six months." A long acquaintance with his doctor was possible yet.

The familiar food satisfied his senses as the pungent sting of the *wasabi* spread through his sinuses and the salty *shoyu* washed through his mouth like nectar. The fish and rice—everything—eased his anxiety.

Restor asked, "Has your doctor been in?"

"Not today. I saw her after surgery but not since. Another doctor, a heart doctor, came by. They say my heart almost stopped, but I do not recall it."

The *sushi* was gone and Tetsuro sipped the tea. Kifume gathered the debris to throw away.

"She's cute," Kifume commented. She continued to speak English.

"Who?" Tetsuro feigned ignorance. His assessment of Dr. Stafford didn't include the word *cute*. *Beautiful* was the adjective he had in mind.

"Your doctor."

"I guess." Tetsuro could not look at the girl. "What is important is that she is skilled."

"From what I understand, she's the top in her field," the manager interjected.

"This could prove fortuitous, Te-*san*." Susumu spoke in Japanese.

"How is that?" Tetsu concentrated on the cold tea.

"If I recall correctly, you have always had a bit of a craving for Western women."

"I do not know what you are talking about." He *did* know but that was the last thing he was going to admit.

"Do not pretend with me! We have known each other too many years and shared too many secrets. You are from Tokyo. America is everywhere there. All Tokyo boys try to be American tough guys. You said yourself you had movie star posters on your walls when you were a teenager and did you not save you money to go to rock concerts at Budokan? Not *sumo* but rock and roll! We poor farm boys never experienced McDonald's or Coca-Cola until we began touring."

"I guess you are correct, but I have not been a teenager for a long time." The memory of himself as a teenager was clear. He'd embraced everything Western, scoffing at the old customs of his grandparents.

"Do not lie to me, Te-*san*!" Susumu playfully punched his good arm. "I remember the story about the public bath and the American tourist."

"What has that got to do with now?"

With ease the memory of the incident came up from Tetsuro's subconscious.

The new surges of puberty had prevented him from keeping the custom of the Japanese bath. From babyhood, he had been instructed that the community bath was not to be viewed as erotic. Sex was far from the purpose of mixed bathing and one did not look upon another's nakedness. To be so overt in his study of the pale skin of the full-bodied woman was the height of bad manners. The woman did not notice the boy's stare and thus had no idea of his insult. His mother, on the other hand, had been very aware and the scolding he received once they returned home had been accompanied by a painful grip on his ear.

Tetsuro didn't know whether his mother was more upset because he was looking or because it was a European woman who'd caught his eye. As an adult, he had kept company with both Japanese and Caucasian women, but had been drawn more to the buxom Western female. Until he met Dr. Stafford.

Listening to Susumu's teasing, Tetsuro wished he could crawl into the cup of cold tea. It might stop the fiery flush creeping up his throat. Even his ears were getting warm. Why had he told Susumu the story? Because they were friends and *very drunk.*

Susumu's face broke into a wide grin. "Maybe you can fulfill your fantasy."

"She is my doctor. Nothing more," Tetsuro protested. "Besides, why would she want to have anything to do with me?"

"I have never heard you be so humble. You who could have any woman you wished?" Susumu whispered now as Kifume came nearer.

While the men talked, she'd opened Tetsuro's duffel bag. Now she placed the portable CD player and a stack of CD cases on the bedside table. She also put out the book she had seen him reading.

"In Japan, that is true," Tetsuro responded to Susumu's comment. Talking was becoming arduous. He pushed the over bed table away and tried to relax further into the bedding.

Kifume pulled the sheet up his chest over the hospital issue gown. "You look tired."

"I am a little." Tetsuro sagged into his pillow. He was glad Kifume had unwittingly changed the subject. With his stomach full, he could sleep contentedly. Except he couldn't seem to take a deep breath.

"We best go. We have to get to rehearsal," Susumu said.

"I will miss you. Please write."

"We will miss you, too!" Kifume placed her hand on Tetsuro's uninjured arm. Although they'd shared a bed a few times, this was as close to open affection as she could show him.

"You get better, Tetsu," Susumu voiced an order. "I want to see your smile back!" He joined Restor and departed the room. Kifume hung back.

Once the men were in the hallway, she addressed Tetsuro.

"You know that…problem I told you about?"

"The one that distracted me so this…" he moved his hanging hand, "…happened?" He winced with the pain the gesture caused.

"Yes, well, never mind. It is not true."

"Was it before?"

"Are you saying I would lie?"

"Are you lying?"

"No." Kifume sounded indignant.

"Then I guess I will believe you." Tetsuro sighed as deeply as he could.

"Goodbye." Kifume left the room without looking back.

CHAPTER SIX

As if drawn by some unknown force, McKenna returned to the hospital. She'd taken an early morning nap to make up for lost sleep, then gone for a five-mile run around her Shaker Heights neighborhood. While both were refreshing, her conscience would not allow her to enjoy her day off until she saw Takamitsu. He hadn't been far from her thoughts all morning. She'd even taken his CD to listen to while she ran. The beat of the Japanese drums had provided a perfect pace and the run had been the best she'd had in weeks.

But her thoughts shouldn't be so engaged with the man and her brain's inability to let go of him aggravated her. He was her patient. He was from Japan. He would be gone soon. All the more reason not to allow an attraction to him to grow. If she wanted anything, and she wasn't sure she did, it was a home and family, not some touring performer who probably saw babies as an entrapment.

Annoyed with her capricious side, she approached Tetsuro's room. She'd declined the charge nurse's offer to accompany her when she passed by the nurses' station.

"Mr. Takamitsu." She entered the room, speaking his name quietly. The room was dark and quiet, the early evening sunlight not strong enough to intrude through the drawn curtains.

There was no reply. As she neared his bed, she saw he was lying quite still. The pole suspending his hand was pulled to the opposite side of the bed and McKenna decided his back was to her. A sheet pulled to his waist covered his lower body. Coming around the bed's foot, she noticed his position was more fetal than lateral. His hair hung over his face. That was odd. Why hadn't Takamitsu brushed it away? Was he so filled with narcotics he was comatose?

"Tetsuro," McKenna spoke louder. Her fingers pushed the light switch recessed in the bedrail.

He remained silent.

McKenna put a hand on his shoulder, gently shaking him.

"Tetsu!" she shouted.

He remained unresponsive.

McKenna shook harder. "Tetsuro, wake up!"

This didn't produce a response either.

McKenna's heart rate sped up. Her breath caught in her throat but her brain took over and told her to concentrate on her assessment skills. She became more aggressive, pushing hard enough on his shoulder to move him onto his back.

"Tetsu!"

McKenna brushed the raven hair off his face. His eyes remained closed as his head lolled back on the pillow. His color was pallid, his full lips dusky. She looked down. His chest labored to rise and fall and he gasped for breath.

"Tetsu!" Her voice rose a pitch. Her hand groped for the nurse call device. When she found it, she followed the cord to yank it out of the socket. This set off the klaxon of the emergency call light.

Nurses rushed into the room in response to the alarm.

"Get some O^2 on him," McKenna ordered. She quickly unhooked the suspended hand and lowered it to the bed, pushing the pole to the corner. In this state he wouldn't feel pain or it would be enough stimulus to rouse him. A nurse pulled an oxygen mask from the cabinet over the head of the bed. "Tetsu!" McKenna jerked the plastic mask from the nurse's hand and put it over his face and mouth.

"Dr. McK…" Tetsuro's eyes fluttered as he tried to speak. He coughed dryly.

A nurse wrapped a blood pressure cuff around his undamaged arm. Another put ECG leads on his chest and an O^2 saturation clip on his finger. The first nurse pushed the start button on the blood pressure machine. The sound of the heart monitor began to beep, the rate of his heart rapid.

The nurse read off the vital signs. "Heart rate's 123, respirations 32,

O^2 sat's 85, BP's 75/32."

"Call a code," McKenna told the nurse. "Tetsu, what hurts?" The more information she had, the better she could treat him.

"*Mune ga kurushii.*" He tried to touch his left upper chest with his right hand. "*Iki ga dekinai.*" His words were forced even in his native language. He coughed again.

"Speak English, damn it! I can't help you if I can't understand you!" McKenna shouted. What was wrong? *Think McKenna! You're a doctor. You know how to figure it out.* Her hands pulled the stethoscope from around her neck and put the earpieces in her ears and the bell on Tetsuro's chest. She listened.

"I cannot...breathe." The translation came in gasping breaths. "My...chest...hurts."

His eyelids began to flutter, threatening to close.

"Stay with me, Tetsu! I need an ABG here!" she shouted to the nurses. When she yanked the stethoscope from her ears, the ends caught in one of her loop earrings. Freeing herself required further yanking, frustrating McKenna even more. "Where's respiratory?" she quizzed as she straightened from the bent position. "Keep your eyes open, Tetsu."

Tetsuro endeavored to stay awake. His color was worsening, his lips almost blue.

The emergency room team burst into the room.

"I'm right here," the respiratory therapist announced. He knelt beside the bed and took hold of Tetsuro's arm. By instinct, he began to seek the spot to stick a needle into the radial artery of Tetsuro's right hand.

"Get me a chest tube tray!" McKenna ordered. *It has to be... What else could it be?*

"What's up, Mac?" Rick Ramirez ran into the room.

"Got it," the respiratory therapist declared success in obtaining arterial blood gas and rushed off with the blood specimen.

McKenna gave the ER doctor her diagnosis. "Tension pneumo. Get me a number ten blade!"

"Want some help?" Ramirez offered from the opposite side of the bed. "Somebody get an IV going," he said firmly. "Maybe he doesn't need a tube. A needle stick might work," he suggested to McKenna.

"No!" McKenna ran her hands over Tetsuro's chest, feeling the distended left side. She searched for landmarks to insert the tube. "There're no breath sounds on the left."

"McKenna," Ramirez said. "You're an orthopod."

"I'm a doctor first," she asserted. "I can do this!" She looked toward the foot of the bed where a nurse opened the sterile chest tube insertion tray.

"I know, but I've done a million of these."

"I can do it! Where are the gloves?" McKenna searched the area of chaos.

"Here, Dr. Stafford." A nurse opened a package of sterile gloves and held the insert out to the doctor.

McKenna pulled the latex gloves on, then picked the surgical knife off the sterile tray. With no hesitation, she pressed the razor sharp point into the firm bronze skin. Crimson rivulets dripped down his side. She applied more pressure to enter the chest cavity. Muscle gave way.

With what breath he had, Tetsuro screamed.

It was the worse sound McKenna had ever heard, cutting into her heart as painfully as the knife in his chest. She pulled the instrument back, replacing it with her index finger.

"Push 10 milligrams of morphine," she ordered as her glove finger probed the surgical incision. She was rewarded with the sound of escaping air. Automatically, she reached out for equipment and a nurse handed her the chest tube. Under Rick's watchful gaze she shoved the plastic tubing into the hole her finger had widened.

"Nice work, Doctor," Ramirez declared.

"For an orthopod?" McKenna gave him a weak smile.

"For anyone."

McKenna began the process of suturing the tube in place while the nurse secured it to a waterseal container.

"Repeat the ABGs," she told the respiratory therapist who'd

returned with the results of the first specimen. The young man held the paper in front of McKenna's face so she could read the results without holding it. The numbers told the story. Much longer and his damaged hand would be the least of his worries. He would have had brain damage. "Thanks."

The tech moved out of the way. "Sure thing."

"Sats?" McKenna finished the sutures.

"Coming up. Ninety-two," a nurse answered. "BP's rising, 98/65 and his heart rate's 96."

"Tetsu," McKenna spoke in a calm voice. His breathing had slowed and color was returning to his lips.

"The morphine's on board," the nurse reminded her, dropping the used syringe into the biohazard container on the wall.

Staring at the soft, relaxed features of her patient, McKenna didn't acknowledge her information. He was sleeping. The crisis was over.

Maybe. A pneumothorax often had its own set of complications.

"I'll dress the site," the nurse said, urging McKenna to step away.

"No. I will. If I can't trust you to monitor him, why should I trust your dressings?" McKenna was hardly aware of the insults she hurled at the nurse. Her concern was her patient. Or was it the man? She cared for her patients' safety and health but she'd never questioned a nurse's ability before. What was so special about Tetsuro Takamitsu that she was suddenly so protective?

The nurse didn't speak as she handed the surgeon 4X4s and tape. Once the dressing was secure, McKenna pulled the latex gloves off. Tetsuro's blood stained her tailored pink shirt and navy twill pants.

"I'm going to go change and be right back."

In the physician's lounge, McKenna went over the event. First an arrhythmia; now a pneumothorax. What was going on? The man had had an operation to repair his hand fractures. The repair, while tedious, was fairly simple. Why was this happening? Ordinarily she'd discharge him today or tomorrow at the latest, but now...who knew?

Another thing she didn't know was why he made her feel so tingly inside. Being in the Japanese man's presence caused her heart to skip a beat and her breath to clench in her chest. Her skin prickled with anticipation, and a flush rushed through her any time she expected to see him. The thought caused her to smile as she walked out of the lounge.

When she returned to the nurses' station, dressed in blue cotton scrubs, McKenna was ready to address the problem of what had happened. Her face no longer held the smile thinking about him had instigated.

"All right, ladies," she spoke to the nurses grouped around the desk. "Let's talk about Mr. Takamitsu. What the hell happened? Wasn't anyone watching him? Weren't his vital signs taken?"

The nurses exchanged looks.

"Well?" she pressed.

"His last BP was 110/67," the charge nurse answered, holding his chart open to the vital sign page.

"When was that?" McKenna reached for Tetsuro's chart. "The man was in critical condition when I arrived."

"I believe it was at mid morning."

"At ten a.m.? Eleven?" She whipped her head around to check the clock. "That was three hours ago! Don't you do vital signs every two hours?"

"Only immediately post op."

"He *is* immediately post op!"

McKenna flipped through the pages to find the sheet with blood pressure, heart rate, and respirations charted there. Over the hours since his surgery, his vital signs had been taken frequently in the recovery room and only twice since he'd been transferred.

"Did someone think I might need to know that his BP had been dropping steadily and he was tachycardic?"

"Your orders have specific parameters for when to call," the nurse defended.

McKenna did some more rapid flipping of pages and read her post op orders. "Mr. Takamitsu's blood pressure is clearly in the boundaries of when I want to be called," she informed the nurse. Taking a deep breath, she collected her thoughts. This wasn't the time to be discussing the nurses' care. She'd have to take the matter up with the clinical manager of the orthopedic floor. "I want vital signs every hour for the next eight. We'll see how he's doing then."

The nurse blanched, recoiling from her words and the sound of the chart slamming on the desk. "Yes, ma'am."

McKenna walked to Tetsuro's room.

An hour after she'd first entered his room that afternoon Tetsuro's situation was more reassuring. The area was tidy and his hand was again suspended on the pole. The oxygen mask remained over his mouth and nose and the monitor equipment continued to bleep reassuring sounds. McKenna read the numbers, pleased with them.

She stood beside the bed and took in her patient. His face was once more a healthy bronze and his lips were enticingly pink. Brushing the unruly hair back off his forehead, her hand was warmed by a tantalizing flicker. The touch stirred something inside her long quiet, making her linger with her fingers on the warm, smooth skin.

"Tetsuro."

As before, he didn't wake.

"Tetsu," she said louder.

Endeavoring to open his eyes, he responded, "Dr. Stafford."

"How do you feel?" She took her hand off his forehead.

"My chest hurts." He put his hand over the bandage on his chest and managed to keep his eyes open. "But I can breathe better. What happened?"

"You had what we call a pneumothorax caused by a small puncture of your upper lung. It probably happened when Dr. Furumiya put the subclavian block in to help with your hand pain. You have a chest tube now and in a day I'll remove it. I want to give your lung time to repair itself."

"You...saved my life, Dr. Stafford." Tetsuro gazed at her with his soulful, deep brown eyes.

"I don't think I did anything so dramatic." Her face warmed. "I'll check on you tomorrow."

"Very well. *Sayonara.*"

McKenna delayed leaving and Tetsuro slipped back to sleep under the influence of the narcotic.

Tetsuro wanted to go back to sleep but it was impossible. He couldn't move without disturbing the tube Dr. Stafford had inserted and increasing the pain. But he could finally breathe.

Staring out the window, he watched rain splatter against the glass in the evening's darkness. The gloomy evening paralleled his mood. The last thing he remembered before sinking into unconsciousness was his friends' visit. Now his mind was full of questions. What would he do now that they were gone? He was completely alone. What would he do if he couldn't use his hand again? His life might as well be over if he could use it for everyday tasks but not for drumming.

And his strange attraction to Dr. Stafford made him question himself even more. The sooner she let him out of the hospital, the less he would be tempted to form a relationship with her. If he pursued her, she could reject him, an event he had not often encountered. Or she could respond but eventually break his heart. His heart bore old wounds that had never healed completely. He did not want to disturb the scar.

The troubling thoughts were still there when he awoke Sunday. The rain continued and the dark skies reflected his mood all the more.

Dr. Stafford's voice broke into his thoughts. "Are you in pain?"

"Depends on what you're talking about." Tetsuro turned to her and she greeted him with a professional smile. Her dark-skinned complexion was light enough to suggest a blush. The soft waves of thick black hair framed her oval face and covered her shoulders. Bangs scattered over her forehead. The carefully arched eyebrows accentuated the roundness of her eyes and Tetsuro was drawn once more into her amber pools.

"I was talking about your hand and your chest." Dr. Stafford approached the bedside. Her slender long legs, exposed by the short skirt beneath the lengthy lab coat, carried her across the floor in a gliding motion. She held herself with an authority earned by years of study and training. A nurse was behind her. "What are you talking about?"

"Nothing important." He certainly didn't want to air his mood to either of the women.

"So. Back to what I was talking about."

"They both hurt. The way my hand throbs, I wonder what is in store for the future." His fears had spilled out despite himself.

"Too soon to worry about that." McKenna tapped the chart. "Says here you haven't asked for any pain medication."

"Did not know I could," Tetsuro confessed. "But it did not really start hurting until this morning."

She touched the fingers nestled in cotton wadding. "Wiggle," she instructed, and he complied with great difficulty and pain. "I would begin to worry about nerve damage if it hadn't started to complain by now. You can ask for medication to help."

"Then I'd like some." He tried to smile. Her perfume dispatched the hospital smell and washed over him with warm familiarity.

"I was afraid you were going to be the stoic *samurai* on me."

"What do you know about *samurai*, *Sensei*? Do you not think they felt pain when those nasty swords cut them?"

"I don't know much. I'm sorry. I didn't mean to offend you." There was a soft luster to her eyes now.

"I am the one who should apologize. I suppose I am feeling a little short-tempered." Tetsuro couldn't tolerate the downcast look she gave him.

"What did you call me? *San say*?" The quiet smile she gave him cleared the doldrums from his brain.

"*Sin say*. It means doctor or teacher." The way her full lips formed around the Japanese word made his heart swell.

Dr. Stafford was back to studying his chart. "I also read that you haven't been eating."

"Did not appeal to me."

"Should I have dietary come and arrange meals more Japanese?"

"No." His upbringing, the custom of never becoming a burden, caused him to refuse. It would be too much trouble for them to cater to his stomach. "I am used to America and your foods. I have been here so many times, and for so long, I could pass as Japanese-American." The muscles of his face relaxed at her concern. The aloneness of his situation had settled in, but the appearance of Dr. Stafford had uplifted his spirit. "*Domo arigato.*"

"How do I say, 'You're welcome?'" Her face relaxed but she clutched his chart to her breasts.

"You just did." He grinned at her.

"No." McKenna laughed a sweet, light giggle. "In Japanese. How do I say it?"

"*Do...*" he enunciated carefully.

"*Do,*" McKenna repeated.

"*Ita...*"

"*Ita...*"

"*...shi...*"

"*shi*"

"*...mash...*"

"*mash*"

"*...te.*"

"*te.*"

"Now put it all together. *Do itashimashite.*"

"*Do itashimashite.*" McKenna stumbled over the syllables as she tried to string them as one.

"Close enough." Tetsuro laughed and the doctor joined him.

"So much for language lessons." McKenna wiped away the laughter tears. She took several minutes to gather her composure

"You should laugh more often. Your face lights up."

"Have you eaten *anything*?" She ignored his remark.

"My friends brought me *sushi* yesterday."

"Ugh." Her face contorted into a mask of disgust.

"Do you not like *sushi*?"

"I must admit I haven't ever tried it, but…raw fish? Ugh!" McKenna repeated. "Cat food."

"You have never been introduced to it properly."

The nurse cut in, "I'll have something for pain brought to you."

Tetsuro glared at the woman, upset she'd interfered with their conversation. He didn't fail to notice Dr. Stafford's sudden return to the decorum of their doctor-patient relationship. Perhaps it was improper for him to think she could become his friend. Maybe it was his abrupt realization of his solitude that had made him reach out for friendship from anyone he could. A flutter deep within, however, assured him this was something deeper.

"Well," Dr. Stafford stammered. "I'll see you tomorrow."

"I will be right here."

"And so you will."

Just as quickly, she was gone and he was alone.

As he stared out the window, Tetsuro noticed a drenched little bird sitting on the high ledge, prompting traditional thought. An easy *haiku* popped in his mind.

These barn swallows
are they looking for nest sites
in the hospital's eaves?

Did it hint of his search? He pulled the sheet higher on his chest and turned away from the window.

CHAPTER SEVEN

In the hallway, McKenna paused to make sure her heart was back to its regular, unflappable pace. Why was she awash with such anxiety and palpitations when she was in that man's presence? He was just a patient, another operation of screws and wires; plaster and ace bandages. Yet when she came into Tetsuro Takamitsu's presence, his eyes captivated her no matter what she tried to concentrate on. A hot flush lit her cheeks as she recalled the dark raven beard over his strong jaws. The smudge above the sensuous full curve of his upper lip hinted at the beginning of mustache.

"Dr. Stafford?" the nurse questioned. "Are you all right?"

"What? Yes. I'm fine." McKenna turned her attention to the chart. She wrote her progress note, additional orders and was finished. "Make sure someone asks Mr. Takamitsu if he would like to shave." She turned to leave.

"Since when do you care if a patient shaves?" The nurse must have thought she whispered too low for McKenna to hear. She was wrong.

"It's not that I care personally, but a man needs to be cared for the way he cares for himself. He was clean-shaven the day I admitted him so he'll be more content if that need is attended to. Please see to it." McKenna handed the woman the chart. She couldn't let her see that she, too, was wondering why she'd mentioned the need to shave the exotic shadow deepening the planes of his face.

She left the floor and headed for her office.

"What are you doing out of bed?" Dr. Stafford confronted Tetsuro as she entered his hospital room and saw him coming out of the bathroom.

"I had to…" He motioned his head to indicate the toilet without description. "You would not want me to…"

"Suppose not," McKenna muttered. She ducked her face to hide the blush by reading his chart. Tetsuro saw through the pretense since he hadn't done anything for the past four days to take note of. The only excitement had been when she'd removed the chest tube, another rather painful event.

"I don't want you overdoing things." McKenna raised her face.

"Very well." Tetsuro moved on the bed. He pushed the IV pole supporting his hand in place and sat on the edge of the mattress. "I am driving this thing better every day."

"It's time we take your hand down." Dr. Stafford reached to unhook the stockinet from the pole. As she lowered it, she cradled his hand in her own.

"Ah," Tetsuro moaned softly.

"Does it hurt?" She held his hand gently at the level of his chest.

"My shoulder is stiff." Tetsuro reached with his good hand and rubbed his shoulder.

"That's normal. How does the hand feel?"

"Throbs a little. I can tolerate it."

"You don't have to *tolerate* it. We have medicine for pain," Dr. Stafford explained. "Or is this a cultural thing I'm unaware of?"

"Perhaps. My drum training is intense and encourages mastering pain and fatigue. It will be all right." With his good hand, Tetsuro took his hand back, brushing against her briefly. He wondered if his touch was the cause of the spark in her eye. "Is it healing well?"

"Seems to be." She inspected the exposed digits protruding from the cotton wadding. "The bruising's fading."

"They almost look normal." Dr. Stafford's head was close to his face and the soft, floral scent of her perfume drifted to him. "You smell nice."

"Excuse me?" She popped her head up and away. She cast a look sideways at the nurse who hung behind her.

"Your perfume is nice," he repeated.

"Thank you."

"And your blush is attractive," he continued. The rush of blood to her cheeks deepened the russet tones of her skin.

"Why are you talking like this? You're my patient," Dr. Stafford chided.

"Can we not be friends, too?" Tetsuro asked.He smiled at her nervousness.

"I don't see why…we can't be friends." Her lips formed a gentle smile not unlike Tetsuro's. Her face relaxed and she said, "I didn't realize you were so tall."

"You expected me to be a little monkey man?" Why did she keep changing subjects? *Small talk must not be easy for her.* He moved to rest his back against the elevated head of the bed and pulled his right leg bent at the knee onto the bed. His left hand rested on his thigh.

"I didn't mean to offend you." Dr. Stafford took a seat on the end of his bed. Her hands were folded around the metal chart back lying on her lap.

"I am not offended. You can blame my unusual stature on a stray Manchurian ancestor many centuries ago. There are many tall men on the island of Kyushu where my father's family comes from. I was born and raised in Tokyo and my six-foot-two height was out of place there." Tetsuro watched her as he spoke. With all of his visits to America, he had met numerous people, but never had any long conversations with anyone, except conversations about drumming.

But conversation wasn't what intrigued him about Dr. Stafford. Her lips, dusty rose with a touch of lipstick, were moist and inviting and formed a soft mouth in an oval face. Her light brown eyes, wide and curved, were framed with heavy black lashes. Balanced by a determined chin, her nose was delicate. The blush coloring her cheeks emphasized their apple-shape. But what attracted him most, besides her eyes, was the heavy mane of waves the color of rich brown shot through with honeyed hues evident in the sunshine beaming through the window after a weekend of rain. The desire to run his fingers through her hair was overwhelming.

"What are we going to do about this?" He gestured at his hand, needing to move the conversation away from the direction he wanted to rush toward. "From here?"

"Healing, then rehab. Normally, I would be discharging you, but…"

"I do not have anywhere to go."

"No. You don't. Social services reports the accommodations we have for visitors are full. The Utilization and Review Committee has allowed me to extend your stay a while longer. And with the pneumo, I wouldn't want you discharged for a few more days anyway. Is it going to be a problem?"

"*Iie.*" Tetsuro picked at the edges of the bandage, then gazed into her eyes. "I do not want to complain, but I am bored. Watching television is good only for a short while. And I've finished the only book I have. Inactivity is something I do not take to well."

"I'll write an order to allow you to leave the floor. There's a gift shop for books and magazines and a gym in the physical therapy unit. One of the nurses can escort you there and then you can go anytime you want. There will be personnel there to help you with your injured hand."

"I would like that. I am used to physical exercise. It is a discipline of my drum school."

McKenna found the trance she fell under each time she came into Tetsuro Takamitsu's presence wrapping its tentacles around her. His statement about being an athlete made her realize her patient was no longer clad in a hospital gown. His golden body rested before her covered with only a pair of shorts inches away from being indecent. She couldn't help noticing his wide, solid chest with muscles rigidly outlined or his long, firm legs stretched out on the bed.

Her gaze swept back over the length of his body upward and she saw he was watching her. His exotic eyes looked at her with a hint of laughter trying to escape from the deep dark chocolate pools. His face, full of life, was saved from softness by the strong line of his jaw and the long, narrow nose.

McKenna was struck by how equine-like Tetsuro tossed the thick raven hair. The river of darkness surrounding his head was board-straight in an even, blunt cut and fell to his shoulders like a smooth veil. He casually stroked a stray strand back behind his ear.

Mentally, she shook her head to free herself.

"I have to make rounds on the rest of my patients." McKenna stood and took a hesitant step toward the doorway.

"What did the cardiologist say about my heart?"

"Dr. Whitman couldn't find anything wrong." McKenna looked again at the report in the chart. "He suspects it was an event caused by the anesthesia. Dr. Furumiya said the same."

"Then I should not worry about having a heart attack?"

"I don't see any reason to worry." McKenna sensed he wanted to keep her in his room. She wanted to stay, but it would be inappropriate. "I must go now."

"Dr. Stafford." Tetsuro spoke from his perch on his bed. He was like a two-year-old putting off bedtime. "Would it be possible for me to take a bath?"

"Haven't the nurses been helping you shower?" She restrained herself from moving nearer to assess his hygiene. There was no doubt it was impeccable. His body was well cared for in every way possible. McKenna held the metal chart before her breasts as a shield between them. She could not let the temptation of Tetsuro overtake her.

"Yes, I am allowed to shower every morning. They wrap plastic around my hand. Bring me towels. Even turn the spigot on and adjust the temperature, but I am…Japanese."

"I am very aware of your nationality, Mr. Takamitsu."

"That I am sure of." Tetsuro's full lips curved into a wry smile. "How much do you know about the Japanese?"

"I told you the other day, not much." She shifted her weight and the heel of her pump tapped impatiently.

"Please, Dr. McKenna, sit." He waved his hand toward the foot of his bed. She gingerly lowered her hip to the bed again, feeling it sag under her weight. Tetsuro shifted to prevent his legs from bumping into hers. "We are an island nation. Surrounded by water, we have made a ritual of bathing. We have been known to bathe several times a day. Shinto, our national religion, and Buddhism both teach the principle of cleanliness. To that end, it is almost inbred in us to immerse our bodies in hot water for long periods of time."

A heat not unlike that of a steamy bubble bath washed over McKenna as she conjured a picture of Tetsuro in a deep tub full of hot water. Nude. Not an image she wanted to form but one she did not rush to push away. The result was a prickling sensation deep inside her. Whether she wanted the vision and the results or not, she had to ignore them both.

"I…I…don't know…what I mean, is…the nurses know more about baths versus showering." The words were stuck inside her, reluctant to emerge and break the spell of the picture of naked Tetsuro. "I…I'll…I'll have them see to it."

"Thank you very much, *sensei*. It does not have to be a Jacuzzi or anything like that."

"Well…" McKenna stood. "If there is nothing else…"

"No. Everything is well." Tetsuro gave her one of his warm smiles, a twinkle in the dark brown eyes.

She had to leave or she would be back to doing those stupid things again. Besides, she had a department meeting and it wouldn't do to arrive with a blush on her cheeks.

"Will I see you tomorrow?" She read anticipation in his solemn eyes.

"Why wouldn't you?"

"Your comment about extending my stay instead of dismissing me makes me think I am no longer a regular patient."

"You don't need hospitalization, but as long as you are here, I'm required to visit you daily," McKenna explained.

"You are…*required* to visit me." Tetsuro's words were spoken in a tone of despondency.

"Then I'll be seeing you." McKenna left the room.

"Diane," McKenna addressed the nurse standing at the nurses' station as several other nurses did paperwork. "Could you have someone take Mr. Takamitsu to the gym in PT? He's bored and wants to work out. And to the gift shop for some books?"

"I'd hate to see *that* body out of shape," a nurse commented. "Did you notice the definition of his abs? My husband spends hours everyday in the gym and would kill for a six-pack like that."

"No wonder you volunteered to give him his bed bath the first day post-op, Libby!" Diane laughed along with the other nurses.

"Hey. I can respect a great body when I see one!" Libby joined her friends' laughter. The petite woman with a head full of red curls came to stand across from McKenna with only the counter between them. "Can't you, Dr. Stafford?"

"Can't say I noticed." McKenna feigned disinterest, but a heat rose to her face. The nurses were their usual friendly selves. She'd apologized to Libby for her remarks during the chest tube insertion and all was well once more between them.

"But, you know, I think I'd have a problem having sex with a man whose hips are smaller than mine," Libby confessed.

"Libby!" Diane admonished.

"Well, wouldn't you?" Libby asked. "Dr. Stafford doesn't have to worry about that with the great shape she's in. That and not having had babies!"

"Libby…" McKenna closed the chart and pushed it toward the unit secretary to transcribe her orders. To stand here and talk about a patient's body was hardly professional, but they did it all the time. Now it had taken a personal turn and McKenna was uncomfortable. Libby didn't know how close she was cutting.

"Come on, Dr. Stafford," Libby urged. "You're a woman. Surely you've looked at Mr. Takamitsu. Especially in the OR. When he was asleep."

"I looked at his hand." She was not going to get caught confessing.

"I bet you caught a glimpse of the rest," Libby scoffed.

"There was no need to pay attention to any more of him," McKenna argued. "I'm an orthopedic surgeon, not a urologist."

"Aha! Nobody mentioned *that* part of him," Libby squealed.

"That's one of the perks for working on urology, but the patients are usually eighty years old!" one of the other nurses declared.

"I don't have time for your erotic fantasies about patients." McKenna picked up her bag.

"Mr. Takamitsu is better dream material than the stuffed shirt you bring around here," Libby said before McKenna could leave.

"Libby, I don't know what you mean," McKenna offered in defense. She should be offended by the personal comments of the nurse, but she wasn't. There was camaraderie between doctors and nurses and the teasing was allowed. In her father's day, doctors had been gods and nurses, their handmaidens. Today, the longer nurses worked with the same doctors, the deeper the friendship. The fact that they were all women made it easier to establish such a relationship, open to free banter.

"Dr. Stafford," Libby scoffed. "Your boyfriend…"

"James is a friend." McKenna didn't recognize her clarification was the same as Tetsuro's in the operating room.

"Okay, but he's so stuffy. Mr. Takamitsu would be an adventure."

"I don't need adventure." McKenna began to walk away.

"We all need adventure!" Libby called out to her.

"Bye, ladies." McKenna waved a hand behind her as she returned to her office.

McKenna sat at her desk between patient appointments. A cup of cold coffee was at her elbow and a pile of paperwork was neatly stacked. She paid no attention to either.

The conversation at the nurses' station echoed in her thoughts. To agree with Libby about the excellent physique of Tetsuro Takamitsu would have revealed too much. Truth be told, his all too visible muscles affected her, whether she wanted to be or not. But he was her patient! Moreover, he was from another country and would leave once the treatment was complete. Pursuing such a relationship would be useless, even if she wanted to! McKenna sat bolt upright. She didn't want to be any more to Tetsuro than his doctor. Suddenly her thoughts were deflected when she knocked the coffee over.

"Damn it!" she spat as she mopped the cold, brown liquid creeping toward the papers. "Why do men make me act so stupid?"

CHAPTER EIGHT

"The last item we need to address," the chief of orthopedic surgery said, "is my position as chief which is about to expire. I would like to nominate Dr. McKenna Stafford as my successor."

There was a smattering of applause from the orthopedic committee members and mumbled agreement.

"Dr. Klost, I appreciate the nomination." McKenna held her satisfaction inside. *If only Father could...* She cut the thought off as quickly as it came.

Dr. Klost read her thoughts. "I am sure your father would be proud."

"I'm sure he would." McKenna drank from the coffee cup she had been toying with. The stares of the other doctors seated around the oblong table bore into her. These men, all orthopedic surgeons, surely envied her the position. Until ten days ago, being chief of ortho had been her ultimate goal. Now she didn't care about the position. Her emotions were caught up in a man, a man who could never be part of her life. Nor should she even think about it. "Thank you for considering me."

"We'll make it official next month. If there's no other business, we'll adjourn." He gathered his papers.

The other physicians rose and left the room, leaving McKenna with Klost.

"McKenna," he spoke in a fatherly tone. "I am sure your colleagues will support you, and I have no doubt you can do a wonderful job, but I would suggest you think about working on your people skills. The chief of orthopedics is required to attend a number of charity and hospital events."

"I have never been much of a social butterfly. Not that I haven't had a perfect example to follow in my mother and oldest sisters." She'd attend all the debutante functions, finishing school socials, cultural events, holding her own with the best of Cleveland's white and black society.

"You followed your father's example and that's what counts. Your surgical skills won you the position. That's all that matters."

Dr. Andrew Stafford had forged a place for himself as one of the first, if not *the* first, African American Chief of Surgery, making friends and enemies along the way. McKenna had both benefited and suffered from his career. Her father's shoes were hard to fill and all her life she's struggled to wedge her small feet inside and walk with confidence. Lately she'd managed not to trip. How long that would continued, considering her sudden distraction with a patient, was anyone's guess.

"I'm sure that's the case, sir. If you'll excuse me, we'll talk more about the position later. I have rounds." McKenna gathered her briefcase and files and left the room, proceeding directly to the orthopedic floor.

As she neared the nurses' station, Libby's boisterous laughter joined by others less distinguishable was audible. Closer to the desk, McKenna saw the women huddled around a man and wondered which doctor had center stage. A familiar voice answered Libby's next question.

"You mean playing drums gave you this great body?" she flirted.

"Not exactly." Tetsuro laughed. "We are taught to maintain our muscle strength so we are able to perform the strenuous routines."

McKenna was near enough to see her patient.

"I never saw Ringo Starr with abs like these!"

Libby, sitting on the desk, leaned forward to run her finger over Tetsuro's thin tank top. She made an attempt to raise the shirt, but he used his good hand to keep her from exposing his lower abdomen. The group around them burst into laughter with them. His laughter was a mellow, warm sound, filled with joy. McKenna resented being out of the loop, but wasn't about to let them know it.

As she entered the U-shaped nurses' station she spoke, "Mr. Takamitsu, I didn't know you had taken up nursing."

"Hello, Dr. Stafford," several of the women greeted her as they quietly dispersed to attend to their duties.

"*Konnichi wa, Sensei* Stafford," Libby said with caution. "Takamitsu-*san* is teaching us Japanese. That's 'good afternoon.'"

"Really?" McKenna looked from Libby to Tetsuro as she approached them. "You've taken up nursing *and* teaching? Tetsu, I am impressed."

McKenna reached to take a chart from the rack behind Libby, who still sat on the desk. Leaning over Tetsuro, her body was so close to his that her breast brushed his shoulder. A sensation like touching a hot ember with her nipple shot through her. She jerked back, almost lost her balance and dropped the chart.

Both Tetsuro and Libby reached to steady the doctor.

"Would you mind letting me go?" she spoke through clenched teeth at Tetsuro who clutched her arm securely. She was so mad she could spit! Once more a man had caused her to make a fool out of herself. There, blame him. Forget it was she who was envious of Libby.

"I was merely trying to keep you from injuring yourself," he explained but didn't remove his fingers.

"I can manage just fine!" McKenna snatched her arm free. "And you, Ms. Loman, should not be seated so unprofessionally." If she could don that ever so remote doctor guise she could handle this situation.

"We sit here all the time, Dr. Stafford," Libby protested, but slipped off the desk. "Geesh, what's your problem?" she spoke *sotto voce* as she reached to pick the chart up from the floor.

McKenna bit her tongue to prevent a sharp reply. The response would only make matters worse. She was angered that the easy companionship between the nurses and Takamitsu eluded her.

The best thing she could do was concede that she could never be so free with her patient, leave and forget about Tetsuro, except as a patient.

But could she forget the fire set off by contact with his body? She walked down the corridor, heading for the stairs and home.

Three days later, Tetsuro found himself in the corridor of McDonald House Hospital, the facility where Cleveland's women were treated and their babies born. He'd begun wandering the hospitals grouped in the University Hospital area once Dr. Stafford wrote a release to allow him freedom. The tedium of his hospitalization was driving him mad. The only thing he looked forward to was Dr. McKenna's visits. Her femininity eased his loneliness. Their conversations, though short, were becoming less medical. And when she left, he was doubly lonesome. His heart ached with their brief separations. How much more would it hurt when he was healed? Soon they'd be apart forever. He'd rejoin the troupe and she would remain in Ohio. How would he deal with it?

Struggling to relieve his doldrums, he had formulated a routine. He worked out in the physical therapy gym for two hours a day and took long walks around the hospital's grounds to help fill the other hours.

He'd come to McDonald House to look at the babies in the nursery, a common ritual for the average visitor, no matter the reason for their hospital visit. Although the common practice now was to allow the babies to room-in with mom, there were always several loners in the nursery.

As he came to the long row of plate glass windows separating the hall and the nursery, Tetsuro recognized the figure at the window staring at a baby in a crib. The large white lab coat couldn't hide the curves of her slender body or the dark hair covering her back in loose waves, free of the ponytail that usually confined it. The hunch of her shoulders and the way her hands were stuffed into her pockets hinted at despondent feelings.

As he approached her, he greeted, "Good morning, Dr. Stafford. How are you?"

The doctor turned toward him.

When he saw her face fully, he questioned, "Is something wrong, *Sensei*?" The deep pain hidden in her eyes made his heart ache. A lifetime of reading what a person didn't want to show had given him a unique ability to see and understand.

"What makes you ask?"

"This." Tetsuro extended his hand and, with a gentle touch of his thumb, wiped away the single tear on her cheek, then cupped her cheek for an instant. "Why are you crying?"

"I...didn't know I was." She raised both hands and wiped her cheeks. "What're you doing here?"

"I am the phantom of the hospital," he answered with theatrical flare, then returned to his somber tones. "And you?"

"I was called to consult on a baby whose arm is deformed." Dr. Stafford faced the nursery again. "I suppose that was why I was crying."

"That could be the reason." Tetsuro looked toward the babies. The tiny humans swaddled in pink and blue striped blankets were lying on their sides with knit caps covering newly minted hairdos. The nurses milled about the next generation, tending to those awake and vocal. "Or maybe you stand here thinking of how your life has played out thus far, thinking about whether or not you have missed something, made the wrong choices. All those thoughts are there before you in the shape of someone else's baby." When he faced the woman, shock glistened in her eyes.

"How dare you imply my life is not as I planned?" Fury colored her cheeks, and the sparkle in her eyes was no longer pain.

"Perhaps I was not talking about *you*." Regretting his boldness, he left her standing before the nursery. Her sputtering reply followed him down the corridor.

As McKenna watched Tetsuro depart, she flushed. Exasperation and humiliation collided within her, rendering her speechless, though a myriad of thoughts sprang to her mind.

Why was she angry? Had his words hit a nerve? How could he know the choices she'd made? Did he assume, since she was single and female, she'd forfeited family for career? Then again, how could he know she was unmarried? Was he assuming once more?

And why was she flustered? She'd stood her ground plenty of times with her father, professors, residents, and fellow doctors. Never had she been shy about telling someone exactly what she thought, even to the point of alienation. Her self-confidence and courage were her strong points. How could a man she'd known only ten days so easily make her act like a child?

McKenna straightened her shoulders, mentally stiffened her back-bone, and raised her chin. She would not let Tetsuro Takamitsu affect her this way. He was a patient, albeit a difficult patient, and as soon as he was healed, he'd be gone and she'd be well rid of the Japanese drummer! She entered the nursery to assess her newest patient.

"So, how was your day, Mac?"

"Horrible." McKenna sat across the round table from James Russell at the Pewter Mug, viciously cutting into the chicken breast on her plate. "I had surgery scheduled for eight, but it didn't start until ten because central supply didn't have my hardware tray sterilized. I was late getting to the office and then had grand rounds."

"Well, we'll have a nice dinner and go to the movies and you can forget all about it," James placated in his patronizing tone. His deep baritone voice matched his dark ebony skin. His build hinted of a former pro football player who'd neglected his workouts, the muscled body becoming just a touch softer after retirement.

McKenna looked closer at her dinner companion. His tight black curls were clipped close to his head. A neatly trimmed beard covered strong jaws and surrounded full lips. Crinkles were at the corners of his deep brown eyes that were dull. Manicured hands held the eating utensils to enjoy his steak. What about James had ever attracted her?

"And then," she continued her tirade on the day still working at her chicken, "when I came to the floor, I found Takamitsu at the nurses' station, distracting the nurses from their duties." She plopped a bite into her mouth.

"How's his hand coming?" James poured a second glass of wine for them both.

"Fine. No surprises." McKenna sipped from the glass. "Utilization Review is after me to discharge him. Since he was visiting Cleveland for a performance, however, he has no place to go. The annex is full so I don't know what to do with him. I can't send him back to Japan half finished."

"Maybe Social Services could find him an apartment." He took a drink of the wine.

"Just for a few months while in rehab? That would be too expensive. He has insurance but cash may be another problem."

"Won't his employer, that drum troupe, pay for it?"

"I should try to keep the costs down for him and the troupe." McKenna watched James carefully slice his meat into small pieces and place each one, in turn, into his mouth.

"Since when do you worry about your patients' finances?" He wiped his lips with the linen napkin.

"I do! I'm on two committees to help lower the cost of heath care. And I spend time in Columbus with the state legislature to enact bills for insurance reform. How dare you say I don't?" She dropped her fork onto the plate. The clank echoed across their table.

"I'm sure you do, Mac." James placed his hand on hers in a placating manner. "Still, why do you worry about what he'll do? He's a patient." He withdrew the heavy hand.

"*A patient*? And I'm sure your clients are just clients," McKenna responded hotly.

"Okay, okay," James relented.

The couple fell into silence. McKenna had dated James off and on for a few years and had been more or less content with their relationship. He filled all the requirements for a Stafford woman, money and position, requirements established by her mother. But tonight little things irritated her. His personality required precision bordering on compulsion with everything. He methodically consumed his food, each bite so exact, that there would be no uneven remains.

His teeth scrapped the fork with an annoying metal clink and his molars came together with the snap she heard in the OR when bone moved against bone.

McKenna rested her utensils on her plate and pushed it away with food remaining. She motioned to their waiter. When he responded promptly, due to James' reputation as a big tipper, she ordered brandy, coffee, and cheesecake.

"My, aren't we audacious tonight," James stated.

"I'll not have you comment on my choices. It's been a long time since I was forced to clean my plate before dessert."

"And testy, too." James continued with his steak.

When her brandy arrived, McKenna took a healthy sip. Her throat burned and fumes flooded her sinuses so she was forced to cough to clear them and regain her breath.

"You should drink that a little slower, Mac."

"Stop telling me what to do!" To spite him, she took another gulp. It went down easier the second time.

"I wish you wouldn't be so hostile." James finished the last bites of his meal.

"I'm sorry," McKenna apologized. "I don't know what's wrong with me."

"You're tired." He moved slightly to one side as the waiter served his coffee.

"I'm sure that's it. Think I'll pass on the movie." If she had to remain in James's company any longer tonight, she'd scream.

"Sure thing, hon. We'll make it an early night." James took a small sip of his coffee.

McKenna ate half her dessert before she spoke again.

"Breathing Room is coming next month."

"Oh?"

"Yes, the twenty-seventh. I've already purchased the tickets." McKenna recognized the look he gave her over the cup's rim. His pale eyes were small and cold, unlike the deep warm ones of her Japanese patient. Why was she thinking about Takamitsu? Before this she had been able to easily put patients out of her mind when she was away from the office or hospital. Takamitsu shouldn't be any different.

"You know I'm not fond of rhythm and blues."

"And I'm not too keen on opera but I go." So that's how it would be? She'd share his interests but he wouldn't hers? This was the first time conflict had arisen, small though it was.

"Maybe someone at work would enjoy it more."

"I'll go alone." McKenna tossed her napkin on the table. "Are you finished? I'd like to go home."

"As you wish." He motioned for the check as she stood and strode angrily toward the door.

The car ride to Shelbourne Road was uncomfortably quiet. Again, McKenna found herself easily annoyed. James's driving, always safe, was horribly cautious, his speed too slow, his stop at lights and signs, too long. After what seemed hours later, he drove into the drive.

"You don't have to see me in." McKenna already had her hand on the door handle. A thumb on the garage door remote in her other hand raised the garage door.

"I've been thinking, Mac, about your patient." James appeared unfazed by her attitude. "Since you're so concerned about him and where you can discharge him to, why not bring him here?"

"Excuse me? Have a patient come live with me?" She was appalled he suggested such! "A man I don't even know?"

"Just temporarily. You'll never know he's in the house. It's huge. You could put him in the other end. You're at work or the hospital most of the time. And you wouldn't have to eat with him if you plan it right."

McKenna stared at him. She hoped her mouth was closed, but she was afraid her jaw had dropped.

"I don't know. I don't think it'd be wise."

"Merely trying to help."

"Thanks for the dinner."

"Any time. I'll call you tomorrow."

"Sure." Suddenly she felt guilty about her demeanor. She leaned across the gearshift and quickly kissed him. His mouth was flaccid. "Good night."

"Good night, Mac."

She left the car and entered the house, continuing to be amazed he'd suggested Tetsuro come live with her! That would be the day!

CHAPTER NINE

Determined not to allow the exotic drummer to work his erotic magic on her, McKenna entered Tetsuro's room. She would discharge him from the hospital and let things fall where they might. Medically, she wouldn't need to see him until she removed the bandage-cast in three weeks.

"Good morning, Mr. Takamitsu." McKenna needed to be more formal with Tetsuro who stood in front of the bathroom mirror.

"*Ohayo gozaimasu, Sensei.*" Tetsuro attempted to comb his lengthy hair, but was successful with only one side. "I guess I will have to wait for Libby-*san* to help me." He replaced the brush and exited the bathroom. His bandaged hand was suspended in a sling across his bare chest and he wore a pair of snug low hung sweat pants exposing the flat plane of his abdomen, the rigid muscles well defined along his torso.

"The nurses do your hair?" McKenna stood at his bedside after he sat in the chair. She waited until he was settled before she looked at his hand. After three weeks, the long and slender fingers were back to normal color and size. The nails were no longer black, only faintly gray, oval-shaped and glossy as if recently manicured. She wondered if Libby was also doing nails.

"Yes, but Libby-*san* takes the time to make sure it is done well," Tetsuro answered. "I think she likes to play with it."

"*I think* Libby likes you. Too bad she's married," McKenna returned, envious of the nurse's ability to casually work with the dark mass.

Why was she so jealous about the nurses, especially Libby? They were in charge of the hygiene of patients and that included hairdressing. If Libby put the luxurious hair into a bundle at his neck, it would be because he wanted it that way.

Tetsuro's facial expression changed ever so slightly.

"I heard a rumor you are discharging me."

"I'm being forced to." McKenna took a seat on the edge of his bed. He'd managed to put her on the defensive again! "We've had a lot of patients lately and we need your bed, but we still have no place to put you. So," McKenna paused. Did she want to make this offer? Tetsuro could hardly say no. He was out of options. *Oh, what the hell?* "I thought you could come stay at my house. It's large and I live alone."

"I would not wish to impose." Tetsuro showed no emotion.

"It wouldn't be an imposition. You'll have a wing all to yourself and I'll be at the office or hospital most of the time. Home health can come do all the things Libby does for you."

"It would be too much trouble for you, *Sensei*," Tetsuro stated.

"Well, if you don't wish to." Her tone changed. "I'll discharge you and you can find your own housing."

McKenna stood and departed the room. She'd tried. No one could say she hadn't. But Tetsuro hadn't taken her up on her offer. Why was she disappointed?

Tetsuro looked at the door that Dr. Stafford had passed through. What was he doing? She'd offered him, a stranger with no one to turn to, a place to stay. And he'd refused her because of his pride. Or was it the cultural bias he'd grown up with against anyone not from Japan? Surely not. He'd learned years ago not to let racial prejudice cloud his thinking. He knew the effects of bigotry well enough not to fall victim to it.

Was he afraid of the obligation it would put him under if he accepted her hospitality? Another cultural dictate was not to owe anyone for anything. If he were honest with himself, he'd admit the real reason. He was afraid of what might result from being in such close quarters to the doctor with the enticing sepia eyes.

Tetsuro moved out of the chair and toward the hallway.

"Dr. Stafford." He spoke loudly to get her attention as she walked away from the nurses' station.

McKenna turned to him. "Yes?"

"I would be honored to accept the offer of your home for my convalescence," he spoke formally. His body moved into a ritual bow.

Rushing to him, McKenna steered him back to his room with a hand on his arm.

"Let's go talk in here." She hurried him away from the nurses who were grouped nearby.

"*Gomen kudasai.* I am sorry. Is something wrong? Did I offend you?" McKenna's flushed face assured him he'd erred.

"It's...all right. I...didn't want everyone to know I was taking you home. They might not think it's...appropriate."

"Then perhaps we should not do it." McKenna didn't retreat when Tetsuro stepped closer. He was drawn to a warmth radiating from her, a magnet-like heat pulling him to her, but he hesitated.

"It'll be fine. It's my decision." Her hand was on his arm lightly. "Sometimes what's inappropriate is necessary. I'll write your discharge for this afternoon and come pick you up after I finish at the office."

"I will be here."

With those plans in place, McKenna left Tetsuro.

"Your home is very...spacious," Tetsuro commented as he and the doctor entered the kitchen through the garage entrance. He carried the heavier of his bags slung from his good shoulder and the backpack in his healthy hand.

"This is obviously the kitchen." Dr. Stafford, with another duffel, led Tetsuro further through the house. "Help yourself to anything. Rebecca'll be here most mornings and she'll be glad to cook for you, except weekends. And this is the living room." She indicated a room to her right. "And the study, family room," she continued as they passed the rooms. "You'll find books in the library at the head of the stairs, television and stereo system in the family room."

They ascended the wide staircase and then turned right.

"My rooms are that way." She waved left. "You'll be here. Rebecca's opened the rooms. You should have everything you need."

They entered a large suite of rooms. The sitting area had a small television, a love seat and chair and occasional tables. The antique furniture was made of solid maple and mahogany. Dark oak paneling covered the walls and heavy drapes hung closed. Someone had placed cut flowers and potpourri to freshen the room. Through one door was a bathroom with a large Jacuzzi tub and shower. Another door led to the bedroom. The king-sized bed and other furniture were arranged for comfort.

"My whole apartment in Japan is only this big." Tetsuro indicated the bedroom. He placed his bag on the bed. "With a tiny bathroom."

"You can unpack your things into these." Dr. Stafford pulled open empty dresser drawers lined with lavender-scented paper. "Make yourself at home."

"I will have to become accustomed to the open space." Tetsuro began unpacking his backpack.

"Well," she stammered. "I guess I'll leave you to settle in. Did you have supper at the hospital?"

"Yes. Thank you." Tetsuro placed his book on the bedside table.

"If you get hungry, don't hesitate to go down to the kitchen. Anytime."

"Again, *domo arigato*."

"Can you teach me 'good night' in Japanese?"

"*Oya...*" Tetsuro began breaking apart the syllables of the phrase.

"*Oya...*" she repeated.

"*...sumi.*"

"*sumi.*"

"*...Na...*"

"*Na*"

"…*sai.*"

"*sai.*"

"*Oyasumi nasai,*" Tetsuro put it all together for her.

"*Oyasumi nasai.*" She smiled as she repeated his words.

"Very good, Dr. McKenna."

Tetsuro noticed a softness to her smile when she departed.

McKenna went to bed with a strange feeling in the depth of her stomach. When she first settled into the warm, snug bed, she thought sleep would come easily. The longer she lay there, the more vivid Tetsuro's presence became, as if he were actually in the room with her. She avoided thinking that given other circumstance he could be in her bed.

It had been a long time since she'd had another person sleeping overnight in her house, especially a man. The thought of Tetsuro, even at the distance he was, unnerved her, but not in a bad way. The feelings were pleasant, almost a comfort.

Once more, she cut the thought of Tetsuro off. Even if he was now a houseguest, he was still her patient, and she had no right, much less reason, to think about him familiarly.

Try as she might, though, she couldn't keep her thoughts from drifting down the hallway to his room. She envisioned him in his own cozy cocoon, his tawny body displayed on the cool sheets. The thought of how his ebony hair would contrast with the pillow was one she couldn't dispel. But the straw that broke the camel's back was the picture in her imagination of him showering before bed. Or would it be a bath at the basin because of the porous bandage on his hand? Whatever, she had no trouble imagining his nude body.

This is ridiculous. I should have no problem sleeping, even if I do have, as Libby would say, a drop-dead gorgeous guy in my house. And he'll be here at least six weeks!

In sheer frustration, she threw the covers back and sat up. She reached for the television remote and angrily punched up the news.

Being in Dr. Stafford's house was the least of Tetsuro's problems. After three weeks of sleeping in a narrow, stiff hospital bed, he found it difficult to get comfortable in a big, soft one, even though he was able to stretch out his long frame. In the hospital, he'd curled his legs to prevent his feet from bumping the footboard. Such problems didn't exist on his *futon* at home. There his feet rested on the wooden floor or *tatami* mats. He fluffed the feather pillows, trying to get comfortable and used one to prop his hand.

The quiet of the house was worse than the bed. At the hospital, there was the low level of noise humming at all times and a nurse came in ever so often. Here, he was alone, open to musings about his doctor. As she moved through his thoughts, the southward region of his body stirred awake. His hand began to pound with pain. If he were at the hospital, all he'd have to do was ring the nurses' station and medication would arrive.

Now, he had to get out of the nest he'd at length managed to create, go to the bathroom, where he'd laid out his toiletries and the small bottle of pain medicine Dr. Stafford had prescribed. Struggle with the childproof cap. Dump as few pills on the counter as possible. Chase two around until he cornered them and could put them in his mouth. Swallow water from a crystal glass to force them down his throat.

Then he could go back to bed and, hopefully, sleep. If that mind-of-its-own part of him would go back to sleep!

As the narcotic worked, filling his bloodstream with a pleasant sedation, Tetsuro thought of home. He would like to share it with his doctor. On the island where the drum school was located, a soft breeze blew almost constantly, keeping the humidity low and lulling a person's senses. At night, the wind, high in the lofty trees, was a source of contentment. The fragrances of the dense foliage and rich soil were carried in on the breeze through the open-sided buildings. The sun during the day lit the island brightly and the ocean was the deepest of blue-greens.

As Tetsuro drifted to sleep, the soft scent of the sheets of Dr. Stafford's guest room bed replaced the heavy hospital antiseptic smell. The aroma of the linens, reminiscent of her perfume, the pressure of a pillow to his back and buttocks, as well as the hallucinogenic effect of the painkiller, gave him the sense of her sharing the bed. The thought made him peaceful.

McKenna woke late Saturday morning, and when she made her way downstairs to the kitchen, she found Tetsuro at the sink, his back to her. She stopped short, not voicing her presence for long seconds, taking in the view of his body. Thick black hair lay over his neck in straight luxurious strands. His bare wide back was a deep golden hue with broad, well-defined muscles. As her assessment lowered, she drank in his narrow waist and small buttocks exhibited by the tight gray sweat pants. She fought the urge to touch the soft, highly erotic, dimpled area of his lower back above the waistband riding low on his almost non-existent hips. He stood on long straight legs and narrow, bare feet. What was that schoolgirl myth about the relationship of manhood and foot size?

McKenna's voice was thick with emotion as she contemplated its validity. "Good morning."

"Good morning." Tetsuro turned to smile at her over his shoulder. "Or *ohayo gozaimasu. Ohayo* is good morning. *Gozaimasu* makes it polite."

"Excuse me?" McKenna approached him.

"You wanted to learn Japanese." Tetsuro looked at her as she came to stand beside him.

"Then good morning is…" She led him to repeat his words.

"*Oh…*" he began the ritual.

"*Oh,*" McKenna fell into the pattern.

"*…hi…*"

"*hi.*"

"*...o.*"

"*o.*"

"*Go...*"

"*Go.*"

"*...zai...*"

"*zai.*"

"*...ma...*"

"*ma.*"

"*...su.*"

"*su.*"

"Good morning," Tetsuro repeated.

"*Ohayo gozaimasu,*" McKenna returned, then addressed the sink. "What are you doing?"

"Trying to cook rice." Tetsuro returned his attention to the pan in the sink. He removed the lid and thick steam rose from the deep sink. "I could not find a rice cooker so I tried the old fashioned way. Did not do such a good job. It is mush."

"How long did you cook it?"

"The normal length of time to prepare *gohan.* Twenty minutes. Guess I am out of practice."

"It's not you. It's the rice. Or should I say *gohan*?"

"You are a quick study." Tetsuro's mouth formed a relaxed smile.

"Always have been," she returned. "You can't cook it a long time. It's instant rice. I'm not a very good cook. I suppose if my ancestors were runaway slaves from South Carolina instead of Kentucky, I'd have a better grasp on rice." McKenna took the lid from his hand and twisted the faucet to run water into the overcooked rice. "You probably wouldn't like it anyway. It's different from the rice I've eaten in Chinese restaurants. It's fluffy and doesn't stick."

"At this point, I would accept a bowl of any kind of rice, sticky or not. Rice is a comfort food for me. Libby-*san* brought me *sushi* as well as some dishes Americans call Japanese."

"Libby brought you food?"

"Yes. And some of the other nurses, too." Tetsuro turned to lean his back against the drain board while McKenna emptied the rice and water down the disposal. He didn't speak again until she had rinsed the food away. When she turned the disposal off, he spoke. "They did not seem to mind."

McKenna made a defense for an unvoiced complaint. "I asked if you wanted a dietitian to come arrange meals for you. You said you didn't care."

"I did not wish to impose. You are a busy doctor. I could not take up your time."

"As your doctor, I'm charged with making sure everything is adequate for you. That includes making sure your diet is to your liking. And the University Hospital takes great pride in serving cuisine satisfactory to the many nationalities who come to be treated here."

"*Gomen.*" Tetsuro bobbed his head forward. "I am sorry. I intended no offense. However, in Japan we are taught never to be obliged to another. Never knowingly impose your will upon another. It is not polite to do so. If my request for a change of food incurred a burden upon you or any of the dietary staff, I would have caused a wrong. I could not do so." Tetsuro pulled at the frayed edges of his bandage near the elbow. "Besides, my brain misses rice more than my stomach."

"Are you homesick?" McKenna noticed how he held his wounded arm across his wide chest and his head drooped.

"I suppose I am." He looked at her with eyes that reminded her of a pathetic puppy. "When we are on tour, we are together, speaking Japanese, eating meals close to those at home, playing our music, keeping my beat. I have never had a reason to be homesick. Now, without my friends and unable to drum…I suppose I am lonesome."

"It must be hard to admit that."

"*Hai.*" It was a quiet 'yes.' "I do not know why I even told you."

The look he gave her bore into her soul. The lost puppy eyes melted her heart. She struggled with the desire to embrace him.

"I'm pleased you did. I'd hate for my patient to be unhappy." She forced her focus back to the pot. He was so near the heat of his body radiated to her.

"Your patient?" Tetsuro gave her another kind of look. This one, caught from the corner of her eye, was hard and maybe disappointed. "I thought we were friends."

"We are," she stuttered.

Her emotions collided. Doctors were taught from early on not to become involved with their patients. If patients became friends, it changed the ability for doctors to be unbiased toward treatment and prognosis. How would she feel if she had to tell Tetsuro, *her friend*, that he'd never use his hand again? It would be easier for her to tell Tetsuro, *her patient*. McKenna began scrubbing the bottom of the pan with a vengeance, even though the over-cooked rice came away easily. This was a mistake. They couldn't be friends!

Even if it were possible to establish a relationship with a patient, why would she choose this one? A man who'd leave the country?

"Dr. McKenna." Tetsuro turned so he could touch her arm. "If you keep doing that, you will have a hole in the bottom. The pan is clean."

McKenna stopped her scrubbing and under his touch, stood extremely still. The electricity of his touch shot through the material of her shirt and coursed up and down her nerves. Her knees threatened to bend. She faced her houseguest cautiously, afraid of what she'd see in his eyes or what she'd do.

She saw the exact look she'd dreaded. The glow it filled her with was one she'd never before had. She liked it.

"Why don't I take you shopping this morning?"

"That would be nice." Tetsuro removed his hand and stepped away from the sink. "I would like to see Cleveland."

"There's an Asian market downtown." McKenna busied herself with rinsing the pan. "I'll fix breakfast while you dress and then we'll go."

"I thought you said you couldn't cook?" His eyes twinkled with impishness.

"Breakfast is the only meal I *can* manage. Now go dress."

"Yes, Dr. McKenna." Tetsuro smiled as he left her at the sink.

CHAPTER TEN

In the time she cooked breakfast Tetsuro changed into a pair of black cotton pants with an elastic waistband. He returned to the kitchen wearing a kimono-like shirt with wide sleeves and an open overlapping front.

"I need some help here."

"Sure. What can I do?" McKenna was thankful he wore a black tank top beneath the shirt so she wasn't confronted with his masculine chest.

"Can you tie the belt so my shirt stays closed?" He dangled the thin black cloth belt from his good hand.

"Okay." She took the belt. *This isn't going to go well.*

Timidly she stepped nearer to wrap the belt around his waist. His male essence swept over her senses, tickling her nostrils, awakening sensual stirrings deep inside. Up closer, the tank top she'd been thankful for failed to hide anything. The delineation of his muscles was clear beneath the stretched material. Her hands accidentally caressed his sides as she brought the belt around to meet at his navel. His breathing was slow and regular, and its whispering sound tantalized her ears. Before the urge to taste his lips overcame her sensibilities, McKenna made quick work of a loose knot and stepped back.

"How's that?" Her voice was thick and deep in her throat.

"*Domo.*"

McKenna stepped further back. Was his voice husky and full? Was he drinking in her nearness as she had his?

"Well." She stepped to the kitchen table. "Shall we eat?"

The rush of blood in her ears made it difficult for her to hear his answer but they sat.

At the Asian Plaza, a small square building near downtown Cleveland's east side, McKenna trailed Tetsuro while he shopped for comfort foods. The market was quiet, filled with smells she found unique and at times offensive. She didn't know how he expected to pay for the items he kept putting in the basket she pushed, nor did she know how to broach the subject.

Tetsuro placed a liter sized plastic bottle emblazoned with Oriental writing in the basket.

She stated, "I have soy sauce."

"That's what you call it. This is *shoyu*."

"There's a difference?"

"*Hai. Shoyu* is fermented longer than regular soy sauce. The flavor is stronger."

McKenna shrugged her shoulders and they continued along the aisles. She wondered if the people they passed thought of them as a couple. Did she want them to? Did she want them *not* to?

A couple.

Two as one.

A unit.

The idea was tempting. She'd shopped alone all of her adult life. Pushing the cart and discussing meals was invigorating. Or maybe it was the nice male form she followed up and down the aisle. His tight little butt was easy on the eyes.

When he was finished, they turned a corner to approach the cashier. An Asian girl who looked less than five ran around the opposite corner and slipped on a wet spot. Before McKenna could react, Tetsuro moved toward the child.

He knelt and spoke what McKenna supposed was Japanese. How did he know the child was Japanese? Wasn't that an awfully big presumption? With gentle tones and soft caresses he wiped the girl's tears away with a tissue. The girl's cries had changed to sniffles by the time he helped her stand and took in her lack of injuries.

Tetsuro's words changed to English, yet his cadence remained that of his native tongue. "Are you all right now, little sister?"

"Yes, elder brother." The little girl looked at him with soft doe eyes. Tetsuro pushed back her long straight hair over her shoulder and moved the shaggy bangs away from her wet eyes.

"Where's your mother?" He wiped the last tear off her cheek.

"Oh, Anna!" a young woman shrieked and came to her daughter's side.

"She slipped and fell." Tetsuro stood and moved away from Anna who watched him with curious eyes. "I do not think she is too injured. Not as badly as me, huh?" He gestured toward Anna with his broken hand.

"No, elder brother." Anna shook her head and began giggling. She stopped abruptly and put her fingers to her mouth as if the laughter was not polite.

"It is all right to laugh, little sister. It does look silly and it does not hurt much anymore." Tetsuro touched her hair one last time.

"Thank you for seeing to her," Anna's mother said.

"*Do itashimashite*," Tetsuro returned with a shallow bow of his upper body.

Mother and daughter departed with Anna keeping her eyes on Tetsuro until she and her mother rounded a corner. When the two disappeared, McKenna looked at Tetsuro, and saw a forlorn expression. She didn't think it had anything to do with his hand so decided not to mention it.

At the checkout, Tetsuro produced a credit card that the checker swiped through the machine. He signed the slip and they were finished. Afterwards, he managed to collect the handles of all the plastic bags in his good hand and carried them to the Jeep. They made two more stops, one for books and one for drugstore items, before heading back to the house on Shelbourne Road.

"I thought the way you handled the little girl was sweet." McKenna could no longer keep from commenting about Anna.

"I was afraid she had hurt herself," Tetsuro replied, his voice low. He kept his face toward the window.

"I was, too, but you acted swiftly and were so compassionate, almost…fatherly." She recalled his words at the nursery in McDonald House. "Do you have any children?"

"Ah…I have never been married." He continued to stare at the passing landscape. "What are these little statues and things?" The statuary he spoke of lined the street on both sides in deep easements of woody areas.

"They are ethnic parks established by the different nationalities of Cleveland. Japan has one here on the right," she explained. "About children. These days you don't have to be married."

"I suppose some people feel that way." The fingers of his right hand tapped a nervous beat against the Jeep door. "Marrying would be better for the children."

"I see." She read a hurt in his eyes when Tetsuro turned to face her, but was afraid to ask any questions.

"In Japan, the father has little to do with children born to unwed mothers except if the baby's a boy. Then he can take the baby and either raise him as his own or give him to a family of his choosing. If it's a girl, she remains with her mother and may be adopted by her mother's future husband."

"Are you…one of those babies?" McKenna asked cautiously. "I'm sorry. It's not any of my business."

"It is all right. No. My father died when I was nine and my mother raised me by herself, although we lived with my father's family. As youngest daughter-in-law she was obligated to care for them," Tetsuro answered freely. "These parks are nice."

"They have been revitalized over years. John D. Rockefeller donated the land and different ethnic groups formed associations to design and keep the gardens. In the sixties, they became rundown, but now they're coming back." McKenna gave him a tour book description of the gardens. She decided Tetsuro was finished talking about babies and his childhood. His fingers moved in a calmer beat.

The cohabitation of the Stafford estate went along smoothly for two weeks. McKenna's schedule prevented her from seeing Tetsuro on a daily basis, but she was aware of him. She heard him moving around, and sometimes his music or television. Under Tetsuro's supervision, Rebecca became proficient in preparing rice and *miso* soup. Other foods he cooked himself or consumed Rebecca's substantial Amish fare.

Nights continued to be the orthopedic surgeon's worst times for dealing with her patient's nearness. No. At night he was Tetsuro. Not her patient. No matter how tired she was, McKenna lay awake with insidious erotic thoughts. Try as she might, she could not stop envisioning Tetsuro in his own bed, usually with the sheet pushed to his feet. It was an annoying yet pleasing fantasy. One night, she gave up on sleep and wandered downstairs.

McKenna encountered Tetsuro in the kitchen. "Couldn't sleep?"

"*Iie*. You either?"

"No. What are you making?"

"Tea. Would you like a cup?" Tetsuro opened a small round tin of fine green powder. "Would you hand me two cups? That is, if you want some. You have not answered." He looked over his shoulder at her. "You are staring at me."

"I'm sorry. I didn't realize I was." McKenna retrieved the teacups as he'd requested, embarrassed he had caught her enjoying the view of his body. Tonight, not aware he'd have company, Tetsuro wore only athletic shorts.

"*Domo arigato*," Tetsuro said, taking the cups.

"*Do itashimashite.*"

"*Tadashii*. Very good," he translated his compliment. While they spoke, he went on preparing the tea, spooning the powder into the cups and pouring hot water into them. Then he stirred carefully until the tea dissolved. Handing McKenna a cup, they moved to the table and sat.

In silence, they tasted the tea. Tetsuro gazed at McKenna over the rim of the fine porcelain teacup held delicately with both hands. The fingers of his bandaged left hand managed to encircle the cup. She placed her cup on the table and reached to touch the fingers of the hand she'd repaired. He didn't move, supporting the cup by resting his elbows on the tabletop. Their eyes locked as she caressed his fingers.

"The dressing comes off next week."

"I am afraid of what you will find underneath."

"It won't look very nice." McKenna pulled her hand back and Tetsuro set his cup on the table. "The tea is good. Is it instant?"

"No. It is from Japan."

"I've heard of the tea ceremony. Can you do it?"

Tetsuro laughed lightly, the warm sound filling the kitchen. "I know as much about the *chanoyu* as the average teenager growing up in Tokyo's urbanity can learn from television. The only people who perform it now are those who do it for tourists." Tetsuro drank the last of his tea.

"I know only what I see on TV. About Japan, that is." McKenna finished hers. "You probably know more about America than I do about your home."

"I do not know about that. I have traveled all over, many years, many tours, but I mainly see the concert halls. Sometimes, especially now that I am older, I make a point of visiting tourist sites, but that still does not give me an understanding of Americans. When the nurses came to my room and talked, on their breaks and after their shifts, I learned much more. And living 'with you' so to speak, has given me a lesson in United States customs."

"I'm glad the nurses were there to entertain you." McKenna abruptly stood and took the dirty cups to the sink. "I think I'll be able to sleep now. Thank you for the tea."

She left her patient sitting at the kitchen table, alone as she'd found him.

After giving the doctor time to hide herself away in her room, Tetsuro returned to his. He sat on his bed, his back against the headboard, and stared into space, thinking about his doctor. He could sense the vibrations of her desire for him as well as her need to keep her distance. He, too, felt an attraction, one that seemed centered in his chest, not below his waist. From the first moment he saw her beautiful crystal-clear, light brown eyes, he had been heading in such a direction. Tonight's tea ceremony had made it clear. His body and heart ached for McKenna Stafford.

Tetsuro had watched her as she sat across the small table from him. Just as he hadn't expected company, neither had she expected him and wore only an over-sized T-shirt. Her breasts, round, full, each enough to fill one of his large hands, were evident and enticing. Then she'd stood and walked to the sink. The view from behind had caused blood to converge in that most unruly part of him. He couldn't have stood if the house was on fire!

Her thin, cotton knit shirt hung to mid-thigh on her long legs. Her calves were curved, her ankles, slender. The nails on her slim, bare feet were polished. Tetsuro smiled. McKenna pretended she couldn't be bothered with such feminine trivialities, but tonight had revealed the truth.

As she leaned to place the rinsed cups into the dishwasher, her buttocks curved against the material. Her hair swung freely over her back. Tetsuro had been tempted to give into the urge to put his face in the waves. When she turned, the remnant of a pout was still on her lips, but her eyes forgave him whatever offense he'd committed. As he sat on his bed thinking about her, his groin had the same reaction he'd experienced in the kitchen.

What had he done to cause her to leave so abruptly? The last thing he remembered talking about was the nurses.

Ah, so, as the American media liked to make Japanese characters say.

Every time he mentioned Libby or another of the nurses McKenna bristled. Was she jealous? Surely she realized he didn't see the nurses, with all their flirtatious gestures, as any more than groupies who were attracted to the drummers. Not that he'd been one to refuse a warm female body in his bed, but he wasn't interested in the nurses.

He enjoyed their attention when, as he'd begun feeling better and working out more, they'd come to his room to visit. The sweat molding his clothing to his body had been like a magnet. They would tease and joke with him, but he didn't have the same dizzying feeling McKenna stirred. He'd never thought seriously about the nurses, for even then, *she* had his heart.

McKenna. As such, he'd always thought of her. Not Dr. Stafford.

There. He'd said it. Or at least thought it.

He was in love with McKenna.

Tetsuro slipped off the bed and walked to the small desk. Sitting in the antique chair, he began a letter using the stationery and pen he'd located inside the desk. Without thought he wrote in Roman characters. Several sentences into it, he was struck by the lettering. He paused and read.

'*Dear Emiko...*' He read no further. Like so many times over the last twelve years, he wadded up the paper and tossed it at the wastebasket. He started once more with the name he'd meant to write in the first place. Susumu.

For half a page, in precise Japanese *kana* and *hiragana* mixed with the *katakana*, a script used for words foreign to Japanese, he explained his problem to his best friend. Disclosing such intimate concerns was not normally done in the ever so staid society of Japan. But bonds formed over long periods of close contact made sharing easier. Susumu had joined Taiko Nihon the same year Tetsuro had. The young boys had grown into young men together. They were as close as brothers.

Relating his emotions and what he suspected about McKenna's returning his affection, Tetsuro added his doubts. What if her attraction to him was superficial, simple lust for a foreigner so different from her African American boyfriends? Did his slanted eyes (to his amazement, he actually *wrote* the word!), call to her? Could she love him, a man of a different race, from a country once an enemy?

He paused to collect his scattered thoughts. The index finger protruding from the bandage slowly tapped out the rhythm of his soul with no pain or stiffness. Minimal though it was, it was functioning. McKenna had said she'd remove the wrapping this coming week. What if he couldn't drum as he had before? He'd be out of a career and have nothing to offer her as a husband, nothing for any woman.

His right hand clutched the pen until it ached. Relaxing his grip, he finished his letter quickly and returned to bed, well aware that sleep would not come.

Using relaxation techniques learned through years of studying *taiko*, he pictured himself strolling through McKenna's garden. His mind formed a *haiku*.

Easy to find
in the Queen Anne's lace:
the dark center.

CHAPTER ELEVEN

"Hello, Rebecca," McKenna greeted her housekeeper as she entered the kitchen. She looked forward to the afternoon off. "How are you?"

"Fine, madam doctor. *Danke.*" Rebecca gathered her coat and tote bag. She always left at noon on McKenna's half day at the office.

"Have you seen Mr. Takamitsu today?"

"No, ma'am. I heard him come from the fitness room about an hour ago."

"He was up late. Maybe he slept in."

"I will see you tomorrow."

"Have a safe trip home."

McKenna flipped through the mail and her messages as she took her time making her way to the stairs. The red 'message light' on the answering machine blinked and she pushed the button to listen to the home health aide's message that he'd not be able to assist Tetsuro. After it rewound and clicked off, she heard her name called faintly from down the hall.

Following the sound, she called, "Tetsuro?" Had she actually heard him calling out to her? The guest wing of the house was so deep, the sound echoed.

"Dr. McKenna!" her houseguest called again. His voice was louder now.

"Tetsu?" She entered the front room of his suite. "Is something wrong?"

"No…but…" His deep voice dropped to a muffled undertone.

"But what?" McKenna continued to follow Tetsuro's voice. It brought her to the bathroom. "What in the…?" Her hand went to her mouth as she turned the corner and discovered Tetsuro sitting in the deep tub.

"I decided to take a bath," he announced sheepishly.

"I see!" She retreated around the doorframe. "What did you call me for? To scrub your back?"

"I cannot get out. An hour ago, I thought I could. Now it is impossible.

I need your help."

"What can I do? Especially since you're…naked." McKenna remained hidden behind the door like a schoolgirl. What was wrong with her? She'd seen naked men before, had sex, had even been married! What was different now? Most of the time when she'd been confronted with a nude man, she'd not been attracted to him, if you didn't count Stephen in their early times.

"That I am, but I do have a towel. If you could give me a hand to get my feet underneath me, then I can manage on my own."

"I'll try." He wanted her to touch his wet, nude body? Would she be able to breathe in such close contact? The brief glimpse of Tetsuro's athletic torso had already sent quivers of passion through her. What would tactile stimulation do to her senses? He needed her help, she reminded herself. She could be adult about this.

She inched her way back into the bathroom on rubbery legs. Tetsuro lay back against the tub, a small towel spread over his midsection. He'd drained the tub and the wet cloth clung to the very masculine bulges. With effort, McKenna used her professional wiles to keep her eyes off his manly attributes.

She came to the edge of the tub. "What do you want me to do?" Her fingers itched to rip away that wet cloth! Her heart raced at the thought.

"Put your arm around my back. I just need a little support," he instructed.

"Very well."

She leaned over the tub to slide her right arm behind the expanse of his muscular back until her hand was in his right armpit. His satiny skin and firm muscles caused her to take a steadying breath. With her cheek at his shoulder, she couldn't help breathing in the aroma of the earthy bath salts. As she held her left arm out to support Tetsuro's bound hand, her cheek brushed innocently against his shoulder. Her heart quivered and her chest was as tight as if she'd been kicked there. A flood of heat lapped her face.

Tetsuro settled his left arm on McKenna's and bent his knees to try to stand. "Ready? On the count of three," she said breathlessly.

"One."

His silky moist skin sent sparks through her.

"Two."

Her cheek rubbed his shoulder again and burned as though grazed by a hot ember.

"Three."

Together they moved.

Tetsuro managed to get his feet beneath him in the slippery tub and moved his hips close to the edge, almost clearing it. His upper arm pinned her hand between his torso and triceps, allowing him to cover his groin with a towel.

Unexpectedly, his foot slipped in the soap residue. Losing his balance, he pulled McKenna with him as he fell backward over the tub's edge onto the floor. They landed, McKenna beneath his length, on the carpeted floor.

Tetsuro struggled to move off her and at the same time maintain the towel's camouflage.

"Are you all right?" His voice was a deep rumble of emotion.

"Yes." McKenna giggled as she imagined the comical picture they made. She didn't want him to think she was laughing at him but she couldn't help it. Moreover, her laughter distracted her from the fact that his weight pressing on her was intoxicating. "And you?"

"Fine." He laughed with her. Tetsuro smiled more than he ever laughed, making his laughter all the more special.

Their laughter bounced off the tiled walls. Without conscious thought, her arms found their way around his upper body Waves of electricity shot from her toes to the top of her head. His fine, thick hair fell across her face, the wet ends wrapping themselves about her neck like soft caresses.

Though Tetsuro tried to wiggle out of her embrace, his movements only brought him closer. They lay stomach to stomach. The swell of his groin pushed against her. With her skirt hiked around her hips, only the wet towel and her silken panties, damp from a source all their own, were between their intimate parts. The blaze threatened to consume them both.

Inches away, Tetsuro's intense brown eyes gazed into hers and his hot breath was against her skin. Frozen still, she couldn't avoid the mouth intent on covering her lips. A tingle started within her when the supple, sweet lips caressed hers. McKenna gave in to the heat of his body. His tongue made gentle movements to gain entry into her mouth. Her lips parted.

What was going on? McKenna broke away from the lusty kiss.

"No," she managed to whisper.

"*Shitsurei shimasu.*" His voice was husky with desire.

Nevertheless, Tetsuro placed his good hand on the floor and shoved himself upward and sat back on his heels. Through it all, the towel remained safely on his groin, albeit stretched to its limit.

"I am sorry. I did not intend to be so bold. I...lost..."

"...your balance. I know." McKenna crabbed backwards until she huddled in the corner, tugging her short skirt over her slender thighs. Her heart pounded in her chest as though she'd run a marathon. She was desperate to be in the arms of the lusty body kneeling before her, desperate to fuse her body with his.

Incredibly, she heard herself say, "If you're okay, I'll be going." McKenna drew her feet underneath her and stood up on legs threatening to buckle at any moment. Her panties were sopping wet. "I have a...date tonight." *James.* The absolute last thing she wanted right now was to be with James tonight. The blood rushing through her veins screamed for Tetsuro. She crossed her hands over her breasts to still the tickling of her nipples.

"*Domo arigato, Sensei.*" Tetsuro's words were so quiet she barely heard them. He bent his body in a slight bow.

Long minutes after McKenna left, Tetsuro concentrated on his breathing, filling his lungs with deep regular breaths in hope of pacifying his heart and softening the passion rushing through his veins. When Kifume had likened *taiko* to a religion, she had been on the mark, especially in the use of mediation and ritual. He'd been taught the meditation early in his drum training, but now it failed to calm him. He closed his eyes and drew deeper into himself. At last, his body was pacified even though his soul still cried out for McKenna.

Once he mastered himself, Tetsuro dressed and went downstairs, fixed a meal and carried his plate to the family room. He inserted a classic black and white movie from McKenna's many DVDs into the player and started it.

He pulled several of the large pillows onto the lush carpet and lay on his side. The food disappeared while he watched the movie without really seeing it. His thoughts were on McKenna.

Every time they had a close encounter, the doctor retreated. Could he hope that someday she would not rush *from* him but *to* him? Did he have the right to wish for that? When he remembered she's said she was going out tonight, the dragon of jealousy squirmed to life without warning. Years had passed since he'd had a relationship close enough to be jealous of another. Would he make a fool of himself with McKenna, as he had before with…?

Fatigue, a full stomach, and a boring movie lulled Tetsuro to sleep on the comfortable carpet and pillows.

Tetsuro dreamt of *taiko*. He sat on the wooden floor in a semicircle with Susumu and others he couldn't name. They struck their sticks carefully against the small drums positioned on their crossed legs. The drumming continued evenly until suddenly Tetsuro's dream-self missed a beat as his left hand fumbled. His dream-self panicked.

He jolted awake.

His broken hand lay beneath him and the pain was incredible.

McKenna said, "That's just great. I worked on that hand for hours and you're going to destroy it."

Tetsuro turned on his right side and looked for her. He first saw the hem of her dark rose evening dress. Slowly, as if he sensed he shouldn't rush the process, he raised his eyes to appraise her. The skirt hung to her curved hips and firm thighs with a light rose-colored belt cinching in the narrow waist. Mounds of pliable flesh pushed against the bodice to form a deep V-neck accentuated by a small gold heart locket on a fine chain rested. The tint of her dress brought out the dusky pink in her bare shoulders and arms.

His appraisal ended at McKenna's face. Her eyes twinkled and there was a tender smile on her glossy plum lips. Her luxurious dark hair was piled on her head with a fluffy spray of bangs over her forehead and tendrils cascading down her slender neck.

When he could speak, Tetsuro commented, "It hurts like hell."

McKenna walked to the television, the silky material rustling seductively.

"You must have fallen asleep." She punched buttons and the DVD slid out. "It's been off long enough for the DVD player to shut off."

"Yes." Moving by instinct, Tetsuro stood and moved to McKenna who had her back to him. With his right arm, he encircled her waist and laid his right cheek against the left side of her neck. "You smell as good as you look. Beautiful."

She lurched out of his amorous embrace and whirled to face him. Without warning, she slapped him resoundingly. Tetsuro stepped back slightly, his hand touching his stinging cheek.

"Oh, my God!" McKenna gasped. Her fingers went first to her mouth. Then she took his face in her hands. "I am so sorry! I don't know why I did that. Oh, my God!"

"*Iie.*" Tetsuro took her hands from his face and moved them to waist level before he released them. "You know exactly why you did it. It is I who must apologize."

He had overstepped his bounds, urged by the events in the bathroom and his desire for her.

"Tetsu," she breathed his name.

"*Iie. Oyasumi nasai.*" He turned and left the room.

"Tetsu, really. I'm sorry," McKenna called after him.

CHAPTER TWELVE

McKenna listened as the sound of Tetsuro's footsteps faded away on the stairs. A tear came to her eye and she brushed it away. What had she done? She'd never struck anyone in her life! Not only had she hurt Tetsuro physically, she'd hurt him emotionally. She didn't mean to do either. What had happened?

His touch, his palm against her midriff, had sent pulses of sparks to the most intimate part of her. His lean body pushed against the swell of her buttocks intensified the sensation. The brush of his lips on her neck when he spoke, his warm breath on her skin and the rough, five-o'clock shadow on his jaw against her cheek had sent her over the edge. With a thoughtless slap, she'd quenched the passionate electricity in both of them. How could she apologize?

There was a way. But it was a gesture that would do neither of them any good and would cause more problems than it would cure. She pushed the thoughts away.

The doorbell rang. McKenna picked her coat and purse from the hall table and left for the opera.

"You look lovely," James commented as he walked McKenna toward the State Theater on Euclid, his arm bent for her to slip her hand through. "As usual."

"*Domo,*" McKenna replied, her thoughts clearly not on the strong ebony man at her side. The casualness with which they touched was so different from the intensity of the rare touch she shared with Tetsuro. A seminar last year had taught her that Japanese culture was barren of friendly touching, allowing only for personal caresses in private. For Tetsuro to embrace and kiss her as he had was proof of his growing affection.

"Interesting." James opened the door for her. "Learning Japanese, are you?"

"I'm…picking up a lot from him. He's fascinating."

"And I thought I put that blush on your cheeks. I can see now where it comes from. Do I sense a rival here?"

"Please!" McKenna scoffed. "As you said, he's my patient. Besides, he'll return to Japan soon, and I'll never see him again."

"Me thinks the lady protests too much."

"James, don't worry. Tetsuro Takamitsu is only a friend." *If you can count a someone with whom you roll around nude on the bathroom floor a friend.*

"I was kidding, Mac." James gave the usher their tickets and followed McKenna to their box seats.

McKenna wiggled back into the deep velvet chair, expecting to spend the evening on the edge of sleep. Opera had been lost on her since childhood when her mother had been on the Cultural Arts Forum and made sure McKenna and her sisters sat through hours of opera and symphony. She'd been to almost every one ever written and had yet to find a thrill. She'd even quit asking which one they were attending. They were all the same.

She had just started to read the program when the curtain rose on a small wooden house with paper-covered screens for walls with a footbridge at stage right. Two men came over the walkway…a U. S. Naval officer and a small Japanese man. McKenna's interest perked up.

Madama Butterfly.

How ironic!

She'd seen the opera about the Japanese teenager wed to Lt. Pinkerton for companionship only many times, but had never really understood the story. This time she brought a different background to it and fell under its spell. Unfortunately, the opera seemed to be reaching the same conclusion she had. Nothing good could come from a relationship between herself and the drummer. While her family, in its most dysfunctional form, might accept it, his probably would not. That is, his mother probably wouldn't.

Wasn't his father dead?

At intermission, James had to practically drag McKenna from her seat to accompany him to the lobby for a glass of wine.

"It looks like you're enjoying *Madama Butterfly*. Usually, you have that bored-to-tears look."

"It's rather impressive. Maybe I have finally seen it enough to understand it." Standing in the crowd of opera buffs, she sipped the white wine.

"Or perhaps you can relate to it."

"Oh? How so?"

"What'll you do if your little Japanese houseboy slits his belly when you spurn his affections?"

"Affections? What the hell are you talking about?" The heat of her passion, be it anger at James or lust for Tetsuro, set her face throbbing. "Tetsuro is my patient. Nothing more, nothing less. It was your idea for him to stay at my house." She spoke emphatically but not loudly so as not to attract attention. "We share nothing more than the house and polite conversation with infrequent meals together. I don't know why you keep hinting at something other than hospitality between us. I hardly ever see him." She took a long drink of wine from the glass she held in a grip which threatened to crush the delicate stemware.

"I've known you a long time, Mac, and you never get this worked up unless it's about bones. Even though your first acquaintance with him was because of his need for your expertise, it doesn't mean you must restrict yourself to that if you are drawn to him. I'm a big boy, I can take rejection."

"I'm not rejecting you! You mentioned it."

"We'll see." James took her glass and walked away.

McKenna swallowed hard, tasting the last trace of wine. She wished for another gallon to wash away the vision of Tetsuro's face after she'd slapped him. And what of James's hint that Tetsuro, if rejected, would follow Butterfly's end? Surely he wouldn't do something so drastic! Would he?

Oh, please!

The lights flashed to indicate that the audience should return to their seats. James came to collect McKenna and with a gentle pressure of his hand on the small of her back, guided her back to the box seat.

All during the drive home, McKenna worried about what she'd find. Her logic told her this was the twenty-first century and that the most traditional of Japanese would be unlikely to commit suicide over something so petty. Tetsuro was not going to kill himself over her! *Hari-kiri* was probably as dated as the *chanoyu*.

Still, when the house loomed before them, her heart went to her throat.

James got out and escorted McKenna to the door.

As they stopped on the porch, he asked, "Did you find someone to go to the Breathing Room concert?"

"No." McKenna inserted the key, punched in the security code on the keypad, then opened the door.

"You'll find someone."

"I'm sure." McKenna entered the cancel code on the keypad and faced him. "I honestly enjoyed the opera tonight. Maybe my tastes are changing."

"I'm sure they are, but not in the area of music." James stepped nearer. He encircled her waist and pulled her to him. Her arms loosely embraced his shoulders.

In James's embrace, McKenna felt nothing. She wished the kiss he was preparing to plant on her lips were over. When he did kiss her, his lips were cold and hard. She resisted his attempt to muster up more passion and pushed away from him.

"Good night, James."

Dismay registered in his eyes. "Yes, I can see a definite change. Good night, McKenna."

James waved as he got into his car and she returned the gesture.

After the door was secured and burglar alarm set, McKenna looked up the long stairway. No lights. No sound except the hall clock striking one. Had she expected Tetsuro to wait up for her?

Determined that she would explain the boundaries of their friendship and apologize for hurting him, she climbed the stairs. Each step was mountains high. The closer she came to the landing, the louder her heart pulsed in her ears. She trembled as she reached the top and paused. One direction led to her bed. The other, to Tetsuro's.

Was he asleep?

Blood rushed to her head.

Was he still hurt by her actions?

She struggled for control.

Could she wait until breakfast to know?

She was dizzy.

Did she dare enter his bedroom?

Her face burned with emotion.

Should she invade his privacy in such a way?

Her guilt increased.

She was desperate for his forgiveness.

She sighed.

McKenna removed her shoes and walked silently toward the closed door of the suite of rooms occupied by her patient. As though taking hold of an exposed electrical cord her hand closed on the knob and twisted. When the door swung open, she was startled, having expected it would be locked. Slow, deliberate steps brought her to the next closed door, the one leading to Tetsuro. Just as tentatively, she placed her fingers on the cold knob. She held it for long seconds while she tried to slow her breathing and still her heart. Her conscience needled her.

He was a grown man and deserved more consideration than to have her, a virtual stranger, enter his bedroom uninvited or unannounced, even if it was only to say she was sorry.

McKenna's grip tightened and she opened the door.

The heavy door swung inward with a whisper and McKenna stepped into the cool, silent room. A wide beam of moonlight streamed in through the open drapes to fall across the figure sprawled on the bed, angled from corner to corner to accommodate his length. Tetsuro was on his stomach, the injured arm extended out to his side. McKenna was breathless. He'd kicked the covers to the foot and the smooth expanse of tawny skin was open to her view unbroken by a garment. For seconds, she could only stare transfixed at the magnificently muscled man before her.

His soft snore broke the spell and when he moved as if to turn over, McKenna fled back the way she'd come. What if he'd caught her staring at the round curve of his buttocks? What was she doing here in the first place? Had she planned to wake him up? Apologies would have to wait until the morning.

As she made her way out of his suite her gaze fell to the floor and her eye caught sight of a wad of bright white paper outside the waste-paper basket.

How did Rebecca overlook this?

Never one to tolerate clutter, she picked it up and carried it to her bedroom, intending to throw it way.

Once alone in her room, McKenna could breath easier. She placed the paper wad on her nightstand and went to the bathroom to ready herself for bed. Crawling beneath the cool sheets minutes later, she remembered the paper. She lifted it from the nightstand and unfolded it before she turned the light off. What she read disturbed her.

Dearest Emiko it began

Tetsuro had written in Roman characters so precise they could have been Japanese characters.

So, he had a *dearest* in his life.

And her name was *Emiko*.

Did she want to compete with the woman who had his heart? A woman of his culture who would understand him, and he, her? But was she worthy of him? *Dearest Emiko* certainly hadn't rushed to his side after the injury! She, McKenna, had been there for his trauma. Not some kimonoed, raven-haired *geisha*.

McKenna placed the paper inside the nightstand drawer, then she tried to sleep.

CHAPTER THIRTEEN

"Good morning, Dr. Stafford," Libby greeted McKenna bright and chipper the next morning at the hospital. "You look beat. On call last night?"

"No." McKenna paused while writing on her patient's chart to brush a stray lock of hair from her face. Physically, emotionally and spiritually she was tired and confused by turmoil she could hardly recognize. "I'm having trouble sleeping."

Libby's sparkly eyes lit up and her eyebrows crept up her forehead. "Oh? Could Mr. Takamitsu be the cause?"

"Libby." Hoping to hide the blush that warmed her cheeks, McKenna recapped her fountain pen and dropped it into her purse. "Why would you presume that?"

"Do you think no one has noticed the chemistry between the two of you?" Libby's face was bright with anticipation.

"Chemistry…between…us?" McKenna walked around the nurse's station to replace the chart. Her pace was quick and anxious. The heels of her pumps tapped on the tiles and her A-line skirt swished against her legs. She forced herself to take a deep calming breath.

"Duh. Yes." Libby came near her. "And since he's living with you, things might be heating up."

McKenna bristled. "How do you know he's staying with me?"

"You don't think we all figured that out the day he was discharged? You two left together," the nurse pointed out the clue.

"I don't know why I think anything around here's secret." McKenna glanced around the area. She and Libby were the only ones there.

Nurses and doctors gossiped nonstop at the hospital, the nurse's station the source of all kinds of conjecture. Their close working relationships and the long hours they spent together fostered the environment of familiarity. And Libby, bubbly, feisty and full of life, was one source of much of the personal tidbits. A good nurse, she was the unofficial party planner and after hours get-together hostess.

"He's certainly taken with you." Libby returned to the subject of McKenna's patient and houseguest. "He used to ask all kinds of questions about you. And I don't think he was concerned with your medical skill."

McKenna took a deep breath. What was she doing standing there talking about her patient? She needed to be at the office, not indulging in gossip.

"I think you should go for it. I don't think the man-woman thing is much different between East and West." Give Libby a chance to talk about men and she'd run with it. "Mr. Takamitsu's nice and sweet. Not to mention he has a body to die for!" Libby's eyes sparkled again.

"Libby! I'm not attracted by his…body!" McKenna's hot face belied her words. How could she expect Libby to believe her? She couldn't even convince herself.

"It's not a bad thing." Libby placed a reassuring hand on her arm.

McKenna couldn't help but smile. "Are you…sure?"

"Dr. Stafford, don't worry so much. Be spontaneous. Ask him out to dinner. A movie. Go shopping and have coffee. Tell him you want to show him Cleveland," Libby suggested.

"I…don't know," she hesitated.

"Mr. Takamitsu might be as timid as you are. You're dealing with culture shock. He's a little more American, but some things are ingrained." Libby pulled a chart from the rack and handed it to a physician who came up to the desk. He gave the women a cursory glance and moved down the hall. "I asked him why he didn't talk to you himself and he said that in Japan, one did not ask another personal questions."

"They go around talking behind each other's backs. How quaint," McKenna remarked. *He'll fit in with my family perfectly.* "I'll think about it." McKenna patted Libby's hand.

"Will you let me know how things go?"

"Certainly. Now I'll let you get back to work." McKenna grinned as she gathered her things. "I have an important patient to see in about an hour. His dressing comes off today."

Tetsuro waited for McKenna in the cast removal room at her office. A fidgety young man, who introduced himself as Greg, sat across from him after arranging and rearranging the doctor's tools. The Japanese drummer was anxious. He worried about the condition of his hand and was equally nervous about seeing McKenna. He'd come to the painful decision of finding another place to stay to prevent any further strain on their situation.

"Is something wrong?" Tetsuro asked the young man who continued to fidget. He wasn't going to think about his personal relationship with his doctor.

"No." He paused, then answered again. "Well, yes. I usually cut off casts and Dr. Stafford comes in afterwards. But she wants to do yours herself. Maybe I'm doing things wrong."

"I am sure she would tell you directly if you were acting incorrectly. She does not appear to be the type of woman to keep her feelings inside." McKenna had made it clear what she thought of him and his actions.

Before they could speak more, McKenna opened the door and entered the room. "Good morning, gentleman,"

Greg jumped up and moved to the equipment. "Morning, ma'am."

"How are you, Greg?" She sat at the examination table across from Tetsuro. "And you, Tetsu? Are you well today?" She reached to take the hand she'd repaired.

"I am fine." Her use of his common name was refreshing. "Thank you, *Sensei*." His words were crisp and precise. Like most Japanese, Tetsuro could use language to build barriers. His native tongue had several layers of language, from the most intimate used with family to the elitist used at the Imperial Court. His always perfect English modeled after Japanese was formal, discouraging intimacy.

"I'll explain what I'm going to do. The first thing is to clip the bandage and cotton as much as possible so I can simply peel it away from your arm." She spoke of the cotton batting and elastic bandage she'd applied in the operating room to keep his injured hand immobile for the initial healing. "It'll be messy and matted, even stuck to your skin, especially where the suture lines are. To get rid of that without ripping your skin, we'll let you soak your hand for about thirty minutes in warm water." She indicated an oblong pan Greg had prepared on the table at his side. "Then I'll come back and clean it off so I can assess the operation. Any questions?"

Tetsuro looked into her face. The twinkling brown eyes worked their spell over him so easily. "Will I be able to use my hand?" He wanted to read the truth in her eyes. The smile on her lips chipped away a bit of the wall between them.

"I can't tell you for sure right now." The heat of her fingers as she stroked his right upper arm raced to the center of his chest. "Let's take one thing at a time."

"Very well." Tetsuro dropped his eyes and respectfully bowed his head ever so slightly toward her.

"Shall we begin?" She accepted a large pair of scissors from Greg.

"*Hai.*"

Carefully and expertly she cut away the bandage encasing his hand and arm. As she leaned over the work her breath was tight. Her head was close to him, and the woodsy aroma of his cologne, the soap from his morning shower and the manly scent of his body's nervous sweat washed over her. His long hair brushed against her shoulder as he tried to see over her and inspect her work. When he sat back the soft hair was moved away too.

The dressing's cotton batting was adhered to his hand and she picked at it with delicate movements. When she turned his hand palm up, the batting over his palm was discolored with dried blood. She stopped trying to remove any more of the dressing when it would not come loose easily.

She sat back. "That's all I can do now. Greg'll help you soak it and

I'll go see other patients until he says it's time."

"*Daijobu.*" Once more, Tetsuro bobbed his head in surrender. "All right," he translated.

"I'll see you in about half an hour." Again, McKenna stroked his arm. The pulse of her touch joined the beat of his heart, becoming one beat. "You'll be in good hands." She stood to leave.

"Not as good as yours," Tetsuro spoke softly. Neither McKenna nor Greg acknowledged hearing his words.

Guided by the medical assistant, Tetsuro placed his cotton-encrusted hand into the warm water.

"Is it too hot?" he asked.

"*Iie.* It is fine." Tetsuro settled his hand in the hot water. It felt alien to him. Unaccustomed to the air currents, the skin prickled. He didn't want to look at his wound and engaged the technician in conversation. "You say usually you are the one to remove bandages?"

"Yes." Greg cleaned up the debris and put away the equipment.

"Would you have done anything differently?" Consoling the young man was a useful distraction.

"No."

"Then you can be assured she did not find disfavor with your technique." Was it that he was than a patient to her? The memory of the slap made him to doubt it.

"You're right." Greg faced him and smiled. "Thanks."

"You are welcome." At least the assistant was pleased.

"Let me go ask the doc if she wants you to wiggle your fingers while in the water. Don't want to tell you to do something that'll mess up her work." Greg left the room.

Finally, Tetsuro mustered the courage to look at his abused hand resting in the water. At first, the water had been rather hot, but now the temperature felt good. Extending from the clumps of batting tiny strands of cotton floated in the water like spider webs. The discoloration he'd seen the night of the accident had cleared and the skin, he hoped, would be normal colored when McKenna finished cleaning it.

When he returned Greg said, "Dr. Stafford says it'll be all right for you to wiggle your fingers. The heat'll make it easier." He placed a porcelain cup of tea at Tetsuro's right side. "She also sent you this." He departed again.

"*Domo*." Touched by McKenna's thoughtfulness, Tetsuro took a delicate sip of the tea. He wished he could understand her mixed signals.

Fifty minutes later, McKenna returned. She was alone.

She retook her seat. "How's it feel?"

"Cold."

"I'm sorry. I was busy with a child who wouldn't let me touch her foot for a long time." She spread a towel out in front of her, between them. "Put it here." She patted the towel as he lifted his hand out of the water. McKenna began to gently scrub the back of his hand with a plastic brush and the cotton clumps came away, adhering to the brush, causing her to pause periodically to pull them from the tiny bristles. At length, she could no longer put off turning his hand over.

"Perhaps the child has not learned to trust you." Tetsuro tensed his arm as she began to turn it over. Could they put it off a few seconds longer?

"Children are very trusting." Her small hands stroked his damp skin. "Greg has a better way with them than I do. I suppose that's because he's from a large, close knit family."

Tetsuro watched her fingers trace the veins on the back of his arm. Sparks of electricity sent his heart to racing and the rush continued to his groin.

"With a child of your own you will become more adept."

"No chance of that anytime soon," McKenna sighed.

"You never know what *karma* has in store," he spoke with Asian astuteness. Even as she spoke, the seed for such a child threatened to spill into his jeans.

"I think I do when it comes to that. Let's look at your hand. You trust me, don't you?" She batted her eyelashes at him.

"With my life."

McKenna rotated his hand, mindful not to cause pain.

The incision line was coated with old blood and half-dissolved sutures. She worked the brush over the palm in an easy yet effective manner while cradling his hand in hers. Even lying still his hand radiated power. Muscles corded his arm. How he'd managed to maintain the tone and strength of his arm was a mystery to her but the warmth spreading through her was pleasant.

When she'd finished with the brush, her fingers lingered to outline the clean incision lines which followed the creases covering his palm. The pink tissue evidenced healing.

"You are staring." Tetsuro broke into her thoughts. "Is something wrong?"

"I didn't realize I was." McKenna took her fingers from his palm, but continued to hold his hand. "Nothing's wrong. It's healed well. Can you move your fingers?"

"*Hai.*" Slowly at first, Tetsuro wiggled his digits; the range of motion was limited but he cold move them. But could he *use* them? "Not well."

"Can you make a fist?"

Try as he might, Tetsuro could not close his hand.

He sighed, "*Iie.*"

"It's all right." She stroked the back of his hand. "That's where physical therapy comes in. In time, you'll do better." With enthusiasm, McKenna said. "I think we should celebrate!"

"*Gomen kudasai?* Celebrate? I cannot use my hand!" Fear and anxiety filled his tone.

"In time, Tetsu, in time." She leaned closer, her elbows resting on the top of the table as she held his hand. Reading the concern in his eyes, she reached one hand to stroke his jaw. "Tomorrow you'll start physical therapy and, with time and use, your hand *will* work."

"I must trust your judgment." He took the hand that caressed his face into his good hand and held it tightly.

"*Domo arigato*. I'm the professional here. You can tell me what to do when I take up drumming. Now go home and find a place you think has the best *sushi*. I want to try it with an expert."

"*Sushi*? Excuse me?"

"It's your *hand* that was hurt, not your *ears*!" McKenna laughed. "Why are you making me repeat everything?"

"I am a little confused after…" Tetsuro didn't finish his thought. "I would be honored to celebrate with you, Ke-*chan*."

For a long period, the two, doctor and patient, sat quietly, each watching the other, and holding hands across the table. The long fingers of his injured hand next to her slender ones entranced her. Yearning to feel his hands on her skin, she was certain his touch would be tender, a soft caress of strong hands. Prickles of passion erupted along her body. When a knock sounded at the door they broke away.

"Doctor?" Greg put his head in the open door. "Do you need my help?"

"No, Greg." McKenna stood. "I've finished…for now. Mr. Takamitsu will need to schedule physical therapy five times a week. Can you see to that?"

"Sure." Greg left.

"Greg'll fix a sling for you to rest your hand as well as a splint. You don't have to wear it all the time, only when your hand's tired or hurts. I'll see you tonight…," McKenna paused, "…at home." They indeed made a home.

"I will look forward to it," Tetsuro answered. "And thank you for the tea."

"You're very welcome. Made it myself."

"Well done, Ke-*chan*." Tetsuro's soft smile brought the heat to her cheeks.

McKenna left the room and headed for her office. She couldn't stop smiling and imagined if someone was watching her, they'd see a spring in her step. She was happier than she'd been in years.

CHAPTER FOURTEEN

Tetsuro sat waiting for Greg, his arm extended on the table. The hand, once so acquiescent to his will, moving without thought in the precise direction his mind willed it, seemed as foreign to him as his doctor. Both were necessary to his soul. If he couldn't drum, his life was over. If he couldn't have McKenna…he had no idea of what would result. He'd been hurt so badly before he wasn't sure he'd survive another disappointment in the area of love.

Love was an emotion the Japanese tried to ignore for centuries, not even formulating a word for it. But he knew exactly what it was even without being able to call it by name. His heart ached every day of his life because of love.

Tetsuro was glad when Greg returned to the room. Determined to ease his melancholy, he focused on the technician's movements. The young man opened a cabinet door, removed a white jar, then came to sit in McKenna's vacated seat.

McKenna. Her name whispered through his head settling in his heart. Tetsuro sighed.

Greg opened the jar and scooped a large glob of white cream on his fingers. He spread it over Tetsuro's forearm, starting at the elbow and working his way to the wrist.

"What is this for?"

"Since your skin has been enclosed for so long, the moisture's gone." Greg worked smoothly with firm strokes. "This is a special cream Dr. Stafford uses to restore elasticity and natural oils. I'll give you this jar and you put it on twice a day, heavily for the first few applications. After therapy, P.T.'ll massage it in, too." When Greg neared his hand Tetsuro drew back, anticipating pain. "I'll try not to hurt you, sir."

"*Sumimasen,*" Tetsuro apologized. "I did not mean to flinch." He struggled to relax and allow the medical assistant to do his work.

"Everyone does. It's instinctive. You've spent weeks with pain and guarding against further injury." Greg continued to massage the cream into Tetsuro's arm. "Dr. Stafford says you're a drummer. What band?"

"I am not that *kind* of drummer." Tetsuro watched Greg's fingers lightly work over his hand. "I am a *taiko* drummer, the traditional drum style of Japan."

"Like in the movie *Rising Sun* with Sean Connery and Wesley Snipes?"

"Yes. Those drummers were actually from our troupe." He had been in Tokyo when the film crew came to the school. Otherwise he was sure *Sensei* Nakamura would have assigned him a role.

"Dr. Stafford loves rhythm and blues. She gave me tickets to Johnny Lee Hooker a few years ago because the guy she dates hates it."

"I do not think you should be telling me this." The mention of McKenna's boyfriend made Tetsuro uncomfortable. He didn't want to remember that she was inaccessible to him on that level.

"I've a Chinese friend. Well, Chinese-American. Anyway, he's a rocker and would love to be in a band. Not many openings for Asian rock stars."

"No, I do not think so. However, if your friend wishes, he can join workshops where we teach *taiko*."

"Where are they held?" Greg finished applying the cream.

"On Nakano Island, in the Sea of Japan."

"Wow. Don't think Mike can make that." Greg stood and washed his hands. "So. Where are you from? Cleveland? I know there's a Japanese community here although it's dwindling."

"I am from the suburbs of Tokyo originally. I now live on Nakano."

"Let me show you how to put the splint on." Greg took the arm and laid it in the hard plastic cradle. "It's easy to fix these Velcro straps around your forearm." He did so to show Tetsuro how to fasten the splint. "Now the sling. You'll need to use it to avoid injuring your hand."

He fastened a canvas sling around Tetsuro's neck, guiding his hand into the sling and made sure it was comfortable.

"How's that?"

"Fine." Tetsuro did his own adjusting of the strap at his neck. "*Domo.*"

"If you don't have any questions, we're done."

"I need a taxi called." Tetsuro again adjusted things. He pulled his hair out from beneath the sling. The raven mass floated down his back.

"Meg'll be glad to do that. She also has your P. T. schedule. Here's your cream." Greg handed Tetsuro the white jar.

"Thank you." He dropped it into the leather bag he carried, then rose to walk to the door, heading to his home away from home.

Back in his room at Dr. Stafford's house, Tetsuro sat at the desk and pondered his next move. What he should do was clear, but was it for the best?

Greg had spoken of Cleveland having a Japanese community. If they maintained Japanese traditions, there would be an association where he could find what he needed. And he had to find the *sushi* bar. Even if he planned to move out, he owed McKenna a meal.

For both tasks, he needed a phone book. He looked through his suite in all the obvious places without success. Rebecca was out shopping so he couldn't ask her where it might be.

He walked toward McKenna's room. Cautious, aware he was invading her privacy, something so valued in Japan, he entered her bedroom and immediately spied the phone on the nightstand. A drawer beneath the lamp and phone must hold the book. He put his hand on the handle and started to pull. When it came open, a familiar looking piece of wrinkled paper caught his eye. A smudge of black ink peeked from beneath the folded edge. Before he could investigate it further, he was distracted by the phone book in the cubbyhole of the nightstand. He shut the drawer and bent to pick up the book, forgetting the slip of paper.

Flipping through the phone book, he wasn't sure what to look for. He really didn't want to be successful in finding another place, but knew no matter how painful, it had to be done for everyone's sake.

Every patient McKenna saw after Tetsuro's appointment came and went without complication. She didn't even remember seeing most of them. She rushed home eager to see Tetsuro and was disappointed he wasn't waiting for her like a schoolboy greeting his prom date. She walked up the stairs, her eyes trained on the hallway, hopeful he would suddenly appear to welcome her.

He didn't.

With dampened spirits, McKenna made her way to her bedroom. A hot bath with plenty of bath salts to leave her skin smelling of lavender revived her anticipation. Expensive, delicately scented lotion removed any ashy look from her skin. Her hair refused to cooperate so the thick cascade remained over her shoulders in natural waves. A light application of makeup gave the illusion of a permanent blush.

For her attire, she chose a flowing skirt of deep orange and red swirls that hung in soft drapes to her knees. Her silk blouse, a lighter shade of orange, fit close to her body, and the front buttoned to the spot between her breasts where her cleavage began. The colors highlighted her coppery tones. A quick spritz of perfume and she was ready to search out her date for the evening.

Tetsuro stood in the family room studying the photos. The sound of McKenna's footsteps on the stairs brought back the memory of the night he'd insulted her with his touch. As if her hand struck him anew, his cheek stung. This dinner was foolish. It would result in nothing and both would be hurt. Still, he wanted to enjoy McKenna's company more than anything in the world, almost more than he wanted to return to *taiko*.

As he turned and took in her appearance in the doorway, he announced, "Those colors make your skin glow."

"Thank you." McKenna came into the room, casually fastening earrings to her pierced earlobes. "You're very GQ tonight with that white shirt and khakis."

"Did you expect me to pull a kimono out of my bags?" There was a hint of laughter in his voice. With the semi-return of the use of his hand, he found it easier to dress in the American style.

"No, I did not." McKenna giggled.

"Are these photos of your family?" he asked, genuinely wanting to know but also to keep from getting into an awkward discussion.

"Yes." McKenna stepped to the wall where portraits of three generations on both sides of her family were hung. "These are the oldest pictures we have of my great grandparents. He made the Stafford family fortune with the first Black taxi service." She pointed to the next photo. "This is my grandfather Haynes and his wife. She was half-white. There are no pictures of the Haynes great grands."

She walked to the last two pictures. "My father and mother."

Tetsuro leaned closer and studied the people. McKenna shared very little with her parents. Her mother had a cold, hard stare for the camera and her father held himself in reserve, revealing little on film.

"You must have inherited a great many of your grandmother's genes." Tetsuro indulged in the desire to touch her hair, pushing the heavy wave back.

"I did." McKenna took his hand as he lowered it from her hair. She clung to it briefly, then released him to approach the bookcase. "These are my sisters." Three small frames lined the shelf.

Tetsuro gave them a cursory glance. McKenna was the beauty of the family it was clear.

"Family must be very important to you."

"In some ways," she answered. "It's become easy to forget we are family over the years. We aren't as close as we once were."

"In Japan, family is the most important thing. *Taiko* has a family closeness. Some of us have no other family members so drumming fills the void." His drum had taken the place of many things in his life. *Taiko* comforted him when he was sad and gave him a way to express his joy.

"The hospital staff makes up for my family's absence. Since my father died, my sisters and I have become very…distant." She took an extra moment's glance at her sisters' photos before asking, "Have you chosen a restaurant for us to start my *sushi* education? I still don't think I'll be able to eat raw fish."

"I made reservations for eight at the Chrysanthemum Bar. It is the only place in Cleveland I have any knowledge of. My friend brought me lunch from there."

Tetsuro came to McKenna's side and helped her into her jacket. As he stood behind her, his hand on her shoulder after pulling the garment up, her tantalizing perfume filled his nose and awoke his body to her sensuality. The urge to place his jaw against her soft hair threatened to overcame propriety, but memory of his earlier trespass and its results restrained him. "Shall we go?"

With a catch in her voice, she answered, "Yes."

CHAPTER FIFTEEN

The couple walked through the house to the garage. Tetsuro opened the driver's door to the SUV and McKenna took her place behind the wheel. He then sprinted around the vehicle to the passenger side. An adolescence spent in the movie theaters showing American movies had given him a vast knowledge of Western manners.

"Ready?" McKenna started the Jeep and put her hand on the gearshift.

"*Hai*." Tetsuro had an easier time fastening the seatbelt when his hand was bandaged than now with it suspended in a sling. Frustrated, he slipped the sling off, laying it in the floorboard, then pulled the fabric of his jacket so it was not wadded beneath the seat belt. McKenna's hand moved from the gearshift toward his face. Tetsuro dodged her touch as she straightened his lapel.

"What're you flinching for? I'm not going to hit you." McKenna started backing out of the driveway.

"*Gomen kudasai.* A...habit," Tetsuro responded in a flustered spate of words. "It is not common for strangers to touch another in Japan."

"Do you consider me a stranger?" McKenna was into the traffic flow on Fairmount.

"No," he spoke softly. Who was he kidding? They'd rolled around on the bathroom floor, embraced, kissed passionately. He hadn't dodged any of those moves. Why now? He couldn't tell her the real reason he'd moved away from her; wouldn't remind her of the pain and hurt she'd caused. Again, his culture prevented such openness which would embarrass both of them. "I consider you a very good friend."

McKenna smiled but remained mute.

Tetsuro watched the intensity on her face as she concentrated on the traffic. Her short, perky nose and the roundness of her cheeks gave her a soft profile that intrigued him. He wished he were bold enough to cup his hand around those cheeks, but he sat stoically in his seat and stared toward the businesses they passed.

Normally, Tetsuro wouldn't have thought twice about pursuing a beautiful woman, as long as it came without strings attached. He would not risk giving his heart away. *Again.* And now, when he could easily offer the heart he had guarded for the past twelve years to McKenna, he slipped into the familiar guise dictated by long ingrained Japanese social customs. He would be polite, hiding behind the facade of etiquette.

Arriving at the restaurant, Tetsuro performed the usual gentlemanly Western moves, holding doors and following behind McKenna and announcing to the maître d' that they were here for their reservations. In Tokyo, his date would concede to tradition and fall behind him, unaccustomed to men holding doors or being concerned about her whereabouts or safety.

"Do you prefer Japanese or Western seating?" the maître d' asked in a clipped Japanese accent.

"Western would be best." Tetsuro looked at McKenna as he said, "I would hate for your legs to go to sleep during the meal."

They followed the maître d' to an out of the way table. A waiter appeared with menus.

"Something to drink, sir?" His Midwestern accent belied his Japanese features. Until he spoke he could have passed for any *sushi* bar waiter in Japan. He wore the same black and white *hanten* with black *hakama* and a white *hachi-machi* over straight black hair that they did.

"*Hai. Sake, dozo.*" Tetsuro turned to McKenna. "Would you like something?"

"Did I understand you ordered *sake* for yourself?"

"Yes."

"Then I'll have it, too."

"Very well."

The waiter disappeared.

"You know, *geisha* have a saying. 'The *sake furasuko kami* often leads to singing and dancing and the truth,'" he commented.

"The truth, you say?" McKenna's face brightened. "That might be interesting."

"*Hai*," Tetsuro breathed regretfully. Was he willing to reveal any truths to McKenna?

The waiter returned and set the flask of *sake* before Tetsuro.

"Are you ready to order, sir?"

"It will be a few minutes." The waiter disappeared. With his right hand, Tetsuro poured warmed *sake* for the two of them. "Have you had *sake* before?"

"No." McKenna accepted the tiny cup he offered her. "This is a night of all new things."

"Well, then…" Before Tetsuro could say anything further, McKenna raised the cup to her lips and took a large swallow. She immediately sputtered and gasped for breath. The alcohol was much stronger than any she'd experienced. Composed, Tetsuro handed her his napkin and took her *sake* cup.

In a soft voice, he said, "I was about to warn you."

"Point taken." McKenna dabbed her chin and finally had breath to speak.

"Now. Unless you wish to repeat the episode with the *wasabi*, listen before you put something into your mouth." The tone of his voice was tender and instructive.

"Yes, master." McKenna took a sip of ice water. "But I have had alcohol before, you know."

"I am sure you have, but *sake* is different." Tetsuro took her napkin to replace the one he'd given her.

"Isn't everything from Japan?"

"Not…everything." There was a tantalizing hint of something in his voice. "Some things are the same the world round."

A tender look crept into in his eyes in spite of his boyish grin. McKenna broke the stare, aware of a warm glow.

"What're we going to eat?" McKenna sipped the *sake* from her refilled cup. The alcohol increased her warmth.

Tetsuro again looked into her eyes and McKenna slipped into the dark pools framed by the oblong lids. She wasn't sure if it were the *sake* or his eyes that made her breath catch in her throat.

"I sense you would rather be eating a well done steak."

"We'll do that some other time. Now, tell me what I want to eat." McKenna stared at the menu as if she understood it.

"Do you trust me?" His voice, full and sultry, came from deep within.

"Are you turning the tables on me? I asked you that once, didn't I?"

There was that mischievous look to his smile. "*Hai.*"

"And your answer was yes. So I, too, defer to your wisdom, especially with raw fish."

"I wish you would stop calling it that. There is more to *sushi* than raw fish."

"*Shitsurei shimasu,*" McKenna apologized in Tetsuro's fashion. The glint in his eyes remained while the smile faded from his lips. Or was he consciously concealing it?

"You are a very quick study."

"Oh? How's that?"

"You used the phrase which literally is 'I am committing a breach of etiquette.' I used it only once in your presence," Tetsuro explained.

McKenna wet her lips with *sake,* recalling the bathroom incident where Tetsuro had said '*shitsurei shimasu*' in apology for falling on her. "I thought 'I'm sorry' was the same words."

"Apologies come in several ways, but we will study Japanese language later." The hint of a smile was back to the full lips moist with *sake.* "You are forgiven. To begin your training, *sensei,* you must learn some basic facts. I think the first reason Westerners are put off by our cuisine is language. *Sushi* is like your sandwiches. It does not have to be raw fish or fish at all, for that matter. *Sashimi* is always raw fish and has no rice. Both are served in two manners. Individual pieces, about two bites worth, are called *nigiri-sushi.* Rolls are called *make-sushi* or *norimake.*

"The second reason is the strange-sounding names. The names are merely Japanese words for the kind of fish. What kind of cooked fish do you like?"

"Shellfish-lobster, shrimp, scallops. Salmon, whitefish, cod. But I *hate* mackerel." Nervousness caused her to take another drink of rice wine.

"That gives me a foundation. You are not allergic to anything?"

"This sounds like you are taking a medical history." The flow of *sake* sent her blood flowing through her veins with a hot sensation. "No."

Tetsuro signaled to the waiter who stood anticipating the call.

"Yes, sir?" the young man responded. His language now was Japanese.

McKenna listened as Tetsuro ordered, but she had no idea what he said. The whole conversation was a blur.

"Now, we wait until the *itamae* does his *sushi* preparation magic. With *sushi*, unlike many dishes, you can count on freshness. In the better restaurants, it is not made until ordered."

McKenna accepted his offer of a refill acutely aware she'd consumed four cups to his two. It probably accounted for her decreased nervousness.

She began small talk. "Have you heard from any of your friends or relatives?"

"Susumu-*san* sent a card from Philadelphia." McKenna watched the elegant way he handled the tiny cup in his large hands, his slender fingers balancing it as he took a drink. His splint didn't prevent his holding the cup because of the manner he employed. Instead of holding it in his hand, he poised the cup on the fingertips of both hands as he brought the rim to his lips. The part of his mouth covering the cup's edge looked soft as he sipped with his sensuous lips.

McKenna broke her stare away from his mouth and drank from her own cup, in hope of washing away the temptation to replace his *sake* cup with her mouth. "You could call your mother if you wished."

"She died ten years ago."

"I thought…I'm terribly sorry." McKenna caressed his arm in sympathy. "She was your only family?"

"Yes. My mother's parents died before I was born. My father died when I was nine. His parents both died a few years ago. Because I study *taiko*, I have been isolated from my extended family." Tetsuro sipped again and tossed his lengthy hair back in that equine way of his. "I suspect that is why I desire children. I enjoy being around the young *taiko* students when I teach. A child of your own would be much more precious."

"Yes." McKenna studied her empty *sake* cup. How had he been able to slip so easily into the one area where she was so vulnerable? His words and the strong alcoholic rice wine combined to bring tears to her eyes. Damn! She couldn't do this! She wouldn't. By an act of will, McKenna pushed back the tears.

The waiter returned and deposited a stone rectangle displaying several bits of food artfully arranged.

Tetsuro thanked him, then addressed McKenna.

"Your raw fish, madam," he announced lightly. "Or, as you once said, cat food."

"I'm sorry. I didn't mean any offense."

"I was teasing, Ke-*chan*." Tetsuro picked up the paper-wrapped eating sticks. "Can you use *hashi* or do you wish a fork?"

"I can use chopsticks. What are *hashi*?"

"Chopsticks are Chinese. *Hashi* are Japanese." He picked up the fine wooden implements. Quickly, he fit them into his fingers and poked at the pieces of *sushi*. "Why not start with *ebi*?"

"Which is that?" McKenna leaned forward to examine the food. There were five pairs, each a different shape, size and content.

"*Ebi* is shrimp." Tetsuro pushed the inch-sized rectangle of rice with a shrimp curled on top of it. "But, first, your sauce. Do you like hot and spicy food?"

"Yes."

"*Wasabi*." He lifted a tiny bit of the green paste on the *hashi* and deposited it in the shallow bowl, then poured *shoyu* into it until he had about half a teaspoon of sauce. "This is for you to dip your *sushi* in. Go easy. It is strong. You can always add more if it is not to your liking."

McKenna adjusted the shrimp and rice between the wooden sticks. She brought the morsel to the small bowl in a flimsy balancing act. With a plop and tiny splash the *sushi* dropped into the sauce.

"Oops!" she giggled.

"Either you need more practice or less *sake*." Tetsuro used his own *hashi* to help her. Even with his aid, McKenna couldn't retrieve it. "Open your mouth." Tetsuro lifted the rice and shrimp and placed it inside like a father bird feeding its offspring. Or, rather, a male cardinal courting the female by feeding her tidbits in hopes of mating for life. "Be careful. It will have a lot of *wasabi* on it now."

Around the large mouthful, she replied, "I can handle it."

McKenna struggled to breathe. At the moment he laid the rice on her tongue, the strong *wasabi* flowed into the nerve endings and erupted. The spicy herb sent its fumes up through her sinuses and down into her throat. Tears rolled down her cheeks as she reached for the tiny wine cup.

"Easy." Tetsuro put his hand on her back and sympathetically rubbed. "It will pass."

"I think...your food's...trying to kill me," she managed to gasp after she swallowed and the fumes subsided. She eased back against the chair and wiped at her eyes.

"You will get used to it," Tetsuro assured her. His hand remained on her back; the soft circles of his fingers caused her to sigh. She took another sip.

"This flask is empty. Should I order more?"

"Why not? I'm developing a taste for it." McKenna regretted her answer when he removed his hand to wave at the ever-attentive waiter.

The *sake* arrived and he refilled both cups. "Are you ready for more? I mean another piece?"

"What's next?"

"You must cleanse your palate." Tetsuro lifted a small piece of finely grated pink substance and aimed it toward her mouth. "This is ginger. It removes the first taste from your mouth so you can experience the second."

"You Japanese think of everything, don't you?" McKenna accepted the ginger and chewed thoughtfully. The pungent spice did wash the taste from her tongue and she welcomed the next taste.

The evening wore on, speeding by too quickly for McKenna. Tetsuro's choices of *sushi* were perfect, each a blend of the familiar with a hint of the exotic. The sensations of taste and texture opened new experiences for her and the *sake* filled her body with a cozy, comfortable glow.

"What's that one called again?" She poked the *hashi* at the second piece she'd tried.

"*Hamachi*. Yellowtail fish."

"That's my favorite." McKenna picked up the leftover bite and plopped it into her mouth.

When she'd swallowed, Tetsuro asked, "Should I order more?"

"Sure. But aren't you going to eat?"

"I only ordered a small amount for you. I was afraid I would have to consume all of it. Since you have overcome your aversion, I will order more for you and some for myself." Tetsuro turned again to the waiter and ordered in Japanese. When he departed, Tetsuro turned back to McKenna. His finger caressed her cheekbone. "The *sake* has caused a lovely flush to cover your cheeks."

The trail of his touch was so intense on her skin McKenna could only drop her face. The heat remained when he removed his finger.

"Do you ever think of having a family, Ke-*chan*?"

"Often." The *sake's* effect sent the reply to her lips unbidden.

"You should have many. You have many maternal qualities. Have you ever…had a child?"

McKenna stared at him in complete disbelief. How dare he ask such a question? Did he know? How could he?

"I…" She was relived of the obligation of speaking what she knew would be the truth as the food arrived. As she peered at his dish, she commented, "Yours is different."

The plate before Tetsuro was filled with several pieces of *sushi* and a bowl of soup. McKenna's meal was the same as he'd ordered before.

"I did not think you would like the more unusual." Tetsuro worked his sauce magic.

"That's very presumptuous. You didn't think I'd like the first." McKenna reached with her *hashi* to take a piece of Tetsuro's food.

Tetsuro sat away and allowed her to take what she wished from his plate.

"Very well."

McKenna put the piece in her mouth and started to chew. Abruptly, she stopped and grabbed her napkin.

"Ugh!" she exclaimed after she spit it into the cloth. "What was that?"

"*Shirako*," Tetsuro informed her while trying not to laugh. "Cod fish sperm sac."

"How disgusting!" She tossed the napkin away in shock.

"To you, maybe." Tetsuro stirred his soup with the wide spoon. "It is one of my favorites."

McKenna picked up the napkin. "Want it back?" She offered the glob toward him.

"No, thank you." He smiled as he pushed the napkin away. "This will be fine."

"Your loss." She giggled.

After a few minutes, Tetsuro said, "You've stopped eating."

"I'm suddenly very full." McKenna rested against the back of her chair. "I didn't notice until I was about to burst."

Tetsuro sipped *sake* under her watchful eye. Even handicapped with his injured hand, he managed to deftly use the *hashi*, alternately dipping the *sushi* into the sauce and then his mouth.

"You know," McKenna spoke with a slurred tongue, "your white shirt brings out the bronze tone of your skin."

Instead of looking at her Tetsuro concentrated on finishing his soup. "Thank you." The *sake* was affecting her just as he'd warned.

"So, tell me how you came to be a drummer." When he looked at her, McKenna stroked the fine thick hair in place behind his ear. "What kind of music do you like?"

"Which question do you wish me to answer first?" Tetsuro wiped his mouth with the linen napkin and sat back. Was there a bit of reluctance in the withdrawal of her touch?

"Music." McKenna drank and Tetsuro poured.

"I like rock and roll."

"That's too pat. Go for the first question."

"Very well. They both go together actually." Tetsuro wet his mouth with *sake*. "My grandfather was a teenager after World War Two. My great grandmother was an apprentice *geisha* before the war. When the school was closed, she worked as a waitress in a teahouse near the Imperial Palace. They said MacArthur was even a customer. As a boy my grandfather listened to the American Occupation Forces radio. He developed a love of Big Band music. When my father died and we moved into his house, I learned to appreciate it also. Especially Gene Kruppa.

"As I grew older, living with my mother and an old man who was not up to the energy and discipline of an adolescent boy, I began to get a little wild. Living in Tokyo made it easy. I was youngest in a gang of neighborhood tough guys. Before we had a chance to do anything terrible, we were arrested and taken to the police station."

"What did you do?" McKenna pressed. The waiter brought them a fresh *sake* flask.

"Me, nothing. I was with four others who were shoplifting. I must have looked pathetic at the station, because the arresting officer took me to his office, away from the others. He made me sit, alone and scared, for what seemed like forever. I sat, tapping my fingers on his desk. By the time he returned, I had picked up two pencils and was beating out a tune." Tetsuro paused to drink. "Wakiya-*san* took pity on me and did not book me. He did punish me. He took note of my drumming, and having *taiko* as a hobby, released me with the obligation of attending *taiko* class with him every Sunday for the next six months. By then, I was hooked. He pulled some strings to have me accepted by Taiko Nihon as an apprentice and, as they say, the rest is history."

"So becoming a drummer kept you from becoming a delinquent."

"There was more to the Sundays than drumming. In fact, I did not touch a drum for six weeks. Up to then, I was being physically tuned.

He had me running, doing physical exercises, biking, and learning martial arts. Anything to turn a skinny kid with no strength into a man who could perform *taiko*. It is not only hitting a drum head with a *bachi*."

"The policeman did a great job." She gave his upper bicep an affectionate squeeze.

"*Arigato*, Ke-*chan*."

"What is that you're calling me now? I was getting used to '*Sensei*'."

Interrupting before Tetsuro could explain, the waiter asked, "Would you like your check now?"

"Yes, *dozo*. And would you call a taxi please?"

"*Hai*." The waiter fled.

"A taxi? Why?"

"You are in no condition to drive and I cannot. So, a taxi."

"I'm fine," she insisted.

"You are all right while sitting. Once you stand and try to walk, the *kami* of the *sake* flask will steal your legs." Tetsuro handed the waiter a credit card with the check. "A taxi is the safest way to get home."

McKenna reached for her purse. "I planned to pay for the night. I invited you."

"Your *sushi* schooling is on me." Tetsuro scribbled his name on the receipt when the young man returned with it.

"Your ride is here, sir," the waiter told Tetsuro as he separated Tetsuro's copy. "Thank *you*, sir," he responded to his tip.

"*Do itashimashite*," he responded to the waiter. "Are you ready?" he addressed McKenna. He stood and stepped to McKenna's side, his good hand extended to help her stand.

"I think so."

Taking the offered support, McKenna put a little more pressure on his arm than usual. With a sudden surge in her grip she staggered against his arm. He tried not to smile at her predicament. *Sake* was such a misleading alcoholic drink. It was always amusing to see a first timer's experience. With his help, she managed to walk out of the restaurant without loosing any dignity.

CHAPTER SIXTEEN

Tetsuro was sorry when they arrived at the house. He had to tell McKenna of his decision, no matter how much he'd enjoyed the evening. He'd do it when they got inside. Remembering his sling, he stuffed it in his jacket pocket before leaving the car.

The walk up the long path to the door seemed to refresh her and by the time they entered the house, she was alert.

"Come in here." She took Tetsuro's hand, the one he'd used to support her, and pulled him along into the family room. "I have something I want to show you."

Tetsuro followed, forced to by her grasp of his hand. Once in the room, she released him and Tetsuro sat on the couch. She went to the wall unit and opened a door. Inside were over a hundred compact discs.

"Have you found this yet?" she asked over his shoulder. "You're welcome to listen to any of them." McKenna took out a CD and placed it into the player at mid-cabinet. "There are a lot of artists. My father was fond of swing music. I have rock and roll, Motown, jazz and rhythm and blues."

She came to sit beside Tetsuro as the first beats of the piece by Benny Goodman started. He removed the splint from his arm.

"What groups do you like?" She was close enough for Tetsuro to push her hair from her face.

"*Sake* tends to make one fail to notice things," he commented. "Led Zeppelin, Cream, the Who, Springsteen, Def Leppard, Journey, Aerosmith, Foreigner, and Breathing Room. There are many more."

"Breathing Room is my favorite group." McKenna lounged back on the couch. She spoke of the R&B band from a few decades before. "I play their CDs in the OR. Drives other surgeons wild."

"My mother did not have much to say that was good about them either." The warmth of McKenna's body radiated towards him and as Tetsuro settled closer to her side, his arm was along the back of the couch, almost resting on her shoulders.

"Did she forbid you to listen to them?"

"No. I was the firstborn son and could get away with anything. Since I did not have any brothers or sisters to lord it over, it did not do me much good." Tetsuro picked up a loose curl of hair.

"I," McKenna began, "on the other hand, have three older sisters. I've been told what to do and not to do since I was conceived."

"Oh, I am sure you have had your way most of the time, Ke-*chan*." Tetsuro placed a finger of his good hand beneath her chin and turned her face toward him. "You are a dynamic woman, sure of yourself and what you want."

McKenna didn't speak. Her eyes were trapped by his. He didn't move his finger, afraid that, if he did, the tears he saw in her beautiful brown eyes would begin to fall.

"You are Dr. McKenna Stafford," he continued, "the most skillful orthopedic surgeon at University Hospital, especially in the area of feet and…hands." Tetsuro dropped his finger from her chin and pulled his arm from the couch to show her. He turned his palm up so her gaze could fall on the healed incision.

McKenna took his hand in her two. Her breathing was jagged and she sniffled. He'd not managed to dam the tears as he'd wished.

"You've had a lifetime of doing what you want." McKenna directed her voice toward his hand. "Years of doing what your heart desired, not what was dictated by your father, your mother, teachers, professors, chief residents, chiefs of staff and…husbands."

Tetsuro heard her gulp. He didn't speak, fearful he'd say the wrong thing. His hand remained in hers.

"To survive in a profession I have…was forced into, I developed a stern manner, a determined personality. It was necessary in a profession run by men. But I had to give way somewhere." She sniffled again and her finger traced the incision line on his hand.

Tetsuro took his hand back, now aware that he would need both hands. At that instant the phone rang. McKenna pulled herself together to answer.

His lips teased into a fey grin as McKenna took a timid wobbling step. The alcohol continued to make her unsteady. The powerful and misleading *sake* spirit also worked to cloud one's decision-making processes. How well he remembered the night when *sake,* a beautiful woman, and his over-eager hormones combined to result in the most devastating event of his life. He wouldn't make that mistake again. He couldn't survive such trauma a second time.

McKenna's absence gave him the time he needed to rethink his plans. As much as he wanted to entwine his life with hers, nothing good would come of it. The end result would be pain and heartbreak. He would not be the cause of such anguish.

She returned to the room, more sober than when she'd left.

"Bad news?"

"On the contrary, very good news." McKenna sat again at his side. Seeking the comfort of his closeness, she was so near their hips met. Her body's heat seared into his like a hot sauna rock used at the mineral baths on Kyushu. The intensity electrified the deepest parts of him. "My friend has given birth to a baby girl."

"Then surely that is wonderful news." Her eyes betrayed her emotions. They again sparkled with unshed tears. He cupped her cheek with his good hand. Her skin was hot and moist. "Is it not?"

"For Claire, yes, but it makes me sad." She swallowed hard as if facing a demon she'd encountered before.

"Why are you sad, Ke-*chan*? We should rejoice in another's good fortune."

"I keep remembering my baby." She closed her eyes and held her hands to her mouth as if holding in the words wanting to rush out. After a deep breath, she spoke. "I found out in the middle of my pregnancy that she would not live because of a malformation of her brain. It was terrible. The time that should have been filled with great happiness was a nightmare. I lost everything then." The look McKenna gave him melted his heart. For moments his own heartache was forgotten.

"Stephen wasn't the best of husbands but his true colors showed during the ordeal. He'd never thought we should have children and held me responsible."

Tetsuro was mute, not daring to intrude on her confession. As she paused to collect herself, he slipped his arm around her shoulders. Her narrow, muscular back trembled beneath his touch.

"The men took charge, doing what they said was best for me," she continued. "But it wasn't. My doctor advised me to have my labor induced. So, after hours of contractions that went nowhere, they decided I should have a c-section." She used the familiar professional words, easier on her tongue and heart. "I wanted to have a regional block instead of general anesthesia so I could see my baby. Stephen and my father said no, it would be too hard for me. I didn't have the strength or will to fight them."

She turned sideways and curled at Tetsuro's side. His arm tightened, bringing her near to his chest. His heart swelled at the agony in her voice.

"When I woke in recovery," McKenna gathered his shirt in a tight wad in her hand, "I was alone and empty. My baby was gone, dying alone without her mother to hold her. They hadn't let me say goodbye."

Tetsuro held her gently while McKenna told him the most intimate thoughts.

"Then I didn't bounce back as fast as they thought I should." Her voice was clearer now, but sadness remained. "They wanted me to put it behind me. It was taking me too long, they said." The clutch on his shirt grew tighter, pulling the shirttail out of the confines of his slacks. "So, I forced myself back into my internship. I had to please them. But I couldn't forget. I still can't.

"Stephen couldn't handle my emotions and I couldn't tolerate his lack of them. He wasn't supportive, resented me for everything from the pregnancy to her death. My marriage was over. It was for the best. I felt like a failure."

Then it happened. Tears, large and sparkling, coursed down her cheeks, filling his heart with her pain.

"Why me? What did I do wrong?"

"I am sure you did everything possible." He couldn't say any more. How well he knew words would not take her heartache away.

He could only envelope her as she collapsed, her face against his chest. Her slender shoulders shook beneath his hands and her tears dampened his skin. Minutes passed before she quieted and the only sound in the room was the swing music.

Tetsuro was content with both her outburst and her quiet. She snuggled closer, her face now turned to rest her cheek on his chest. Compelled by the soft air caressing the notch in his neck as she exhaled, he laid his lips against the soft tresses so comfortable beneath his chin. McKenna moved in his embrace, her body against his. Blood rushed south, making thought complicated. He resisted the urge to act upon the fiery flame it stirred in him.

"Ke-*chan*," he whispered. Lying over his chest, her heart met his and the beat of hers echoed that of his, a tempo never matched until now.

"What does that mean?" McKenna turned her face up to him. The *sake's* effect was still there in her tear-wet eyes, but they were no longer sad.

"A pet name." His voice was soft. His lips were drawn toward hers as if magnetized.

Her breath was on his lips, yet they had not met. "What does it mean?"

"I will tell you…some other time." Tetsuro wanted to give her all of himself and receive every bit of her in return, but he drew back before he could make the mistake of kissing her. The meeting of his lips with hers would be his undoing.

"Oh," she pouted and her head lolled. As she succumbed to the rice wine's sedation, he kept her from falling backwards.

For a few seconds, he waited for her to wake, but she didn't. He moved off the couch, and carefully laid her down. Standing beside the couch, he realized how vulnerable the doctor, the woman, really was. Her face was relaxed, no furrow between her eyes as she often had when thinking. The crinkles of her eyes smoothed, and her thick lashes curved luxuriously beneath the lids. Her mouth was pliable, her lips moist and full. She was at ease in her slumber.

She spent her days erecting a facade of strength and determination so sturdy she found it hard to lower it in private. Only the honesty of the *sake* bottle freed her, allowing her to open up to him. She was now defenseless against whatever he wished to take or give.

Using more of his left arm than his injured hand, he lifted the sleeping McKenna. Tetsuro carried her up the stairs after settling her against his chest and ignoring the pain in his hand.

Tempted to act on the sensations starting in his heart and spreading through his groin, Tetsuro laid her on her bed. McKenna barely stirred. The soft movement of her breasts, rising and failing with each breath, enticed him, but he could not accept the invitation. She challenged him more than any woman ever had. To chastely loosen her clothes and remove her shoes was a Herculean task. He pulled the covers up to her shoulders and leaned to kiss her forehead.

Reluctance hung from his heart like a heavy drape as he left her.

CHAPTER SEVENTEEN

The bright summer sun crept over McKenna's bed until it rested on her face. She woke, her eyelids heavy and her mouth sour. Once her eyes were open, a sharp stab of pain pierced her brain and her head began to throb. She hadn't had a hangover in years. And she didn't much like the prospects of experiencing one now.

Taking great care as she moved, McKenna noticed she was dressed but her clothing was undone. The silk blouse was twisted and her unhooked bra had slipped around her chest. No wonder she hadn't slept well.

And just how did I get into bed without undressing? A beat passed before she remembered. *Tetsuro! He must have put me to bed.*

She'd passed out. How embarrassing! Of all things for her to do, she'd gotten drunk. The wonder was that she hadn't ended up in bed with him. He could have taken advantage of her. She lifted the blanket to confirm that all her lower garments were intact. No. Tetsuro was too much of a gentleman to do such a thing. She halfway wished he weren't so noble.

How could she face him at breakfast?

McKenna left the bed and looked at the clock. One-fifteen. She'd slept all morning! She must have been very tired or very drunk. Much to her chagrin, she suspected the latter.

The house was eerily quiet when McKenna went down to the kitchen after she'd showered and dressed. On the kitchen table she found an envelope propped up against a vase of fresh irises from her garden. Rebecca often cut flowers, but McKenna knew she hadn't arranged these.

These were the work of her Japanese houseguest/patient. The letter was addressed to her in Tetsuro's crisp handwriting.

As much as she desired to rip the envelope open, she couldn't face it without coffee. The pot, ready for use, quickly produced coffee. McKenna sat down at the table to read, armed with a mug.

'*My dearest McKenna.*' Her heart skipped a beat as she recalled his stray paper with '*Dearest Emiko*' written in the same manner. He was awfully free with his endearments.

McKenna returned to the letter. '*I hope you have managed to out sleep the sake kami,*' Tetsuro's fine lettering across the white paper looked like Japanese calligraphy. '*I regret I was not more watchful in the amount I allowed you to consume.*'

Allowed? Who do you think you are to allow me anything! Indignation brought a flush to her cheeks.

'*I must confess that I, too, indulged a bit too much. But the truth, which sake creates, makes my next actions clear. First, may I say the evening was one of the most special in my life. Your laughter and presence are something I shall always recall. I wish the evening had never ended.*

'*Yet the time also made me understand the need to distance myself from you. Because of any number of things, all of which need not be spelled out here, it is best that we remain friends through your profession. To that end, I have made other living arrangements.*'

McKenna's heart threatened to stop.

Oh, no! She gasped and struggled to read on.

'*I have enclosed what I hope is a proper sum for payment for my stay. I can never truly repay your hospitality, opening your home for a stranger, the way you did. I will be eternally grateful.*'

Ten travelers checks issued by American Express at the Bank of Tokyo were paper clipped to the letter.

'*Rest assured the things you shared with me will remain our secret and I shall never speak of them. It is my deepest desire that the wound you have received will heal.*

'*My fondest regards, Tetsu.*'

McKenna saw a smudge, a mark through not quite obliterated. 'L'.

Had he intended to sign 'Love?'

She supposed the pen flourish he added beneath his name was the Japanese character for it.

Stunned, McKenna dashed upstairs, desperate to find him. The rooms he'd occupied were quiet and clean, the bed made and the towels in the bathroom neatly folded. The drapes were closed, giving the room a cool, shadow quality. None of Tetsuro's personal items remained. The suite could have been in any five star hotel in the world.

McKenna sank to the bed and a single tear rolled down her cheek. He was gone and until this very moment she hadn't realized how much she wanted, needed him. He had fled from her without a way for her to reclaim him. Her heart ached and she wept.

As McKenna gathered her things to return to her office after rounds, Libby spoke, "Dr. Stafford, you look miserable. There are dark circles under your eyes. You don't care how you dress."

Stunned, she studied the perky nurse for a minute then answered, "What a thing to say!"

"It's the truth. And as your friend, I don't want to see you this way. What's up?" Libby asked.

McKenna turned her attention away from the nurse who professed to be her friend. No matter if she did voice her concern out of friendship, it hurt. And it wasn't something she didn't already know. In the past three weeks, she doubted if she'd slept more than four hours. Personal hygiene had dropped to only the necessary attention, pulling her hair back in a ponytail and forgoing the time it took to apply cosmetics. It was as though the depression she'd had after her baby's birth had returned.

"I'm fine. It's just been a busy month." She pulled a chart from the rack and tried to focus on the lab results. "Mr. Peters needs blood. I'm ordering a unit." She scribbled, closed the chart and handed it to Libby.

"I'll take care of it. Want a post infusion H&H, too?"

"Right." Another chart, radiology results for her this time.

"Mrs. Long's fracture is still approximated," Libby told her what she read. "She could go home today."

"I'll probably discharge her." Why were they talking about patients? She wanted to talk about Tetsuro but she couldn't. She couldn't speak his name without tears.

"He's down in PT." Libby seemed to be reading her mind.

McKenna was accustomed to the nurses anticipating her orders, but for Libby to be clairvoyant about her personal life was eerie. She covered her surprise by capping her pen and lifting the flap of her purse. The ivory stationery crinkled as she touched it. The note weighed heavily on her heart.

"He doesn't want to see me." She sagged to the chair, thankful there were no other personnel around.

"Did you ask him?" Libby leaned against the desk and awaited the physician's answer.

"No!" McKenna responded quickly.

"You need to talk to him."

"I'm scheduled to see him next week for his hand." She was bound and determined to forget Tetsuro's daily visits to University Hospital.

"What did you do that makes you think he doesn't want to see you? Some of the other nurses and I have been down to see him several times," Libby told her. "And he *always* asks about you."

"I couldn't show up." McKenna straightened her shoulders and stood. She didn't even think about responding to the nurse's question.

"He might be as miserable as you are."

McKenna dropped her shoulders in resignation. "I can't lose anything by asking."

"No, you can't, but," Libby put a hand on the slumped shoulders, "you've got to get that 'I'm a doctor, damn it!' attitude back to your spine."

"You're right." McKenna stood perfectly straight the way she always carried herself and left the nurses' station.

Spurred on by Libby's talk, McKenna ventured boldly to Physical Therapy. Part of her wanted to find Tetsuro. Another part wanted him not to be there.

"Hi, Dr. Stafford," the head of Physical Therapy greeted as she stepped inside the door.

"Good morning, Paul." McKenna tried not to be obvious as she searched the room with her gaze.

Paul gestured toward the back of the gym. "Your patient's over there."

"How's he doing?" McKenna tried not to sound as if she were overly concerned.

"Well…" He hesitated. "Not so good. Finger movement's improving, but he can't close his hand. In fact, he barely moves it at all, only his fingers."

"Time will take care of that. We'll keep up the exercise."

"He spends long hours working out the rest of his body." Returning to his work, Paul added, "He's not so interested in his hand."

"I'll talk to him." Paul's information was a good excuse to approach Tetsuro. She never ceased to be amazed at how she could talk and deal with men professionally, patient or colleague, but be hopeless when it came to social settings.

A number of patients and physical therapists filled the room, but Tetsuro was alone at the lat-pull-down machine. Since he was unaware of her presence, she was able to watch him work. As he sat on the bench, his back muscles, exposed by the black tank top, flowed gracefully as he moved and sweat glistened on his skin. He pulled the bar by holding it through his crooked elbows. McKenna was amazed that Tetsuro could pull the bar down to his chest and release it so smoothly without the use of his hand.

When he finished, she said, "Excuse me."

"*Konnichi wa, Sensei.*" Tetsuro let the bar return to its resting place and bowed his head toward her.

"*Sensei* is it?" She attempted to sound indignant but friendly. "I thought we were on a first name basis."

"*Gomen nasai*. You caught me off guard."

He would not meet her eyes and there was a bit of a blush to his face. That she could evoke such a reaction in the Japanese drummer pleased her.

"Can we talk? Privately, if you're through."

"I am, but where…"

"Paul will let us use his office for a few minutes."

McKenna turned and led the way, assuming Tetsuro would follow. When she reached the door he was behind her, as obedient as a puppy. They entered the physical therapist's empty office. McKenna poured them coffee and set a cup on the desk in front of the chair where Tetsuro sat. She took the seat at the corner opposite him, near enough to touch him, although she didn't.

"How are you?" Tetsuro broke the silence and ignored the coffee.

"Fine. And you?" They were in the uncomfortable area of small talk.

"Well." Sweat soaked the edges of his tank top around the neck and underarms. He wiped droplets from his face with the ends of the towel around his throat.

"Paul says you're not progressing as well as he would like." McKenna entered into the area where she was comfortable and the most knowledgeable.

"As you said," he looked at his hand, turning it back and forth, "it will take time."

"But he says you aren't working your hand."

"It is difficult. Perhaps with more time."

He was delaying the enviable. "Do you work it at all?"

"*Hai*. I do the exercises the therapist wishes. Just not as well."

"That's important. Without the exercises your hand will not be functional. It'll freeze and then where would you be?"

"Useless."

"Yes."

They were disquietingly silent again. McKenna watched Tetsuro. He glanced at her frequently and his fingers tapped a furious beat on the desktop. She didn't know why he was anxious or why his drumming matched her own rapid heartbeat.

"Why did you leave?" she blurted out.

"It was…best…for both of us." His fingers slowed their tempo. Her heart continued its cadence.

"Did I do or say something to offend you? I don't know what is acceptable and what is not in your culture. I can only act as I know how." Her heart tried to pound its way out of her chest. "If I did, I am sorry."

"Nothing you could ever do would offend me in any culture." Tetsuro's eyes held hers now. "I can honestly say it was one of the most pleasant evenings I have ever had, here or in Japan, made so because of you."

"Thank you." McKenna lowered her face to hide her blush.

"I was honored that you allowed me to learn about the woman you are in addition to being a doctor." His tone was sincere.

"I enjoyed hearing about your life." She raised her eyes to meet his once more. "But you didn't have to leave."

"It is best. I do not think things would be so…virtuous if we remained in such close quarters." His eyes were filled with hunger. Did hers reflect the same? If he wanted her, why didn't he say so? She would gladly give herself to him.

"We're adults. Nothing would happen between us unless we wanted it." Perhaps there was another reason he'd not shared.

"Could it have anything to do with this?" She turned to her purse and removed a piece of wrinkled stationery. Until this moment, she'd been unaware of why she'd stuffed it in her bag.

Tetsuro took the folded paper and deliberately opened it until it lay exposed between them. His own handwriting confronted him.

"Where did…?" The words caught in his throat.

"On the floor." She didn't say she was in his room or when.

"I thought I'd thrown it away."

"You did. It was beside the wastebasket. I picked it up and read it," McKenna confessed. "Does it have anything," she repeated, "to do with us?"

His reply was soft. "No."

"May I ask about Emiko?"

"I would rather you not." Tetsuro met her gaze. The look in his eyes made her acutely aware of his desire not to speak of the woman he addressed the letter.

"If we don't have Emiko to contend with, why do you feel the need to abandon my house?" McKenna needed to know even if it hurt her.

"We have no hope. My hand will heal and I will rejoin the troupe. Your work is here. Parting would be too painful if put off any longer."

"Do you not think I can make such a decision for myself? I can protect my heart," McKenna defended.

"But what about mine? Do you think only you are vulnerable? Because I'm a man, my heart cannot break? Or because I am Japanese? Though we hide it well, we are capable of emotion."

"I didn't mean *anything*. And if I had, it wasn't because you're Japanese. I only stated what I'm sure of myself. I find it hard to know what you're feeling."

"In my society, we do not wish to burden others with petty concerns regarding our emotions. I find it necessary to protect us both from what lies ahead."

"You can't spend your life worrying about others. Don't take the choice from me." It had taken her years to reach the place where she could confront anyone who attempted to map out her life, as Stephen and her father had done. Her heart wanted Tetsuro enough to assert herself.

"I worry most about my hand," Tetsuro admitted.

"I know." She took his hand, cradling it and tracing the lines on his palm with her fingers. They were safer talking about his injury, each comfortable in the area. "You placed your trust in my hands. Let me worry about it."

"I do not wish you to worry alone." Tetsuro put his hand over hers.

"I don't know where you are. How you are." She looked deeply into his exotic eyes, but couldn't read the emotions there.

"It is better you do not."

"But you're my friend, Tetsu." Was she actually begging or did it just sound that way?

"And you are mine."

"Tetsu," McKenna increased the pressure on the hand she held. "I want you in my life."

Tetsuro hesitated. "Is it wise?"

"If I promise not to get drunk or tell you any deep dark secrets, will you join me at the Breathing Room concert next week?" She pressed for a commitment to see him at least once more. She had to win him back.

Back? I've never had him!

"I would like that."

Tetsuro's defenses fell away and a pleasant smile crept to his supple mouth. Tempted, her fingers touched his lips for a brief second.

"Tell me how to say 'thank you.'" McKenna returned the smile.

"Have you not figured it out?" Tetsuro's eyes twinkled at her as he took her fingers from his mouth.

"Just do it," McKenna requested.

"*Domo…,*" he began the phrase. He continued to hold her hand.

"*Domo,*" she followed.

"*Ari…*"

"*Ari,*" McKenna struggled not to start giggling.

"*…ga…*"

"*ga,*"

"*…to,*" he finished.

"*to.*" The two concluded the impromptu language lesson.

"*Domo arigato.*"

"*Domo arigato.*"

"My pleasure."

"Where can I call you?"

"I will call you." His smile softened.

"Won't you let me know where you are?" McKenna pressed.

"We will see."

Before she could reply, McKenna's pager sounded. She retrieved her hand to check it.

"My office," she stated. "I'm late and have a waiting room full."

"I will see you soon." Tetsuro withdrew both his hands.

"I wish you'd return to my house."

"You cannot always have what you want, when you want it."

"I can hope."

"*Ke-chan...*" he began.

"Okay. I'll wait for you to call me." McKenna stood and Tetsuro followed. They parted at the doorway.

CHAPTER EIGHTEEN

When he returned to his new lodgings, Tetsuro was met by Mrs. Soto, a plump, gray-haired woman. She was his landlady, of sorts, allowing him to use her guest room. He'd been put into contact with Mrs. Soto after explaining his dilemma to the president of the Japanese Society of Cleveland. For three weeks, they'd shared the large house on the west side of Cleveland.

"Takamitsu-*san*." She bowed and greeted him.

"*Ohayo, Oba-san*." He addressed her as 'grandmother' out of respect for her age.

"You are *uchite*, no?" She used the Japanese term for a drummer of *taiko*. Her words and accent told Tetsuro she'd not used her native tongue for a long time.

"*Hai*."

"My grandson is visiting," Mrs. Soto explained as they walked into the family room. "He is always tapping on the tables. I thought perhaps you might give him some instruction. Nothing elaborate. I would be pleased if he could find something to relate to from the land of my birth."

"I can tell him of *taiko*, but..." He gestured with his damaged hand.

"I would be so pleased. I do not wish to impose." Mrs. Soto bobbed her head at the young man.

"It is no imposition. As *uchite* it would be my pleasure."

"*Arigato, sensei*." Mrs. Soto bowed. He returned the gesture in precisely the same manner, as low and as long, to indicate they were equals.

Tetsuro found comfort in the return to the rituals, language and behavior of his native Japan. Mrs. Soto had yet to look him in the eyes, a habit everyone else he'd encountered in the States took for granted. He had to be careful with himself lest he confront the woman with a direct look. She would sense displeasure in her action if he did so because he was a man.

He missed McKenna's searching look, the way she had of fixing those deep honey-colored eyes so firmly on his. And he'd never once thought it impolite. Her visit to the physical therapy gym had stirred the emotions he'd worked to suppress over the past twenty-one days.

Teaching would distract his mind and body. "When will your grandson be here?"

"He is here now. Would you wish to meet him at this time?" Mrs. Soto's eagerness radiated from her face.

"*Hai.*"

With a quick informal bow, she led him upstairs. A teen-aged boy sat on the bed of the second guest room. He was reading a comic book. *Spiderman* if Tetsuro read correctly.

"Richard, this is my guest, Tetsuro Takamitsu," she said in English. The woman used the American form of his name, first then last, instead of the Japanese form, last then first. "Takamitsu-*san* is from Japan and is a drummer."

"Hi." Richard barely glanced up from the comic book.

"Nice to meet you." Tetsuro looked at the boy. His longish black hair came to his eyebrows in front and his collar in the back making him look like any teenager in Japan. "Your grandmother says you like to tap on things."

"Yeah. My mom fusses about me banging on stuff, but she won't let me have a drum set." He set Spidey aside and became interested in what Tetsuro had to say.

"You do not need a whole set. Only one is required."

The two males fell into a serious conversation as Mrs. Soto disappeared. Minutes later she returned with two small drums, each with a head about ten inches across and six inches deep.

Tetsuro took the drums and sat down in the chair at the student desk.

"This is a *namitsuke-daiko*, Richard-*san*. I learned on the same type of drum." Placing them on the desk, he tapped on one lightly with the single stick to test the tautness. "Your grandmother wishes me to tell you about *taiko*. Do you wish to learn?"

Richard moved nearer Tetsuro. "Yeah. Sure."

Mrs. Soto left them alone.

"*Taiko* is an ancient art in Japan. Originally, the drums were used to call villagers into the heart of the town for messages and meetings. Over time, the temples began to use them and the role of the *uchite* came into being." Tetsuro glossed over the history. The young man wouldn't care about much more. "Do you have a favorite rock group?"

Richard's face brightened with the reference to something contemporary. "Several actually."

"Put in a CD," he pointed to the small stereo on the bookcase, "and start your favorite song."

Richard shuffled through a stack of compact discs and finally decided on one. He flipped the plastic lid open and dropped the silver disc into the tray protruding like a tongue from the black portable player. After punching the play button, he joined Tetsuro in waiting for the music to begin.

When the song started, the older male commented, "Def Leppard."

"You've heard of them?"

"I know many rock and roll bands. Def Leppard is an interesting and good group. You know the drummer only has one arm, do you not?"

"Sorta like you." Richard pointed at Tetsuro's arm in its sling.

"But I will be able to use mine again." He hoped he spoke the truth. "Rick Allen had to learn to drum all over again. Now. Listen closely to what he is playing. Picture his beat in your head."

The way Richard's face contorted as he struggled to produce the image in his brain was amusing.

"Using the *bachi*," he handed Richard the drumstick, "begin to tap lightly and match the beat."

Tetsuro took his hand out of the sling and removed the splint, then laid his hand over Richard's smaller one. Guiding him, he led the boy into the tempo, the stick striking the drumhead in time. Tetsuro released him and the boy continued to match Def Leppard's unique drummer.

On his own drum, with his good right hand, he began a rhythm slightly counter to the song. As the boy became aware of their beats' peculiar joining, Richard's smile stretched from ear to ear. The CD song ended but the two continued with their sound. Subtly, he changed his beat and a touch to Richard's hand produced a different, matched rhythm. They continue this way, Tetsuro changing and showing Richard how to join it, for a period of time.

Tetsuro enjoyed teaching others the skill of *taiko*. One of his responsibilities now after so many years with the troupe was to lead workshops. Interacting closely with fans who later became students was rewarding. He often thought if he could get a toddler or preschooler, he'd be able to develop a perfect drummer, but it wasn't easy to interest parents in enrolling young children. When he got tired of traveling maybe he'd pursue that idea.

They came to the end of their impromptu piece.

"See. It is not mere *banging* on stuff," Tetsuro said.

"Yeah. That was cool."

Mrs. Soto returned to the room. "*Uchite*, could you do me favor?"

"Another, *Oba-san*?" He wasn't accustomed to people asking favors at all. In Japan, it was not done.

"*Hai*. When I was a girl, my father took me to a shrine and I heard *taiko* for the first time. Could you play a piece that would have been performed there?"

"I am limited to what I can play, having only one hand."

"Oh." Her sigh made him reconsider her request.

"I will do something you will like, *Oba-san*. Richard-*san*," he addressed the grandson. "I may need your help. I do not know what will come from my *ki*. I will motion to you if I need you."

"Your what?" Richard questioned.

"*Ki.* My center of being."

"Oh. Soul." Richard responded.

"More spirit. Let us play something for *Oba-san.*"

"She's my grandmother. What's *Oba-san*?"

"Do you not speak Japanese?"

"No, sir."

"*Oba-san* means honored grandmother. Let's play."

Tetsuro paused, his head bent, eyes half-closed, and let the rhythm come from within. It rose from his lower abdomen to his chest and out his arms. The stick vibrated against the drumhead, a soft quivering beat, reminiscent of a butterfly's wings brushing against a rice paper panel. He opened his eyes and the sound grew louder. At intervals, with a touch of his injured hand to Richard's, the boy struck his drum to add a deep resonant timbre.

The tempo changed to that of a frantic bird caught in a net. Picking up the beat easily, Richard struck his instrument. Tetsuro slowly brought the sound down to a gentle tapping and kept the rhythm steady, all the while watching the old woman.

Mrs. Soto knelt on a cushion she'd placed on the floor. Her hands were on her lap in the way she'd been taught as a child. The way *he* had been taught. Her face, with its closed eyes, was serene. A slow tear escaped the corner of her eye and made its way down her round cheek to the corner of her mouth, coming to rest in the tiny wrinkle there. Her torso swayed ever so slightly with the tempo.

The song continued to rise inside Tetsuro, emerging from the pit of his stomach. He heard the beat in his chest and head. It was minutes before he felt the composition finish. The sound faded, ending as the soft drops of rain on a straw roof.

No one moved for a full minute as the beat echoed and died. Tetsuro motioned for Richard to leave. As the boy passed her, Mrs. Soto opened her eyes.

"The *taiko* has taken you home, *Oba-san*?"

"*Hai.* When I first heard the *taiko* struck," she spoke in Japanese, "it filled my spirit. Your song was so much like that." A flicker of light sparked in her eyes as she spoke of the temple drum.

"Do you miss home?"

"You speak of *home* as Japan, but my home is here. I came to America as a bride over forty years ago. My husband was an economics professor at Case," she explained. "I buried my husband here. My children are here. My grandchildren. Soon, great-grandchildren. Here…," her small fist struck her breast, "…is home. Do you know where your heart is, *Uchite*?"

"*Hai, Oba-san*." Tetsuro lowered his face and began to fix the splint. His hand had started to ache. "I know clearly where my heart is." A vision of McKenna rose before his mind's eye. He could almost hear the beat of her heart joining his.

"Then that is your home." Mrs. Soto rose and came to help Tetsuro, who fumbled with the splint.

"I am afraid that is not possible." A sharp stab of pain ran through the palm of his hand.

"You must bring heart and home together, *Uchite*." Mrs. Soto pulled the Velcro straps snug and put the drummer's wounded hand into its sling. Her fingers went up and around the material at his neck to smooth it. "Your heart aches, *Uchite*." She put her hand on his cheek. "You must fix it."

Then, in an uncommon gesture, she placed her lips on his forehead and kissed him as a mother would her baby.

"You must mend your hand and your heart," she said and left the room.

After Mrs. Soto departed and Richard returned to his room, Tetsuro went to his. The woman's words echoed in his conscience. She was right. Home was where his heart lay. Unfortunately, his heart was divided between two sides of the Pacific and he knew too painfully where the larger part was.

He walked to his suitcase and removed a leather portfolio. Unzipping the case, he opened it. His most important papers were inside—travelers checks, passport, birth certificate, immunization records, visa, and a small silk packet. He took this out.

The knot in the thin red ribbon of silk had set firmly from the long period it had not been undone. He tugged the bow loose and opened the flap. He paused before he brought the contents into the light.

Why? Why was he visiting his painful past? Because his heart dwelt here? Or was there some other reason?

A black and white five-by-seven slid out into his good hand. He picked up the picture of his mother and studied it. This was one of the few times he remembered her smiling. He had been a source of anguish for too many women. Could he inflict himself on anyone else?

Iie.

Tetsuro pushed his mother's photo back inside the envelope and closed the silk packet. Two other photos picked out of the packet, urging him to pull the out. His heart squeezed and he pushed the pictures back inside without viewing. They were his past. His future was elsewhere. His heart and home were not with her. With difficulty he tied the ribbon and returned it to his portfolio.

CHAPTER NINETEEN

On the sidewalk of the Agora Theater, McKenna waited for Tetsuro. When he'd called to accept her invitation, he'd refused her offer of transportation. She couldn't understand why he was so secretive, but she didn't argue with him.

McKenna felt like a large rock in the ocean surf as the crowd, made up of mostly forty-somethings, flowed around her. The noise level steadily increased. The tickets she held were to third row, center, and although they'd be there when she got there, she was anxious to be inside. She was also nervous about Tetsuro.

She'd seen him once in the office to assess his hand, but she'd been so busy she'd had to cut it short. Now, with the prospect of spending several hours together, she was as giddy as a schoolgirl.

Tetsuro appeared on the sidewalk without warning. She waved to catch his attention and he returned the gesture as he moved toward her.

When he arrived at her side, he spoke. "*Konban wa.*"

"That's a little easier than your other phrases. *Konban wa.*"

"Perhaps you are getting a better ear for Japanese."

"What did I say?"

"Good evening."

"That's what I thought." McKenna took note of him. He wore faded Levi's with the Japanese style shirt he'd worn when his hand was in its cast. "Having problems buttoning your shirt?"

"What makes you think so?" They stood together on the walkway amid the shifting crowd.

"You're back to wearing your *yukata*. That is the correct term, isn't it?"

"That is what they were called many years ago. This is actually a *hanten*. We wear them in performances." He pulled at the overlap of his black and white silk garment. "Where did you learn about *yukata*?"

"I read it somewhere," she responded coyly, not about to tell him about her recent research on things Japanese. "You're doing better with your hair," she commented. The top was pulled back and tied at the crown and the lengthy sides hung down to cover his shoulders evenly. He must have been to the hairdresser's for a trim.

"My landlady fixed it for me," Tetsuro confessed.

"Your...*landlady*?" She didn't recognize the ice in her tone.

"Yes." Tetsuro crooked his arm and offered it to her, his attention on the crowd. "Shall we?"

Did she a grin tugging at his lips? "By all means." McKenna put her hand through his arm and they entered.

"She's over seventy," Tetsuro said, his face forward.

McKenna suspected he'd break out into laughter if he caught her eye. Her hand slid down his forearm to entwine her fingers in his. "It looks nice."

"*Arigato.*"

Taking their seats, McKenna and Tetsuro were only minutes ahead of the beginning of the show. Accompanied by flashing lights, the group took the stage, quickly whipping the crowd into a frenzy. Like others, McKenna stood, swaying, clapping and singing along. At her side Tetsuro tapped his right palm against his thigh. The splint but no sling supported his left hand.

Over the crowd noise after the second song, she asked, "Are they not great?"

"Yes," Tetsuro shouted back. The excitement built, enthusiasm pouring out and through the crowd, making it impossible for them to talk.

The energy of the crowd and music pushed McKenna's sensual response to Tetsuro's nearness to its limits. Each casual touch sent prickles along her spine. The heat of his skin brushing hers radiated through to her center. Her knees were weak and she had to fight the desire to fall into his arms. Concentrating on the music was nearly impossible.

Six or seven songs in the program, the band settled into a gentle ballad. The crowd, now calm, remained standing. Tetsuro encircled her waist and drew McKenna to him. With his touch, a glow filled her and her heart skipped a few beats before reviving up a notch. She leaned into him and they swayed with the crowd. Then Tetsuro moved behind her, his arms wrapping her waist to hold her snugly against his torso. His groin pressed against the swell of her hips and the contact produced an intense fire. She sagged against him, welcoming the closeness. The soft rhythm and loving words of the song cast a spell on them. His embrace tightened and he dropped his chin to the top of her head.

The scent of his body drifted over her and she closed her eyes to drink in his touch, his essence. This was what she wanted. She yearned to make love to him. If she had her way tonight would be the night.

The spell was broken when the ballad ended. They were once more a part of the crowd's energy that increased with one rousing song after another. When the tempo lulled, McKenna and Tetsuro sat. His arm draped her shoulder with his hand resting on the start of her upper breast. His fingers kept the rhythm as the band played its Grammy-winning song from the past year and his movement matched the drummer's strokes. Her heart's raced with his touch.

When the group began another ballad, the theater quieted and McKenna cuddled with Tetsuro. The warmth of his body was intoxicating. When the tune ended, the group paused only an instant before swinging into the next song that brought the crowd to their feet. The kinetic spirit continued through the third encore.

"That was the greatest concert I've even been to!" McKenna collapsed into her seat, exhausted, as if she'd performed instead of Breathing Room. "How'd you like it?"

"They were in excellent form." Tetsuro sat calmly, a grin tugging at his boyish mouth.

McKenna turned sideways to face him.

"Are you ready to leave?"

He didn't move. Instead he brought his hands up so his elbows rested on the armrests and his fingers templed as well as they could with the splint in place.

"We should wait until the crowd thins."

Impatient to get him home and into her arms, McKenna said, "That could take some time."

"I know that." The sight of his full lips curling ever so gently into a smile only increased McKenna's erotic agitation.

"Then why are we sitting here?" She crossed her arms across her chest in exasperation.

"Do you have somewhere to be? Are you in a hurry to go home?" His eyes twinkled in the subtle lighting.

"No, but…" McKenna was aggravated. She couldn't come out and say she wanted to take him to bed and she couldn't see any purpose for sitting in the Agora after the crowd left.

Tetsuro reached out to cup her cheek in his good hand.

"Patience."

McKenna sat back in the chair. As if to keep her there, Tetsuro took her hand in his. She forced herself to relax. Soon enough they'd be together at the house on Shelbourne and she could bring Tetsuro back into her life.

A security guard approached them.

"Takamitsu-*san*?"

"*Hai.*"

"Mr. Stillwell would like to invite you backstage."

Tetsuro turned to McKenna.

"Do you want to meet the band?"

"You're kidding, right?" McKenna leaned forward. "You *know* Breathing Room? Of course I want to meet them!"

Tetsuro didn't answer, only stood and held his hand out to her. When she took it, the security guard led them backstage. Tetsuro was as at home in the crowded wings of the stage as she would be in any hospital. Trusting his knowledge, McKenna went along a narrow hallway with dressing rooms and crowds of people. The ordeal was akin to salmon struggling upstream. She pressed close at his back in an effort not to be separated. The security guard commanded respect, thus space, but the river of humanity closed quickly behind them.

When they reached the door of the band's dressing room, Tetsuro stopped and pulled McKenna around in front of him. The security guard opened the door and they entered the inner sanctum.

McKenna, sure her mouth had dropped open, scanned the room of wall-to-wall people. Some stood, others loitered on couches lining the walls. Women sat on men's laps, tangled in a knot of limbs, making out as if they were alone.

People stood in small clumps with arms around waists and shoulders, opposite and same gender alike. The conversation level was loud to compensate for the recorded music playing in the background. No one was concerned with the addition of two more people until the lead singer caught sight of the Japanese drummer.

"Takamitsu-*san*!" Gene Stillwell rushed to greet Tetsuro and when he got close enough bowed to him. "I knew it was you out there, man!" he said when he straightened. The singer then wrapped his arm around Tetsuro's shoulders to welcome him warmly.

"How are you, Stillwell-*san*?"

"Great! You see how well we're doing. First gig of our world tour." He led Tetsuro, and Tetsuro led McKenna, deeper into the sea of human flesh. "Man, I'm so glad you made it. Did you get tickets from one of the guys?"

"*Iie*. I am the guest of with my doctor and friend, McKenna Stafford." Tetsuro turned toward her.

"Lovely lady doctor." Stillwell extended his hand and she shook it. "Read about the accident, man. You the doctor putting my man's hand back together?"

"I am. We're working on rehab now." McKenna had been afraid her voice would fail her when Tetsuro first introduced them, that she would make a fool of herself. She was relived to speak about medical facts.

"Did he ever tell you how he messed his hand up once before?"

"No, he…" McKenna couldn't finish her comment because Tetsuro interrupted.

"Stillwell-*san*, I do not think Dr. Stafford is interested in such foolishness."

"As you say, Takamitsu-*san*." Stillwell dropped the subject. "Are you still seeing Emiko?"

"*Iie*."

The rock star looked at the drummer, his eyebrow cocked. "Oh?"

"It was not to be," Tetsuro answered without answering.

"Glad you're here. Help yourself to food and drink over there. I'll talk with you later." He slapped Tetsuro soundly on the back. "Happy to meet you, doc."

"Me, too." McKenna watched Gene Stillwell move back into the crowd as another member of the band approached.

"Hey, Tetsu-*san*! Long time, no see. Really sorry about your hand, man. I feel for ya." The tall thin black man was the group's drummer and could understand Tetsuro's pain, physical and mental.

"Thank you," Tetsuro said, acknowledging his sympathy.

"Who's yer lady?"

"Dr. McKenna Stafford. McKenna, Patterson Porter."

"Hi ya, doc." Patterson was a bit on the drunk side.

"Hi, Patterson."

"Why don't you go get your lady-doctor something to drink, *Uchite*?" He came nearer McKenna's side. "I'll keep her company."

"Would you like something?" Tetsuro asked.

"A Sprite would be nice."

"I will be right back." Tetsuro made his way through the throng.

"He's the greatest drummer in the world and a great guy," Patterson commented.

"I think so. How do you know him? All of you?"

"Thirteen or so years ago, we attended one of the workshops the Taiko Nihon holds every summer. I learned more about drumming from Tetsuro-*san* than I ever thought I could."

"Did you meet Emiko?" McKenna thought maybe she could sneak the question in.

"Nah, just heard about her. It was about the time he broke his finger. Did Takamitsu-*san* tell you about her?"

"No."

"Then I'll leave it there. He wouldn't tell anyone anything I didn't want him to, so I won't break his confidence either."

"That's very honorable." McKenna was disappointed she couldn't get the scoop on this Emiko person. Maybe Patterson wasn't as drunk as he appeared.

"Tetsuro-*san's* very honorable. But I'll tell you something not many people know." Patterson moved nearer as if in conspiracy. "You know the song we won the Grammy for last year?"

"Yes."

"Well, since I was having a hard time trying to work something out, Tetsuro-*san* sent me the drum arrangement. When we got the Grammy, we sent him a check; you know, to compensate for his effort. He returned it."

"Really?" This was an interesting side to her patient.

"Yep. Said he didn't do anything to deserve it. He did suggest we donate it to a music school for elementary kids. So we did."

"What did you call Tetsuro? *Uchi*-something?'

"*Uchite*. Japanese for a *taiko* drummer. And, I'll tell you something else about our friend," Patterson seemed to be a fountain of information except about Emiko. "You remember that Japanese emperor that died a few years back?"

"Yes."

"Well, in the funeral procession, they used two drums, the large *O-Daiko* drum and another *nagado-daiko*, a smaller ceremonial drum. Takamitsu was selected as drummer for the small one. It was a very prestigious position. I've heard talk about the Japanese government considering naming him a national treasure, but he'd have to be a lot older for that honor." Patterson was so wound up with his enthusiastic news, he hardly paused to take a breath. "I feel privileged he's my friend."

"I had no idea he was so highly regarded." She watched Tetsuro with a renewed respect and admiration as he made it to the table loaded with refreshments. His manner was confident but quiet.

She shared the awe Patterson exuded as several of the women and a couple of the men checked him out as he picked up drinks for them. Her body and mind reminded her, again, of her desire to make him hers. If she couldn't have him forever, she would settle for tonight.

On his way back, Tetsuro watched McKenna standing with Patterson. She gave him a curious stare. What, he wondered, was the drummer telling his doctor? Surely he wouldn't divulge the Emiko incident. Although Emiko's choice had been best for both of them, it still hurt, even after twelve years.

"Your drink." He offered the Sprite to McKenna. Patterson disappeared discreetly.

"Thank you." She took the bottle.

"They did not have any glasses."

"I'm not so much of a lady that I can't drink out of a bottle." McKenna put the lip of the bottle to her mouth and took a tiny drink.

"I did managed to get you…," he put a finger into the splint on his hand, "…a napkin." He pulled out the white paper napkin.

"Thanks."

He wiggled his hand in the splint. "This thing comes in handy."

"That's not what it's for." McKenna grinned at him.

"What were you talking to Patterson about?" He took a long drink of his Coke and tried not to act concerned.

"He had a lot to say about you, *Uchite*. He admires you very much."

"Do not believe everything you hear." Looking deeply into her eyes, Tetsuro read the desire revealed by the soft mistiness.

"I think he told the truth." McKenna held his gaze. "Are you ready to go home?"

"Do you not want to meet the rest of the group?" Tetsuro couldn't stop looking into the brown eyes he'd first seen in the midst of severe pain. Now the only thing that hurt was the pressure his passion for her caused in the stride of his tight jeans.

"No," she breathed softly. "I want to take you home with me."

"As you like."

Tetsuro put an arm around her waist and they walked out of the room. The feel of her body next to his made the blood rush to his head and groin. He was dizzy with anticipation.

CHAPTER TWENTY

On the ride home, they spoke little, each consumed by private thoughts. McKenna was full of desire, a passion she was hard-pressed to conceal. Although sure that Tetsuro wanted her just as badly, she resisted jumping on him in the middle of the garage. She wanted to make love to Tetsuro in the most exquisite ways she could devise.

When they entered the kitchen, she said, "Tetsu, would you fix us tea?" An authentic Japanese tea service and other utensils necessary to prepare tea in the traditional way sat on the table.

"I would be most honored." His appreciation for her gesture was evident in his tone.

"While you do that, I'm going to change clothes."

"The tea will be ready when you return." Slipping his hand out of the splint, Tetsuro went to the stove and turned on the burner beneath the kettle. In an opening caress McKenna's hand grazed across his broad back as she passed behind him.

She managed to walk out of the kitchen in a dignified manner but once she was out of his sight, she sprinted like a teenager up the stairs and into her room. She came out of her clothes and pulled down her hair in almost one motion. After quickly attending to personal hygiene, she slipped on new lingerie. On her way back down the stairs she paused at the last step to catch her breath and thought of something else that needed to be done.

In the family room, she opened the cabinet with the audio equipment and placed five CDs into the machine. Soft jazz from the house-wide speaker system began to fill the air. She made herself calmly return to the kitchen. And to Tetsuro Takamitsu.

He stood with his back to the doorway, preparing the tea as she'd requested. The pulse of sexual energy raced from her breasts to the moist area between her thighs.

With her arm extended over her head, McKenna struck what she thought to be a sensual stance. The soft folds of the peach-colored silk robe, tied loosely around her slender hips, clung to her frame. She stretched her long shapely leg out of the silk material and arched her back to accent her breasts. She cleared her throat to get his attention.

When he faced her, she asked, "Is tea ready?" She felt silly.

"*Hai.*" McKenna noticed how the word stuck in his throat as he stared at her.

Tetsuro put his hands behind him and held onto the sink's edge to keep from running to McKenna and assuaging his passion on the cold tile floor. The view of his surgeon standing in the doorway in a most unprofessional, or at least not a *medical* professional way, made it impossible for him to say anything but the one syllable Japanese word for 'yes.'

He had no way of telling her it was not necessary to strike such an alluring pose, that he would be attracted to her dressed in the lowliest of rags. As he stood looking at her, he marveled at the attractive woman who offered herself to him in the middle of her kitchen. The feathery tresses of brown with flecks of gold hung down over her shoulders. Her tawny skin looked dewy, smooth and tender. A blush touched her cheeks and her eyes sparkled with invitation.

When he took note of the inviting, moist lips curving in a gentle smile, he could say nothing. Only actions would express his feelings. He took the first step toward her.

Tea was forgotten.

McKenna moved at the same time. She'd watched him watch her, and performed the same inventory of him. While she was changing, Tetsuro had removed his shoes and socks. His *hanten* hung open and she caught brief flashes of his tight stomach as he moved toward her. As they met, his hands went to her robe's belt and he used his good hand to carefully undo the loosely tied knot. The edges of the silk fell open, displaying her unclothed body. She didn't speak as her hands teased their way along his satiny skin over his flat stomach. His flesh was hot and she stepped closer. There was no space left between them.

As she wanted for so long, she received the most ephemeral and sweetest of kisses. They exchanged a caressing sigh as East and West joined for the briefest of instances, culture and race forgotten.

He pulled her closer and breathed, "Ke-*chan*."

Her mouth whispered over his chest, "Take me upstairs, Tetsu."

No further prodding was necessary. He lifted her into his arms, thankful that his exercise had kept his muscles strong, and carried her to her bedroom.

Overcome with the sense of coming home, McKenna nestled in the exotic man's warm arms and enjoyed his firm muscles moving against her. She was swept by a contentment she never remembered feeling before. The comfort she had longed for was Tetsuro's embrace. She wanted to curl against him and surrender to his strength.

He laid her on the open bed and the silky robe fell fully open. She looked up at the man who stood over her, content to be open and exposed. Anticipation grew in her lower abdomen, the desire churning wildly.

Tetsuro shrugged the open shirt off his broad shoulders. She chose to move then, her own garment sliding off as she rose up onto her knees. Her arms encircled his waist and pulled him to her. Her lips, hot and wet, caressed his stomach just above the waist of his jeans riding low on his pelvis. Her fingers worked at the buttons until his fly was open. As she pushed his jeans over his narrow hips, his jockey shorts followed and her mouth moved over the beginning of the soft hair of his groin. His fingers entwined in her hair as she moved downward and soft moans of passion came from his throat.

Inflamed by her touch, he interrupted her. With one smooth movement, he brought them together in the middle of her bed. His body covered hers as he rested on his elbows alongside her head. Between his palms, he held her face so he could kiss her lips.

His mouth rested against hers in a tender kiss. His lips moved cautiously, then with abandon. A hunger between them rose to fuel their desire, and McKenna returned his eagerness in equal measure. His breath was ragged against her face. She couldn't figure out if it were lust or the effort of holding himself over her on his weak hand. Her mouth still next to his, she moved upward, an arm around his shoulder and her breasts pressing against his chest, to change their positions. Now McKenna straddled his narrow hips, breaking their kiss and rising up to give Tetsuro full play of her breasts.

She signed, arching her back, as he took each round mound in turn. His fingers, tongue and lips worked over the firm nipples. Fire coursed through her to the hidden folds between her thighs. He slipped his right hand between their bodies, his long fingers stroking the moist area. Learned fingers played over her.

Her body was consumed with the wondrous sensations and she reached the peak of passion easily. Wave after wave of sensation washed over her as he stroked the erotic flesh pressed against his groin. His firm flesh pulsed beneath her bottom. His mouth nuzzled her breasts as she rocked against his hand and hot fluid coated his fingers and a deep-throated moan came from her. Spent from the climax McKenna folded forward, the heat of Tetsuro's body soothing her. She nestled into the curve of his throat and he held her tightly.

"That…was…wonderful." She spoke in breathless pants. "How…did you…?"

"To play an instrument, one must study it closely." Tetsuro's lips moved against her skin.

"You have studied other…instruments?"

"Not…many." He stroked her breasts. "An artist must have a passion for the composition or his efforts are merely meaningless strokes. Although I have learned to play many types of *taiko*, I have my favorite."

"You have certainly played this…well." Her body awoke once more under his touch. She took him in her hand. Blood pulsed at her palm. "You have not…"

"All in good time. You cannot rush an opus."

Her body still straddling his, electrical waves shot through her. Tetsuro reached off the bed and brought his hand up. He handed her a foil package. Taken aback for an instant, McKenna was more curious about how he'd reached the jeans on the floor beside the bed than that he'd presented her with a condom.

Once the latex sheath was in place, Tetsuro returned to the artistic, arousing melody of their excitement. The coarse scar tissue of his hand rubbed erotically over her nipple, adding to the sensation. Tetsuro moved in a deliberate, unhurried beat, pushing up into her. McKenna's body welcomed him with strong tugs of intimate muscles. Rising and falling in the direction of his body, his hands on her hips, McKenna allowed him to orchestrate their lovemaking.

The tempo began gradually, each stroke perfect, touching the deepest part of her. The probing flesh pushed deeper into her swollen folds, the cadence rising. She followed his pace, until they both reached the cataclysmic end. Afterwards, Tetsuro's muscular arms held her secure against his wide chest.

Sated, McKenna dozed through the night in Tetsuro's embrace, the soft spot between his shoulder and chest making the perfect pillow. His breath was gentle and quiet against her cheek and her hand on his abdomen felt his faint movements. When she could manage to open her eyes, she saw he was looking at her.

"Hi."

"Hello yourself." Tetsuro brushed his lips across her hair.

"Tetsu." McKenna couldn't hold back the words coming out of her mouth in a matter of seconds. "I…I'm in lo…"

His fingers came up to still the words from her lips.

"Do not speak." The hint of naughtiness hovering in his dark eyes an instant before faded. "We do not know what will happen. *Karma* may have nothing further for us. To speak of our hearts would make the end that much more difficult. We can only concern ourselves with today."

McKenna settled her head further down on his chest. The beat of his heart moved against her cheek. The press of her breasts was hot and damp from their lovemaking. His hipbone against her stomach was comforting. She lifted her leg and laid it over his groin. When the arch of her pubis brushed his thigh, the fire of passion rekindled.

"You…are correct, Tetsu." She loved him and was certain he loved her, but without a commitment, such admission would be worthless.

"I do not wish to be." His voice was foggy with their spent ardor. "I wish I could remain by your side."

"I wish you could too."

"Ssssh. To speak of such desires so openly only invites the *akuma* to thwart our wishes."

"We are not drinking *sake* at six o'clock in the morning!" McKenna laughed.

"I am not talking of the *sake furasuko kami*. I refer to those little imps of Japan, spirits seeking to perform mischief on those in the real world. And to give them ideas is not a good thing." He adjusted his hold on her, his fingers tapping contentedly, and once more dozed.

McKenna lay in a quiet contentment. This was the place she had longed for all her life. She was next to a man whose only concern was Her happiness. No hidden motive or desire. While Tetsuro demanded nothing of her, he would give her what she wanted fully and without question. To give him her heart would be her choice. And it would be his choice to tell her about Emiko. She would never press him for answers.

Tetsuro roused. "It has been a long time since you have given your-self to a man." He pulled her up onto his chest and cupped her buttocks.

"It has. I'm glad I waited." She kissed his chest.

"I am glad you have given yourself to me." Tetsuro shifted and laid McKenna on her back. He covered her like a blanket. "I want to be here with you, Ke-*chan*, for as long as we have. I *need* to be with you."

Resting on his forearms, his hard, athletic body pressed hotly, but she didn't notice the weight of him. His hands roamed her and his touch reawakened the rhythm of her soul.

Tetsuro pressed his mouth to hers and their tongues danced. She wrapped her arms around his torso to hold him as tightly as she could. His fingers explored her and she sighed as his erection replaced them within her. The tempo of his thrusts built until they wrote their own song of passion and finished with a great crescendo of sensation.

Neither noticed they had forgotten a fresh protective sleeve.

When she awoke again, McKenna stretched her arm out across the expanse of her king-sized bed and found it empty. Coming further awake, she heard the shower stop. She rose, picked up his *hanten* from the floor and pulled it on. His aroma clung to the soft silk, pleasing her. Flipping her hair out from beneath the cotton garment's collar, she walked to the bathroom and knocked softly at the door. She was answered with an equally soft, "Come in."

Her lover stood toweling dry his lean body. Then he wrapped the towel around his slender hips blocking her view of the patch of coarse coal-colored hair and his sleeping body.

"*Konnichi wa,* Tetsu."

"That is good evening. Good morning is '*Ohayo gozaimasu,*'" he corrected gently.

McKenna approached and encircled his waist with her arms. "I need help to learn how to say it."

"*O...*"Tetsuro began as he rubbed another towel through his long hair.

"*O,*" McKenna echoed and brushed her lips across his velvet skin.

"*...hay...*" Tetsuro dropped the towel and embraced her.

"*hay,*" she spoke into his body.

"*...o.*" He pulled her close to him.

"*o.*" She kissed his chest wetly.

"*Go...,*" he started the next word, his mouth against her hair.

"*Go.*" A lump rose to her throat with the press of his body.

"*...za...,*" their affection-punctuated language lesson moved on.

"*za.*" Her heart thumped wildly, the beat sounding in her ears.

"*...i...*" His finger teased the folds at the juncture of her thighs.

"*i.*" The way his other hand rubbed her breast beneath the *hanten,* she didn't think she had breath in her body to speak.

"...*ma*..." The rise of his body beneath the towel pushed against her.

"*ma*." She took hold of him, stroking him further alive.

"...*su*." Tetsuro's jaw, morning beard rough, rested against her cheek.

"*su*." McKenna raised her face and accepted Tetsuro's toothpaste fresh kiss.

Once he released her mouth, she said, "*Ohayo gozaimasu.*"

"Well done." Tetsuro rewarded her with another kiss.

"I love the way you teach Japanese."

"And I love the way you learn it."

The couple sank to the soft bed of plush carpet. Mindful of the injured hand, McKenna lay above Tetsuro with his shower-moist body beneath her. With tender strokes he reawakened her passion, then sated it just as completely.

After they ventured downstairs and ate breakfast, Tetsuro took the opportunity to visit the garden behind her house. He offered to help with the dishes, but McKenna declined. He used the time to read the letter that had arrived in the morning mail. He'd delayed until he was alone because he was afraid if his friend had replied in English, McKenna would inadvertently read something that might hurt her. He began reading the letter in Japanese *kana*.

Dear Tetsu,

I received your letter two weeks ago and am now able to answer. I am sure it will be weeks before you receive it, so I hope you do not do anything stupid before I can answer your questions. I will not be much help as the only thing I can tell you about the situation is to follow your heart. I know your past and how much you have been hurt, but I still believe you can find happiness. You must consider closely what you want in life. Do you wish a family or are you content to remain alone with only taiko to fill the void?

I also have a warning to impart. I heard in a roundabout way that Emiko is looking for you. Restor received a letter she sent to you and returned it to her. I do not know if he told her where you could be found, but you should be aware that she might contact you.

We are having a great tour, but miss you and your artistic guidance. I hope your hand heals and you are soon back leading us.

See you soon,

Su

"Just like you, Su-*chan*. Short and to the point," Tetsuro muttered.

McKenna appeared just as he put the letter back into the envelope and into his pocket.

"Your garden is lovely," he commented.

"I don't spend much time out here. My landscape company takes great care of it." She looked around the expanse of greenery and flowers. "Are you sure you want to visit my friend and her baby?"

"I said so, did I not?" She had received an announcement in the morning mail and issued the offer over breakfast.

"I called Claire and she's expecting us."

"I would like to cut some flowers for your friend. It would be a nice gift."

"Sure. I'll get scissors."

McKenna returned to the house and back to the garden in a flash. Tetsuro had already chosen the blooms he wished to cut and made quick work of a bouquet for Claire and her new baby.

CHAPTER TWENTY-ONE

At Claire's newly remodeled house on Monmouth, a maid showed McKenna and Tetsuro into the foyer. She accepted the bouquet of fresh cut flowers Tetsuro had wrapped in the front section of the newspaper.

"I'll put these in a vase and bring them in, sir. Mr. Ikuta's in the library," she said. "If you'll follow me."

The couple trailed her down hall toward the back of the house. She turned a corner and waved a hand toward the library. When the maid left, Tetsuro held McKenna's arm as she started down the hallway.

"Your friend is married to the baseball player, Kentaro Ikuta?" His eyes narrowed as he asked about Claire.

McKenna didn't miss the surprise in his voice replied, "I thought you knew."

"I knew Ikuta-*san* had married an American woman from Ohio, but…" Tetsuro's bewilderment was amusing. The shoe was on the other foot now.

"You didn't know I grew up with her," McKenna finished his sentence. She failed to suppress a grin.

"I was…surprised." Again the angled eyes narrowed in disbelief.

"Like I was at the Breathing Room concert." *Touché.*

"I see your point." He conceded defeat.

They met the Cleveland pitcher in the library.

"Kentaro, hello." She entered the room with confidence. The Japanese baseball player stood behind a desk, reading the morning paper laid out before him.

"McKenna, welcome," Ikuta stepped forward to shake her hand.

"We dropped by to see that new baby."

"Claire will be happy to see you." He released her hand. "She misses you when we are in Japan."

"I miss her, too." McKenna recognized Kentaro's uneasiness at making small talk. He was as uncomfortable with idle chatter as Tetsuro was.

"I'd like to introduce you to Tetsuro Takamitsu." McKenna was struck by the resemblance between the men. Both were handsome, their faces angular and lean. They both wore their long, raven-wing black hair pulled back into ponytails at their nape. Tetsuro was a little taller and heavier than Ikuta but they were both fine physical specimens. She felt a pang of quilt as she considered that she had once thought all Japanese looked alike—short, round-faced, and slit-eyed. And hardly erotic. *Boy! Is that ever racist!*

"Takamitsu-*san, kangei suru,*" he welcomed the drummer.

"Ikuta-*san.*" Tetsuro bowed to the pitcher.

Once the men finished their salutations, McKenna left to visit Claire. She made her way through the house until she found the maid who sat Tetsuro's flowers now in a vase on the table in the living room. The house evidenced its remodeling but retained its vintage charm. She'd always envied Claire and her homey house on Fairmount, unable to have the same family life herself. Now her friend was making a new home in the same fashion. McKenna was sure this house, the Ikuta house, would be like the Ferris house-filled with love and family warmth.

"Miss Claire's in the sunroom with the baby," the maid said as she made her way up the staircase. McKenna followed, anxious to see Claire and discuss the changes in their lives.

"McKenna!" Claire rushed to embrace her as she entered the room upstairs. "I'm so glad you came!"

"I'm happy to see you, too!" The women hugged and then McKenna went to the bassinet. "But I really came to meet your daughter."

"Here's my little angel. Chikako Kathryn." Claire lifted the baby out of the frilly crib.

"Oh, Claire, she's beautiful." McKenna held Chikako to her breast. McKenna's heart throbbed with delight when the baby snuggled against her. The baby's large oblong eyes studied the new face. She stroked the baby's downy black hair and memories that came all too often these days crashed upon her. Tears welled in her eyes; she stepped to the bay window.

She put her back to Claire in hope of composing herself before she faced her friend. Batting back her tears, she shifted the baby up onto her shoulder. The soft curls ruffled against her cheek and the baby tried to suckle at her neck.

Claire placed her hand on her friend's back, "McKenna, are you all right?"

"I bet my biological clock's ticking so loudly even the baby can hear it." She turned back to Claire.

"Then you should find a man and have a baby," she said as though it were as easy as that.

"Maybe I have." Claire was her closest friend, the only person she could really share things, especially personal secrets, with.

"Anybody I know? Like James Russell?"

"Heavens, no! James is a friend." She turned from the window. They walked to the chairs and sat. "No, I've met someone new recently. He was my patient. And now I'm...sleeping with him." She gasped and laughed at the confession, then buried her face in the baby's stomach as she lay across the length of her thighs.

"McKenna!" Claire laughed. "I can't believe you said that!"

"Neither can I!" McKenna rose. "Actually, last night was the first time."

"And who is this great guy? I'm trusting he's great."

"Oh, yes he is. Like I said, he was a patient. I met him the night of your shower. Remember when I was called to the ER? It was for him. I fixed his hand and he's in rehab now."

"What's his name?" Claire leaned forward.

"You're going to laugh." She played with the baby's hands, allowing her to curl tiny fingers around one of hers.

"Why?" Claire questioned curiously.

"Because it's very ironic." McKenna directed a look Claire's way and took a deep breath. "Tetsuro Takamitsu."

"A Japanese man?" Claire's eyebrows arched inquisitively.

"Isn't it weird? You've married a Japanese baseball player and I'm...involved with Tetsuro." She played with the baby who lay in her lap cooing and gurgling. "We just get more and more alike."

"Wasn't that one of your sister's concerns? That you were more white than black?" Claire asked.

"That was Bailey's attempt to connect with her roots," McKenna explained. "I wonder what her comments would be now?"

"You can bet she'll have comments. Which will be strange since she's married to a white guy and lives in England. But for you and me to both be attracted to Japanese men...that's scary."

"It's natural for me since I'm a linguist, holding a doctorate in Japanese. Come on, tell me about him," Claire pushed.

"He's from Nakano Island and is a member of the Taiko Nihon drum troupe. Sensitive, smart, talented and, of course, *gorgeous*." Both women laughed. The two-month old baby seemed to understand and smiled with them. "You'll meet him in a few minutes. He's visiting with your husband. Yes, he is," she said to the baby. "Tetsuro's talking with your daddy."

McKenna's heart warmed with the baby's innocent smile.

"Claire, I'm curious about something and you'd be the one to ask." McKenna cuddled the warm infant in her arms. "I sometimes wonder about Tetsuro. He's very quiet, stoic almost. Often he's kind of...mechanical, if you know what I mean. Except in bed and then he's *very* animated. I don't know if I offend him and he's too polite to say anything or he doesn't care. Have any hints for me?"

"Well, the Japanese are very inward people. They don't wish to offend another, no matter their personal feelings. The closer you become to him, the more he'll open up. Because you'll matter to him. Don't get your feelings hurt. It's early in the game."

"Oh, wow. Baseball metaphors. You never liked sports!"

"But I love a baseball player. That's all that matters. Just as you are...*fond* of a Japanese man, you'll learn to be fond of Japan."

"I think it's more than fondness." She shouldered the squirmy baby. "I'm in love with Tetsuro." Speaking the words aloud caused her heart to swell with emotion.

"Well, let's go get the guys. I want to meet the man who puts that blush on your cheeks." Claire rose and started out of the room only to be stopped by her husband and the gentleman in question.

"Where are you going, Claire?" her husband asked.

McKenna approached Tetsuro to help him feel at ease. "Claire, this is Tetsuro Takamitsu."

"*Hajimemashite. Dozo yoroshiku,*" Tetsuro addressed Claire with a bow.

Claire returned his bow. "*Genki desu ka?*"

"That's enough of that," McKenna announced. "I'm the only one who doesn't speak Japanese, so cut it out."

"I suspect you'll learn it soon enough," Claire said with a laugh in her voice.

"Tetsu, come look at this beautiful little baby. She's the reason we came over here, not for you to talk baseball."

"You are correct. She is beautiful." Tetsuro touched the chubby cheek of the baby. "May I?" He looked to Kentaro for permission to hold his daughter.

The proud father answered, "*Dozo.*"

Tetsuro took the bundle into his arms. His face gazing into the infant's was soft and tender with a glint of paternal fondness in his sober eyes. He caressed her cheek and in response, the baby reached a tiny hand to grasp the lock of raven hair that hung down the side of his face. McKenna stepped closer to his side.

"Makes you want one of your own, doesn't it?" she asked softly.

"Yes, it does."

Chikako chose then to begin to cry. A loud wail filled the quiet of the room. Startled, Tetsuro looked around as if he were holding a bomb and didn't know what to do with it.

"Don't panic." McKenna noted the scared look on his face and took the baby. "I'm sure Claire can fix whatever's wrong."

"The only time she makes noise like that is when she's hungry." Claire took the baby in her arms. "McKenna, come to the nursery with me while I feed her. You men entertain yourselves."

As she left with Claire, McKenna caressed Tetsuro's arm briefly. "You can get back to talking about baseball."

"*Hai.*" His eyes glistened as he smiled at her.

In the nursery, McKenna watched from her perch in the deep seat of the bay window next to Claire's rocker as the mother first prepared, then offered her breast to the hungry baby. Chikako suckled eagerly, and the women returned to their talk.

"How did you adjust to Kentaro?" McKenna asked.

"Adjust? How do you mean?"

"You know. The culture differences."

"I never thought of our idiosyncrasies as cultural. I see him as a man and the differences we have are the same as with any man and woman. We learn from one another by being together. Every day I discover something new."

"But when you're in Japan, doesn't he expect you to act…less Western?"

"Why should he? I'm the woman he married, in Japan or Cleveland." Claire paused to remove Chikako from her breast and raise her to her shoulder to be burped. "McKenna, it's the twenty-first century. Kentaro doesn't have any of those medieval ideas. He and Tetsuro are men of the new Japan. I suppose, if they were from a village in northern Japan, they might have old-fashioned customs. But they both have spent time away from home, learning and living in the West. They've absorbed our culture."

Chikako obliged her mother with a resounding burp and Claire rewarded her with the other breast.

"The things we find as different, we manage to compromise on. For example, with Chikako, we have two nannies. Martha takes care of her in the States, and Hanaju takes care of her in Japan. Both nurses travel with us."

"So you're saying I should go with it and anything I need to know will explain itself?"

"Well, yes." Claire giggled. "You've always made everything so difficult. Enjoy being with him. Love him, if you do. Have fun even if you only *like* him."

"I do love him, Claire." McKenna liked the way she felt when she uttered the words.

"I thought so." Claire finished feeding her daughter. Martha entered to take the baby for her nap. "McKenna," Claire turned all her attention to her friend. She leaned forward in the rocker and took McKenna's hands in hers. "You and I have been friends forever. So I want to say something that might be hurtful, but it's the truth."

"Go ahead."

"You've spent all of your life living for others. Your father's been dead for three years and your mother and sisters have all moved away to their own lives. It's time for you. You should sell that house and everything in it. Maybe even change hospitals. Anything but continue living vicariously as you do. You've got to live for you."

Afraid to look into Claire's eyes for fear of what her friend would see in hers, McKenna focused on their joined hands. Claire was so right. Her life had been spent trying to make everyone happy. What did she want from her life now?

Tetsu.

"You may be right."

Claire took her friend's face in her hands to tilt it up so she could see her eyes.

"You know I am. McKenna, three years ago Dr. Ramstein gave me some pretty harsh advice. If I hadn't listened to him I wouldn't be where I am today. Happier than I've ever been."

"Tetsuro says we can only be concerned with today, what with his career and mine being so opposite. But I know I'm going to enjoy the ride. Thanks."

"What are friends for?"

The two women embraced warmly.

"*Sumimasen*?" Kentaro interrupted.

They came apart.

"Come in," Claire said.

"I am going to the stadium. I will see you after the game."

"Certainly." Claire then changed to Japanese and her husband replied in kind as he left. Claire turned to McKenna. "Why don't you and Tetsuro come to the game with me? We'll go out to dinner afterwards."

"I'd love to. Let me go find Tetsuro and see if he wants to."

CHAPTER TWENTY-TWO

McKenna entered Jacobs Field, her hand in Tetsuro's and her arm entwined in Claire's. The women laughed and the lone male walked along with a slight smile tugging at his mouth. They made their way along the outer walkways lined with food vendors providing fans with hot dogs, beer, soda, cotton candy and Peterson peanuts. The crowd noise poured from the concrete tunnels leading to the field.

"We've got to get you a hot dog and beer," McKenna announced to Tetsuro. "Have you ever been to a baseball game?"

"He's probably been to more than you have!" Claire laughed. "I don't think you've *ever* been."

"Until three years ago, you hadn't either," McKenna countered.

"I have been many times in Japan, but only twice in the States." His gaze fell on McKenna. "It is ironic. I had tickets to a game the night I broke my hand and we met."

"I'm not sorry you missed it." She moved her hand from Claire's arm and touched his injured hand supported by the splint. "Only sorry about your hand."

"*Shigata ga nai,*" Tetsuro replied, the words accented by a shrug of his shoulders.

"Okay, Claire. What'd he say?" McKenna implored.

"'It could not be helped.' It's a general phrase used by the Japanese to express a resignation to things one can't change," Claire translated as she led them to their section of the stadium. "How about that hot dog? Have you ever had one?"

"No. But since McKenna so graciously experimented with *sushi*, I would be happy to indulge the two of you."

"*Sushi*, McKenna?"

"Don't start, Claire." She changed the subject. "We need to get in line somewhere."

"Over there." Claire pointed to the right. They fell into line behind a family of six.

McKenna took in the area around her, blinded at intervals by flash-bulbs as the paparazzi snapped pictures in their direction. Tetsuro was playing with the toddler held in the arms of the woman in front of them. He soon had the little boy shrieking with laughter at his funny faces. McKenna hoped the photographers wouldn't capture the twisted features.

"Claire, why are these people taking our picture?" she asked in a whisper.

"They probably think Tetsuro's the Japanese Crown Prince or something. Someone'll ask Kentaro who he is after the game."

Tetsuro ignored the women and continued to play with the child.

Claire moved up to the counter after the family completed their purchases and moved away. The little boy kept an amused eye on Tetsuro.

"You're like the Pied Piper," McKenna commented.

His eyes narrowed as he asked, "Who?"

"The Pied Piper of Hamlin. A Grimm's fairy tale. Don't you have them in Japan?"

"We have fairy tales. I do know some Grimm's fairy tales. What did the Pied Piper do?"

"Played a flute to draw the rats away from the town. When the town didn't pay him for his services, he used his talent to lead the children away. You are a child magnet."

"What can I say? I like them."

"And they seem to like you."

Tetsuro grinned. "I am a nice guy."

"You are a great guy." McKenna wrapped her arms around his.

Claire turned to them laden with a tray of food and drinks. Tetsuro reclaimed his arm and took the cardboard tray.

"*Arigato*, Takamitsu-*san*. We'll go down to the next entry. We have seats behind home plate under that ledge. There'll be a policeman at each end so don't be surprised."

They went through the crowd and turned to enter the stadium, passing vendors selling everything imaginable.

"What's that?" McKenna asked Claire about a large quilt hung on the wall.

"The players' wives' quilt. We donated pieces of fabric, helped sew it and are now selling chances to win it. The money goes to League charities."

"You sew?"

"Some. We had help from the Amish community out in Geagua County. My contribution was a square of Japanese weaving from Kyoto. It's unique, but since I have a whole kimono of it, I could part with the piece I bought before Kentaro gave me my kimono."

"I remember seeing that when you came back from Tokyo. You were so proud of it you had it framed." The apricot and gold square of silk had adorned the wall of Claire's office when she'd returned from Japan. "I'm gonna get a ticket." McKenna walked to the woman manning the booth and purchased five tickets for the raffle. She had quilts made by her great great grandmothers put away in the attic; her sisters had also taken their share of family heirlooms. These things seemed to be the only connection to black culture the Staffords held on to.

When McKenna returned to Tetsuro and Claire they began to move again, Claire said, "Good luck."

The Cleveland police officer acknowledged Claire and the three entered the row. The players' families' seats were half full. Claire nodded and waved to a number of people. Their seats had a clear view of the field where players were warming up. Tetsuro took a seat with McKenna between him and Claire. Once they were settled, McKenna took the cardboard tray and began to parcel out the food.

"The soda's yours, Claire?"

"Yes." Claire took the plastic cup. "You know breastfeeding and alcohol don't mix well."

"It'd just make the baby a little sleepy." McKenna handed Tetsuro his beer and a paper-wrapped hot dog, then handed Claire her food.

For a few minutes the trio gave their attention to preparing to eat.

"Where's Kentaro?" McKenna raised her eyes from folding the wrapper away from her hot dog.

Around a mouthful, Claire said, "In the bull pen." She wiped her mouth with a paper napkin. "Over by first base."

"I see him. I didn't recognize him with his hair tied back."

Claire looked at the gentleman at their side. "Don't you like your hot dog, Tetsuro?"

"I have not tasted it yet." He unfolded the wrapper.

McKenna turned her head to see him take a tiny bite. "Oh, no, *that* will *not* do." She reached for his hot dog. "You have to take a regular bite like you made me take of *sushi*."

Carefully guiding the oblong bun with the sausage into his open mouth, she fed him the hot dog. He bit off a considerable portion and she lowered the sandwich, then wiped mustard and relish from his lips as he chewed.

"That's better. Isn't that tastier than some ole fish's scrotum?"

Claire sputtered, spewing the mouthful of soda into the air. Fortunately, the seats in front of them were empty. "McKenna! What on earth are you talking about?"

"*Shirako*, Tetsu's favorite *sushi*," she answered, proud of her ability to use the Japanese word.

"I don't want to know any more about it." Claire waved a hand in her direction.

"So, Tetsuro," McKenna turned back to him. "What'd you think?"

"Not bad." Tetsuro continued to consume the hot dog, washing it down with the beer.

Twenty minutes later, the teams took the field and the game was underway. Kentaro Ikuta pitched three innings without a hit.

McKenna slumped down into the seat, her head resting against the back, and placed her hand on Tetsuro's arm. "You and Kentaro have beautiful long hair. What is it with you two?"

"I suppose it is our *samurai* heritage." His arm moved to lie along her shoulders. "Young men like to have longer, less *sarari-man* fashion hair. We think 'What did those short-haired military types get us in the past?'"

"What's a *sarari-man*?"

"Businessmen," Tetsuro answered before Claire could.

"Weren't *samurai* military?" McKenna continued her barrage of questions.

"In a way. *Samurai* was a class of Japanese society, usually warriors, but not all entered a battle."

"And they had that bald spot." McKenna cuddled closer to his side.

"Again, not all. That was done only when they went into battle because of the heat and sweat of the helmet." Tetsuro nuzzled her hair. "Besides, maybe we wear it long because we are rebels in a land of conformity. Most all drummers have long hair, again due to tradition."

"Are you going back to drumming soon?" Claire asked.

"I hope so. My physical therapist says I need more work, but should be able to return."

"I'm happy to hear that. I attended a concert of Taiko Nihon a few years ago. Were you with them then?"

"I am sure I was. I have studied for sixteen years and been on tour for ten."

"I enjoyed the concert," Claire concluded. "Especially the flute. It was so haunting and sweet."

"*Domo arigato.*"

The game continued with McKenna lulled by sun and alcohol, as well as little sleep the night before, into a brief nap on Tetsuro's shoulder. Reluctantly, she roused to allow him to leave. He hadn't returned by the last inning.

"I wonder where Tetsuro went?" McKenna pondered. "Maybe he got lost."

"The restrooms are around the corner. If that's where he went, we'll probably run into him as we go to the locker room." Claire picked up her purse and stood. "Let's go look."

They joined the river of people heading for the upper deck.

"He might be over at the children's play area," McKenna said. "He was playing with the little boy in line and he was fascinated by Chikako. I wonder if I should be concerned that he's a pedophile."

"McKenna, please. Not every man who likes children is a pervert," Claire admonished as they made their way through the crowd.

"The news media would have you thinking so." McKenna was sorry she'd said such an ugly thought in regards to the man who held her heart.

"Most Japanese men," Claire continued. "have a soft spot for children from infancy to about school age. Then culture sets in and they are given more structured lives. For fathers to pamper their children would be detrimental to their schooling."

"That's a good thing to see in a man." They emerged from the tunnel into the vendor's area.

"Tetsuro will just be a great father," Claire commented.

"What if I…" McKenna broached the subject both knew was raw.

Claire touched her arm and gave her a sympathetic smile. "It doesn't mean it'll…"

"Look," McKenna broke in. "Let's just drop it." She searched the crowded walkway. "Oh, there he is." She pointed to the area where the charity's quilt was displayed. "Buying a ticket?" She took his arm and rubbed his bicep.

"He's purchasing a hundred," the player's wife answered while counting off the raffle tickets.

"A hundred? Aren't you generous?" Claire commented.

"It is the least I can do to help unfortunate children." He finished signing his travelers check and handed it over to the woman in exchange for the tickets. "*Dozo.*" He gave the woman a brief nod of a bow, then turned to McKenna and Claire. "Since I have no need for a quilt, what would you suggest I do with these?" He waved the tickets toward McKenna.

"I already have one chance and don't really need a quilt," she thought aloud. "Let's give them away to everyone we pass," she suggested.

"Great idea." Tetsuro tore off three sections, giving McKenna and

Claire each a part while keeping his. He followed the women's lead and handed a ticket to people in the crowd of exiting baseball fans. They received the occasional odd look, but everyone took a ticket. Their task was quickly completed.

"I feel really good," McKenna said.

"Maybe *karma* will now reward us," Tetsuro whispered, leaning closely toward her. His lips tickled her ear.

"Oh, you had an ulterior motive, did you?" She hugged him.

"Come on, lovebirds." Claire began walking away. "Let's go down to the locker room and get Kentaro so we can go eat. You'll join us, won't you?"

"That all right with you, Tetsu?"

"I am all yours, Ke-*chan*."

"You're so easy." McKenna kissed his cheek. She was close to Tetsuro's side, clinging to his arm and tried to push back the thoughts of how brief their affair could be. She didn't want their encounter to be a sweet short interlude and nothing more.

The evening wore on with the couples enjoying a leisurely meal with wine. Claire abstained because of her nursing Chikako, even taking a leave from the table to pump her breasts. McKenna kept her company in the ladies' lounge and they chatted about friends and family.

"I'm glad this is such a nice restaurant that the ladies' room has a couch and room to do this." Claire indicated the apparatus at her breast she had hidden beneath a baby blanket.

"Why are you doing that?"

"You must have slept through your obstetrical rotation. I haven't nursed in six hours. My breasts are like rocks."

"I didn't sleep through it. I just try not to think about anything connected with…babies." McKenna turned away.

"I think you want a baby."

"I'm…scared to try," she whispered when she looked at her friend.

"What if...?"

"It happens again? You know the chances of that are rare." Claire touched her cheek. "You deserve to move forward. Now. Have you told your mother or sisters about Tetsuro?"

"I didn't know there was an *us* until yesterday." She looked at her friend who was discreetly redressing.

"You must have had a clue." Claire began to repack the small breast pump into the tote bag.

"Well, yes, but not enough to *tell* anyone. Especially my family." She stood and walked to the sink, patting a stray strand of hair back into place.

"As I recall, your mother doesn't take to surprises well." Claire pressed the Velcro patches together to close the bag.

"No, she does not." Claire joined McKenna at the sinks to wash her hands. "Your mother, on the other hand, loves surprises."

"You're right about that." Claire pulled several paper towels from the dispenser and dried her hands.

"How'd she take Kentaro?" As she looked into the mirror, McKenna wondered if the warmth in her cheeks was from the wine or was a light case of sunburn from the afternoon game.

"Wonderfully, especially after the Jason incident. I think Kentaro made a permanent place in her heart because of the way he took care of me."

"I don't think I want to get raped so Mother will like Tetsuro." McKenna turned from the mirror and Claire picked up the tote bag. "My mother would end up blaming me for it."

They stepped to the door, but Claire stopped and faced McKenna, her hand firmly on her friend's arm.

"*She* doesn't have to like him. You do! Stop trying to make everyone happy. It doesn't matter what people think. You and Tetsuro are all that matter."

"But, Claire," McKenna spoke softly, "he's going to leave. Then where will I be?"

"Don't think that way. You can't see the future and anything can happen. You may end up hating him or he, you. Or he could stay or you could go to Japan. Be happy *today*."

"You've always said the right things." McKenna hugged her. "Let's get back to our rebel *samurai*."

They left the lounge.

"I want you to teach me Japanese," McKenna stated as they approached the table.

"Be glad to."

"I'll let you know what I want to know later."

The women reclaimed their seats and the attention of the Japanese men who shared their lives.

CHAPTER TWENTY-THREE

Because everyone except the new mother had been drinking, Claire drove McKenna and Tetsuro home. Saying goodnight, McKenna giggled her way into the house. Tetsuro followed without complaint, a hand on her at times for support as she wavered. The beer at the game and wine with dinner had left her inebriated. He himself, while drinking, had not achieved the same buzz.

"McKenna." They stood at the foot of the stairs where she'd taken a misstep twice while trying to ascend. "Perhaps you should not drink."

"Excuse me?" she whirled around to defend herself. "Who are you to talk? You had as much."

"I do not think so. In any event, I can walk up the stairs." The comment had been innocent, he thought.

"I can walk!" She made it up three more steps before she stumbled. Tetsuro was behind her to prevent bodily damage.

"Here." He lifted and carried her up to the landing and set her on her feet.

"Thank you." McKenna clung to him, her arms around his neck, her mood now amorous.

He kissed her. Her mouth was hot and inviting, and she pressed her body into his. His gut contracted, ready for action, but his conscience nagged. To take an inebriated woman to bed was poor form. He'd done that before and the result had not been pretty.

"Alcohol does not agree with you, *Sensei*." He stepped out of her embrace.

"Who are you to talk to me like that?" she bristled. Her eyes flashed angrily.

"It was merely an observation. I apologize for interfering." He reached to push a stray curl back behind her ear, but McKenna slapped his hand away.

"Don't touch me!" she growled and whirled to rush down the hall. "I'll not have you telling me what to do!" The quick movement unsteadied her but she caught hold of the wall before she fell. Staggering, her fingers trailing the wall, she stomped down the hall.

"I was not…" Tetsuro began to explain as he followed. The slammed door cut him off. Caught off guard, he stood for a few seconds before he turned and went downstairs.

With tears clouding her vision, McKenna furiously yanked off her clothes. As she scrubbed her hot face with cold water, thoughts raced through her brain.

How dare he?

What right does he have?

He's just like any other man, wanting to run my life! Only to abandon me!

Tears ran down her cheeks. She crawled into bed and clutched a pillow to her breasts to muffle her sobs. Tetsuro was right, she realized. Alcohol had never served her well. The joy of having Tetsuro with her had led her to want to celebrate.

Finishing school sermons on the decorum of young women and the use of alcohol echoed in her head. Her mother's words, her head-mistress's scolding, her professors' lectures about alcohol abuse, all were clear in her ears.

Finally, the tears dried and she rolled over. It dawned on her she'd closed Tetsuro out of her room and now wondered where he'd gone. Was he asleep in his former bedroom? Or was he downstairs having tea?

McKenna rose and washed the tears from her face. Pulling on a T-shirt and sweat pants, she ventured out to eat crow.

The first floor was quiet, the lights off except for one in the foyer. Tetsuro was nowhere to be found. *Damn!* Once again, she'd let him slip away. She'd destroyed whatever they had before their allotted time was completed. It was her fault.

McKenna sniffled and tossed her hair back, trying to affix a renewed stiffness to her backbone. So, it was over. She'd be all right. Hadn't she managed before? She didn't need a man, much less Tetsuro Takamitsu.

But as she crept back up to the empty bed full of the scent of his body, her heart ached.

McKenna made rounds the next day with a pounding headache. It was a wonder she even understood what her patients told her. Even luckier, Libby, the brassy and cheerful nurse, was not on duty. She swore she'd never drink again.

Although her head hurt, her heart was the most painful. There was little hope of Tetsuro's return and no way of contacting him. Yet, he'd be in P.T. sometime today.

She picked up the phone at the nurses' station.

"Hi, Paul. Dr. Stafford," she said to the physical therapist. "Is Mr. Takamitsu scheduled today?"

"He's come and gone, doc. He was here before I arrived at six forty-five."

"Well, thanks." She replaced the receiver.

She grasped the Styrofoam cup of lukewarm coffee and sipped diligently to assuage her headache. Caffeine and sugar, the cure-alls of the world.

"Good morning, Dr. Stafford," Greg greeted her at the doorway to the medical suite. "You're needed in your office immediately."

McKenna had barely put her things down when Greg approached her. "What for?"

"I'm not sure." Greg, a nurse and the two secretaries disappeared.

"What are you up to?" McKenna pulled on her starched white lab coat and walked to her private office. She lifted the heavy hair out from beneath the collar. Her pounding headache eliminated any thought of pinning it up.

The door was closed. She opened it slowly, afraid of what she'd be confronted with.

As she let the door fall open completely, she exclaimed, "Oh my word!"

On her desk was a vase holding two-dozen red roses. Several large heart-shaped balloons floated above them, tethered with ribbons. She approached the desk, her hand trembling as she reached to take the card supported by a plastic holder.

A voice came from behind the door, "I hope you do not have any surgery scheduled. You could hurt someone as badly as you are shaking."

McKenna whirled to see Tetsuro calmly close the door, a quiet snick indicating he'd locked it. She fought the urge to rush to him.

"Oh, Tetsu," she sighed after she lifted the card and read it.

When he came to her, McKenna had strength only to lean into his body and sink into his embrace.

"*Gomen nasai.*" He whispered his apology into her hair. "I should have known better than to even hint at telling you what to do."

"You called it as you saw it." The guilt was hers. He had nothing to apologize for. Tears inched down her cheeks silently.

"Can you forgive me?" his deep voice rose from low in his chest.

"Yes." McKenna raised her face from his chest.

"I love you." The tender words caressed her heart with their warmth.

"*Watakushi wa aishimasu,*" McKenna replied with the phrase Claire had taught her. Her chest swelled and her knees were wobbly.

Tetsuro's mouth touched hers. From between slightly parted lips, their breaths mingled. Then he pressed farther, pushing against her mouth until his tongue passed her teeth. His mouth crushed hers as he tried to devour her. He pulled her closer, his arms tightly wound around her. His healing hand slid up beneath her hair, sending shivers down her spine as he spread his fingers over the back of her head, interweaving through the tresses. He couldn't make a fist but the slender digits were capable of creating all sort so new sensations.

McKenna responded, eagerly working at his mouth. She slipped her hands down, cupping his jean encased buttocks to her. Grinding her pelvis against him, she felt the hard ridge of his erection. If only they were anywhere but in her office.

What the hell... McKenna released him, bringing her hand to the front of his shirt. The buttons flew away when she ripped it open. Her mouth never left his as she tugged his shirt from his jeans, then began to unzip his fly.

Tetsuro took his cue. He pushed the starched coat off her shoulders and worked his hand down into her skirt. Long thin fingers stroked her buttocks, tracing the gluteal cleft. Tremors rushed through her, centering between her legs. She moaned into his mouth.

"Ke-*chan*." He returned her emotions.

"Tetsu." It was a husky breath.

He pressed harder. In desperation, McKenna broke the embrace, fumbling with her clothes to remove them. Blouse open, her lacy bra proved no challenge to Tetsuro. A quick snap at the front and the cups fell away to reveal her full breasts, nipples taunt with excitement.

Circling an arm around her waist, Tetsuro pulled her back to him. His jeans were open, his erection full and throbbing. It pressed into her soft abdomen as he once more probed her mouth with his tongue. McKenna was sure she'd come before he ever entered her. He kneaded her breasts as he covered her throat with kisses. At last his mouth found one breast and he sucked a hard nipple between his lips.

McKenna sighed, arching her back. She held his head to her, awash in sensation. She burned with a passionate fire. Her inner thighs were saturated, having to have him in her. Without care, she yanked her skirt up and ripped her pantyhose away.

"Now, Tetsu," she encouraged.

Wordlessly, he obeyed, gently lowering her to the plush carpet. McKenna held his shoulders, wrapping her legs around his hips as he slid into her. Thrusting slowly at first, he built the fire, stoking it until her hips rocked in the same powerful rhythm. Faster and faster he moved until neither could control their body and the wave of fulfillment crashed over them.

Tetsuro covered her body, holding her tightly to him as his heart slowed its pace. McKenna gulped for air as she slowly came back to earth from the lofty air of his passion. How could she ever let him go?

McKenna gathered enough breath to say, "I have patients."

"They can wait." Tetsuro pressed his mouth on hers again.

"No they can't. I have to go." She snuggled against his neck, her arms around his shoulders.

"Very well." He raised his long lean body from hers and stood. McKenna pulled her clothes back around her and got up.

"I have...a bathroom over there." She pointed to the corner.

"I am fine." He'd already righted his jeans and shirt. The missing buttons would be hidden beneath his jacket.

"I'll..."

Tetsuro took her arm. "Am I forgiven?"

"You have a doubt?" She smiled as she stared into his eyes.

"No, but I brought chocolates in case it took more than flowers." Tetsuro pointed to a gold square box on her desk.

"Really?" Holding her blouse together, McKenna went to inspect it. "Oooh, Godiva. I'm impressed."

"That was my intention." Behind her Tetsuro encircled her waist. His palm was hot on her bare midriff.

"I guess I'll *have* to forgive you now." McKenna opened the box and picked a candy to place in her mouth. As she savored the creamy chocolate, she sighed. "Wonderful."

Tetsuro nuzzled her neck as she purred.

"Can I expect you at my house tonight?"

"*Hai*. And in your bed."

"I can hardly wait." Claire was right. The closer they got, the more animated Tetsuro became.

"This…" he pushed his hand down between her legs and rubbed the erotic area, "…will have to do." His hand worked over her until she shuddered, her body arching against his touch. She sighed.

As the climax faded and she rested against him, she muttered, "You are evil. Evil but good."

"I have to leave." His breath teased her cheek. "I have a drum lesson to give this afternoon." Without releasing her, Tetsuro turned McKenna to face him. "*Sayonara*." He kissed her and moved away. "You taste of chocolate."

"It's your fault." McKenna regretted having to leave his embrace.

Mrs. Soto met Tetsuro at the door as he entered the house. "*Uchite*," she said, a bit out of breath.

While hanging his jacket on the hook behind the front door, he greeted, "*Konnichi wa*, Soto-*san*." He didn't expect the matron to ask him about his missing buttons.

"Come quickly. You have a phone call." She took his sleeve and ushered him toward the den. "From Japan."

"*Domo*." Tetsuro picked up the receiver and Mrs. Soto departed. "*Moshi-moshi*?" he spoke into the mouthpiece.

"Tetsuro-*san*, how are you?" a familiar voice said from the other side of the world.

"Su-*san*! It is wonderful to hear from you. I am well." He took a seat on the couch.

"When are you coming home?"

"I…do not know." Tetsuro studied his injured hand, working the fingers in and out of a loose fist. Would McKenna give him a release from her care now? He didn't look forward to the day when she would. "I am still in physical therapy. I do not think I can hold a stick securely enough to control my beat."

"Too bad." He heard the sigh and labored pause in his friend's conversation. Finally, Susumu spoke again. "I have bad news."

"Is someone dead?" Tetsuro's heart began to pound.

"No, nothing as dire. Emiko-*san* is looking for you. I wanted to warn you since I did not think you wished to see her. Not after what happened the last time."

"It is not something I look forward to repeating." *Emiko*. Would she never leave him alone? Could he ever forget the humiliation and pain she'd caused? What more could she want? She'd already ripped his heart away. "Have you talked to her?"

"*Iie*. I have been avoiding her calls. But Kifume-*san* did. I think she told her where you are. That is why I am calling."

Kifume probably took great pleasure in revealing all she knew. "*Domo arigato*, Su-*san*. You are truly my friend."

"Have you made a decision in regards to your...doctor?"

"I am following the path *karma* has lain for me."

"That is the only thing one can do," Susumu agreed.

After several minutes of small talk about the troupe's tour, Tetsuro replaced the receiver and broke contact with Japan. The call had reminded him of his life, the life he was ignoring. He dreaded returning to Japan. The lure of drumming was not enough to overcome his love for McKenna.

CHAPTER TWENTY-FOUR

The next month passed quickly, faster than McKenna thought possible. Her hours at the office or in the operating room were the longest, but they, too, seemed to fly by. She looked forward to her time off, a purpose now to her leisure. That purpose was Tetsuro. If she were on call, they spent their evenings quietly. If she wasn't, they ventured into the nightlife of Cleveland.

"You know, the last time I was on the *Good Time 4* it was named the *Good Time 2*," McKenna informed Tetsuro as they stood at the rail of the excursion ship while it pulled away from the dock. "I was ten."

"I have never been on such a large ship." Tetsuro watched the shore closely. "There is only a small ferry between Nakano and Honshu."

"I'm glad you're interested. I thought it was sorta silly at first." McKenna wrapped her arms around one of Tetsuro's as she stood at his side. "I'd forgotten how much fun it can be."

As the trip continued, McKenna couldn't pull Tetsuro from the rail. They listened to the tour guide as she told of the history of Cleveland's shipping industry and the Cuyahoga River. They concluded the day trip with dinner in The Flats, an area of trendy restaurants and bars along the shore of Lake Erie.

"So," Tetsuro started as they walked up the sidewalk to enter the Rock and Roll Hall of Fame and Museum. "Has it been twenty years since you visited here, too?"

"No." McKenna playfully slapped his arm.

"I had planned to visit with Susumu-*san* when we were here for the concert."

"Another plan ruined by the accident." She took hold of his recuperating hand and interlaced their fingers. Unexpectedly, he tightened his grip in response. McKenna glanced at Tetsuro. He seemed enthralled by I. M. Pei's glass triangle building. Was he aware he was using his hand so well? She didn't say a word about it, hoping to forget he'd closed his hand around hers. Once he realized he was working his hand, he would disappear from her life.

He purchased tickets in the lobby and began the tour of the featured exhibit, *Drummers—The Beat of Rock and Roll.*

As they read the placards and displays of sheet music, posters and letters, she said, "I couldn't have planned it better if I'd tried."

"You did not know of this exhibit?" Tetsuro glanced up from the display describing Buddy Rich's style.

"No. But I did think you'd find the museum interesting."

"I do."

They walked through the hallway between exhibits behind glass, encountering other visitors. At the end of the corridor drums were sat up for those who wished to try their hand at playing part of several computerized songs.

"Sorta of like karaoke but with drums instead of vocals," McKenna commented as she walked to the control console. "Why don't you play?"

"What? Me?" Tetsuro placed his hand on his chest. "You are joking, right?"

"You are a drummer, aren't you?" She was reading the play list.

"*Hai*, I am but…here?"

"That's why they put it up. The museum is famous for its interactive exhibits. Besides," she looked around the area, "these people might never have heard a *taiko* drummer before."

"McKenna, these are not Japanese drums."

"I know that. Come on. Show me what you've learned from Breathing Room's drummer."

"Very well."

He stepped onto the platform and took a seat on the stool behind the large bass drum. Picking up the wood sticks resting on the head of the snare drum, he manipulated the stick in his good hand, but the one in his injured hand was still. McKenna pushed the buttons for the song to start.

When Tetsuro hesitated to join the music, she asked, "What's wrong?"

"I do not know if I can play with my broken hand."

"Just do what you can." McKenna came to stand behind him, her hands on his shoulders. "It's just for fun."

"I cannot give the piece the proper respect." Tetsuro set the drumsticks aside and stood. "We have more to explore."

Disappointed, McKenna nevertheless understood his refusal. If he couldn't meet his own standards, then he had no wish to play. Drumming was in his soul. He reacted to *any* music, his fingers tapping on whatever surface they found. At the exhibits and video presentations, he drummed to the real music from the sound system or to music only he could hear. That he didn't attempt to use his hand was bittersweet. The longer his hand was not completely rehabbed, the longer he would be with her. His talent was like another woman in their relationship. Drumming would take him away from her and she hated it as if it were another woman.

The night was still as McKenna lay in Tetsuro's embrace, his body a soft pillow for her as they reclined in the tub submerged in fragrant bubbles. Candles flickered around the antique claw-footed tub and were reflected on the ceramic tiled walls. Steam rose, giving the air a moist feel and strains of soft music surrounded them. McKenna caressed the arms embracing her.

For so long she'd yearned for the satisfaction she felt now. With Tetsuro, she felt comfortable and safe, free to be herself. She didn't have to please him or worry about doing what he wanted. And she instinctively knew he would support her in any situation. For better or for worse.

He asked nothing more than to be with her. For her part, she wanted him with her forever. But she'd never tell him so. She couldn't. It would destroy the spell. They'd agreed to enjoy the now and not worry about the future. To tell Tetsuro she wanted him permanently in her life would put a pressure on them that would dispel the magic.

Lethargic from the heat of the bath, the busy day and the passions of their lovemaking, she could barely summon the energy to ask, "Are you comfortable?" She twisted in his embrace to look up at him.

"Yes." Tetsuro cupped his hand and drizzled water over her throat. "And you?"

"Uh-huh." Settling back again, McKenna took his hand and turned it over to inspect the palm. "How is it?"

"This does not look like my doctor's office." He moved his wound from her view. "Paul says it is getting better. I am using the next to smallest squeeze ball. By next week, I should be using the smallest."

She recaptured his hand. "Show me."

"Do you really want me to?" Tetsuro used the hand to run a sensuous finger from her jaw to the top of her bubble-covered breast.

"Why not?" McKenna stilled his movements.

"You might not like what you see."

"Don't you think I want your hand to work?"

"I will reserve comment."

Tetsuro extended his arm and slowly closed his hand into a loose fist. His hand worked! Maybe not perfectly, but he was almost whole. It was both thrilling and disheartening. Soon, their idyllic romp would come to an end. Could she go on without him? Would she be happy with only her work to fill her days, no one in her house or bed? Sitting in Tetsuro's lap, immersed in the warm bubble bath, she couldn't bear to think of him leaving. They rested in silence, each lost in their inner thoughts, soothed by the hot water.

"I'm going to sell this house," she suddenly announced, shifting on her human pillow to turn the hot water tap on. "I spoke with a real estate agent and it goes on the market next week."

Tetsuro rewrapped his arms around her upper body when she eased back. "Why?"

"Too many bad memories." McKenna stroked his forearm. His skin was satiny with soap.

He began his titillating shower of warm water. "You grew up here?"

"I've lived here all my life."

Tetsuro continued his erotic shower. "Are you the youngest?"

"Yep, I'm the baby."

"Were you spoiled? In America it seems the youngest is pampered. In Japan, the oldest male is the only one to get away with everything, even up to old age."

"Well, yes and no. As the baby, I was spoiled by nannies and my sisters."

"Did you have a happy childhood?"

"Not really, but I didn't know it until I grew up." She snuggled closer against his silky skin.

"What made you unhappy?" He rubbed his chin across the top of her head.

"I missed having parents."

"How so? You were fortunate enough to have both."

"Our mother was aloof, busy with social obligations. By the time I was born, the nursemaids were in place to care for us and we spent most of our days in another part of the house. When we were old enough, we were sent to boarding school.

"I thought if I became a doctor, I'd have my father's attention and admiration. But the more I accomplished, the more he wanted. He was a cold, strict authoritarian and ruled the family as if we were his hospital or office staff. We girls were taught to respect him, but in reality, we feared him."

"My family was very close." Tetsuro's fingers drizzled water over her breasts. "I remember my father warmly. When he died, it left a large part of my life empty. From the time I was nine, I had no strong father figure. My grandfather tried but he was too old to deal with me. My mother's hands were tied by our culture. She had been taught to allow me to do as I wished. When I was a baby and toddler, she coddled me, lavishing affection on me. I think, too, she spoiled me because I was the only tangible tie to her husband. I was disrespectful and defiant and didn't even receive the minimal discipline an eldest son receives. If Lieutenant Wakiya had not interceded and given me direction, I would be *yakuza* or something worse.

"What's *ya-ku-za*?"

"Japanese Mafia." Tetsuro gathered her sleek wet hair away from her neck and tantalizingly kissed her throat.

She sighed, drifting in the calming effect of his caress. "I have an invitation to Sawyer's next weekend when my mother comes to visit. Want to go?"

"I would be most honored to meet your family."

He continued his sensual touching, and McKenna reveled in the waves of sensation. His fingers kneaded the soft flesh of her breasts, rubbing the nipples into firm peaks. Beneath her hips, his body swelled, throbbing into the valley of her buttocks. His hand stroked down her stomach, his finger circling her naval, before moving beneath the warm water. He caressed the yielding folds, awakening the hidden erotic area. She writhed against his hand.

His mouth worked over her neck, nibbling her collarbone and jaw. McKenna wiggled her bottom against his groin, further rousing his passion. Before she reached her climax, Tetsuro rotated their bodies, exchanged their positions. With McKenna beneath him, he pulled her leg up around his waist as he explored the depths of her mouth with his tongue.

Water and bubbles overflowed the tub as he pushed his erection into her moist, hot sleeve. The bubble bath had transformed the tightly curled hair of her sex to satiny strands that erotically rubbed the base of his sex.

As his body pressed against hers, McKenna wrapped both her legs closely around his hips. The tight muscles of his buttocks flexed under her calves as he moved harder and deeper inside her. The waves of passion pushed away any further thought of her mother's annual visit. Any thought of what Leila Stafford might say when McKenna arrived with

A DRUMMER'S BEAT TO MEND

Tetsuro Takamitsu on her arm vanished in the explosion of his love within her.

CHAPTER TWENTY-FIVE

"Watch out, Tetsuro!" From the passenger seat, McKenna took hold of the steering wheel and directed the Jeep to the correct side of the road. "Stay on the right!"

"*You* are the one who is going to cause an accident." Tetsuro shook her off. "I learned to drive where the right side is the *wrong* side of the road."

"I should never have agreed to let you drive." McKenna laughed and settled back into the passenger seat. As Tetsuro navigated the twists and turns of the Ohio country road, she tried to concentrate on the forest scenery passing by in order to put off thinking about where they were going and what they'd encounter. "I forget how pretty this area is."

"Reminds me somewhat of Japan."

"Do you miss…home?" McKenna dared to broach the subject of his returning to Japan.

"Of course. As you would if you came to Japan and broke your leg."

"Turn right at the next road," she directed. She wasn't going to talk about his leaving.

Tetsuro cautiously made the right turn. "Do you wish to give me a clue as to who I will be meeting?"

"Not really," she muttered. After noting Tetsuro's disapproving look, she relented. "Okay. My eldest sister, Sawyer, is married to the CEO of one of Ohio's major corporations. That explains the estate in Hunting Valley. In my opinion, the most important thing they've ever done is have four beautiful little girls, ages five to twelve. They are precious and I love being 'Aunt Mac.' It's the only time I really like being called 'Mac.'"

"I could never call you such. 'Ke-*chan*' is much nicer."

"You promised a long time ago to explain that."

"It is the Japanese way of making a pet name. We do not call our loved ones by names like 'Honey,' 'Sweetheart,' or 'Dearie.' So we take the first syllable of your name and add the *chan* to make it affectionate. In your case, Mac-*chan* did not work. So…Ke-*chan*."

"That's sweet." Yet he'd called Emiko 'Dearest.'

"As it is intended to be." A flush of red washed over his face as he talked. "Who else will be there?"

"My mother. That's why we're all meeting in the first place. Morgan, my third sister, might be here."

"What is your other sister's name?" He steered the Jeep skillfully with minimal use of his left hand.

"Bailey. She lives in England and won't be here."

"Are not your names usually last names for Americans?"

"Yes. You know so much about America but I don't know that much about Japan."

"When you travel the world, it is easy to learn things about where you are. If you remain in one area all your life, you do not tend to investigate further." He strained to see down the road. "When do I turn again?"

"About a mile and it'll be to the left. It's a private road with a locked gate about two hundred feet off the main road."

Conversation paused as they watched for the turnoff. When they reached it, Tetsuro stopped at the gate and McKenna called off the code numbers. The ornate iron gate swung open.

Tetsuro drove up the long winding lane slowly. Stately pines lined the road and acres of green pasture rolled gently out from each side. Behind white board fences horses grazed on the lush grass.

"Your sister has horses?" The questioning tone in his voice suggested awe at the possibility.

"A few. Do you ride?"

"I have never had the opportunity. Horses are an expensive luxury in Japan. Even in ancient times, horses were owned only by important and wealthy *samurai*."

"We'll plan on a ride this weekend. It'll be a pleasant escape at some point." An escape plan was always necessary at family functions. It was a means of survival.

"What makes you say that?"

"My family can get on your nerves. My mother is overbearing. She has this misplaced sense of self. Our father wanted all of his daughters to become doctors, but I was the only one who did. Now my sisters make me feel as though they resent me for it. They don't see that it didn't make him happy. I sometimes wonder if it's made me happy."

"You are very successful. That should make you happy."

"Success doesn't necessarily create happiness. I enjoy my work, but the other parts of my life haven't been so great." McKenna placed her hand underneath the loose hair on his nape. "Until now."

"I am honored that I have brought pleasure to you." His healing hand steadying the wheel, Tetsuro took the hand from his neck and kissed her palm.

They approached the house.

"This place would be a *whole* neighborhood in Tokyo. A swimming pool?" Tetsuro's astonishment was in his voice as he saw the large pool at the side of the house.

"Surely you can swim, since you live on an island."

"I'm a very good swimmer. It would do my muscles good to have a different kind of exercise."

"You take your exercise seriously." His body was a fine example of what gym time could achieve. He never mentioned being concerned about his diet and there wasn't an ounce of fat anywhere on his long body.

"*Taiko* is strenuous even though I enjoy physical exertion." He guided the Jeep into the curve of the driveway, careful to avoid a collision with the stone barrier around a rose garden in the middle of the drive.

"I'd love to join you in a swim." McKenna wasn't the most exercise friendly, even though she ran several times a week. Running gave her the opportunity to think. Swimming with Tetsuro would be a different story. Just imagining him in a Speedo sent a flush through her.

"I will look forward to it." Tetsuro held her hand. "Ke-*chan*, enjoy your visit with your family and remember, I am here for you."

"I know." She squeezed his hand. Each minute they shared could be the last and she wanted to build as many memories as she could manage. She hoped her family wouldn't cause her to have unhappy ones of this weekend.

By the time Tetsuro parked the Jeep at the apex of the curved driveway the sun had begun to set. Just as he came around the vehicle to open her door, the front door of the house opened. Arm in arm, they walked up the steps and were met by a butler. After greetings were exchanged the butler told McKenna that the family had retired to dress for dinner.

"Great," McKenna mumbled. "I knew we should've come earlier in the day."

"What does 'dress for dinner' mean?" Tetsuro leaned into her to whisper softly. His breath tickled her ear.

"Formal and fancy." She turned to the butler. "Has everyone else arrived?"

"Yes, ma'am. Madam Stafford has been here since Wednesday and Ms. Morgan and friend arrived yesterday." The stiff man went to the Jeep to collect their luggage. Tetsuro started after him.

"No." McKenna touched his arm to stop him. "He'll get our things. Let's go up."

Certain her sister would give them the same room she always gave her, McKenna led the way through the house to the staircase.

"We will...share the room?" He was whispering again.

McKenna embraced him. "Don't you want to?"

"Of course." Tetsuro wrapped his arms around her. "But will your family approve?"

"Why should they care? No one tells my sisters what to do. I'm an adult. So are you. They are not going to boss me around."

The butler with their luggage interrupted their kiss. Tetsuro followed McKenna, who trailed the butler to their suite.

When she finished showing Tetsuro where things were, she asked, "Do you want to bathe before you dress?"

"I would not be Japanese if I turned down a bath." Tetsuro worked to lighten McKenna's spirits, but wasn't succeeding. "Would you like to join me?"

"We shouldn't delay. Cocktails are in the library at six-thirty followed by dinner at seven-thirty." McKenna gathered her toilettes. "Nothing changes. We're bound by the same routines whenever we gather. I'm afraid Sawyer keeps her own family to the same standards."

"Perhaps you should bathe first. It will take me less time." Tetsuro searched his bag for the items he'd placed in it several days before when they began planning the trip.

McKenna left him alone in the bedroom.

Tetsuro busied himself with laying his clothes out on the bed. Then he sat in the chair at the bedside and looked around the room. The room was depressing, or more properly, oppressing. The somber drapes on the tall narrow windows darkened the large room. The dressing table with its wide mirror and the chest of drawers were dark oak. A king-sized bed and other pieces of furniture crowded the space. He longed for the airy, uncluttered style of his native land.

When he removed his shoes and socks, he wondered about the American predilection for covering the floors with thick carpeting, although he had to admit it felt good to his bare feet. And to his body when he made love to McKenna on the floor.

He pulled the tail of his T-shirt out of his jeans and yanked it off over his head. By the time he stood and unzipped his jeans, McKenna had returned with a heavy bath towel around her.

"All yours."

"There you go tempting me." He approached her, his finger tickling the swell of her dark breasts over the stark white towel. "And I thought you said we did not have time?"

"You're such a bad boy!" McKenna took his hand away and stepped out of reach. "Go. Bathe. We have to meet the jury."

"You, my lady, are as bad as I." Her laughter pleased him.

When he returned, McKenna had donned her underwear, panty-hose and slip. The dress lay on the bed and she was applying the last touches to her makeup. He came behind her, moving aside the lengthy hair she'd left down and kissing her neck. His bare chest pressed against her back and his arm encircled her waist.

"You're being naughty again," McKenna admonished. "Dress."

"You are no fun."

Her uptight attitude hinted at her nervousness. Her demeanor, so professional at the hospital, and in control most other times, was crumbling. He had seen many of his friends revert to children in the presence of their parents. There was little he could do for her except remind her of his support.

He moved to the bed and dropped his towel. In the mirror's reflection, McKenna watched him pull on the tight boxer briefs and then a shirt. As he buttoned it, he winked. Embarrassed at being caught, she flushed. He finished dressing, still under her gaze, and joined her at the dressing table to comb his hair.

"Here. Let me." McKenna, still only in her slip, reached to take his comb. "Sit on the corner of the bed."

Tetsuro complied and McKenna knelt behind him on the bed. The warmth of her body radiated to his back. Closing his eyes, he enjoyed the strokes of the comb pulling through the length of his thick fine hair.

"I should have known my family would do this," McKenna spoke as she gathered his hair at the back, then combed again. "They can't meet you casually. We have to be formal."

"As you said, this is how it has always been. Customs are what keep society together, allowing people to live together civilly. A person knows how to behave in structured environments." More than anywhere on earth, Asia was a land and people dictated to by centuries old customs. Without a reverence for such antiquated etiquette, *taiko* would no longer exist.

As they spoke, McKenna combed his hair more vigorously.

"I suppose you are right. We might be shuffling around lost without the organized schedule." The comb painfully connected with his scalp. "I want them to like you."

"I am sure we will find a meeting ground. I…care for you, their sister and daughter so we do have something in common." He winced at the ferocity with which she combed.

"I'm not too sure they care for me." A rare tangle in his hair pulled violently.

"They love you in their way. You must learn to accept their terms." Tetsuro allowed his head to follow her stroke to release the pull at his scalp.

"I have tried to do that for thirty-two years." She gathered his hair together into a low ponytail and pulled it tightly. The precise surgeon's hand fumbled with the elastic ponytail holder.

The pulling of her grip was intense. Finally, Tetsuro could tolerate it no longer.

He took the comb and moved off the bed. "I will finish."

"I'm sorry. They just make me so angry," she growled as she came to stand with him, watching as he bound his hair back.

"Do not let them. They only have power if you give it to them."

"I want them to be nice to you." She hugged him. Tetsuro dropped his arms to hold her.

"I can take care of myself. I have dined with kings, queens, movie stars, rock and roll groups and even our emperor and crown prince."

McKenna kissed him.

"Put on your dress. Or we *will* be late." Tetsuro released her.

"You look nice. Those black slacks are sinfully tight." McKenna stepped away to dress. "Do you have a jacket?"

"Yes. Or perhaps you wish me to wear kimono?"

"I was just checking." McKenna stepped into the bright blue soft jersey dress that clung to the curves of her body.

Tetsuro was sorry they didn't have time to make love. The response of his body threatened the strength of his trousers.

CHAPTER TWENTY-SIX

Fifteen minutes later, Tetsuro escorted McKenna into the library where her family had gathered for cocktails. Even though he had boasted of meeting VIPs and the rich and famous, he was more anxious about meeting the average American family and, after listening to her stories, specially this one. His greatest concern was that they would upset McKenna. At the mere thought of it, his long-suppressed anger threatened to resurface.

As they stepped into the somber room with book-lined walls, he glanced around. Three men and three women sat on straight, barely-cushioned chairs, clad in tea length dresses and dark suits, hair coifed perfectly, makeup equally tended. Each one held a glass with slowly melting ice which Tetsuro figured from their demeanor would not dare to melt any further than necessary to chill the dark brown fluid at the bottom of the Waterford crystal. No one moved or spoke. Their eyes were directed at him as he stood behind McKenna.

McKenna approached the older woman sitting at the most prominent place in the room. She leaned and embraced the thin shoulders of her mother who, in turn, embraced her daughter.

"Mother, I'd like you to meet Tetsuro Takamitsu. Tetsu, my mother, Leila Stafford." He couldn't help but notice her mother's ebony skin was dry and the underlying muscles were loose.

Tetsuro took McKenna's place to greet her mother. He moved warily, pondering how he should say hello. A deep formal Japanese bow? A good old-fashioned American handshake? A very continental kiss to the back of the hand? She eliminated his most natural of choices by extending her hand to him. He took the fragile-looking hand and bent to lower his lips. He stopped before he touched the thin skin, giving the illusion of a kiss.

"How do you do?" Leila asked rhetorically. Her voice was husky, as if she'd only recently, if ever, stopped smoking.

"I am very well, thank you." Tetsuro straightened. As he looked at Leila Stafford, he realized he found exactly what he had unconsciously looked for in the sisters. Leila had given McKenna the beautiful light brown eyes he'd been drawn to the first time they'd met. But Leila's were dimmed and watery whereas McKenna's were bright and sparkly. Tetsuro hoped she would never lose that glitter.

"I'm sorry, I don't know your name." McKenna spoke to the Latin looking young man who stood behind her mother's chair.

"Marco Fuentes," the man introduced himself. He had the look of an Acapulco cliff diver, wide-shouldered, narrow-waisted. Oily black hair was slicked back on his head like a raven's feathers.

"You're my mother's...guest?"

Tetsuro would bet good money that Mrs. Stafford had purchased the tailored suit clothing is muscular body and that Marco was just one in a long line of lovers.

"Yes," Leila Stafford answered for him.

"I'm going to make the rest of this simple," McKenna addressed the room. "Tetsuro Takamitsu, my sisters, Morgan and Sawyer." She pointed first to the woman closest to her and then the other who sat beside their mother. They resembled their mother in skin tone but their facial bone structure was more their father's, if Tetsuro remembered the photos correctly. "Sawyer's husband, Andrew Reichert. I'm sorry, Morgan, I don't know your friend."

"Ronald Bates," Morgan said and sipped from her drink.

Tetsuro nodded his head to each woman and stepped up to shake the hands of the men. There was little warmth in the male hands or the female faces. Except for him and Marco, the members of the Stafford clan were African American, as well as the staff he'd met thus far.

"McKenna, how have you been?" Leila turned to her daughter. "I expected a visit this spring."

"I...I...couldn't get away," McKenna stammered. Her cheeks darkened and she lowered her face to avoid her mother's look. "I'd repaired Tetsuro's hand and couldn't leave town."

"Oh?" Leila raised her finely-penciled eyebrows and looked at him. "You're McKenna's *patient?*"

"*Hai.* I had an unfortunate accident which turned into a very fortunate meeting with McKenna." The derogatory lilt in her voice hadn't escaped his notice.

"You're dating your patients, Mac?" Sawyer chimed into the conversation, as if Tetsuro weren't in the room or was deaf. "Don't you think that's a little unprofessional?"

"I don't think now is the time to discuss such matters." McKenna crossed the room to the bar. She took a glass from the shelf and dropped several ice cubes from the ice bucket into it. "It doesn't matter anyway." Her fingers closed around the neck of the bourbon bottle. "I don't know why I wanted you to meet the man I love. I thought maybe you'd be happy for me."

"Oh, McKenna, don't be so melodramatic," Sawyer remarked.

"Ke-*chan.*" Tetsuro came to her side, mutely stopping her from picking up the bottle. "Would you split a soda with me? I do not wish to spoil my appetite."

For an instant, McKenna's eyes flashed hotly, but then changed to the usual laughing sparkle the minute he gave her a soft smile.

"Love to." McKenna poured them each a soda. When she turned back to the group, her mother spoke.

"How long are you staying in the States, Mr. Takamizzu?"

"McKenna has yet to release me from her care." Tetsuro didn't bother to correct her pronunciation of his name. Sometimes it just wasn't worth the effort.

"I bet Mac will hate to do that," Morgan stated. She was the plainest of the three girls with McKenna obviously the prettiest. Morgan's form was full and round, disguised by the draping of flowered material. Her hair was clipped close to her head, allowing the tight curls their freedom.

Her boyfriend was rail thin, a lighter cocoa brown with the same sort of hairstyle. Morgan clung to his side as though she needed his support. Were all the Stafford women so needy?

"*McKenna*," Tetsuro corrected, his words and attention toward Morgan.

"Excuse me?"

"I believe your sister prefers to be called 'McKenna.'"

"Mac? What is he saying?" Morgan's wide eyes shot to her little sister.

"He told you. I don't like being called 'Mac' except with the girls." McKenna raised her glass to her lips to forestall speech.

"Come now," Leila interjected. "We've called you that all your life."

She lowered the glass and glared furiously at her mother. "But I haven't liked it *all my life!*"

Before they could disagree further, there was a burst of activity and Sawyer's four daughters arrived.

"Auntie Mac! Auntie Mac!" they squealed and hugged her, all four huddling around their favorite aunt. The two youngest were lively with the two older girls trying to suppress the same youthful zest.

"Hello, girls. I'd like you to meet my friend, Tetsuro Takamitsu. You can call him 'Tetsu.' It's easier. Tetsuro, this is Brianna, Amber, Stephanie, and Christina Reichert."

"Hello," the older girls, Brianna and Amber, said in unison.

"Glad to meet you," Tetsuro replied. The little girls all looked with surprise and wonder at the strange man before them. "I think you have met someone from Japan before."

"No." Amber shook her head, her long curls swinging.

"Oh, yes, you have. His name was Hotei and he left you something." He reached behind her right ear and withdrew a *sen* coin. He displayed the shiny item for the little girl.

"Thank you." She took it, enraptured with the gift.

"And me?" The third little girl tugged at his sleeve. "Have I seen Hotei?" Stephanie had an ear for languages, saying the name easily.

"I do not know. Let me see." Tetsuro looked her over. The adults watched him with as much expectation as the girls. He turned her around, inspecting the back of the beautiful frilly dress with its lace and bow. She faced him again. "What is this?"

He performed another parlor trick and a paper fan appeared in his hand. Flicking it open, he fluttered it in her face. Stephanie responded with giggles as she took the fan in her two small hands.

"You are very quiet, Elder Sister. Are you sure Hotei has not visited you also?"

"Nooooo," Brianna scoffed, her pre-adolescent face trying not to show that she was impressed with his simple slight of hand.

Tetsuro began the magic ritual once more, screwing his face up thoughtfully as if seeking the tiniest of things.

Andrew, the children's father, asked, "What have we here? Qua Chang Caine meets Santa Claus?"

The adults laughed as though trying to dispel the anticipation.

Without taking his eyes off Brianna, Tetsuro answered, "Merely pleasantries for lovely children. Ah so!" He fell into the stereotypical jargon. "He seems to have left you something very special. I do not know why this is not irritating you."

Withdrawing his hand from the neck of her lace collar, Tetsuro held a two-inch piece of ivory.

"Ohhhhh." Brianna stopped all her pretense, thrilled with the gift. "Aunt Mac, look!" She held the carving out for inspection.

"That is very nice, Brianna." McKenna studied it. "What is this, Tetsu?"

"A *netsuke*. A bear."

"Oh, I see. A sweet, cuddly bear cub." McKenna handed it back to Brianna. "What do you say?"

The girls' soft, high-pitched voices joined in a chorus of 'thank yous' and Tetsuro gave them his most formal of bows.

The smallest girl stood quietly waiting, looking from sister to sister and to the Japanese stranger. Her mouth was held in a threatening pout. Big brown eyes eagerly beseeched his. Tetsuro knelt in front of her, taking hold of both her tiny hands. He smiled and winked at her.

"McKenna, do you think Hotei left something for the little one?"

McKenna looked bewildered. "Huh, what?"

Tetsuro raised his body up and turned back to McKenna.

"Maybe something's in her pocket?" Tetsuro indicated the large pockets of the pinafore apron the youngest girl wore.

She followed his lead and reached into the pocket. When she found a tiny stuffed animal, she gave Tetsuro a questioning look. The little girl took the toy excitedly and left with her sisters when their nanny came to remove them.

"You haven't lost your touch with the girls." Sawyer came near McKenna at the bar and refreshed her drink.

"They are so great. I'd love to have children just like them." *They are what make me willing to come up here.*

"You know what happened...," Leila joined her daughters.

"Mother...," McKenna spat, cutting off her mother's words.

Sawyer changed the subject. "Are you still seeing James?"

"No." McKenna faced her. "Didn't you hear what I said? I am *dating* Tetsuro!"

"You don't have to get so excited," Leila chastised.

"Mother..." McKenna began again. The color rose to her face. They were surrounding her, closing her off from escape. Their words assaulted her, tearing down any defense she erected. She couldn't breathe! Her eyes flashed around looking in desperation for rescue. As her mother and sisters continued to speak, she couldn't understand the words. The room was spinning.

Tetsuro stepped nearer.

Before he could save the day, a maid announced, "Dinner is served."

The gentlemen offered their arms to the ladies and the four couples entered the dining room.

As Andrew seated her at the foot of the table, Sawyer announced, "I've resorted to place cards."

McKenna and Tetsuro moved to her left. Finding her seat, Tetsuro assisted McKenna with her chair.

"Sawyer, you missp…" McKenna began.

As he pushed her chair up to the table, Tetsuro whispered "Ssssh" into her ear, stealthily brushing her ear with his lips. "It does not matter." He subtly removed the place card from the table to his pocket.

"But…," McKenna continued to protest.

"*Iie.*"

She obediently dropped the matter and Tetsuro took his seat.

"I sat Mr. Takamissa next to you, McKenna, so he'd have someone to talk to. With his limited English," Sawyer explained as the others settled around the table, separated from their partner as etiquette required.

Tetsuro swallowed to prevent responding. His cultural upbringing precluded his saying what he thought. *I do not see how that would have benefited either of us. Unless you think your sister has taken a crash course in Japanese since March.*

Before anyone could respond, the meal began with the salad course. When the maid poured the wine, Tetsuro declined and McKenna followed his choice. Once served, the family began to eat and the conversation was safe and sterile, if not boring.

Tetsuro identified the second course as cream of asparagus soup. He relaxed his guard. With the idle pleasant conversation, he could sip calmly. In the drawing room when he had stepped to McKenna's defense, his Japanese side had been appalled at the rudeness of the family. Such confrontations and personal attacks were never publicly displayed in his native land. When strangers were present, relatives were on their best behavior and the most polite. He hoped the family would remain polite during the meal as a normal Japanese family would.

Everything went smoothly until the main course was served.

"If any of you want anything from the house," McKenna announced to the table, "you better come down and get it. I'm selling it."

"You're what?"

"Selling our house?"

"You can't!"

The chorus was loud and bewildered.

"It's my house," McKenna defended. She replaced the silverware on the table. Tetsuro figured it was so she wouldn't be tempted to hurl the weapons at someone. "I can do anything I want to with it."

"Well, I'm not too sure of that, Mac," Andrew said. "Have you checked your deed?"

McKenna picked her fork up from the plate. "It's mine. After Father died and his will was probated, each of you got a fourth of the value because you didn't want the house. You wanted it over with. It was your choice."

Tetsuro kept an eye on the implement in her delicate hand. Could he move fast enough to prevent danger?

"You can't up and sell it. Especially without our permission," Sawyer said.

"I can! I asked my lawyer before I called the real estate agent." Her knuckles were white on the fork. The muscle high on her jaw twitched. "It's my house! None of you wanted it or anything in it. Till now!"

"Whose idea was this, Mac?" Andrew inquired. "You've been happy there all these years. 'Until now' to use your words."

Tetsuro felt the man's stare. He remained calm, watching the exchange.

"What are you insinuating? That Tetsuro wants me to sell my house? Please!" McKenna turned her attention to her food, angrily slicing the chicken breast.

Tetsuro gave up eating and quietly replaced his fork and knife. He leaned to whisper into McKenna's ear, then slid his chair away from the table and stood.

"If you will excuse me, I will take my leave." Tetsuro confidently departed.

While not really wishing to leave McKenna vulnerable, he'd decided it would be best if he distanced himself from the family quarrel. Walking up the stairs and across the corridor that overlooked the first floor, he pulled the place card out of his pocket.

Tatsuru Takemistzu

It wasn't uncommon for him to have his name misspelled but this was the worst he'd ever seen. He chuckled and returned it to his pocket. Listening carefully, he heard youthful laughter and followed the sound. He came to the girls playing in the nursery.

They had been fed and bathed and were now entertaining themselves before bed. Sitting around the small table dressed in their pajamas, they played cards. A nanny sat in the corner. She glanced up at him briefly from the book she was reading.

Tetsuro entered the room and said, "Good evening, ladies. May I join you?"

"Hello, Mr. Tetsu," Brianna greeted him. "Is dinner over?"

"No." Tetsuro took a seat in one of the small chairs, his knees almost at chest level. "I was not very hungry."

"Are you really from Japan?" Amber asked.

"Yes. I was performing when your aunt had to operate on my hand."

"We studied Japan last year in school. Do you wear kimonos?" Amber was the inquisitive one.

"Sometimes. Usually when I am going to a very special event. Weddings, funerals, formal dinners and parties. What else did you learn about Japan?" He picked up a picture book the toddler Christina had been looking at.

"About the royal family and the war," Amber answered, suddenly seeming grown up.

"Very boring things, huh?" Tetsuro teased. "What is this?" He pointed to a picture.

"Doggie," Christina replied, hopping from foot to foot.

"Nooooo," Amber replied to his question, trying to be diplomatic. "I just don't remember much more."

"I do not either," Tetsuro fibbed. "And this?"

"'Angaroo," the little girl squealed.

"Have you ever seen a kangaroo?" He folded another page over.

"Auntie Mac took us to the zoo. We saw 'angaroos there." She put a finger in her mouth.

Brianna joined in. "Could you tell us about Hotei?"

The nanny came over and pulled Christina's finger away from her mouth in silent admonishment.

"Certainly." Tetsuro closed the book and faced the girls. "Hotei is a Buddhist deity, one of the Seven Gods of Luck. You have probably seen pictures of him. He has a big round tummy." He unbuttoned his jacket and pushed his own stomach out and pretended to caress a more substantial one. "He cannot keep his kimono closed over it. And he always has little children around him."

Stephanie spoke up. "Are you going to marry Aunt Mac?"

"I do not know. Do you think I should?" *Out of the mouths of babes.* He realigned his body but didn't rebutton his jacket.

"Yes," she announced.

"We will have to wait and see what *karma* has planned for us."

Christina launched herself into Tetsuro's arms. "You're funny!"

"What are you playing?" He perched her on his knee, an arm around her tiny waist.

"Go fish," Brianna answered. "Wanna play?"

"You will have to teach me," he told Stephanie on his right. "I have never played."

"Okay," she giggled.

Christina remained in Tetsuro's lap and he pulled his chair closer to the table as the girls began to tell him the rules. He tried not to think about McKenna downstairs playing what seemed to be the parlor games of the American rich.

CHAPTER TWENTY-SEVEN

After Tetsuro left the table, McKenna tried to hold her own but failed. Convincing her family of anything was useless if they didn't want to be convinced. It didn't matter. She excused herself before dessert was served.

Their room was empty, so she went searching for Tetsuro.

"Here you are." McKenna stood at the threshold of the nursery. She should have come here in the first place.

"Good thing you arrived. I keep losing." Tetsuro faced her. "I think they are cheating."

His tall, lean body dwarfed the child's chair. He reached to draw a card from the pile in the center of the table, careful not to jostle her youngest niece who was curled in his lap, asleep with the thumb in her mouth. Her head rested on his chest and one hand extended upward to clutch a clump of his hair in her small fist.

Amber left the game table to hug McKenna. "Auntie Mac."

"Hi, girls." McKenna entered the room with Amber close at her side. Ribbons, barrettes, and bows cluttered the floor. Tetsuro's hair was released from the elastic that normally held it neatly at his nape and now a barrette was fastened to an uneven clump. "You've been playing beauty parlor."

"Yeah. It's fun. His hair feels different." Amber left her favorite aunt's side and began to run her fingers through Tetsuro's hair. His head came back sharply as her little fingers caught an obvious snag.

"Careful." McKenna took the small hands in hers. "Don't want to hurt your client. Why aren't you all in bed?"

"We get to stay up until dinner is over and Mother comes up to say goodnight," Stephanie explained.

"Well, she should be up soon. Can I take your playmate away? It's past his bedtime." She casually removed the barrette.

The nanny came to take Christina from Tetsuro.

"Show me where and I will carry her." He stood with the girl cradled in his arms.

The nanny led him through the suite of the girls' rooms and he deposited Christina in her bed. She snuggled into the pastel sheets decorated with fairies as Tetsuro tenderly tucked her in. He returned to McKenna and the other girls.

"What's wrong?" McKenna asked. "You look sad."

"I did not wish to release her. Someday I wish to know such a daughter."

McKenna kissed his cheek. "Let's go to bed," she whispered.

The couple said goodnight to the girls but not before the three remaining sisters demanded Tetsuro tuck them in also. He rose to the occasion. He seemed born to minister to children. He pulled up covers and in turn tickled and teased the girls, appearing to enjoy it all. McKenna wished she would be the one to provide him with daughters.

"You're so good with children." McKenna was curled at Tetsuro's side in bed.

"It is the children who are special." He rubbed her back gently. "Are we going to make love?"

"Other than the nursery, this house is not conducive to love."

"You should not allow others to dictate your emotions."

Tetsuro turned, moving McKenna to her back. He brought his body over hers while gently brushing his lips across hers. His hands tugged her nightgown over her head. His mouth migrated down her body and easily awakened her passion.

She relaxed beneath his tender foreplay, responding readily to his touch. Once she'd climaxed, he lifted her hips and drove himself deep inside her. Quick strong penetrating strokes brought them both to orgasm and they drifted into a sated sleep.

Morning came and McKenna awoke alone. She didn't like not knowing when Tetsuro got up or that he'd done so without waking her. Once out of bed, she pulled back the drapes of the window that overlooked part of the back and side of the house. The pool was in clear view and occupied by recognizable swimmers.

McKenna watched in fascination from the window as Tetsuro coached Brianna on diving. The man and girl stood at the deep end of the pool. Brianna was listening intently as he first instructed and then illustrated the dive. A sleek flash of bronze as he smoothly entered the water, he came up at the edge and easily pulled himself out to stand beside her again. His hair was tight against his skull and neck. The brief cut of his dark swimsuit was the only interruption in the tawny skin.

Then both Tetsuro and Brianna dived into the water. He timed his movement seconds ahead of Brianna so that he could emerge before her and still her fears. As she thrashed to the surface in the deep water, he held his strong arms out to her for reassurance.

How so like our relationship?

McKenna felt as though she'd struggled all her life with only herself to depend on. Now she had Tetsuro.

But for how long?

Her heart cracked as she stepped away to dress and join them in the pool, eager not to lose a minute of Tetsuro's time.

"Morning all," she addressed her mother and sisters who lounged around the pool. Lucky for her, juices and muffins were set out on the table and she helped herself. "Sleep well?"

They muttered responses and she walked to the edge of the pool.

"Are they trying to drown you?" she asked Tetsuro who knelt low in the shallow water. While Christina sat on his shoulders, he had Brianna and Amber on each side, pulling his arms in opposite directions. Stephanie vigorously splashed them all from behind.

"I am not sure what they are trying. It may be to draw and quarter me."

To the thrill of the girls, he rose and moved his body like a giant monster, shaking the older two girls off. But Christina held on tenaciously and Tetsuro resigned himself to having her on his shoulders. The girls gave him little reprieve before pouncing again. McKenna moved away to sit beside her mother.

Large sunglasses and a floppy straw hat hid Leila's face. A flowing caftan protected her body from the sun. "Should we worry about your Jap friend being a child molester?"

"Mother! Don't call him that."

"Well, that's what he is," Sawyer said.

"He is *Japanese* not a...Jap." The derogatory word was bitter on her tongue. "And how could you think someone I love would hurt children? He happens to like kids. And they like him." Did they think her judgment was that poor?

"Was it his idea to sell the house?" Leila moved to another sticky subject.

"No. He doesn't care what I do. He'll be going back to Japan." The words hurt her heart.

"How sordid, Mac." Leila reached to the table and sipped her orange juice heavily laced with vodka.

She used the term Tetsuro had taught her. "*Shigata ga na.* It cannot be helped. I can't go to Japan and practice medicine. I've been nominated for Chief of Ortho at University Hospital. He can't live here. There's little call for *taiko* drummers in Cleveland."

"Sure he can, Mac," Sawyer said. "He can marry you. Then he'll have a green card and a wife to support him."

"I don't like the way you're talking about the man I'd gladly share my life and *money* with." McKenna walked to the table and started to pour herself a glass from her mother's special pitcher. Her hand rested on the handle for long seconds before she turned and approached the pool's edge.

Morgan called to her, "I don't much like you talking of selling the house in Cleveland."

"It's mine to sell!" McKenna whirled around. "I'd appreciate it if you'd keep your comments to yourself. About my career, my house and my love life! You don't bother to call or check on me and when I come to visit, I'm attacked! I've had enough. I'm doing well without any of you."

McKenna dove into the pool and came up near Tetsuro. With young Christina firmly attached to his shoulders he played with the three girls in waist-high water. She joined in the horseplay, taking the girls' side against Tetsuro. Eventually the girls were worn out and left the water to rest before lunch.

McKenna floated to Tetsuro, and her outstretched arms hugged him. He held her close, buoyant in the water.

"I'm ready to go back to Cleveland," she said. "My family's driving me nuts!"

"Only because you let them." He twirled her through the water.

"I know." She put her feet on the pool floor and hid her face in the warmth of his chest. "Take me home."

He nuzzled her cheek. "If it is your wish."

"I love you." McKenna looked up at him.

Tetsuro lowered his lips to hers. "Shall we go upstairs?"

"*Hai.*" She smiled at him, the taste of his lips on her mouth.

He picked her up and carried her out of the pool and into the house, leaving behind McKenna's mother and sister too astonished to speak.

McKenna dressed, packed, then carried the smaller piece of luggage down to the front door. Tetsuro would come down with the larger ones. When she asked the butler to have the Jeep brought around, it was as though the burden that had been building over thirty years was lifted from her shoulders. Relief washed over her in its place.

"McKenna," a man called from down the hallway.

Walking toward the voice, she questioned, "Andrew?"

"Could you come in here, please?" her oldest sister's husband asked. He was a short man, stocky with a coffee skin tone. Gray colored his temples and mustache.

A mental warning alarm sounded as she entered his office.

"What do you want?"

"I just got off the phone with a friend of mine who's on the board of the Cleveland Museum of Art." He came around to the front of the desk. "That 'little carving' your friend gave Brianna is worth somewhere in the neighborhood of five hundred dollars. Do you think that's a proper gift for a twelve-year-old?"

"I don't know. You buy her expensive things."

"We're her parents. He's some stranger you've brought in here. Where'd he get it?"

"How should I know?" Her voice rose with exasperation. "It's a gift, Andrew. You don't ask someone where they got something they give you. He wanted to be nice. Can't you understand that?"

After her mother's accusation that Tetsuro had ulterior motives for playing with the girls and Morgan's implication that he wanted a green card and money, she was wary of where Andrew's thoughts were leading. "What do you think his motive is?"

"Where'd he get the money for something that expensive? He's a performer, for God's sake!"

"While it is true I am an artisan, I am not a thief," Tetsuro spoke quietly as he entered the room to stand in front of McKenna. "I am well paid for my performances. I also receive royalties for my compositions that are performed worldwide. Although you do not deserve an answer, I would appreciate your asking me about my business instead of McKenna.

"The *netsuke* is from my collection. I received some of them from my grandfather who received them from his father. I have over two hundred pieces that are mine to do with as I choose. However, I purchased the one I presented to our daughter."

McKenna was dazed. The power Tetsuro projected was awesome. He was confronting Andrew, man to man, in an intense but calm way.

She was quite capable of telling her brother-in-law where to go, had done it often enough, but to have her *samurai* come to her rescue was a new experience. Tiny shivers fluttered up her spine and the hair on her nape stood on end.

"I wish for Brianna to have the *netsuke*, to do with as she wishes. I have told her it is for her alone. If she should notify her Aunt Mac about something having happened to it, I will not be pleased and will take action accordingly.

"Now. While McKenna and I appreciate your hospitality, I think it is time we departed. Good day." Tetsuro faced McKenna.

Unable to utter a word, McKenna stood with her mouth open. Tetsuro's strength sent a rush to the center of her chest, swelling her heart and making her short of breath. That someone would do this for her was remarkable.

"Ke-*chan*, if you will go to the car, I will bring the luggage and we can be on our way."

She followed his instructions wordlessly. So in awe was she that she took the passenger seat. Tetsuro got behind the wheel and, with a squeal of the tires on the drive, sped away from the estate.

CHAPTER TWENTY-EIGHT

"Are you bored, *Uchite*?"

"What makes you think that, Richard-*san*?" Tetsuro played his fingers over the keys of the old upright piano in the Soto family room. He and Richard had been playing a piano and drum duet. The last notes still echoed in the high ceiling.

"I don't know. You've been here a long time and the only things you do are go to the hospital, teach me drumming and Japanese, and visit your lady friend. I'd think you'd either be bored out of your mind or really homesick. Don't you miss home?"

"Of course I miss home but my hand must heal." He removed his fingers from the keys and placed his hands in his lap. The piece had been simple, using mostly his right hand but his left had moved with only a slight stiffness.

"What do you miss most?" Richard tapped quietly on the drumhead.

"My friends. The *Taiko* School. The ocean and mountains. The festivals we perform for. I have already missed the *Kanda, Aoi,* and *Sanjo* festivals. We also play at the Imperial Palace at this time of year."

"Cool. When do you think you'll leave?" The boy's eyes sparkled beneath the mop of hair. Tetsuro remembered his first brush with the celebrity of the Japanese imperial family.

"Are you trying to rush me off?" He gave the boy a joking smile. His hand ached and he tried to rub the pain away. To leave America was to leave McKenna. His love for her was greater than for any other woman he'd ever known. His heart had been broken once in his life so he was well aware of the pain ahead. Already he felt the pulse in his chest.

"No. I really like learning Japanese. It's neat to be able to talk with

Oba-san in her first language."

"I am sure your grandmother appreciates it, too."

"Don't you have any family who miss you?"

"No. No family to miss me." Tetsuro's voice was soft.

"Someone must miss you." Richard was an inquiring child, wise for his age.

"My friends do, I suppose." The more he thought about leaving McKenna, the harder the pain in his chest pulsed.

"I'll miss you when you leave here," the teenager said.

"Maybe you can come visit." Tetsuro looked at his student. "Your grandmother would like to show you where she was born."

"That'd be great! And you could always come back."

"*Hai*. Now we should return to your lesson." The only way to stop the pain was to play and avoid thinking of the inevitable.

"Your hand must be better. You can play the piano really well."

A sharp stab surged in his chest. Even a boy could see how healed he was. Could Dr. Stafford put off discharging him much longer?

McKenna was sitting across from Tetsuro enjoying a quiet dinner when her beeper sounded.

She fished her cellular phone out of her purse. "I have to call the hospital."

Without comment Tetsuro continued to swirl butter and sour cream into his baked potato before he tasted it. His taste for American food was expanding and so would his waistline if he didn't run five miles a day. A diet laden with carbohydrates and dairy products was not meant for the Japanese frame.

McKenna punched in the number, then held the phone to her ear. As she waited for the emergency room to answer, she took a bite of her steak.

When someone answered the phone, she said, "Dr. Stafford. I was paged." She ate as she listened. "I'll be right there." She folded the phone and returned it to her purse. "Dr. Macdonald wants me to assist with a case involving a five-year-old who was hit by a car." McKenna gathered her things to leave and handed Tetsuro a credit card. "Use this to pay the bill and a cab. I'll meet you at home."

"I will go with you." Tetsuro returned the eating utensils to the table. He didn't take the card. "I can wait for you in the cafeteria at the hospital."

"No. You stay and finish your meal. I don't know how many hours it'll be. They'll repair internal organs first." After a caressing touch to his cheek, she stood. "I'll see you later."

"Very well."

Tetsuro watched his lady doctor hurry out with a calm dignity. Her carriage signaled that her attitude had shifted from a woman on a date to that of a consummate orthopedic surgeon. He compared it to the way he had of directing his mind to the drum when he began a performance.

Unable to face the rest of his meal without her, he waved to the waiter and called a cab. He sipped his wine as he waited. Suddenly, he was aware of his injured hand cupping the bowl of the red wine glass. The easy movement, without pain or hindrance, was something else he couldn't face.

An hour later, Tetsuro entered the silent house on Shelbourne Road, moving through it with familiarity. He placed several CDs in the player in the family room and, with the volume low, settled in the easy chair to start the novel he'd purchased the afternoon before. He discovered the mail he'd stuck inside the hardcover book. One interested him and he stuck a finger beneath the flap and ripped it open.

Takamitsu-san,

I was happy to receive your letter and learn that your hand is healing. The tour wraps up in Washington, D.C. If you are able to join us there, let me know and I will arrange your trip.

I replied to Emiko's letter seeking your whereabouts, but did not give her your address or phone number. Hers is enclosed. Hope to see you in Washington.

Restor

Tetsuro read the location. Emiko had remained in Tokyo. He folded the sheet of stationery and replaced it underneath the cover of the book. Staring into the space across the large room, he wondered why she would wish to find him *now*? And why be so persistent? She'd put an end to their lives together thirteen years ago. The hole in his heart was a souvenir of that day.

Yet the hole seemed smaller now. He'd had a hand destroyed and repaired by a love he'd found to be greater than the one he shared with Emiko. He wouldn't contact her, could not do that to McKenna. He was going to hurt her badly enough in the future. Emiko could not be another source of pain.

As he contemplated his position, Tetsuro toyed with a fifty-cent piece given to him by the physical therapist to exercise his fingers. He maneuvered the coin from digit to digit, laying it atop the end of his fingers, manipulating it with precise dexterity. He hated the way the coin moved so freely and painlessly. After several rotations, he palmed the coin and squeezed it as tightly as he could. The only pain was the pressure of the metal into his skin.

He angrily threw the coin across the room. His burst of hostility scared him and he took a deep breath, struggling for calm. To achieve tranquility, he strove to put his feelings into the form of *haiku*.

A flash of lightning
the leaves have already turned
on that old tree.

McKenna showered in the physician's lounge and dressed to return home, excited about seeing Tetsuro, even if it had only been three hours since they'd parted.

She bound into the house, throwing her purse and keys on the table as she moved through the kitchen. "Tetsu! Are you up?"

He stood to greet McKenna when she entered the family room. "*Hai.*"

"I'm glad you waited up." McKenna stepped into his embrace as if it were instinct that drew her there. She'd never had anyone at home to share her day with, but had never noticed until Tetsuro so eagerly took in every word she said.

He kissed her, then led her to the couch and they sat. "How is the little one?"

"I think he'll be all right, but he has a long road to recovery."

She snuggled against his side and he pulled her close. They caressed each other as the music from the stereo continued. His fingers kept the tempo against her shoulder. She closed her eyes and let the warmth of his love cover her.

Startled by the sound of the phone ringing, McKenna realized she'd fallen asleep. She pushed herself up as Tetsuro reached to lift the receiver from the cradle on the end table.

He handed her the phone and left the room.

"Dr. Stafford."

While she listened to the words being spoken to her, tears came to her eyes. The message was overwhelming. When Tetsuro returned to the room carrying a tray with tea, she was sobbing violently, the phone still in her hand. He placed the tray on the table and took the receiver, which buzzed loudly with a dial tone, and hung it up.

He held her in a tight embrace, allowing her to cry. "What has happened?" Minutes elapsed before she was composed enough to answer.

"The little boy died." McKenna sat away and accepted the tissue Tetsuro handed her. "There'll be an autopsy, but it was probably a fat embolus."

Tetsuro pushed her hair back from her face. "What is that?"

"A clot of fat, usually released from a break in a long bone, that goes to the lungs. It's common in children because of rapid bone growth." She blew her nose loudly and he gave her more tissue. "That was why I was called. Because of my specialty and the size of his legs. He was terribly mangled."

"Could you foresee this?"

"It happens unexpectedly and we can do nothing." The tears began again and Tetsuro held her until she was quiet. "I don't know why I'm acting like this. I've never been so emotional."

Once she composed herself, he announced, "You should have tea and go to bed."

She sat away from him and dried her eyes. "Tea?"

"Yes. I have made a special blend to help you relax."

Tetsuro turned to the tray and the iron pot sitting there. Fastidiously, he made the tea and handed her the small cup. They drank silently, each comforted by the tea and the other's presence.

"Ke-*chan*," Tetsuro broke the silence. "I have been thinking about what you told me the night we first went out."

"Yes?" McKenna raised her eyes to his. He was treading on thin ice.

"I believe your child's death has clouded your spirit. I see the sadness hidden in your eyes and I know of a way you might remove the shadows."

"Oh, you do?" McKenna sipped the hot tea. How could he know a way to obliterate the pain caused by the death of a baby from defects incompatible with life? The baby's death was a blessing but the way it had been handled had wounded her heart. Although she was the mother of the child, but also a surgical resident, her father and husband had taken over the arrangements. She had not been consulted even once. To make matters worse her husband had never comforted her. Their marriage crumbled as she struggled alone with the pain and emotions along with her residency. She could fathom anything that would alleviate the hurt.

"*Hai*. As I am Buddhist, I believe in the reincarnation of spirits. In such a belief, I am aware of a ceremony performed which allows a mother to apologize to the child she…aborted or lost by no choice of her own." Tetsuro watched McKenna's face closely. She could tell he was gauging how much further he should speak. "It is named *mizuko kuyo* or 'water children.' During the memorial service, offerings are given for the baby in the hope it will be reincarnated soon and will wait patiently, in peace, without taking revenge on the mother who was denied its arrival. It strives to tell the baby it will be welcome again."

"It sounds...nice," McKenna whispered. "*Denied its arrival.* A nice turn of a phrase, Tetsu."

"I only tell you of this in hope of showing you a way to resolve your grief." He took her hand.

"Thank you." She snuggled against him. "You make me feel...comforted."

"That is what a...friend is for," Tetsuro replied, his arm encircling her to pull her tightly next to him.

A friend? It was what a husband or lover was for. She didn't voice her thoughts. "Where would I...have this service?"

"Any Buddhist temple will provide it. I will find the nearest one."

McKenna yawned, her eyes closing.

"It is time for you to go to bed." Tetsuro brushed her forehead with his lips.

"You're right," she said but her only movement was to snuggle deeper into his embrace. The warm cocoon allowed her to forget all her cares. Never had she felt so burden-free.

McKenna barely stirred when she felt Tetsuro carry her up to the bed they shared.

CHAPTER TWENTY-NINE

Within several weeks and assisted by Mrs. Soto, Tetsuro located the Buddhist temple. Although not Buddhist herself, she was in contact with those in the Japanese community who were.

"Are you sure I'm dressed appropriately?" McKenna asked. They'd left the Jeep in the parking lot at the side of the long, low building separated from East 214th Street by only a narrow sidewalk and now made their way sedately up the steps of the temple. The area around the Zen Shin Meditation Center was stark but neat. Small yaupon hollies, precisely trimmed into spheres, were at the four corners.

Tetsuro directed his eyes over her from head to toe, taking in the knee-length gray dress, black cardigan, and low black pumps.

"*Hai*." He enfolded her hand in his strong one and the warmth crept up her arm across her shoulder, and into the center of her chest, and even into her soul. McKenna was at ease with the situation. She could handle this, with Tetsuro at her side.

"Remind me what's going to happen." He'd gone over the ritual the night before, yet she remained unsure. Buddhism was not as interchangeable as some religions. She certainly didn't want to insult his beliefs.

"The *mizuko kuyo* is a simple, private ceremony," he said as they arrived at the wooden double doors. Tetsuro paused. "We will be ushered in by the priest. Our names will be inscribed on a small wooden tablet after we pay the fee." He subtly touched his left breast and McKenna heard a crinkle.

He released her hand to open the heavy door. McKenna passed into the cool dark interior. Tetsuro followed. A soft, deep-toned chant emanated from the depths of the temple. Small prayer flags hung over the statue of Buddha and incense teased her nostrils with its unfamiliarity.

"Welcome," an orange robed young man greeted. He bowed modestly, his hands clasped before his body, his shaved head reflecting the flickering candles in the foyer.

"*Domo arigato*," Tetsuro returned the greeting and the bow. "We are here for the *mizuko kuyo*."

"Yes." The young man was standing erect now.

Without a word, Tetsuro removed a red envelope from the inside pocket of his gray suit coat. The monk received it, placing it inside the fold of his robe. McKenna had no idea how much Tetsuro was paying for her cleansing.

"If you will please follow me," the monk said.

McKenna was close on Tetsuro's heels as they walked sedately through the hallway to an isolated altar room. Before they entered the secluded room, he put a gentle hand on her arm as he removed his shoes. Understanding his signal, she did the same and they entered.

"This is the shrine of Jizo," he whispered. "He is the protector of aborted, miscarried, or stillborn infants. Also infants and children who have died."

The carved stone statue of an infantile-looking man faced them. Smaller icons adorned with red capes and bibs were around the larger one. There were several tiny stuffed animals also. More incense burned in holders. Large rectangular cushions of red and black cotton were arranged before the altar. An older priest knelt at the shrine. He could have been fifty or one hundred and fifty for all McKenna could discern. His body looked frail beneath black cotton robes and the skin on his shaved pate was wrinkled, as was his face. Yet he had a calm countenance.

Her heart pounded. What was she doing here? Would it truly help her heartache? Tetsuro gestured for her to kneel as he bent his knees easily to settle on a cushion. McKenna followed suit, resting on her stockinged heels. The priest had now turned to face them.

He uttered a greeting, followed by a blessing. He then handed Tetsuro the wooden tablet. A tray with ink and brush sat on the bare wooden floor near where he sat. He lifted the brush, dipped it into the ebony fluid, and began to write.

"What was your baby's name?" he asked McKenna. He was already writing in Japanese *kanji*.

"Sara," McKenna answered and watched the quick flicks of the brush as he made the strokes of the name. He handed the *toba* back to the priest who passed it to the young monk who'd led them to the room. The assistant set the tablet by the statues, then joined the priest to face the altar.

His words were Japanese but McKenna sensed their reverence. She bowed her head and closed her eyes. Tetsuro had told her the ritual was an internal discourse between the lost child and herself. She breathed deeply, inhaling the heavy incense, and waited for her brain to conjure up the words to apologize to Sara.

Gentle tears leaked from her closed eyelids as she mentally spoke to her baby.

A soft drumbeat, almost like the quiet, rapid beat of a baby's heart, entered the room. The beat continued while she created words for her child. The priest's chants became a repeated mantra. The drumming slowed and her heartbeat settled to the same calm beat. She lifted her eyelids enough to peek to her right. Tetsuro was the drummer. His own eyes were closed, the thick sooty lashes wet with his own tears. Did he weep for a child of his or for hers? His soft full lips were mouthing the words of the *Lotus Sutra*, words in Japanese that she didn't understand, followed by one she did.

"...Sara-*chan*."

McKenna smiled, closed her eyes, and prayed to Sara, as the drumbeat and chants lulled her despair. Through the hour, they continued. The pain of her baby's death eased and the burden on her shoulders lifted. Her soul felt lighter than she'd ever imagined it could be. With the sorrow and the spilling of her apology, another emotion filled her heart. Peace, or ease, flowed over her much as the chanting of the Buddhist priest did.

Afterwards, McKenna and Tetsuro stood alone in the hallway. The priest had offered light refreshments in the reception room but they had declined to socialize with other families who had performed their own apologies to lost infants and children. McKenna felt closer to Tetsuro than she had ever been, even after lovemaking. The ritual had been so cleansing and comforting.

"Are you all right?" Tetsuro asked once they emerged from the temple.

"Yes." She wrapped her arms around his right one and snuggled closer to his side. "You were right. It helped."

"I am glad." A gentle smile curled his lips. "It is only right I return the favor of repairing a broken part of you."

"A heart for a hand?"

"Something like that."

The breeze lifted her hair and cooled her face as they walked toward the parking lot.

"Thank you."

Several days after the *mizuko kuyo*, McKenna dressed for work and went to her dressing room for the hand cream she used daily. The intense scrubbing she did for surgery caused her skin to dry and crack if she didn't take care with her hands. Tetsuro stood in the narrow room, combing his hair. She was filled with a comfortable feeling when she reached across him to pick up the jar.

"Damn!"

Tetsuro put the comb down. "What is wrong?"

"It's a new jar and I can't get this lid off!"

"Let me try."

McKenna handed him the jar. He placed his left hand over the three-inch wide lid. She hoped the shock of seeing him his use his injured hand didn't register on her face. His knuckles turned white with effort as he tightened his grip and twisted the lid. Watching his simple act of opening a jar was the most horrifying experience of her life. Her own hand trembled as she took the opened jar.

"Thank you," she stammered. *His hand was healed and functional.*

"Are you all right?"

"Of course." But she faltered as she took a glob of cream and rubbed it into her hands. "Why shouldn't I be?" She couldn't look him in the eye.

"Because you are as pale as a *geisha*." Tetsuro placed his hand on McKenna's shoulders and turned her to face him. "Tell me."

"There's nothing…" His finger under her chin lifted her face to study her eyes. She couldn't bring herself to tell him the truth. "…wrong." She rose on tiptoe to kiss him briefly. "I'll see you this afternoon."

Afraid she'd react to the breaking of her heart, McKenna breezed past him so quickly she didn't hear Tetsuro's goodbye. All she could hear was her brain shouting, *His hand is healed!*

She drove to the hospital in a mental fog. Moving through the traffic-clogged streets, passing the tall hospital buildings rising up over the city, all she could see was Tetsuro's hand moving without difficulty. *He's well. He's ready to leave.* The words repeated over and over again in her head. She couldn't face this. It couldn't happen. Maybe if she ignored it, it *wouldn't*.

Yet she knew in her heart it was real and she'd have to face it. Stumbling into her office, she dropped into the comfortable leather chair behind her oak desk. Unable to think further than the realization that Tetsuro could abandon her at any minute, McKenna knew what she had to do.

She turned to her computer and pulled up a blank form on the screen. The cursor moved angrily across the spaces as she typed.

> *To Whom It May Concern-*
> *This is to advise you that*
> *Tetsuro Takamitsu is released*
> *from my care effective this date.*

She printed the form.

Tears clouded her vision as she signed her name. Placing it in an envelope, she left her office and went to that of the physical therapist.

"Good morning, Dr. Stafford," Paul said.

"Hello. How are you?" McKenna began small talk to avoid the reason for her visit.

"Okay, but you don't look so great. Got a cold?"

"Allergies," she said, explaining away the red eyes and running nose. "Ah…could you give this to Mr. Takamitsu when he comes in for therapy?" She held the envelope out to him, reluctant to let go of it. "It's his medical release."

Paul didn't attempt to take it. "He doesn't come anymore."

"Excuse me?"

"*I* released him two weeks ago. Didn't he tell you?"

"No." McKenna retracted the envelope. Now how could she do this? She couldn't face Tetsuro. Why hadn't he told her?

"He still comes down to use the gym. I could give it to him then." Paul held out his hand.

"Later would be…all right." McKenna handed the envelope over. Her eyes clouded once more.

"Here." He gave her a tissue after he took the letter.

"Looks like that allergy's acting up. Must be the dust in here."

"Yes." She wiped her nose. "Must be. Bye." She hurried away so she would not fall apart in front of the physical therapist.

She saw patients the rest of the day, filling her hours with routine. Easily distracted, she needed Greg to remind her what she was doing. Lunch passed and she couldn't recall what she eaten. Or if she had.

"Rebecca," she spoke by phone to her housekeeper. "Is Mr. Takamitsu home?… No! I don't wish to speak with him. Give him a message. I've a late case and probably won't be home until ten or eleven. He shouldn't wait up for me." The words hurt her throat and she was forced to cough. "Thanks." She replaced the receiver.

Her next call was to Claire Ikuta.

"Hi," she spoke softly. "I need a favor."

CHAPTER THIRTY

Richard Soto watched his teacher demonstrating how to achieve a different tone to the drum.

"You're drumming pretty well, *sensei.*"

"It is getting easier." Tetsuro tightened his grip and released it. He studied his hand as if it were someone else's.

"Does it hurt?"

"A little stiff only. Now, you repeat what I played."

Richard replicated the piece.

"Well done," Tetsuro complimented the boy. He enjoyed watching him learn. A sense of accomplishment and pride filled him.

"Wow! That's the first time you've told me I was doing well." Richard's face beamed in response to the praise.

"Teachers in Japan never compliment even their best students. If we are good, we are encouraged to do better. We know we are poor students if they do not push. In your case, it is well deserved praise." Tetsuro touched the boy's shoulder. "This is our last lesson. I will be leaving in a few days. I have some song pages, and will see if I can find a *taiko* teacher to continue your lessons."

"*Domo arigato gozaimasu, Sensei Takamitsu.*"

Tetsuro noticed the boy's attempt to bow and returned it.

Tetsuro left Richard and walked into the backyard of the large, old house. He wondered if Mrs. Soto had tried to recreate the Japan of her youth with the landscape and foliage. Tall cedar trees lined the borders and a small fishpond sat in the farthest corner surrounded by large rocks and lush grasses. Azaleas, hostas and chrysanthemums grew profusely with other greenery whose names Tetsuro didn't know. Large trees shaded the yard, giving it the illusion of isolation. He sat in the open area designed for watching the orange, gold, and black *koi* swim through their clear waters and reflected on his life.

He was an *uchite*. *Taiko* had been his life since he was a teen. It was all he had until he'd given his heart to Emiko. Because she was a performer also, she'd given him a glance at what his life could have been, *taiko* and family joined symbiotically, if only for an instant. His heart ached each time he recalled how close he'd come to achieving his goal. Now he was risking heartbreak once more. *Karma* did not hold a family in his future. Taiko Nihon and its members was the only family he'd have.

Cleveland was an illusion, a dream that would vanish into the mists. The time had come to say Goodbye to McKenna, and he knew how he would do it. But could he?

His thoughts came together.

The hosta blossoms…
how far away from the leaves
their trumpets sway.

"Come on in," Claire Ikuta opened the door for McKenna. "Tell me what's going on!"

"I'll tell you everything, but first," McKenna entered the foyer and hugged her friend, "I need to change clothes."

They walked upstairs and Claire showed her into the guest room. "You can sleep here."

"Thanks for agreeing to do this." McKenna crossed to the closet to find the clothes she'd asked Rebecca to take to Claire's. Now that she'd arrived, she moved in slow motion. The afternoon had crept by like molasses in winter while she made phone calls, planning her escape. She would not let Tetsuro hurt her. Even though the center of her chest was going to explode if she never saw him again, surely the pain would go away.

"Are you hungry? Do you want to talk first or eat?"

"Talk." McKenna unzipped her skirt and let it drop to the floor. Food was the last thing on her mind. She needed to talk to Tetsuro, but she'd have to settle for Claire. "Let's take a walk."

"I'll go change shoes." Claire left McKenna to finish dressing.

The two women met downstairs and left the house. The cool autumn weather greeted them with yellow, orange, and brown fallen leaves, and chrysanthemums blossoming brightly in the yards they passed. Buckeyes, crisp leaves and acorns crunched under their shoes.

After they'd struck out on their walk down Monmouth, Claire prompted, "So?"

"Tetsuro's going back to Japan," McKenna tried to make her answer sound matter of fact.

"When?"

"I don't know." She added a shoulder roll to make a feeble attempt of indifference.

"Then how do you know he's leaving?"

"Because his hand's well and I gave him his release form." She looked everywhere but at her friend.

"What did he say when you gave it to him?"

"He didn't say anything." She rolled her eyes upward to hold the tears starting to fill them. Crying was the last thing she wanted to do.

"He took the form and didn't say a thing?" Claire repeated.

"I don't…know what he said when he got the form. He probably doesn't even have it yet." She sighed deeply, pushing the tears further back.

"McKenna, I'm don't want to have to pry each word out of you. Tell me what you did."

McKenna lowered her gaze to the sidewalk and her vision cleared. "I gave it to Paul in physical therapy and he's going to give it to him when he comes in tomorrow. I can't face him. I'm afraid of what he'd say."

"You big chicken!" Claire took her hand. "You have to give him a chance to tell you *something*. What if he wants to tell you he's staying?"

"There's nothing for him in Cleveland. His life is in Japan." She clenched Claire's fingers tightly, holding on to keep her composure.

"You're here. Maybe he wants to stay with you."

"He doesn't."

"Are you sure?"

"No but…we both said when we started that it wouldn't be forever. I agreed to suffer the cost. I wanted to be with him that badly." McKenna swallowed with difficulty, her head down. "I love him, Claire."

"I know." Claire embraced McKenna gently. When she released her, they walked in silence for a block. Then Claire pulled several pieces of paper out of her jacket pocket. "I didn't want to burden you with this, but I can't keep it to myself."

McKenna took them.

"I got it off the Internet. It's from the show biz paper in Japan. Like *Variety*. It's old, about thirteen years, I think. I thought you might be interested."

McKenna read the article as they strolled down the street. Occasionally she raised her eyes to make sure she wasn't about to step into traffic although sure Claire wouldn't let that happen. The article explained how, while at a nightclub, Tetsuro Takamitsu had been seen in a fistfight with a man known only as Emiko's escort. After landing several punches, Tetsuro was pulled away from the man, who left with Emiko.

"I guess that was when he hurt his hand once before," McKenna said. "After the Breathing Room concert, we went backstage and I met the band. The drummer was drunk and made a comment about him breaking his finger. I guess it was the right since I didn't see any healed fractures on the x-ray of his left. The Japanese press must like gossip as much as we do."

"They do. Kentaro has always had a problem with the media," Claire agreed.

"This fight must have been something on the order of our rowdy actors and their brawls."

"I've been to that nightclub. It's in Tokyo on the *Ginza*. Very nice place. They wouldn't take too well to fight." When McKenna handed the papers back to her, Claire asked, "Did you know about that?"

"I didn't about the fight, but I know about Emiko. I asked him about her when I found her name written on a piece of paper." McKenna hoped Claire didn't ask her *where* she'd found such a paper.

"What did he say?"

"That she was someone he used to know and it was over. He didn't give any clue as to why he would get into a fight with her date." They came to a corner and made a right turn.

"The article gives the impression that he left the drum school without permission," Claire commented. "They're serious about the students who study *taiko*, almost like when someone joins the priesthood or military. You can't run away from boot camp and Nakano Island goes by the same rules. Thirteen years ago, he wasn't one of the stars. He was under house rules. They'd have restricted his performances if they didn't throw him out. His punishment would have been for six months or more."

"Not being allowed to tour for any time must have been hard. But his inner discipline is so great the extra practice and physical exercise were probably fun for him." A smile teased at McKenna's lips with the thought of the rock hard body Tetsuro's discipline had created.

"So, he's not going to return to Japan to a woman or a family," Claire pointed out. "You might be surprised to find out he's planning to stay with you. If you give him a chance."

"Claire, he's a traditional Japanese drummer. That's the only thing he's ever done, the only thing he knows how to do. I wouldn't mind supporting him, but I can't tell him that. He's got his pride. A *samurai's* pride. No, Claire, it's not going to work out and I can't let my heart be hurt any further."

The women came to Arabica's Coffee.

"Let's get a cup," Claire suggested. They entered, ordered and settled at a small table. "What are you planning to do now?"

"I'm going to stay with you until I'm sure he's gone."

"Oh, that's mature." Claire took a drink from her mug. "Big smart doctor and really dumb woman." Her comment was made in jest.

"It's not smart, but I can't do anything else. My heart won't let me." McKenna tasted her cocoa, smearing whipped cream over her upper lip. "If you'll let me."

"Kentaro's on a road trip and Mother and Daddy are in Vegas for an oncology convention. I'll be glad for the company." She handed McKenna a paper napkin and wordlessly indicated she should wipe her mouth. "What about your patients? Surgery? What about your call rotation?"

"I took a leave of absence. You're the only one who knows where I am and you're not going to tell. Are you?"

"Are you sure about this?"

"Claire, I know he's not going to hurt me on purpose, but eventually I'm going to be hurt. I have to get myself together without worrying about Tetsuro appearing and destroying all the resolve I've mustered. He's taking part of my heart with him, a part I'm glad to give him, so it may take me a long time to heal. Maybe I'll never feel whole, but I have to try. I'm going to do it on my terms."

"McKenna," Claire touched her friend's arm. "I wish things could be different."

"I do, too, but I entered the agreement with my eyes open. I just didn't realize it would hurt so much." She sighed deeply. "All of my life men have let me down or broken my heart. They've never been there when I needed them. Not this time. If my heart's going to break, I'm going to do the breaking." She wiped at her eyes with a napkin and pulled her emotions together. "You won't tell him where I am, will you?"

"No," Claire answered softly.

Blind to McKenna's leaving, Tetsuro went to the physical therapy department the next morning for his usual workout. After Rebecca gave him McKenna's message, he'd returned to his rented room at Mrs. Soto's for the night. An early morning drummer lesson with Richard kept him away from the hospital until late morning. He hadn't called McKenna, afraid his call would wake her after a long night in surgery.

"Good morning, Mr. Takamitsu," Paul greeted him.

"Good morning." Tetsuro began loading the weight bar with additional weight.

"Dr. Stafford dropped this off yesterday. I told her I would give it to you this morning." Paul offered the envelope to Tetsuro.

For long seconds Tetsuro stared at the long white envelope with his name written in McKenna's hand across the face. Intuitively he knew his freedom was in that slim packet. His ticket home to Japan. His backstage pass to performing. His liberty to go where he pleased or didn't please. His emancipation from slavery to his rehabilitation. His independence from his doctor.

He didn't want it.

As though putting his hand in the mouth of a dragon, Tetsuro reached for it. His fingers wrapped around the paper-thin envelope and Paul released it into his grip. The paper burned his fingertips and he wanted to fling it across the room, deny he ever saw it, much less held it.

He didn't.

As if reading his thoughts, Paul said, "Now you can go home."

"Yes." Tetsuro nodded toward the physical therapist. "Home."

"Bet it will be nice to get back to reality." Paul had no way of knowing how painful the conversation was.

"I will have a lot of work to do to get ready for performing." Tetsuro's mind was not on drumming. The beat of his heart, rapid and tender as it faced separation from McKenna, was the only drumming he was aware of. "Have you seen Dr. Stafford today?"

"No. Like I said, she left that yesterday. We did get a memo about her being out of the office. Her associate's taking her patients. I guess she's taking a last vacation before she takes on the responsibility of chief of orthopedics."

"Yes. That is possibly what is happening." He couldn't very well tell the young man their private business. "She is a very respected physician."

"Yes, she is. Ah, I hate to break it to you, but since she's released you, I can't let you come to the gym anymore. Regulations. You're no longer a patient."

"Very well." Tetsuro turned to his towel and water bottle. McKenna's life was moving on without him. He needed to do the same.

"You are free to finish your workout today. I'm gonna miss seeing you." Paul shook his hand, then returned to his office.

Tetsuro threw his leg over the bench and lay back. He gripped the bar tightly, his mind not on the weight he was about to bench press. The bar lifted without effort and he held it poised over his chest. All he could see was McKenna as she had lain over him, her bare satiny, cocoa breasts brushing against his chest. All at once the iron bar was resting on his chest and he struggled to find the strength to replace it in the rack.

He had to find McKenna.

Tetsuro began searching for McKenna, unaware of the grail-like quest he embarked on. He arrived at the house on Shelbourne to find Rebecca alone. The young Amish woman welcomed the Japanese drummer and offered him tea that he declined.

"Is Dr. McKenna expected soon?" He fidgeted in the straight chair at the kitchen table.

"I do not think so, sir." Rebecca didn't miss a beat as she put away the clean dishes. "She has left the house for a awhile. I have a note with things to do, but it does not say when she will be back."

"Thank you, Miss Rebecca." He stood and left McKenna's house.

Tetsuro returned to Mrs. Soto's house, intent on continuing the plans he'd decided on. Days passed, days he filled with shopping, and phone calls to John Restor, the agent for the drum troupe, to set up travel times and hotel arrangements. Moving through the details, his heart was heavy. Desperate to relieve himself of the burden, he decided to make a last ditch effort to find his heart.

CHAPTER THIRTY-ONE

Claire burst into the guest room and jerked the drapes open allowing sunlight to fill the room.

"Come on, McKenna. We're going to Baltimore."

Beneath the comforter in the four-poster bed, McKenna turned over and stretched. "Why are we going anywhere?"

"Kentaro's pitching tomorrow and he wants us to join him on the road. He also has tickets to a play tonight." Claire sat on the side of the bed. "Were you asleep?"

"No. I was reading. For the first time in years, I have no reason to get up."

"That was what you said three weeks ago." Claire pushed away the hair dangling over McKenna's face. "You could go back to work."

"What if I don't want to go?" McKenna didn't know if she meant work or to Baltimore. She pulled the comforter over her head. "I'll be a third wheel between you and Kentaro."

"All you've done is sleep. And eat. Without exercise, you're going to get as big as a house. You've already put on a few pounds." Claire patted her rear.

McKenna lowered the cover long enough to say, "Thanks a lot!"

"It's not healthy. You can't retreat into yourself like this." Claire pulled the comforter down to look her in the face. "You'd say the same thing to your patients."

"That's just it." McKenna sat up, tugging the bedclothes around her. "I don't want to have a patient or be concerned with them. I'm not sure I want to be a doctor anymore."

"Are you going to quit?'

"I need time to think, to decide what I want to do. If I weren't a doctor, I'd never have met Tetsuro. Never have fallen in love so deeply. Never had my heart broken so badly."

"You can't blame that on being a doctor."

"I blame it on my father. If not for his pushing, I'd never have entered medicine. Don't get me wrong. I like putting people back together. Seeing them get better. I'm just burned out."

"You're not burned out. You're depressed. And it's your fault. You ran away from Tetsuro. You didn't give him a chance. Now it's time for you to get out of the bed you've made and get on with life."

McKenna sighed as if a great weight had been lifted from her shoulders. "I guess I'll let you drag me away."

In the first class section on the plane headed toward Baltimore, McKenna spoke to her friend beside her. "You're mean."

"Why's that?" Claire flipped distractedly through a magazine.

"Because you're making me do this." McKenna laid her head back against the seat and closed her eyes. For the last two weeks she'd had a dull headache and was at times dizzy. On top of everything else, the movement of the plane made her nauseous.

"I can't be accused of being mean because I want you to get on with your life." Claire closed the magazine. "I'm the one who left her child for the first time since she was born."

"You're right, but I still think you're mean."

"What I want is for you to be happy and have a good time. I don't have anyone to hang out with on road trips, except other wives, and having a friend along will give me someone to do things with. Kentaro thought it would be fun, too. That's why he accepted the play tickets."

"I feel horrible," McKenna commented, tilting her head back on the headrest. The plane's engine hum rumbled in her skull. "I'll try to be a good companion. That's all I can promise. To try."

"And that's all I'll ask of you."

When the plane reached the gate, McKenna asked, "Why are we in Washington, DC?"

"Ah," Claire stuttered and looked out the window of the plane. "It was the only place Kentaro could get rooms for us. He's picky about where I stay. And the play's here."

McKenna rubbed her stomach. "I shouldn't have eaten that airline food."

"It was bad, wasn't it?" Claire picked up her purse and jacket. "We have to get a cab. Kentaro's got practice and as soon as we get to the hotel we have to get ready for the play. We'll get dinner after."

The women made their way through the airport. They'd packed only carry-ons and a garment bag so they weren't burdened with waiting for their luggage. A trip to the taxi stand found them transportation to the hotel. Claire hurried McKenna through the lobby after a brief stop at the desk for room keys.

At the door to her room, Claire told McKenna, "You grab a shower and get all pretty."

"Don't know why I should bother getting pretty," McKenna mumbled trudging down the hall.

"Just go! We're going to be late as it is," Claire ordered. "Come back here when you're finished."

"Aye, aye, captain!" McKenna entered her room.

After hastily undressing, McKenna stood in the shower beneath the torrent of hot water. Because they were so rushed in their preparations that she wouldn't have time to wash and dry her hair, she'd piled high on her head and covered it with a plastic shower cap. She didn't know whom Claire thought she needed to get dressed up for.

The soap she lathered over her body cascaded in a bubbly stream over her slender curves. She let her fingers play over the slippery surface of her skin. Claire was right. She had gained weight. Not much, but enough for her knowledgeable fingers to perceive. She hoped her dress fit.

There was little to worry about. The folds of crimson crushed velvet hugged her shoulders in the cap-sleeved bodice with a neckline dipping into a 'V' between her full breasts. The dress was close to her sides at her hips, flaring then into an a-line skirt. Caressing her legs at her knees, it swung gently with her moves.

Applying a last touch of makeup, she ran a brush through her hair, which draped over her neck and shoulders. She'd pulled the top back to the crown and held it with a clip. Full, curved bangs brushed her forehead.

When she returned moments later to Claire's room, she asked, "How's this?"

"Perfect." Claire smeared lipstick over her mouth. "Ready?"

"Sure." She picked up purse and coat. "What play are we going to see?"

"I...don't know. Taro didn't tell me." Claire closed the door behind her. "He should be downstairs with a limo."

"A limo?" She walked briskly to keep up with Claire, her heels making clicky sounds as they stepped into the tiled elevator.

"We thought we'd be fancy. To cheer you up."

The men they passed in the lobby cast captivated looks toward them. Kentaro Ikuta met them outside the lobby.

As they slipped into the backseat, he said, "You ladies look lovely."

"Thank you," the women replied.

The driver merged into the busy traffic of Washington and McKenna became excited about the evening out. Having been to Washington before, she always found it a new adventure. She longed to have Tetsuro at her side to share the experience of her nation's capital.

The limo pulled up to a side entrance of Lincoln Center. Other cars moved around in controlled chaos, and people walked briskly across the streets to enter the theater. When the limo stopped, Kentaro helped the women out and they walked to the side door. An Asian man spoke to Kentaro in what McKenna recognized vaguely as Japanese. He opened the door and led them through the dark hallway to their seat in the auditorium. The seats were perfect, front row, center.

She whispered, "What are you up to, Claire?"

"What makes you think I'm up to something?"

"This is all too suspicious. And you haven't looked me in the eye since the plane landed."

Before Claire could, or would, answer, the lights dimmed and the curtain rose. McKenna's hand rose to her mouth and her eyes clouded with tears.

At the front of the stage, Tetsuro Takamitsu stood behind a waist-high drum. For all she knew, he stood there alone because McKenna was oblivious to anything else. Her heart sounded wildly in her ears as her gaze traveled up from his bare feet, over the black cotton pants to the familiar black and white *hanten* tied with a black cloth belt. His movements caused the shirt which was crossed right over left on his wide chest and shoulders to gap, giving her a glimpse of his firm skin at the cross point. His raven hair was in a small, curved ponytail, low on his nape, and a white canvas headband held it securely as he looked down, intent on the drumhead.

In his hands were the sticks he'd use to play. He raised them slightly and began the beats. The rhythm dropped into a gentle wave of strokes between his hands, then was abruptly joined by his voice issuing short tonal sounds to indicate rhythm changes to his partners who merged their beats with his.

Now his eyes, the laughing, oblong eyes, were directed her way and she was drawn into them. Her breath caught in her throat when he smiled. She had to press her hand against her lips to keep from calling out to him. Claire clutched her arm as if sensing her urge to rush the stage. Her arm curled around her waist as a wave of excitement induced nausea rose to her throat.

The piece continued. The men kept up the singsong shouts to one another, evidence of their joy in drumming.

When Tetsuro finished and left the stage, she could finally breathe.

Had she really held her breath for the long period he performed the first piece? Tears seeped down her cheeks..

"You should have warned me."

"Then you'd have stayed in Cleveland."

"When did you plan this?"

"I didn't, but I agreed with it. He called Kentaro and they set it up," Claire explained.

McKenna barely relaxed before Tetsuro and several other drummers returned. Tetsuro moved over the stage in a dance that, to McKenna, seemed extemporaneous. As the performance continued, her gaze followed only Tetsuro. He was absent from the fourth number, but returned for the fifth with a flute that he played with the same skill as his drum. The fingers of both hands tapped over the holes faultlessly.

The sixth song brought the emotions of first seeing him back to McKenna's chest. It began with Tetsuro and two men playing a soft rhythm on medium-sized drums suspended from their shoulders by wide leather straps. Others played large, stationery drums. Another three instruments were set at the front of the stage, resting unattended on angled stands.

Halfway into the piece, Tetsuro and his fellows put down the drums they carried and, in a motion reminiscent of the Chippendale dancers, removed their cotton pants with a quick jerk. Their shirts followed. Left clad only in white silk cloths wrapped tightly around their hips, the three men took their posts at the angled drums, lying beneath them with their bare feet hooked under the stands.

Tetsuro lay flat, his hands holding heavy sticks, until, abruptly, he lifted his upper body off the floor and, holding himself erect with superb abdominal strength, pounded the drum with a vigorous beat. His legs were extended, braced under the drum stand. The effort all three men used to hold their bodies up and play at the same time was reflected on their faces. From her close proximity, McKenna could see the sweat rolling back into Tetsuro's hair. She held her breath in sympathetic agony. To McKenna, this lasted number forever.

Finally, it was over and she could exhale.

During the encores, Tetsuro positioned himself in front of McKenna, even winking at her as he took his final bow. He was dressed, but the wide expanse of his chest was erotically evident with his *hanten* flapping open. A small part deep within her abdomen responded with a pinch. He disappeared with the troupe, and McKenna was left with an ache in her body and soul.

The crowd, reluctant to depart, continued with sporadic applause.

"Is he coming out here?" McKenna asked Claire.

"I honestly don't know. This is as far as his instructions went, except for your return flight in the morning."

Before McKenna could respond, the Asian man who had ushered them through the side door appeared with paper-wrapped flowers. Wordlessly, he handed them to McKenna and departed.

McKenna's hand trembled as she opened the envelope. She found a card with a short note in Tetsuro's exquisite hand.

> *Ke-chan,*
> *Please join me here tomorrow night at nine.*
> *Tetsu*

She recognized the Cleveland address.

"Well?" Claire urged, having read over McKenna's shoulder.

"I'll meet him and give him the opportunity to either make my life perfect or break my heart completely." She raised the note and inhaled the trace of his scent.

The next morning was spent traveling. She felt as if a million butterflies danced in the pit of her stomach. McKenna tried to sleep to ignore her queasiness. She'd declined the Ikutas' invitation to a late dinner after the performance and, once in bed, hadn't slept well. Her thoughts and dreams had been crowded with Tetsuro. Claire had accompanied her to the airport, then remained in Washington to join Kentaro.

A DRUMMER'S BEAT TO MEND

At home in Cleveland, she napped. For the past week, it had been as if she couldn't sleep enough. Before she was to meet Tetsuro, she made herself eat a late afternoon meal, then left for the rendezvous.

CHAPTER THIRTY-TWO

At a stately old but well-kept house, a note was tacked onto the front door with instructions for McKenna to enter the backyard through the side gate. Inside, another note on the mudroom door told her to change clothes. A silk kimono, deep pink with muted embroidery, lay neatly on a stool with empty coat hangers for her Western dress. The kimono was simple to put on without cumbersome layers or *obi*.

Returning to the garden, she followed the stone pathway. The stepping-stones were smooth and, even though there had been neither rain nor dew, were splashed with water. She came to the end and ducked beneath a low living arch of vines to emerge in an idyllic spot, wide and secluded, before a *koi* pond.

There, Tetsuro knelt on a *tatami* mat wearing a kimono identical to hers. His hair was down except that the top was pulled back and tied at the crown. His face was solemn.

As she knelt in front of him, she breathed, "Tetsu, have you decided to…"

"Ssssh." Tetsuro placed an affectionate finger to her lips. "We have much to discuss but first, we will take tea." He pulled his hand back and waved at the table between them. "You once asked if I knew the *chanoyu*, and I answered with a lie. I did not know you well enough to know you meant no disrespect with the request. Now, I shall honor you with a tea ceremony because you honor me and my culture."

McKenna sat in silence. The hundreds of words rushing through her brain would remain unsaid. *Why was she there? What did he want of her? What was he willing to give her in return? Did they have a future or was this an end?* All these questions sang loudly while she sat in repose with her hands folded in her lap, watching Tetsuro move through the ancient ritual of tea.

First, he rose to his feet in the most elegant way McKenna had ever seen anyone rise from a kneeling position. The movement began with a forward roll to rest on his knees and position his feet so his toes were bent to push his body up when he rocked backward. He was then standing and went to a fire with an iron cauldron. Using his kimono sleeve, he picked up the kettle and moved it to the table. He then knelt once more, the elegant movement reversed.

Overcome with emotion, McKenna dabbed her eyes with her kimono sleeve while he cleaned the already pristine tea bowl. He ladled hot water into the bowl then wiped it using a fine silk cloth that he folded and handled as though afraid he would hurt the fibers. He cleaned the tea whisk and scoop, both made of bamboo. Lifting the lid off the tea container, he dipped the scoop into it and placed three portions into the bowl. Hot water was ladled in until he had enough for a thin paste. This he stirred together. Adding more water, he whisked it into a pea soup liquid.

With a bow of his head, Tetsuro lifted the bowl in both hands and presented it to McKenna, as though handing her a rare gift. She raised her hands, cupping them around his for an instant before he released the hot bowl into her palms. It was then his turn to caress her hands. He held them firmly for long seconds as his gaze studied hers.

"*Tanoshimu,*" he whispered. "Enjoy," he translated.

McKenna lifted the bowl to her lips and tasted the hot elixir. She then handed the bowl to Tetsuro who drank from it also.

When he placed the bowl on the table, he said, "The *chayano* is a ceremony representing *yin* and *yang*."

He set the table aside and moved nearer McKenna. His knees touched hers and he took her hands in his. "It is used to bring balance between two people. In the past, it joined families, destroyed hostilities between enemies, fashioned alliances between *samurai*." He studied her face intently. "Ke-*chan*, I have selected the most Japanese of ways to tell you Goodbye. If we must part, I wish tonight to be one of joining. Should you not agree, please feel free to depart now with my warmest wishes."

"I cannot leave you, Tetsu." Tears were in her voice as she clutched his hands. No longer were questions sounding in her brain. She could think no further than his words.

"Yet we must part. We knew our short time was made longer only because I refused to recognize my healing. Last night, I experienced the renewing of the joy of *taiko*. I must return to what feeds my soul, Ke-*chan*, as you must continue to do as yours leads."

"I don't want you to." McKenna's hair swayed across her shoulders as she shook her head.

Tetsuro's cupped a hand around her cheek for an instant. "Nor do I wish to leave."

"Then," she reached to take his hand, "why?"

"You know as I do. Our paths diverge here. But we shall have tonight. Come."

Tetsuro pulled her into his arms and McKenna curled against his chest as his hands caressed her. Her hands slipped between the folds of his kimono and stroked the smooth skin of his chest. As more of his skin was exposed, she kissed him, her tongue tasting the broad, male breast, teasing the nipple firm.

Lowering his mouth to hers, Tetsuro's tongue parted her lips. The touch of his hands and mouth sent powerful warmth through her body. She responded by caressing his body and exploring his mouth in the same manner he did hers. The evening's breeze was cool on her body as he removed her kimono and folded it down her back to the ground. She pushed the silk off his shoulders and it pooled around his hips.

Savoring the essence of her skin, Tetsuro took great care to cover her body with intense kisses. McKenna succumbed to the sensations escaping on the surges of passion until he rose to cover her body with his and filled her with his special beat, a rhythm her soul matched effortlessly. As the pulse of their hearts joined the tempo of their passion, they shuddered with the rush of climax and clutched desperately to one another in the darkness of the night.

"Tetsu," McKenna's voice was soft on the night's air, "don't leave."

"I must, Ke-*chan*." His breath was warm against her neck. He rolled to his back. Pulling her atop of him, he held her tightly to his chest.

"No," she whispered, her voice full of tears.

"Do not worry." Tetsuro stroked her hair out of her face. "We have a night to share. Let us fill it with only happy tears."

Tetsuro began touching McKenna once more, and she followed him higher and higher on the rhythm of desire.

McKenna woke beneath the warmth of a soft quilt Tetsuro had covered them with deep into the night and their passion. Water lapped gently against the lush edges of the pond and the fish moved up to the surface, flipping their tails in an angry slap when they found no food. A gentle wind filled with the scent of sweet flowers moved high in the cedar trees. She stretched in a languid movement, tender from Tetsuro's touch, and smiled at the memory of the night. She turned to greet him.

"Tetsu…"

She was alone.

Or was she? There was movement at the entrance of the garden and a short, round Japanese woman emerged.

McKenna grabbed the edges of her kimono and held it to her body. With her other hand, she groped for the quilting. "Who…are you?"

"I'm Mary Soto. This is my home." The woman came to McKenna. "I'm also Takamitsu-*san's* friend." She knelt on the ground with a grace McKenna thought would not have been possible by a woman of her obvious age. "He asked me to prepare breakfast and to give you this." She offered an envelope.

"I'll pass on the food." When McKenna sat more upright, the movement caused her to be queasy. "If you'll excuse me." She made to put the kimono on.

"Certainly." Mrs. Soto lowered her eyes to give McKenna privacy to dress.

"I'll take that letter now." McKenna accepted the envelope.

"You may use my house for your needs," Mrs. Soto offered. "Until then, I'll leave you." She left the area.

McKenna slipped a lavender card from the envelope and read the one word Tetsuro had written in both English and Japanese, a word that caused her heart to fracture into painful pieces.

Sayonara

CHAPTER THIRTY-THREE

"Oh, no," McKenna sighed. She sat at her desk in her office and stared at the plastic stick resting on a paper towel. If she stared at it long enough, the results would fade.

"Yeah, it'll fade," she spoke aloud, "in about nine months."

Three days later her gynecologist assured her. "Oh, yes. You're pregnant. About ten weeks, I'd say."

McKenna lay on the exam table in the darkened sonogram room and tolerated the uncomfortable pressure on her lower abdomen as the probe reflected what grew in her uterus. A tiny speck moved in the dark void. A faint flicker evidenced its heartbeat.

The rhythm of Tetsuro.

"So, that's the situation." McKenna sat back against the chair and looked across the lunch table at James. "I'll be an unwed mother unless you're willing to help me."

"I don't understand why you care." James stirred his coffee. "This is the twenty-first century. People don't care much about things like that. And you know that most of society thinks it's standard procedure for black women to have babies without fathers."

"I'll not be a stereotype. My mother drilled that into my head every day of my life." She sipped from her tea glass. Leila's words came back to haunt her. "As a professional, it wouldn't be very prudent. Especially since I take the post of chief of ortho next month."

"It'll be very obvious I'm not the baby's father when it's born."

"Not necessarily. There're a few African Americans with Asian features. But people'll overlook that. To have a ring on my finger and a marriage license will make it more palatable to my patients."

"I'm curious. Why me?" As he leaned back in his chair, James templed his fingers over his paunch of a stomach. The intensity of his stare was palpable. The steel of his CPA eyes was cold and analytical.

Why indeed. Why had she decided to ask James to marry her? And why ask *anyone*?

"You and I have an easy relationship. We're comfortable," she tried to explain. "I need…or think I need, a father for my baby. But maybe it's a husband for me."

"That's more accurate. This baby has a father. Have you told him?" His dark eyes squinted at her, his heavy eyebrows furrowing together.

"No. Tetsuro's life is in Japan. For him to return because of a baby is not fair to either of us. He'd have to give up the vocation of his life and would come to resent me. As he became a house husband, I'd resent him."

"And you don't think that'll happen with us?"

"I hope not, but…"

"You wouldn't see it as painful," James finished.

"Not exactly." McKenna was certain James was capable of reading her thoughts. The gentle pinch in her pelvis that came at intervals distracted her from the disturbing conversation. Her hand caressed her lower abdomen comfortingly. She didn't remember much from her obstetrics class, especially the part about pregnancy causing cramping. Maybe it wasn't normal. She'd have to check with her obstetrician.

James acquiesced to her proposal. "When do you want to do this?"

"Next month? We'll have things arranged by then. Your lawyer and mine will have the pre-nuptial papers drawn up. And you'll have time to back out if you decide you don't want to go through with it."

"Mac," James took her hand, "your proposal is so romantic, I have to accept." His craggy face molded itself into the semblance of a smile.

"I didn't know any other way to present it. It's just a…oh, God, a marriage of convenience!" McKenna laughed. "I didn't know they still existed!"

"Finally, you smile. That makes it worth it. Yes, McKenna Stafford, I will marry you."

"Thank you, James Russell." McKenna forced herself to sit up and kiss him across the table.

"So you conned James into marrying you." Claire sat at McKenna's kitchen table over coffee and cake.

"Sure did." McKenna had prepared a light supper and invited Claire over to discuss wedding plans.

"I don't see how you did it."

"You know James. He's always been a friend. Since his mother died, he's been at loose ends, so to speak." McKenna stood and began to clear the table. "It works for us."

"Well, I'm not going to try and tell you what to do." Claire rose and helped McKenna attend to the dishes. "Does James know you don't have any furniture?"

"I *have* furniture," McKenna replied emphatically. She turned and planted her hands on the sink behind her. "What do you think you just ate on?"

"But the rest of the house?"

"Well, most of it *is* gone. The auction house has taken all but this, my bedroom, and the family room, along with all the bric-a-brac."

"Your family didn't want anything?"

"They got some stuff. I had to ship it to them. They're so angry with me they wouldn't come get it."

They rinsed the dishes and placed them into the dishwasher.

Claire walked toward the front door. "Have you had any offers for the house?"

"The real estate agent said it'll be hard to sell because of the price. He suggested I try to make it a school or something like that since it's so big." McKenna opened the closet and removed Claire's coat.

"That's a good idea. However, your neighbors will be furious."

"Probably. I haven't told James about selling the house."

"He shouldn't have much of a say about it."

McKenna helped her into the coat. "I hate to be rude, rushing you off like this, but I've got to go to bed. I have early surgery. I usually schedule surgeries for afternoons because of my morning sickness but it didn't work out this time."

"You just want to get rid of me." Claire gave her a hug.

"No, I'm just tired."

"You're pregnant. I'll go and you can get to bed."

"I'll talk to you tomorrow."

The women said good night and parted. McKenna locked the door and went upstairs.

McKenna rose from her bent position over the ankle of one of Cleveland State University's track stars. She stretched the small of her back. The surgery had been long and tedious

"You okay, Dr. Stafford?" the circulating nurse asked.

"I'm tired and hungry." McKenna wondered if the frequent pinches in her abdomen showed on her face. They were getting closer and more painful. "Will you put the dressing on without me?"

"Sure." The nurse pulled blue paper drapes from the operative site.

McKenna stepped back and began to remove her gown and gloves. The pain in her abdomen still nagged, making her back hurt and her stomach nauseous. Food, the immediate thought seconds ago, was out of the question now. She walked to the patient's head.

As Leslie Furumiya worked over the patient, she whispered into the anesthesiologist's ear, "Could you come check on me in the physician's lounge when you finish?"

"As soon as I get him to recovery."

McKenna left the operating room. She pulled the paper hat and mask off and made her way to the lounge.

The room where doctors changed for surgery or merely relaxed was empty. McKenna went into the bathroom, intent on emptying her entirely too full bladder. As she untied the string of her scrub pants, a cramp in her abdomen caught her off guard and she bent double. Bracing herself on the sink, she managed to pull off her scrubs. Blood saturated the stride. In one motions she tugged down her panties and sat on the toilet.

"God, no!" she screamed when she glimpsed the bloody mass in her panties.

"McKenna?" Leslie called.

"Here," McKenna managed. Pain of both body and heart made it a struggle to speak.

In a fog, she sensed Leslie kneeling beside her. She had no idea how she'd come to lie curled on her side on the hard tile floor or how long she'd been there.

"Oh, my God!" Leslie's hands moved over McKenna's body in the standard routine of a physician's assessment. "Are you hurting?"

"Yes," she gasped and moved to her back to allow the anesthesiologist to do her job. Her knees were bent to ease the pain and she guarded her abdomen from Leslie's painful prodding.

"Who's your OB?"

"Abrams."

"Be right back."

Leslie's rapidly spoken words seemed as though they came from a great distance.

"Bring a gurney to the physician's lounge and the crash cart. No, don't call a code, but I need it now! And page Dr. Abrams STAT."

Suddenly the room was full of people—nurses, doctors, surgical techs—everyone she worked with was working over her. In physical and emotional agony, she let them do as they would.

Someone clipped her scrub top and bra off, then got her into a hospital gown. A stabbing pain in her arm told her another someone was starting an IV. Then two men lifted her to a gurney. A sheet floated down to cover her and a blood pressure cuff tightened on her arm. She tried to relax in the care of her colleagues.

"What's going on?" Dr. Abrams's deep voice asked.

"She's bleeding out," Leslie answered. "I sent an H and H."

"BP's 52 over 22; heart rate 150; respirations 8 and shallow," another voice chimed in. To McKenna, the voices sounded as if they were coming from deep underwater.

Dr. Abrams probed beneath the sheet into her body.

Trying to push him away, she cried, "No. Don't!"

"Now, now, McKenna, let me see what's happening here," Dr. Abrams cajoled calmly.

McKenna sat up and screamed, "My baby's dead! That's what's happening!"

As quickly as she rose, she fell back, managing to gesture at the obstetrician with her closed hand.

"What's that?" Dr. Abrams asked.

Leslie pried her fingers open.

Softly, she said, "The fetus."

With those words, McKenna surrendered to darkness.

Two months later, McKenna flipped through the papers the messenger had delivered an hour before. Curled up in the overstuffed chair in the family room with a fire smoldering in the corner fireplace, she was content enough. She'd put the sale of her mansion on hold, purchased enough new furniture to fill the rooms used most often. The rest of the house was closed off, leaving the living area with a condo-like feel. Across the room, James sat reading. She looked up when she heard the paper rustle. He stared at her.

"So," he said, "you're returning to work?"

"I have an ortho meeting tomorrow. It'll be the first since I was elected chief." She lifted the file. "This is the agenda."

James stood and walked to her chair. "I guess I'll be leaving then."

"Leave? Why?" McKenna looked up at him. After the miscarriage, there had been no need for a marriage, but he'd spent the last eight weeks with her.

He turned from the doorway. "You don't need me."

"There's no reason for you to rush off." McKenna uncurled her legs and sat up.

James returned to her side. "McKenna, you're ready to move on and I have to also."

James had been there when she arrived home from the hospital after the miscarriage and he'd stood at her side at the funeral service for Tetsuro's baby. Now he was deciding to leave her.

"I was happy to be here for you," he broke into her thoughts, "but you need someone else to make you happy."

"You're my friend, James." She took his hand.

"I'll always be that but we both need more." He squeezed her hand, then released it "You need a *taiko* drummer. If you'd told him about the baby, he would be the one here. And you'd be happy. We can't go on this way."

"You're right." Tears came to her eyes with the thought of Tetsuro. He would have been there for her. And he would love her. James was merely a friend, a very close friend. They both deserved more.

"I'll leave in the morning." James kissed her forehead. "Good night and Goodbye."

"Bye."

McKenna looked at the file in her lap but she wasn't thinking of the orthopedic meeting. She was thinking about a *taiko* drummer.

CHAPTER THIRTY-FOUR

Kneeling on the east coast beach Tetsuro watched the sun rise over the Sea of Japan. He looked toward the main island of Honshu, but wished he could see all the way to Cleveland. The cool morning air blew over his bare back, stirring loose hair to tickle his neck. He'd finished his ten-mile run long enough ago for his breathing to return to normal, but sweat still ran down his torso and gathered at the waistband of his cotton pants. The sand against his bare legs and feet had been cold when he'd settled there but now had warmed from his body's heat.

He enjoyed this time of day, when he was exhausted from physical exertion and alone. Only then could he allow the thought of McKenna to intrude. He had tried to put her out of his mind, yet she haunted him. Her presence seemed to be around him, permeating his being. He had to force her memory away.

"Tetsu?"

"*Hai*, Kifume-*san*?" Another part of his painful history.

"How are you?" She sat at his side.

"I am well." Her question annoyed him.

"Your hand is hurting?"

"Some. Probably the cold air." *Would you go away?* His cultural politeness prevented him from dismissing her.

"Let me help."

He didn't resist when Kifume began to massage the injured yet healed hand. Nor did he look at her as her fingers moved from palm to wrist to fingertips. She continued in this way for long minutes. When she finished, the sun was fully up, but she didn't release his hand. Her small ones cuddled it in her lap.

They sat quietly until a young voice interrupted them.

"*Sensei* Takamitsu?"

"*Hai*?" Tetsuro reclaimed his hand from Kifume's grasp.

"You have a visitor." The prepubescent boy offered a small card.

After Tetsuro read the business card, he said, "I will be there as soon as I dress."

"*Hai*." The messenger disappeared.

"Who is it?" Kifume asked.

"Someone I once…knew." Tetsuro stood and she followed as he moved up the beach.

Tetsuro bathed, changed into jeans and shirt, then entered the visitor's room. He hadn't see the woman sitting on the *tatami* mat in a dozen or so years and had met the man at her side only once before. At that time, Tetsuro had punched him in the face and broken his own finger.

"Emiko-*san*." Tetsuro approached. It had been so long since he'd dare to utter the name so dear to him once, he was amazed he remembered how to say it.

"Tetsuro-*san*."

Emiko's head bobbed. She was the petite flower who'd haunted his dreams until only recently. An American woman had been the only antidote to the Japanese woman's spell.

"You recall Shinzu-*san*?" Politely she included her companion.

"Yes." After twelve years, Tetsuro could civilly greet Emiko's husband. "I trust you are well"

"And I, you, Takamitsu-*san*. I will leave you and Emiko-*san* to talk." Shinzu caressed Emiko's arm before he stood up and departed the room.

"You are looking well," Tetsuro said, although she appeared older than her years. Her once raven hair was sprinkled with gray and chopped closely to her head. The round face he recalled was lean with sunken cheeks, and her eyes were cloudy with dark circles beneath them. Her lips were held as tightly as she clasped her hands together.

"You have never lied convincingly." There was a slight smile. He could only briefly glimpse her perfect, small white teeth. "Could we walk?

I have been sitting too long on the journey here."

"We can leave this way." He helped her to rise and they exited a door-way into a secluded garden.

"Why have you come?" Tetsuro prodded though it was not the Japanese way to rush conversation. Along the stone walkway, azaleas bloomed profusely and, in spaces, fine sand was sculpted into perfect areas of repose. Tall trees towered over the couple.

She stopped and looked up into his eyes. "A favor."

"You wish *me* to do *you* a favor?" How dare she ask him for something, considering what she'd taken from him!

"I do not ask for myself. I have no right."

Tetsuro watched her thin shoulders shudder.

"I wish you would make this easy for me."

"I do not feel you have that right either. You took…much from me."

"Tetsu, my favor is for *her*."

His heart dropped to his stomach and the air in his lungs escaped in a rush. At first, a buzzing in his ears deafened him to Emiko's words, but then it cleared and he heard her ask her favor.

"Dr. Stafford," McKenna's secretary rapped on her open office door.

McKenna sat behind her desk writing on a chart. "Yes, Deb?"

"This was faxed to us," Deb gave her a sheet of paper, "from Japan."

McKenna took the page and read aloud, "Dr. Stafford, please send to this office the complete medical records of Takamitsu Tetsuro." A Japanese doctor and Tetsuro signed it in both Roman lettering and *kana*.

"Should I fax it?"

"Yes," McKenna stuttered. She felt as if her breath had been knocked out of her and she was losing Tetsuro all over again. Now, with the trans-fer of his medical records, she had nothing to hold him to her.

A DRUMMER'S BEAT TO MEND

The cold, sterile room was large and unfriendly. The sounds around Tetsuro were metallic clanking and muttered whispers in Japanese. No music entertained him except for the internal beat that he drummed on his right hip as he lay on his left side.

"You must lay your arm here." An indifferent nurse adjusted his wayward limb to lie atop his other outstretched arm. She then opened the hospital gown to expose his hip and began to paint it with iodine scrub.

Tetsuro recalled the last time he'd visited an operating room and had his body parts painted orange by surgical prep. The eyes staring at him now above the paper masks were the same as his. He couldn't find *her* light brown eyes anywhere in the room. Tetsuro hated them all. He wanted it to be McKenna operating on him. His hand ached in sympathy with his thoughts.

Standing at Tetsuro's head, Dr. Hirabayashi explained, "Because of the heart problem with your last operation, I will give you intravenous sedation, then a regional block so you will not feel pain."

Tetsuro nodded. As the sedative filled his blood stream, Tetsuro drifted away. He dreamed of McKenna, as she'd been that first day.

He smiled.

Hours later Tetsuro walked with a distinct limp into the waiting area of the bone marrow transplant unit. Emiko and Shinzu sat side by side on the couch. They were well suited for one another. Shinzu had provided Emiko with what he could never have given her, at least not when he was twenty years old and confused about himself.

"Tetsuro-*san*?" Emiko faced him. Her eyes were brighter than before but sadness was still over her. "How do you feel?"

"My hip is sore." Tetsuro adjusted the fit of his jeans, made tighter by the gauze dressing on his hip. He'd completed his part of the favor. Now, he'd claim one of his own.

"You look tired," Emiko commented.

"They gave my own blood back to me after the procedure to make up for what I lost. To return my energy," he explained.

"I want to thank you, Takamitsu-*san*." Shinzu approached him. "For all you have done."

"*Shigata ga na,*" Tetsuro answered but he directed his next statement to Emiko. "It is my turn to ask a favor."

In slow motion, Emiko came to stand in front of him. Horror and shock clouded her face as she anticipated his request.

"You can not ask…" she began.

"I can and do. I wish to see her." There, he'd said it. And he'd charge the nurses' station if Emiko refused. He'd resorted to violence once before to try and keep her but lost. He wouldn't lose this time.

"You will not tell?" Emiko asked.

"No." The incision site on his hip throbbed. "She does not need to be burdened any further."

"I do not know, Emiko," Shinzu interjected. "She could begin asking questions."

"You cannot deny me," Tetsuro replied. "You have had her thirteen years. I have seen her only once. Now you come and ask me to give what you cannot." Tetsuro's anger welled up inside him. "I would think a brief visit would be a fitting reward. After all, Aiko is *my daughter*." A relief washed through him as he uttered the words he'd never said. It was as if he'd emerged from underneath the ocean's waves and could, at last, breathe.

"It will be all right, Shi-*chan*. Tetsu has kept his word all these years, doing what we asked. He stayed away. He deserves to see her for all the pain he has been through."

"Very well, Emi-chan. You are her mother." The man appeared to deflate as Emiko and Tetsuro stepped from the room.

Tetsuro followed Emiko's lead through the hospital corridors. A million questions sprang to his mind, but he couldn't form one on his tongue.

Perhaps it was just as well he not know Aiko too personally. It would make it even more difficult to part from her again.

The two adults came to an isolation room on the pediatric cancer ward.

"This is a laminar air flow room. I am sure they explained to you how Aiko's immune system would be defenseless after the chemotherapy and radiation to destroy her own bone marrow." Emiko took a yellow paper gown from a cart at the doorway. "You will need to also wear a mask and gloves." She took these items out of the boxes while Tetsuro donned the yellow gown. "We do not wish for her to recover from the leukemia and die from a common cold."

Tetsuro put the paper mask over his mouth and nose.

"She would not recognize me in this outfit, even if she knew me."

"You must promise not to tell her!"

"I only wish to see my child."

"Very well." Emiko stepped aside. "There are two doors. Make sure you close the first before opening the second."

"I understand how to go in. I do not wish to compromise her health any further."

Tetsuro entered the small anteroom, pushing the door firmly closed behind him. The second door had a window through which he could see a small form lying still on a narrow bed. He opened the door and approached the bed where his daughter lay. She was a tall girl, rail thin, with a colorful scarf around her head to cover a skull devoid of hair because of the chemotherapy. As he studied her sleeping face, Tetsuro saw his mother when she lay dying. The thin face, dark-circled eyes, and pale thin lips were enough to wrench his heart from his chest.

On the bedside table was a picture taken when Aiko was healthy. In it, she was already taller than her mother, an inheritance Emiko would have to explain someday. Long black hair swung freely and the girl's face was alive. Surely she'd return to the beauty she was destined to be.

An IV drip, almost finished, sent his bone marrow into her arm. Aiko was a part of him, a piece of his heart he could never take back, never wanted back. He'd given himself to Emiko and created Aiko by accident and now, on purpose, his marrow gave her life once more.

He had no right to force his way into her life, even if he would go against his promise not to. She was a sick little girl, almost a teenager, and any change in her life's situation would not be beneficial. Upsetting her world would not set his right. He continued to watch the slow, shallow breaths Aiko took and thought about the women in his life. Because of stupidity and pride, he had lost Emiko so many years ago. And she had taken the one most precious thing in his life when she left. After years of agony and solitude, he'd allowed a stranger to enter his life and now McKenna was only a memory, her career and his separating them. Their lives were on opposite sides of the earth.

He was incomplete. His soul was empty. What had he done in a former life for *karma* to treat him so?

Then again, maybe things did not have to stay the way they were now. Buddhism taught that one should attempt to correct the mistakes of the past in this life to reach Nirvana. This was his duty. He hadn't given things a chance to be right.

As if a light were turned on, a decision was made. Although painful, he would close his heart to Aiko. She was Emiko's, and she'd given her to Shinzu. They were her parents. He was nothing to the girl.

Silently, Tetsuro leaned over and kissed Aiko's forehead through the paper mask over his lips. He rose and left the room. Sadness dragged at his heart but it would ease. He knew what he had to do.

CHAPTER THIRTY-FIVE

McKenna sat on the couch in the physician's lounge after morning surgery. Her feet were on the low table and her head rested against the back cushion. She was tired. Three months after the miscarriage, she continued to take large doses of iron to increase the hemoglobin in her blood. This morning she didn't have the energy to change from her scrubs to start rounds without a brief nap.

"Dr. McKenna Stafford, please call 2149," she heard the overhead page call. "Dr. Stafford, 2149."

She moved lethargically to reach the phone at the end of the couch.

"This is Dr. Stafford."

"Dr. Stafford, this is Libby, on five west. Are you in the middle of something?"

"No. I just finished in the OR."

"Then come to the floor, STAT."

Before she could respond, Libby hung up. McKenna pulled herself up and started to the orthopedic floor.

The minute she stepped from the elevator and turned toward the nurses' station McKenna heard Libby's lively laughter. From a distance, she saw the large group of nurses gathering around the desk and wondered what was going on. It must not have been something bad since all McKenna heard was giggling and girlish squeals.

As she approached the desk, a familiar deep timbre joined the high-pitched feminine voices. Her heart skipped a beat, then rushed blood to her ears in a deafening roar. Her breath caught in her throat and she had to force her feet forward. Could it really be true? Was her mind playing tricks on her?

As if in slow motion, the group of women parted to reveal the center of their attention.

"Oh my God. Tetsu," McKenna whispered as she saw the *taiko* drummer standing with the nurses.

Her trembling fingers went to her lips as she stopped in her tracks. Then, without thought to professionalism, she flew down the hallway to throw herself into his open arms. In response, Tetsuro pulled her to his chest, lifting her feet up off the floor. Around them, nurses and doctors applauded the lovers' reunion.

Her lips were covered with his and she welcomed the passionate kiss, short though it as it was. Released, she buried her face into his neck, the silk of his hair covering her. And she wept.

Continuing to hold her to him, Tetsuro whispered, "I have come back, Ke-*chan*."

She pushed away, her emotions calming. "Are you here to stay?"

"*Hai*. If you will have me," Tetsuro said, oblivious to those around them.

"I'd have you under any circumstances except temporary. You must promise it is forever."

"*Eien*. Eternally." Tetsuro returned his mouth to hers.

As McKenna pulled him after her, Tetsuro spoke quick farewells to the nurses.

"We have only a short time before I have to leave for the office," she explained as she dragged him down the hall. "I have to change and then we'll have coffee."

Tetsuro's arm encircled her waist and they walked as one.

"It is not coffee I want," he said hoarsely, his mouth at her ear.

"Behave!" McKenna shook him off to take his hand as he walked beside her. "I'll sneak you into the physician's lounge because I'm afraid you'll disappear otherwise."

She could hardly believe he was with her and planning to stay. It was all too good to be true.

Slowly entering the sanctuary of female doctors, she found no one in sight. Tetsuro followed her lead.

"Go in here." McKenna shoved him into the bathroom. "I'll get my clothes and be right in."

She shut Tetsuro in the small room and rushed to her locker to grab her clothing. When she returned to the door separating them, Tetsuro yanked her into the room and into his arms and began to kiss her hungrily. McKenna locked the door, then eagerly joined in the fondling.

Like teenagers just learning about sex, they devoured each other. Hands pulled at clothes so mouths could taste and caress skin. Tetsuro's touch set her body on fire. Her scrubs fell away and she felt the coarseness of his jeans against her thighs and the soft silk of his shirt against her breasts. His tongue on her breast sent waves of electricity through her body.

Her hands struggled with his jeans' buttons until she at last freed Tetsuro's rigid flesh. Anxiously, he lifted her off the floor and, with her back supported on the wall, moved into her. She sighed, her arms clinging to his neck and her legs secured around his hips. Tetsuro drove into her and she readily accepted him. Try as she might to avoid it, she found herself moaning aloud.

"Hey! You okay?" a colleague asked at the door.

"Yes. I'm…fine," she managed to reply.

Tetsuro made one last deep thrust and the hot surge washed through her. McKenna sighed as he held her pinned to the wall, her face against his shoulder.

"I am home," Tetsuro murmured.

"*Hai*."

Rolled in an Amish quilt after a repeat performance of lovemaking, they huddled that evening before a smoldering fire at the house on Shelbourne Road.

McKenna snuggled against him. "What's going to happen now?"

"We need to talk." Tetsuro moved away. "But it may not be a conversation you will want to hear. You may not want to be near me when we finish. Why do you not get us something to drink while I stoke the fire?"

"Is it that bad?" McKenna sat up. Tetsuro pulled on a pair of sweat pants and sweatshirt and went to the fire.

"I do not think so, but…" He began to work at the embers.

"I'll fix cocoa." McKenna stood, wrapped her heavy robe around her body, and walked to the kitchen.

McKenna returned and they sat, each with hot mugs in their hands. Tetsuro stared into the flames he'd stirred up. "Now what do we need to talk about?"

"You once asked about Emiko," he began, staring at the fire.

"Yes," McKenna answered in a soft voice. "I read something about the situation in a trade paper."

"It is not honorable to brawl like that. I was young and stupid. If I had been a man, I would have done many things differently. But if I had made different choices, I would not be free to be with you." Tetsuro reached to run his fingers through her wavy hair. "Emiko is the mother of my daughter. We met when she came to the school to study. When she became pregnant, I offered to marry her. She refused, saying she could not make a home with such a man, that I was too brash for her to trust. I was a boy. She left Nakano without telling me where she was going or what she planned to do. After brewing my anger for months, I discovered she'd gone to Tokyo. Aiko was two weeks old when I visited her. I saw her briefly before Emiko threw me out."

McKenna kept her silence, trying to envision a young Tetsuro full of immature rage. That person was so counter to the man at her side.

"Back at the school, I was served with legal papers giving my daughter over to the man she had married a month prior to the baby's birth in a marriage her parents had arranged. I signed and never saw either of them again. Until three weeks ago."

"You saw your daughter?" McKenna's chest hurt with the knowledge of her miscarriage, another child he would be denied.

"Yes." Tetsuro hung his head and looked at his cocoa. "Emiko came and asked that I become a bone marrow donor for our daughter."

"She has leukemia," McKenna said, her hand going to Tetsuro's shoulder in sympathy. "That's why you have a horrible bruise and cut on your hip."

"Yes. Afterwards I asked to see her." He set his mug aside.

"How is she?"

"They say she has a better chance. While I was at her bedside, I released her." Tetsuro looked at McKenna now. "It was there I made the decision to return to you. I gave up happiness once before. I could not do it again."

"I'm happy you're here, but sorry you had to give up your child."

"Legally I was forced to give her up thirteen years ago, I had not done it emotionally. While she will always be in my heart, I am now free of that heartache."

"I'm afraid your heart will hurt again." Putting aside her own cocoa, McKenna took his hand. "After you left, I discovered I was carrying your child."

"Oh, Ke-*chan*." Tetsuro moved to embrace her.

"No. Let me finish. I lost our baby."

Tetsuro pulled her to him and whispered in an emotion-filled voice, "I am so sorry you went through that pain without me."

She allowed him to enfold her. "I found a way to resolve that pain. I went to the temple and participated in a *mizuko kuyo* as you taught me." Contentment settled over her in his embrace. This was home, a place where she longed to be.

"All of this is history. We have a new path to travel." His heart beat a slow steady pulse beneath her ear on his chest.

"Won't you regret not having *taiko* in your life?" Her own pulse increased, dreading the answer to her question.

"It will not be out of my life. I have a plan. While coming to Ohio, I traveled to San Francisco and gave my *netsuke* collection to Christie's auction house. With the money, I want to open a drum school here in Cleveland."

"That is wonderful!" McKenna moved out of his arms abruptly so as to study his eyes. "But your *netsuke*? All of it? I could give you the money to set up the school."

"I could never take your money. All I want from you is your love. Besides, I kept the important and sentimental ones for our children."

"You have my love. You always will." McKenna hugged Tetsuro

tightly and kissed him.

"I love you."

He allowed her to guide him back to the nest of quilts and taking off his sweats, she began to stroke him alive again.

CHAPTER THIRTY-SIX

"Are you ready?" Leslie Furumiya was out of breath and rushing toward McKenna.

"We have to wait until Tetsu finishes." McKenna stood in the wings of the Allen Theater. Leslie took a place beside her and they watched Tetsuro Takamitsu in full *taiko* regalia but wearing the black pants instead of the scandalous *fundoshi*. He played the flute while guiding three four-year-olds in the drum piece.

"It's amazing how he can get those kids to play so well, especially after only six months."

"He's the Pied Piper," McKenna answered, pride evident in her voice. "Kids'll do anything for him."

"Are you sure you can wait?"

"I'm fine. I want to see the older kids play the *O-Daiko*. If it wasn't for that drum, I'd never have met him."

"Does he know?"

McKenna shook her head. "He's too nervous about the recital. It's the first and means a lot to the success of *Takamitsu's Taiko*."

Tetsuro looked toward the wings and, when he caught her eye, winked. McKenna stroked her pregnant abdomen and recalled the day she'd told him about the coming baby. Excited, he'd composed a *haiku* for her and she'd committed it to memory.

A roll of thunder
so begins the steady rain
for this new crop

Now was the time. Labor had begun an hour ago, but she hadn't told Tetsuro. She'd wait until he finished the recital and they'd go to University Hospital where she'd deliver a healthy child, one no one would ever take away from him.

Over two years ago, McKenna Stafford had mended Tetsuro Takamitsu's hand. With the birth of their child, she would heal his heart. The mending of the drummer's beat would now be complete.

ABOUT THE AUTHOR

Kei Swanson was born in Dallas, Texas, on a hot July day. From there she grew to adulthood in Arlington, Texas. Obtaining a degree in nursing, she began a career in obstetrical nursing, married and gave birth to her only child. She managed to see the world on the tails of her USAF husband and they are now retired in North Texas indulging a very spoiled granddaughter. Visit Kei at www.keiswanson.com.

Excerpt from

HAND IN GLOVE

BY

ANDREA JACKSON

Release Date: December 2005

CHAPTER 1

Tyson McAllister stepped onto one of the patios at the rear of the Kingston estate. A sistah could get used to this life. She paused and gazed at the mansion with its windows sparkling in the sun. Even at this early hour, servants bustled through the house preparing breakfast and tidying up. She turned to take in the spectacular view. The rising sun filtered through the trees that ringed the grounds, laying a shimmer of magic to the swimming pool waters and the Italian marble tiles of the extensive patios. She could hear the chirrup of birds in the woods.

A wry smile curved her mouth as she methodically stretched her muscles in preparation for her morning jog. Sometimes she couldn't believe how far she had come. She still couldn't believe her luck in landing this assignment to help cover a big house party in a wealthy suburb of Atlanta, Georgia. But the morning was too intoxicating to waste thinking those thoughts. Light-footed and confident, she jogged along the hedges that ringed the patio; sure, nothing could stop her now. She felt invincible, until she slammed into a hard body coming around the corner of the hedges and fell on her butt with the breath knocked out of her.

There was a startled silence as Ty gathered her shattered thoughts. Jarred more than hurt, she began to giggle hysterically. It figured. Every time she thought she had it made, life knocked her on her ass. Ty McAllister couldn't forget that she had to watch out for herself every step of the way.

As the other runner helped her up with apologetic concern, she breathlessly assured him she was unhurt. When she took in his appearance, the breath swooshed out of her again.

The man before her epitomized the old cliché tall, dark and handsome. In tight-fitting leggings, a pullover jersey with a hood and high-priced running shoes, he could be a model in some touched-up photo in a physical fitness magazine. His exercise clothes emphasized his trim waist and narrow hips, yet at the same time seemed to show off the broadness of his chest and shoulders. His legs stretched fantastically long, the powerful muscles in his thighs accentuated by the sheen of the leggings. Is he real? The casual touch of his hands assured her that he was vibrantly real.

He thrust out his hand with a grin. "Hi. I'm Victor."

She gulped and took the hand. "Ty," she managed to respond to his slight Spanish accent.

He scrutinized her from head to toe, warm approval revealed in his flickering smile. "Are you going for a run?"

"Huh? Oh, yeah." She frowned. Good grief I sound like an idiot. I had better start acting like a television producer. "Were you out already? How's the trail?"

"I just got back. It's beautiful down by the gardens. I love this time of morning." He glanced toward the east and lifted his chin to take a deep breath. Ty's senses went into a tailspin once more. Wow, that sensual mouth, that strong jaw line. He seemed unaware of his effect on her emotions.

"Uh-huh," she sighed. She reined in her reaction once more. "Yeah, great morning. You must have been out early. Did you have a good workout?"

"Yes, but you're the only person I've seen so far."

"Really? I guess most folks are sleeping in."

"I guess so. Maybe we can talk over breakfast when you get back?"

Her heart did another little flutter. "Maybe," she said, with a slight shrug. "I'd better get going now."

She eased past him, turned with a wave then picked up her pace. He was still watching her when she turned the corner.

Heartthrob! She felt all warm and tingly with attraction. He wasn't precisely handsome, she decided; yet something about that square jaw, penetrating black eyes and well-conditioned body made a woman take a second look. And of course, he possessed that devastating slow smile that enticed like honey oozing from an overturned hive. She shook her head over her own whimsy. She wasn't about to indulge in a weekend flirtation. Ty McAllister never did foolish things like that. Her career had been the center of her life for some time. To avoid distractions from the challenge and competition of her job, she'd dumped her last serious relationship. She had no time for a steady boyfriend or social life. No time for coddling some man's fragile ego. She knew how to focus on what needed to be done.

She wasn't here to mingle with the guests, she reminded herself. She was here to work. This was the first big on-location assignment since her promotion to producer. A twinge of nerves sent a shiver down her spine. She had to prove her ability to her boss, Patty Sheldon, as well as the network executives.

Still, she couldn't help wondering exactly who this Victor was. He had to be a guest here at the party, which gave him immediate status. This house party was a small part of one of Atlanta's annual traditions. The rivalry between Clark Atlanta University and Morehouse College, two premier Black schools, was almost one hundred years old. The annual football face off in September was an opportunity to raise scholarship money for both schools. The days preceding the game were filled with lively rivalry and energetic festivity among the alumni and the community. No doubt, Victor was one of the successful alumni.

She didn't see her heart throb for the rest of the morning. After her morning jog, she went straight to her room to change and get to work. By that afternoon, she had all but forgotten him as she directed a taping sequence for the show. The director was busy with Patty taping interviews while she and the camera operator recorded some background sequences. She watched a dozen or more laughing, fashionable women burst out of the double doors of the mansion. They ignored the large staring lens of a television camera aimed at them.

"Steady, Pete, steady," Ty murmured to the cameraman. She watched the scene over his shoulder as he videotaped. This would definitely show the upscale nature of the party. Most of these women, wives of prominent celebrities and executives from around the country, seemed to spend most of their time on their appearance or their entertainment. She hadn't seen so much fake hair and designer clothes since the last Grammy Awards on television. She wondered what would turn up if the glittering surface were scratched.

She felt a little smile tug her lips as she continued to shadow the camera operator. Trust Patty to find any dirt to uncover. The woman was a bloodhound when it came to gossip. She wasn't naïve, but Patty's ability to sniff out secrets still disconcerted her at times.

"Backing up," warned Pete in a low voice. Keeping her hand on his shoulder, Ty started to ease backward so that he could swing the lens on the women as they walked across the green lawn toward the tennis courts.

"Ouch!" So of course, she was the one to bump into someone, jostling the cameraman and almost losing her footing.

Pete lowered the video cam and glared at her in exasperation. She turned and found herself facing two more annoyed individuals.

One of them was Vanessa Sweetlove, a close friend of the host, Duke Kingston. The other was a man with a beard and thick glasses. Ty had noticed them with their heads bent together when she and Pete first set up a few minutes ago.

"Watch where you're going with that thing!" shrilled Vanessa.

"Cameras?" Her companion scowled, his lips pouting from saggy jowls. "What the hell are you trying to do to me, Vanessa? Don't you appreciate my position? I can't be seen here! Those reporter parasites can ruin everything. Everything!"

In his poorly fitting polyester suit, he turned and scurried into the house, leaving Ty gazing after him.

Now that reaction seemed a little extreme, she mused. Most of the people at this fling were glad for a little promotion. This guy didn't quite fit in with the other men at the house party, many of whom occupied positions of power in corporate offices all over the South. Mr. Cheap Suit didn't have that executive air.

Vanessa Sweetlove showed no sign of fleeing. Ty observed a beautiful hazel-eyed woman of color with peachy skin and sandy hair. Chiffon in bright ocean colors floated around her shapely curves. She frowned at Ty. "Honey, if you can't stay out of the way of the guests, I'll have Duke ask you to leave."

"I apologize," Ty said. She nodded to Pete, who began rolling up cords and collecting his lights.

"Miss Sweetlove, isn't it?" Ty went on in her best professional voice. "I'm Patty Sheldon's producer. I understand that you're a well-known psychic. Perhaps you could give me a few minutes of your time later, so that I can ask some preliminary questions for Patty. I'm sure she'd love to have you on the show. Have you seen Eye on Atlanta?" As she named the popular local talk show, she pasted on a smile to hide her real thoughts. Or maybe you can read your crystal ball on the 1-800 Psychic Rip-off Line.

Ty's preliminary research had revealed that Vanessa Sweetlove was "involved" with Duke Kingston. Vanessa had suddenly dropped her weekly radio call-in talk show, "Sweetlove Predictions" just a few weeks ago. The tabloids speculated that she was preparing to venture into a new area. Ty had a shrewd idea that Duke Kingston would finance the new area.

At the mention of publicity, Vanessa's frown cleared, replaced by smiling approval. "I'd love to talk to Patty. I think your audience will find my powers unique and fascinating."

"Good," Ty said, her mind racing to find an excuse to put Vanessa

off until later. "I'll just go and check Patty's calendar. I'll see you at dinner, won't—" she slid a step to the rear in preparation for flight. "Ouch!"
Once more, she slammed into something warm and solid. This seemed
to be her day for bumbling into people.

Hands caught her from behind, and she twisted around to free herself. "Excuse me. Oh, it's you!" she exclaimed and felt her mouth stretch
into a wide, admiring smile.

"Easy there. Oh, hi!"

Just like this morning, the sound of that voice sent a shiver of bone-
melting sensual awareness down her spine, and she found herself gulping
to get her emotions under control as she turned to face good-looking
Victor. This time she noticed that when his generous chiseled lips
stretched in a smile, a little indentation appeared on one side of his
mouth.

They both recovered at the same time; he released her and she
stepped away.

"Hi," he said, still smiling that slightly lopsided grin. "Did you enjoy
your run this morning?"

"Mr. Santiago," cooed Vanessa Sweetlove's fluting voice behind her.
Ty had almost forgotten about the beautiful psychic. "Mr. Santiago, I've
been looking all over for you!"

The name sank into Ty's brain. She froze, staring at him in conster-
nation. He was Victor Santiago? She'd heard all about the mysterious,
ruthless, and fabulously successful investment consultant who'd popped
up on Duke Kingston's doorstep last night. The guests had been buzzing
about him all day, and Ty had hoped to get some footage of him. But the
last thing she'd expected was that he'd turn out to be this heart-stopping
brother.

She might have imagined that his smile tightened a little as he turned
toward Vanessa. "Were you? I don't believe we've met, have we, Miss…?"

"Vanessa." The psychic stepped up and hooked her arm into his.
"I'm helping Duke entertain the guests. You must tell me if there's anything you need to make your stay more pleasant." She fluttered her lashes at him with seductive invitation.

Victor hesitated, casting another look at Ty. She hastily busied herself with a notebook she had managed to hang onto through all the jostling.

"Well," said Victor. "I did want to ask you about the gentleman you were talking to a minute ago. I believe we're acquainted."

"Dr. Franklin? Shall we go and find him?" Vanessa began to tug Victor's arm with firm determination.

He hung back. "I'll see you at dinner, Ty?" he asked.

She avoided his compelling gaze. "Oh, I expect I'll be working," she mumbled. "I'll see you around."

Vanessa, chattering, led him away. Ty peeped after them from beneath her lashes. Trouble, she decided. No thanks. Tyson McAllister knew how to focus on what was important.

Victor forced himself to lend an attentive ear to Vanessa's flirtatious prattle. Something fresh and soothing about Ty attracted him. Perhaps he'd have time to pursue an acquaintance with the young producer later this weekend. Despite his oddly compelling attraction to Ty McAllister, he did need to focus on his primary goal.

He and Vanessa found Franklin standing at the edge of the side lawn watching while some guests performed cheers for their favorite college team.

"How do you do?" Victor said after Vanessa introduced him.

Franklin's gaze shifted, avoiding Victor's face, as he hesitantly took the hand Victor extended. He grunted a brief acknowledgement.

"I thought I might have met you when I attended Morehouse a few years ago," Victor went on. "I majored in history under Dr. Berengi. Do you know him?"

Franklin stiffened. "I've always been at Clark-Howard," he muttered.

"Yes? I thought you might know Dr. Berengi since your field is history, too. He's one of the leading authorities on the African Diaspora."

"Berengi," Franklin said as if the name curdled his tongue. "Berengi is a do-gooding show-off who's managed to get a couple of books published. I have a lot of problems with his theories."

"In what areas?" asked Victor with an air of interest. "I thought his book on the Nakisisi was considered a standard."

"Berengi knows nothing—" began Franklin in a strident voice.

"You men aren't going to start discussing history?" exclaimed Vanessa with a little laugh. "This is a party, gentlemen. Wouldn't you rather talk about who'll win the game this weekend?"

Victor flashed her smile. "Sorry to bore you. Why don't the professor and I go inside so you can get back to your other guests?"

She took a quick step closer to Victor as if to hang on to him. "Well, I—"

"I was just about to go to my room anyway," said Franklin in a quieter tone. Tight-lipped, he added, "Excuse me, Santiago. It was nice meeting you."

"Perhaps we can talk about the Nakisisi later then," said Victor.

Franklin's only response was a non-committal grunt as he turned and walked away.

Victor offered Vanessa an apologetic smile.

"Maybe you and I could talk about the Nakisisi," she said over the rowdy crowd.

"Are you familiar with the tribe?"

"Perhaps. A little," she said. Then she smiled. "But we'll talk later. When it's quieter."

He let her change the topic. How much did Vanessa know? She enjoyed a close relationship with Kingston, apparently. Perhaps she might prove useful to him. He had a couple more days to try to get the information he had come for.

Ty spent the remainder of the afternoon setting up camera angles around the house and grounds, storyboarding ideas, talking to Patty, and taking pages of notes.

As she studied the notes on the guests, she saw that there were several interesting leads to follow up. As she had come to expect, many of these seemingly upright citizens hid personal baggage, some more dramatic than others. She only had to pick which would work best for the show.

Because this wasn't a simple party; this was high stakes business, the way the wealthy and powerful did it. She had a feeling that there were some interesting secret dealings going on beneath the festivities. This party promised to provide plenty of footage for Patty's show. Duke Kingston had invited a number of leading black Georgia businessmen, people who contributed heavily to the scholarship funds of the Atlanta universities.

Kingston was one of the city's most notorious businesspersons. Some dozen years ago as a handsome young man with charm and a fascinating Caribbean accent, he had snared a wealthy older widow in matrimony. The new Mrs. Kingston, known to have chronic health problems, had died just a few months ago. After a brief period of mourning, the bereaved husband was now living large, partying, wheeling and dealing as hard as he could.

As evening approached, Ty retreated to the mansion's magnificent library to work on her notes. She'd found the library was the least used room in the house.

As she walked in, a man sitting on one of the couches behind a low coffee table lifted his head with a frown.

"What are you doing here?" he demanded.

Ty recognized Vanessa's flustered companion from this morning. He still wore the same rumpled blue suit. The gruffness of his tone set her defenses alight.

"Am I disturbing you?" she asked coldly. Her gaze flickered down to the papers spread on the table before him. He began to rake them inside a scuffed leather briefcase without regard for neatness.

"Yes, you're disturbing me," he snarled. "What are you doing, following me around with that camera?"

"I'm not following you."

"Do I look like a fool? I know your kind. You stay away from me. You come near me with that camera again and I'll smash it! Do you hear me? I'll have you thrown out of this house!"

"Excuse me?" Her voice turned even chillier. "Mr. Kingston made an agreement with Ms. Sheldon to record this weekend. I think you're over-reacting. Believe me, you're not the type our show takes an interest in, Mr.—"

He didn't supply his name, but descended into a strident rant about reporters and privacy, his voice rising with every word. She remembered, though, that Vanessa had called him Dr. Franklin.

"What's going on in here?" demanded a new voice from the doorway, which Ty had left opened behind her.

She and the irate Franklin turned to face their host, Duke Kingston. He was a mahogany-skinned man of medium height, in fairly good shape without looking as if he worked too hard at it. His Armani suit was clearly custom-tailored, with creases sharp enough to cut. His thin mustache was so perfectly trimmed it might have been drawn on. Ty had already decided he had the practiced smoothness of a pretty boy hopelessly in love with himself.

Franklin sputtered at him. "Why have you brought these television people here, Kingston? I won't have it! They'll mess up everything if you don't get rid of them. I demand it! They go or I go."

Ty gaped at the blustering man, all her internal alarms clanging. What the hell was this guy hiding? Who was he to deliver ultimatums to a man as influential as Duke Kingston was?

"Calm down, Franklin," Kingston said, lifting his palms in a soothing gesture. "There's no need to upset yourself." He turned to Ty, his expression going stern. "Ms. McCall, isn't it?"

"McAllister," Ty corrected, her throat tight with anger.

"I've allowed Ms. Sheldon to bring her crew into my home as a favor. I advise you to stay away from my guests. I wouldn't like to have to make a complaint to your employer." Kingston still had a faint Caribbean accent, which would have been intriguing at any other time.

Ty was in no mood to appreciate it just now as she felt her blood boil. "Don't concern yourself," she spat out in a low, furious tone. "I'm sure I can manage to keep to my place without disturbing any of your guests."

With a jerky turn, Ty stalked from the room. How dare that man speak to her as if she were one of his servants? She started to climb the stairs, but paused on hearing the front doorbell.

Standing at the banister over the entrance foyer below, Ty saw a uniformed maid open the door and admit more guests who were dressed in glittering evening finery. A smiling Kingston emerged from the library to greet them.

Ty turned and stumbled along the second floor hallway. She didn't think she had the stomach to sit through dinner with these people tonight. She would work in her room.

A DRUMMER'S BEAT TO MEND

2005 Publication Schedule

January

A Heart's Awakening
Veronica Parker
$9.95
1-58571-143-8

Falling
Natalie Dunbar
$9.95
1-58571-121-7

February

Echoes of Yesterday
Beverly Clark
$9.95
1-58571-131-4

A Love of Her Own
Cheris F. Hodges
$9.95
1-58571-136-5

Higher Ground
Leah Latimer
$19.95
1-58571-157-8

March

Misconceptions
Pamela Leigh Starr
$9.95
1-58571-117-9

I'll Paint a Sun
A.J. Garrotto
$9.95
1-58571-165-9

Peace Be Still
Colette Haywood
$12.95
1-58571-129-2

April

Intentional Mistakes
Michele Sudler
$9.95
1-58571-152-7

Conquering Dr. Wexler's Heart
Kimberley White
$9.95
1-58571-126-8

Song in the Park
Martin Brant
$15.95
1-58571-125-X

May

The Color Line
Lizzette Grayson Carter
$9.95
1-58571-163-2

Unconditional
A.C. Arthur
$9.95
1-58571-142-X

Last Train to Memphis
Elsa Cook
$12.95
1-58571-146-2

June

Angel's Paradise
Janice Angelique
$9.95
1-58571-107-1

Suddenly You
Crystal Hubbard
$9.95
1-58571-158-6

Matters of Life and
   Death
Lesego Malepe, Ph.D.
$15.95
1-58571-124-1

2005 Publication Schedule (continued)

July

Class Reunion
Irma Jenkins/John
  Brown
$12.95
1-58571-123-3

Wild Ravens
Altonya Washington
$9.95
1-58571-164-0

August

Path of Thorns
Annetta P. Lee
$9.95
1-58571-145-4

Timeless Devotion
Bella McFarland
$9.95
1-58571-148-9

Life Is Never As It Seems
J.J. Michael
$12.95
1-58571-153-5

September

Beyond the Rapture
Beverly Clark
$9.95
1-58571-130-6

Blood Lust
J. M. Jeffries
$9.95
1-58571-138-1

Rough on Rats and
  Tough on Cats
Chris Parker
$12.95
1-58571-154-3

October

A Will to Love
Angie Daniels
$9.95
1-58571-141-1

Taken by You
Dorothy Elizabeth Love
$9.95
1-58571-162-4

Soul Eyes
Wayne L. Wilson
$12.95
1-58571-147-0

November

A Drummer's Beat to
  Mend
Kei Swanson
$9.95
1-58571-171-3

Sweet Repercussions
Kimberley White
$9.95
1-58571-159-4

Red Polka Dot in a
  Worldof Plaid
Varian Johnson
$12.95
1-58571-140-3

December

Hand in Glove
Andrea Jackson
$9.95
1-58571-166-7

Blaze
Barbara Keaton
$9.95
1-58571-172-1

Across
Carol Payne
$12.95
1-58571-149-7

Other Genesis Press, Inc. Titles

Acquisitions	Kimberley White	$8.95
A Dangerous Deception	J.M. Jeffries	$8.95
A Dangerous Love	J.M. Jeffries	$8.95
A Dangerous Obsession	J.M. Jeffries	$8.95
After the Vows	Leslie Esdaile	$10.95
(Summer Anthology)	T.T. Henderson	
	Jacqueline Thomas	
Again My Love	Kayla Perrin	$10.95
Against the Wind	Gwynne Forster	$8.95
A Lark on the Wing	Phyliss Hamilton	$8.95
A Lighter Shade of Brown	Vicki Andrews	$8.95
All I Ask	Barbara Keaton	$8.95
A Love to Cherish	Beverly Clark	$8.95
Ambrosia	T.T. Henderson	$8.95
And Then Came You	Dorothy Elizabeth Love	$8.95
Angel's Paradise	Janice Angelique	$8.95
A Risk of Rain	Dar Tomlinson	$8.95
At Last	Lisa G. Riley	$8.95
Best of Friends	Natalie Dunbar	$8.95
Bound by Love	Beverly Clark	$8.95
Breeze	Robin Hampton Allen	$10.95
Brown Sugar Diaries &	Delores Bundy &	$10.95
Other Sexy Tales	Cole Riley	
By Design	Barbara Keaton	$8.95
Cajun Heat	Charlene Berry	$8.95
Careless Whispers	Rochelle Alers	$8.95
Caught in a Trap	Andre Michelle	$8.95
Chances	Pamela Leigh Starr	$8.95
Dark Embrace	Crystal Wilson Harris	$8.95
Dark Storm Rising	Chinelu Moore	$10.95
Designer Passion	Dar Tomlinson	$8.95
Ebony Butterfly II	Delilah Dawson	$14.95

Erotic Anthology	Assorted	$8.95
Eve's Prescription	Edwina Martin Arnold	$8.95
Everlastin' Love	Gay G. Gunn	$8.95
Fate	Pamela Leigh Starr	$8.95
Forbidden Quest	Dar Tomlinson	$10.95
Fragment in the Sand	Annetta P. Lee	$8.95
From the Ashes	Kathleen Suzanne	$8.95
	Jeanne Sumerix	
Gentle Yearning	Rochelle Alers	$10.95
Glory of Love	Sinclair LeBeau	$10.95
Hart & Soul	Angie Daniels	$8.95
Heartbeat	Stephanie Bedwell-Grime	$8.95
I'll Be Your Shelter	Giselle Carmichael	$8.95
Illusions	Pamela Leigh Starr	$8.95
Indiscretions	Donna Hill	$8.95
Interlude	Donna Hill	$8.95
Intimate Intentions	Angie Daniels	$8.95
Just an Affair	Eugenia O'Neal	$8.95
Kiss or Keep	Debra Phillips	$8.95
Love Always	Mildred E. Riley	$10.95
Love Unveiled	Gloria Greene	$10.95
Love's Deception	Charlene Berry	$10.95
Mae's Promise	Melody Walcott	$8.95
Meant to Be	Jeanne Sumerix	$8.95
Midnight Clear	Leslie Esdaile	$10.95
(Anthology)	Gwynne Forster	
	Carmen Green	
	Monica Jackson	
Midnight Magic	Gwynne Forster	$8.95
Midnight Peril	Vicki Andrews	$10.95
My Buffalo Soldier	Barbara B. K. Reeves	$8.95
Naked Soul	Gwynne Forster	$8.95
No Regrets	Mildred E. Riley	$8.95
Nowhere to Run	Gay G. Gunn	$10.95

Object of His Desire	A. C. Arthur	$8.95
One Day at a Time	Bella McFarland	$8.95
Passion	T.T. Henderson	$10.95
Past Promises	Jahmel West	$8.95
Path of Fire	T.T. Henderson	$8.95
Picture Perfect	Reon Carter	$8.95
Pride & Joi	Gay G. Gunn	$8.95
Quiet Storm	Donna Hill	$8.95
Reckless Surrender	Rochelle Alers	$8.95
Rendezvous with Fate	Jeanne Sumerix	$8.95
Revelations	Cheris F. Hodges	$8.95
Rivers of the Soul	Leslie Esdaile	$8.95
Rooms of the Heart	Donna Hill	$8.95
Shades of Brown	Denise Becker	$8.95
Shades of Desire	Monica White	$8.95
Sin	Crystal Rhodes	$8.95
So Amazing	Sinclair LeBeau	$8.95
Somebody's Someone	Sinclair LeBeau	$8.95
Someone to Love	Alicia Wiggins	$8.95
Soul to Soul	Donna Hill	$8.95
Still Waters Run Deep	Leslie Esdaile	$8.95
Subtle Secrets	Wanda Y. Thomas	$8.95
Sweet Tomorrows	Kimberly White	$8.95
The Color of Trouble	Dyanne Davis	$8.95
The Price of Love	Sinclair LeBeau	$8.95
The Reluctant Captive	Joyce Jackson	$8.95
The Missing Link	Charlyne Dickerson	$8.95
Three Wishes	Seressia Glass	$8.95
Tomorrow's Promise	Leslie Esdaile	$8.95
Truly Inseperable	Wanda Y. Thomas	$8.95
Twist of Fate	Beverly Clark	$8.95
Unbreak My Heart	Dar Tomlinson	$8.95
Unconditional Love	Alicia Wiggins	$8.95
When Dreams A Float	Dorothy Elizabeth Love	$8.95

Whispers in the Night	Dorothy Elizabeth Love	$8.95
Whispers in the Sand	LaFlorya Gauthier	$10.95
Yesterday is Gone	Beverly Clark	$8.95
Yesterday's Dreams, Tomorrow's Promises	Reon Laudat	$8.95
Your Precious Love	Sinclair LeBeau	$8.95

Order Form

Mail to: Genesis Press, Inc.
P.O. Box 101
Columbus, MS 39703

Name _____
Address _____
City/State _____ Zip _____
Telephone _____

Ship to (if different from above)
Name _____
Address _____
City/State _____ Zip _____
Telephone _____

Credit Card Information

Credit Card # _____ ☐ Visa ☐ Mastercard
Expiration Date (mm/yy) _____ ☐ AmEx ☐ Discover

Qty.	Author	Title	Price	Total

Use this order

form, or call

1-888-INDIGO-1

Total for books _____
Shipping and handling:
 $5 first two books,
  $1 each additional book _____
Total S & H _____
Total amount enclosed _____

Mississippi residents add 7% sales tax